J.D. LINTON
The Last Draig

Copyright © 2023 by J.D. Linton

All rights reserved. No part of this publication may be reproduced, stored or transmitted in any form or by any means, electronic, mechanical, photocopying, recording, scanning, or otherwise without written permission from the publisher. It is illegal to copy this book, post it to a website, or distribute it by any other means without permission.

This novel is entirely a work of fiction. The names, characters and incidents portrayed in it are the work of the author's imagination. Any resemblance to actual persons, living or dead, events or localities is entirely coincidental.

First edition

Proofreading by The Fiction Fix
Editing by Natalie Cammaratta
Cover art by MoonPress Designs | www.moonpress.co

This book was professionally typeset on Reedsy. Find out more at reedsy.com

To those who prefer to read stories that hurt because it allows you to cry for pain other than your own.

Contents

Preface	iii
Chapter One	1
Chapter Two	10
Chapter Three	26
Chapter Four	38
Chapter Five	49
Chapter Six	63
Chapter Seven	76
Chapter Eight	86
Chapter Nine	103
Chapter Ten	113
Chapter Eleven	120
Chapter Twelve	130
Chapter Thirteen	143
Chapter Fourteen	154
Chapter Fifteen	163
Chapter Sixteen	172
Chapter Seventeen	183
Chapter Eighteen	198
Chapter Nineteen	212
Chapter Twenty	221
Chapter Twenty One	236
Chapter Twenty Two	253
Chapter Twenty Three	266

Chapter Twenty Four	280
Chapter Twenty Five	294
Chapter Twenty Six	302
Chapter Twenty Seven	319
Chapter Twenty Eight	334
Chapter Twenty Nine	350
Chapter Thirty	367
Chapter Thirty One	384
Chapter Thirty Two	400
Chapter Thirty Three	409
Chapter Thirty Four	411
About the Author	413
Also by J.D. Linton	414

Preface

CONTENT WARNING

The Last Draig is a fantasy romance based in a fictional realm and while fun, the story contains elements that may not be suitable for some readers — Explicit sexual content, anxiety, panic attacks, profanity, physical and mental abuse from a parent (in the form of flashbacks), suicide, kidnapping, drugging, mutilation, loss of a loved one, and violence (blood, war, death).

Readers who may be sensitive to these elements, please take note.

Pronunciation Guide
  Ara Starrin: Ar-ah Star-in
  Rogue Draki: Row-g Drah-key
  Doran: Door-in
  Thana: Than-ah
  Alden: All-din
  Iaso: Eye-ah-so
  Elora: Eh-lor-ah
  Delphia: Dell-fee-uh
  Ewan: Eh-win
  Correnyk: Cor-ri-nick
  Orrys/Rys: Or-ris/Reece
  Adonis: Ah-dawn-is

Adon: Ay-din
Adrastus: Ah-drah-stus
Vaelor: Vah-ler
Auryna: Or-rye-nuh
Ravaryn: Rav-are-in

Chapter One

Ara

Rogue blinked, and something flickered behind his luminous eyes—a flicker of something...else. Something primal.

Animalistic.

My breath hitched, and he blinked again, his eyes returning to their normal maroon. I shuffled toward him as he staggered to his desk. His knuckles gripped the wood so hard, they turned white as he groaned.

"Rogue?" I gently placed a hand on his shoulder, careful not to touch the split skin revealing his newly-found scales.

His face swiveled to me. "Don't. I don't want to..." He scrunched his eyes, gritting his teeth as the wood splintered beneath his palms. "Get back!"

I stumbled back a few steps, my breaths leaving me in shaky cries.

With a blood-curdling scream, he jerked, his spine bowing as his arms stretched out to either side. I gasped as a snap rang through the room, echoed by another cry. The clouds of smoke around us thickened instantly, blurring out his form, leaving only his silhouette illuminated by the hazy daylight shining through his bedroom window.

My hands flew to my ears at the sound of crunching bones, but not even that could shield me from his screams, the agony in his voice. Tears spilled from my eyes, my body trembling as my legs threatened to give way beneath me.

I choked on my own sob as I watched, unable to tear my eyes away. His form twisted and grew with each broken bone, shifting into something entirely different. His wings doubled, tripled, quadrupled in size.

They just kept growing.

He kept growing, filling the room from floor to ceiling.

My feet shuffled back until my back pressed against the wall, my heart pounding painfully as nausea rolled in my gut.

After what felt like an eternity, it all stopped—the noises, the movement, the air.

Everything stilled, frozen in anticipation.

Then, the enormous shape moved. The smoke cleared, just enough for me to see two glowing eyes peering back at me, the same glowing fiery eyes I had seen moments before, but this…

This was not Rogue.

There was no recognition in his gaze. He didn't see *me*.

The smoke dissipated, revealing a Draig in all his glory.

My lips parted as chills erupted over my body.

Where tanned skin had once been, shining red-black scales now armored him from head to toe. His slitted eyes bored into me as I studied his face—elongated with the same armored skin. Black, razor-sharp spikes protruded from his cheekbones, following up and around his head, growing larger as they trailed down his spine between his leathery

CHAPTER ONE

wings. Each knuckle was now tipped with a curved claw. His arms had shifted into legs, and he stood on four now instead of two.

He took a step toward me, and the sound of claws scraping the floor filled the heavy silence between us. As he inched closer, I pushed back into the wall, turning my cheek to the cool stone as his snout nuzzled my hair roughly, sniffing.

He nudged me again, harder this time, nearly knocking me from my feet.

"Rogue," I whispered.

His eyes flickered again, only slightly, before hardening. A growl reverberated from his chest as sparks lit his throat, illuminating the red scales from the inside.

"Rogue," I repeated.

His head snapped toward the window, like he hadn't even heard me this time. He stilled as if listening to something before taking a step back, and then another.

"Rogue, wait." I stepped toward him as my eyes brimmed with tears. He didn't even acknowledge me—not my voice, not as I followed him, not as I reached for whatever I could, my fingers sliding down the massive scales of his tail. Nothing. "Wait. W-Wait, please."

With a few more steps, he leaped from the window, shattering it with minimal effort. The wall around the edges crumbled, pieces tumbling to the sea below.

"Rogue!" I ran the remaining steps to the window and skidded to a stop before tipping over the ledge. I watched through blurred eyes as he coasted down the cliff face and across the ocean, casting his massive shadow over its choppy waters.

He flew north, silent tears sliding down my cheeks as he

became smaller and smaller, moving farther and farther away until he was nothing but a dot above the horizon.

Then, he was gone.

Rogue was gone.

Lost.

* * *

My feet were frozen for far longer than I should've allowed, but I just kept staring at the horizon, looking but not seeing.

A knock on the door sounded, and I didn't bother turning around as Iaso rushed in.

"I saw him." She slowed as she entered. "He...He..."

"He's gone." The words were a whisper on my breath, but saying them aloud broke something in me, destroying the flimsy floodgates holding back sobs. I fell to my knees as my body was wracked, and a cry sounded from deep within my chest. "He's gone. He's gone. He—"

Her hands were on me in an instant; warmth flooded from her palms as she wrapped her arms around me.

"What happened, child?"

"I marked him. I-I—" I couldn't force the words from my mouth as another wail escaped me. *My fault. Always my fault.*

My fault.

"Ah..."

I pulled back to peek up at her. "Why? Why did this happen? What could..." The realization flooded me before I could finish the sentence.

I marked him, just as he had marked me. Our magic, both bound and gagged, both released by the claim.

CHAPTER ONE

"I marked him," I breathed.

She sighed, shaking her head. "It makes sense. Your curse prevented your magic and he broke that with a mate mark. The curse must have mingled with your bond...been sent *down* the bond to Rogue. That would explain why he couldn't shift when he was thirteen. That..." Her voice shook, and she inhaled deeply, rubbing her forehead as her eyes darted about. "I..."

Her eyes widened a fraction before she averted her gaze, an audible breath leaving her as she slumped at the shoulders. My heart sank with understanding.

"Hey, no," I whispered. "No, no, no. Don't do that."

She nodded forcibly, but the look on her face gave away the panic spiraling behind her eyes.

"That... That is something we don't have time to dwell on right now. I..." Her eyes pricked with tears as she lifted them to meet mine. "I did that." She motioned to her neck. "If I hadn't—then that wouldn't—"

She choked, a tear slipping from her eye. Her breathing quickened as she fell back and braced her hands on the floor behind her.

"Iaso, no. If you hadn't placed the spell, *I* wouldn't even be here. You saved my life. Please, don't. Rogue wouldn't blame you. You *know* that," I said, reaching forward to brush the curls from her face, desperately wishing I could calm her in the same way she did for others.

Still, I did all I could. I wrapped my arms around her, hugging her tightly as she collapsed on my shoulder, sobbing.

My heart broke for her, and I squeezed tighter, placing a hand on the back of her head.

"It is not your fault, Iaso. It's not."

She tensed.

"Yes. Yes, it is." She pulled back, wiping her cheeks. "But that is something I will deal with later. Alone."

"Iaso—"

"No. Thank you for being a friend, for letting me do… that." She rose to her feet as her gaze bounced around the room, landing anywhere but on me. "We need to focus on Rogue. We need… We need to talk to the rest of the group, let them know what's happened."

I remained seated as she wrung her hands, blinking rapidly.

"Iaso," I said quietly.

Her gaze returned to me, her face tight, barely holding the emotion back. She shook her head once, and her throat bobbed as she swallowed hard.

I dropped my eyes, nodding as I stood.

"Let's go." She strode to the door without another word.

I glanced out the window one more time. There was nothing but a crying, cloudy sky and a choppy ocean accepting its tears. No Rogue in sight.

Biting back tears of my own, I sighed and followed behind her.

As we neared the library, Commander Correnyk Lee entered through the front door with Ewan right behind him, laughing and shaking out his hair, wet from the rain. Lee was Doran's next in command and had unofficially taken his place since his passing, maintaining order and training within the remaining army but unwilling to claim the title of General—not that anyone had pushed him to. I don't think anyone was truly ready to accept that the position was even open. Not yet.

While Lee towered over Ewan, he was leaner with brown

CHAPTER ONE

skin, hazel eyes, and dark hair cropped short.

Lee clapped Ewan on the shoulder, and Ewan looked past him, finding us. His face lit up before his eyes darted to Iaso, and the smile slid from his face at her expression.

He climbed the stairs two at a time, Lee right behind him. "What—"

She dipped her head toward the library, and he nodded discreetly in response.

We found Alden in his office, poring over a thick, leather-bound tome as usual. His long, white hair was pulled back in a braid, his glasses on the tip of his nose.

His eyes lifted to us, landing on me. My expression must have been grave because his grew serious as he pulled his glasses off and closed the book.

They all looked to me to explain. A heartbeat passed. Another. I opened my mouth to speak but froze. My throat was still tight with tears, and I knew if I spoke the words again, they would fall and never stop.

I blinked rapidly, inhaling deeply when Iaso placed a hand on my shoulder, giving it a light squeeze. "Rogue has shifted."

"Shifted? Into a dragon?" Ewan asked. "I thought he couldn't shift."

"He couldn't," Alden answered. "How..."

"I claimed him." I lifted my chin. "I marked him, and it broke whatever piece of my curse remained over him."

Alden's eyes darted to Iaso, and her shaky inhale was audible.

He nodded, running a hand over his chin. "So, where is he now? I'm assuming by the lack of destruction that he's left?"

"Destruction? Why..." The lack of recognition in his eyes. It—He—"He's not in there, is he?"

My heart raced, my chest constricting. My hand rubbed at my sternum, willing it to slow before I imploded.

"Oh, he is. He's just…lost for now," Iaso said, sitting in the chair behind her. She propped an elbow on the armrest and rested her head in her palm. "The first shift is…hard, painful, and confusing, especially when they don't have an elder to guide them."

"Right now, the animal instincts of a dragon have taken complete control. It is that way with all Draigs on their first shift until they're brought back. Once Rogue regains consciousness, he won't lose it again, but usually, Draigs have an elder walk them through and bring them back. I don't know how we will be able to do that."

"I'll bring him back," I said, my voice laced with a finality that weighed over the room.

Iaso nodded, her expression unreadable.

"I hate to be the one to say this," Lee said hesitantly, "but if he's lost in there, if he doesn't realize what he's doing, how do we know he will come back?"

My gaze locked on his face. That wasn't something I'd considered, and the question sent me down a panicked spiral.

Air evaded me. My chest rose and fell quickly to no avail, and I could feel another attack threatening to consume me as my throat closed, my mind black and empty.

My hand slid up to my throat as it tightened. I was choking. I—

My fingers grazed across the tiny marks at the base of my neck.

The mirror to his.

"I marked him," I whispered. "I marked him. I can find him, right? I could find him."

CHAPTER ONE

I closed my eyes, trying to feel something, feel *him*.

It was different than sending out the feelers of my magic. It wasn't me reaching out at all; it was a call, and I was its answer. A beacon—just as he said. A distant lighthouse, shining only for me.

My heart raced as I felt his form, still flying north.

So far north.

"I can feel him." My eyes snapped open to find their hopeful expressions.

"Where?" Iaso asked in a rush.

"North. That's all I can tell. He's still moving."

"North?" Alden asked. "I don't know of any land north of Draig Hearth."

Iaso shook her head as she spoke. "Neither do I. Maybe a few scattered islands like the ones off our coast?"

Ewan shrugged. "Either way, no matter where or how far we need to go, I can have my ship prepared if you wish to follow, Ara."

I looked to Iaso, Alden, and Lee.

They were looking at me, waiting for my answer.

I took a deep breath to settle my nerves and nodded.

"Yes." I paused as my thoughts gained momentum. "Yes. I'm assuming your ship is in Nautia?" He nodded. "Have it sent here."

"It can be ready to sail within the next hour and will reach Draig Hearth's dock by the end of day tomorrow," Ewan said.

"All right, then. We'll give him the night and tomorrow to return. If he doesn't..." My gaze shifted from one face to the next. "We set sail after him."

Chapter Two

Ara

My mind reeled as Alden walked out Iaso, Ewan, and Lee, leaving only me in the study.

The silence opened the door for panic, and I was desperately fighting to regain control of my own body, even as my lungs burned, my heart raced, and my thoughts wouldn't form. Panic was a vicious, sadistic beast that my body had an incredibly hard time fighting off, but I had practice. As Alden taught my mother and she taught me, we looked for things calmer than we were.

My eyes darted around Alden's small office and landed on the clock. *Tick. Tick. Tick.*

The sound, while normally irritating, was oddly comforting in this moment—something steady I could focus on, if nothing else.

I closed my eyes and swallowed hard as I clutched the chair's arms. They were made of a solid, unyielding wood, smooth and cool beneath my palms.

Tick. Tick. Tick.

I took another deep breath.

CHAPTER TWO

"We'll find him," Alden said as he stepped back into the office. I jumped, pulled from my shrinking world of hysteria, and nodded. He hesitated before extending an elbow to me. "Come on. I want to show you something."

I glanced up at him and stood, sliding my hand into the crook of his arm. I paused, focusing on the feel of his warm, skinny arm, clothed in the soft fabric of his robe. He was steady—my third and final thing calmer than me in my pursuit of peace.

"I think it might be time for you to learn about the Draigs."

A defeated laugh escaped me. "Yeah, I would say so."

He led me into a back corner of the library. Hidden in the shadows was a doorway, covered in thick dust.

"What is this?"

"A special room, one that has been abandoned for too long."

The hinges creaked as he pulled the door open. It was pitch black inside, and warm air wafted from the room. As we stepped over the threshold, a massive fireplace lit in the back corner, and an audible gasp escaped me. The entire structure was made of shining, black stone.

"Obsidian," Alden answered my unvoiced question. "The stone of Draigs."

"It's beautiful," I whispered. My eyes followed it up, all the way to the ceiling, and my mouth fell open—all along the ceiling were intricate carvings of dragons. Dozens. *Hundreds.*

"Every known draig in history is carved in this ceiling, even the ones before the time of Draig Hearth. It was a way to honor their memory."

Goosebumps erupted over my skin. There were so many—every color and size. They flew and danced across the ceiling, mingling with each other.

"Incredible," I breathed. *The history. The connection.*

I peeked at Alden to find his face was also turned up, admiring the dragons in their flickering orange light.

"That it is. A new carving was added upon each Draig's first shift."

My heart sank as I glanced up again, studying the family of dragons in a different light, knowing Rogue wasn't up there.

The draig left without a shift, all because of my curse.

"Rogue needs to be added," I said quietly.

Alden turned to me, his face solemn. "He will be. I'll make sure of it."

Turning, I studied the rest of the room. It was incredibly large—tall and wide. The sparse furniture was huddled around the fireplace, leaving the rest of the room bare, which confused me until I saw the back wall, or lack thereof. A few stone columns held the ceiling; otherwise, it was entirely open to the sea, shielded by nothing but a protection spell.

The moon hung low on the horizon, its reflection bright as it bounced off the waves below. The rain had finally relented, but I stared at it a moment too long; thick clouds swirled, blotting it out.

"This was the shifting chamber. They could come and go from here," he said, gesturing to the sea.

"That explains why it's laid out like this," I mumbled as I walked over to a nearby wall. There was a small bookcase of sorts, lined with a few journals but mostly just trinkets—small stones, shiny objects, bones, a few carvings. "What are these?"

I reached a hand out and ran my finger along a golden ball, tarnished and dented.

CHAPTER TWO

"Draigs tend to…collect what they consider treasure—items that appease their dragons. Each Draig has one, and they keep it for their entire lives. They usually find it on their first few shifts and grow extremely attached to it. These are the pieces of former Draigs." He stepped closer and pointed to the ball. "*That* one was Adrastus' piece."

I snatched my hand back, wiping it on my trousers.

"Oh."

My mind wandered to Rogue as I studied each object, wondering what he would choose, where he would choose it… Where he was now.

My heart ached for him. He was alone—lost and confused. I wished I could go to him and help him in some way. I wished I could do *anything* other than sit here, but there was nothing I could do other than hope and wait for him to return of his own volition.

It felt pointless. We were essentially just twiddling our thumbs as the most important person in my life was lost—even more so with each passing second.

He was still flying ever more north.

Where are you going, Rogue?

Still, the hardest part was that it wasn't Rogue flying away from his home, his people, his family. *He* had no choice in the matter; he wasn't even aware of what he was doing. No, in this moment, in his mind, he was a dragon and nothing more.

There was no telling how far he would go. If he would ever return.

Why would he? If there were no thoughts in his mind other than those of an animal, why would he return to a castle, to people?

I swallowed hard, pushing down the rising panic as my hand paused on a black, jagged stone. I lifted it and it glimmered in the light. It was made of the same dark stone as the fireplace.

"Whose was this?"

"Stryath's. He built Draig Hearth."

This stone was old, then. A millennium, at least. I studied it a moment longer as if I would somehow see the age and history in its reflection, but I saw nothing, save my own face and the red-orange flicker from the fireplace. Replacing it gently, I turned to the fire and strolled to one of the massive leather chairs.

"Does Rogue come in here?"

"No, not really." He didn't continue. There was no need. We both knew why he didn't.

With a deep sigh, I sat and pulled my knees into my chest, wrapping my arms around them as I rested my chin on top, letting my eyes follow the ebb and flow of the fire.

The flames were stable, unwavering. It felt safe. It felt like Rogue.

My eyes burned and pricked with tears. I tightened my grip on my legs, begging the tension to stop the tears, but it didn't. Nothing would.

One dripped down my cheek, followed by another and another, falling in silence. Rain released from the clouds as the sky cried with me. It fell slowly, sadly, rather than the angry downpour I was accustomed to.

It was different—more heartbreaking—and I scrunched my eyes against the sound.

My heart was confused more than anything, the emotion tearing me in two directions. On one hand, I felt guilty I'd subjected him to his first shift, afraid and alone. He was lost out there with no elder to guide him.

On the other hand, I knew what it felt like to be cut off from my magic; the discontentment, the uneasiness, the feeling of something…missing. If I hadn't claimed him, he would have never connected with this half at all, and I have to think that everything he said about me must have applied to him as well, even if he didn't see it.

Perhaps this was just my mind attempting to rationalize the situation, to dampen the guilt that weighed down on me, but either way, when a Fae is separated from their magic, they never feel whole.

He may never have applied that to himself, but now I couldn't unsee it; he *was* cleaved.

The way it happened was jarring and messy and chaotic. It was painful, but I *had* to believe that in the long run, he would be better for it—more complete, just as I was.

Closing my eyes, I took a deep breath. *Or maybe that's just what I'm telling myself so I can sleep at night.*

Alden sat in the chair next to mine, and I slid my legs back to the floor, turning to face him.

"So, tell me more about Draigs."

"What do you wish to know first?" he replied, resting an elbow on the chair's arm.

"I… I don't know." I didn't know anything. I never did. "So, when they shift for the first time, their dragon is in control. What does that mean? Are they two separate entities?"

"No, they're not really. What we refer to as his dragon is just the primal side of him. It's the animalistic part that houses his dragon and knows how to shift, how to fly, how to hunt, how to *be* a dragon."

"So it's like what? Two sides of the same coin?"

"Right now it is, yes, but it won't always be. Once he comes back to us, that coin will melt down and there will be no sides at all. Just Rogue."

Melt...

"Will that change him? Melding with his dragon?"

Alden paused. "It may. Draigs are known to be... unpredictable. Wild even, sometimes. While Adrastus was an extreme, they are all known to be a bit merciless and territorial. It's their nature."

"Ah..." My gut twisted.

My eyes rose and landed on the ancient painting above the fireplace. It was chipped on some parts, the paint faded and muddy, but the faces were clear. It was a family—a man with black eyes and even blacker hair, a woman with blonde hair and red eyes, and a child no older than thirteen. "Who is that?"

Alden followed my gaze. "Stryath, his mate, Roella, and their son, Drakyth."

I studied their faces, so clearly related to Rogue—dark, sharp features, red eyes. "It's incredible how much Rogue favors them."

"Well, that was only three generations ago."

My face snapped to Alden as he squinted at the painting. "What? How—"

He turned to me. "You know Fae live longer. Stryath was Adrastus' grandfather. That little boy was his father."

My eyes bulged. "How old was Adrastus when he was killed?"

"I think somewhere around two hundred."

"Oh, wow. That is so... I don't know why that shocks me.

CHAPTER TWO

I mean, I knew Iaso was alive when Draig Hearth was built, but I just assumed… Wow. Did Rogue know Stryath, then?"

Alden chuckled. "No, he didn't. Adrastus didn't even know him. He was killed in battle during the War of Two Brothers."

"The War of Two Brothers?" A chill ran up my spine.

A war between brothers. *How history repeats itself.*

"Stryath was king when he built Draig Hearth. He was the reigning Draig with the Obsidian Crown, deeming him the undeniable ruler of the realm, but like Rogue, he also had an angry brother. About five hundred years after Draig Hearth was built, his brother attacked with a full army. Tired of living in Stryath's shadow, I suppose. The war led to the demise of most of the Draig line. Everyone chose sides and in the end, they both died. Stryath's son, Drakyth, was the only one left to continue the bloodline."

The devastation Drakyth must have felt to have watched his entire family be decimated in one fell swoop…

"If he was ruling, then how did Vaelor become king? Would the crown not have passed to Drakyth?"

"Under normal circumstances, yes, but Drakyth didn't want it. He actively refused, actually. After watching his entire family be massacred by the hunger for power, he chose a new successor, and with Vaelor being the Storm Bringer, he was the obvious next choice, blessed by Goddess and all."

"He was the next best choice solely because of his magic?" I asked for more reasons than one. My heart skipped a beat, and I placed a hand on my sternum as if that would soothe the palpitations.

"Being a Storm Bringer is a gift from the Goddess herself. That magic is not bred or created; it is given. Your father was favored by the Goddess, and so are you. That blessing, that favor, is a means for ruling in Ravaryn. The Goddess *chose* you both, set you down an incredible path, destined for greatness."

I choked—literally choked on nothing but his words. I did *not* want to rule and had never even considered the possibility before now—not even as Rogue's mate, much less because of my magic, which in my humble opinion, was horrible grounds for deciding who ruled an entire kingdom.

I hoped I never had to.

He peeked at me, furrowing his brows before giving me a flat look and continuing. "While he couldn't wear the Obsidian Crown—only a Draig can wear that—he was still named King of Ravaryn within weeks of Stryath's passing, and the realm needed him *desperately*. He fostered the kingdom as his own child and returned the realm to peace, within the borders of Ravaryn and with Auryna."

My head spun at the information overload.

While fate had a sense of irony, it seemed history had a love for repeating itself. I just hoped this war wouldn't end in the same way.

Another thought popped into my head, and my chest ached.

"Is that why Adrastus killed Vaelor? Because he felt entitled to the throne?"

"Yes," Alden said, his voice barely above a whisper.

* * *

The first rays of sunrise woke me the next morning. My eyes stung from lack of sleep as I reached up, stretching and cracking my joints.

I had stayed awake most of the night, pacing restlessly.

CHAPTER TWO

While I was grateful for the history lesson and distraction, it felt wrong to do anything other than worry, almost like I was betraying Rogue in some way.

I knew it was ridiculous, but he was out there. He needed us, and yet, we were here, sitting by fires, safe, sleeping.

Just a few hours before sunrise, I had resolved to sleep in Rogue's room. When I'd laid down, the bed smelled of him and the scent enveloped me—the warmth of smoke and evergreen spice. Clutching his blankets to my chest, I had cried myself into exhaustion, falling asleep surrounded by what remained of him.

But with the first rays of daylight peeking in, I couldn't force myself to lay here any longer. I needed to move, to work off this anxious energy.

I jumped out of bed and strode to the door. With one final look around, my eyes landed on the shattered window, revealing the same horizon Rogue had disappeared on only the evening before, but it felt like days, years since I'd seen him.

I tore my eyes away with a sigh and hurried to my chambers. I pulled the dresser drawer open with the intent to pack for the journey we would inevitably make tonight, but upon opening it, I paused.

It was summer. The air was hot and sticky with humidity, and yet, I reached in and pulled out a fur coat and fleece-lined leggings.

Where were we going? I thought as I slowly pulled out the heavy winter clothing and stuffed it into the bag. If the dresser was giving me this, then it knew we were heading somewhere cold. Somewhere north.

My hands shook as I took everything it gave me.

Eventually, I closed the drawer and reopened it again, pulling out my classics for the day—black trousers and a sleeveless blue-gray tunic.

Glancing in the mirror, I pulled my hair back into a braid, revealing my pointed ears. They had been this way for a while, but the sight always caught my attention. I leaned in, running a finger along the edge as I examined them.

They felt so foreign, yet natural. I couldn't explain it, but... I liked them. It made me feel connected to my father, to Ravaryn—an outward display that I did belong here.

Grabbing my dagger from the side table, I slid it into its sheath as I jogged down the steps, not stopping until I reached the bailey, immediately making a beeline for the sparring circle. In the corner by the extensive weaponry rack sat a few straw dummies meant for practicing, and I was grateful to see them still there.

Without hesitation, I picked up a sword and did a few warm-up exercises before turning to the dummy. I swung hard, and the sword sliced, but the straw didn't budge. It didn't fall or damage.

A spell.

With that, I swung again. And again. And again.

I went through the motions for hours. The sun peaked in the sky, warming the bailey, and the stagnant air lacked any breeze, blocked by the stone walls. Sweat rolled down my spine, soaking through my shirt. My muscles screamed with exertion, but I pushed harder, urging the pain in my muscles to overtake the pain in my chest.

With one final slice, I spun on my heel and kicked, knocking the dummy back a few feet. Breathing heavily, I wiped the sweat from my brow and replaced the sword just as Iaso

CHAPTER TWO

joined me outside with water and iced tea.

"How are you?"

"Fine," was all she said, but the circles under her eyes told another story.

She eyed me cautiously, and I bit back anything I was about to say.

Sitting on a nearby bench, she handed me a cup of cold tea that I chugged gratefully. "What's this for?"

There was always a purpose for her teas. They were never random.

"Fatigue." She glanced sidelong at me as she sipped from her own cup. "It just helps keep us awake, revitalize us for the time being."

We sat in silence for a moment as I caught my breath.

"Any word from Ewan?" I finally asked.

"Yes, he set sail hours ago. Right after sunrise."

"Good." My next words caught in my throat as I jerked to my feet.

A woman with violet hair entered through the front gates with an older man and woman, both resembling different parts of her.

"Thana!" My steps were frantic as I strode to her.

She stopped as she saw me before taking off in a sprint, and we collided in a hug. I must have been crying or breathing erratically because she pulled back with concern rather than relief.

"Hey, hey." Her eyes roamed over my face, her hands still on my shoulders. "What is it?"

"Rogue. He's gone. He-He—"

"What do you mean he's gone?" Her eyes widened.

I peeked back over my shoulder to motion Iaso over, but

she was already gone. My head shook with a deep breath as I turned back to Thana, but my eyes fell to the rescued Fae trickling in through the gates.

I stilled, appalled as nausea rolled in my gut. My hand rose, covering my mouth as I fought back the bile rising in my throat.

They were starved. Skin and bone. Some were mutilated with scars or marks along their skin—clearly tortured and abused.

"Oh my Goddess," I breathed.

"I know. There's no telling how long some of them have been there. It could've been years…decades."

I swallowed hard.

"Most chose to return to their homes, but some didn't have anywhere to go, and well," she sighed, gesturing around us, "we have the room."

"Absolutely." I nodded, my eyes trailing after the Fae. Some smiled as they passed; others hardly spared us a glance.

"Delphia never rejoined us," Thana said. "No letters, either."

"She was there at the battle. She watched it all unfold, and it was…tragic." I scrunched my eyes as the memory of her screams echoed through my skull, of the devastation that sank into her features as she watched Doran fall to his knees. "I'm sure she just needs time."

"Time." She nodded slowly, but the look in her eyes was distant. "Time I can give her. She can take as much as she needs. Take an eternity if need be, but how long do we have to wait to just know she's okay? I don't know how long I can continue like this, wondering if she's even alive. I know that's selfish to say, but I just want to know she's breathing." A sad, breathy laugh left her, the sound defeated

CHAPTER TWO

and heartbreaking. "If she doesn't want to come back here, that's... That would be fine. Of course, it would be fine. Completely understandable."

I couldn't tell if she said the words for me or herself, but they were true all the same, regardless of the pain they sparked behind Thana's amethyst eyes. It would be unsurprising if Delphia never wanted to return; the memories and reminders would be painful and constant.

"She may never want to come back to this castle," I whispered.

Her eyes flicked to me as if she wanted to argue, but she clamped her mouth shut, her eyes brimming with tears.

I took her hand, clutching it with both of mine. "But that doesn't mean she won't come back for you. She may leave us and this castle behind, but she would never leave you, Thana."

Her bottom lip quivered as her hand tightened around mine. "She shouldn't be alone in this. I want to be there for her, to hold her and kiss her tears away. I know there's nothing I could truly do to help, but I just…" She exhaled audibly as her forehead fell to her palm. "She shouldn't be alone. Not right now."

She was painfully right. Grief was heavy—too heavy. It was a weight permanently tied to our souls after loss, only lessening with time, and it could all too easily drag us to the deep, unending bottom of our sorrow if given the opportunity. Without help to lighten the load, that was exactly what it would do: drown the hurt and vulnerable.

Delphia needed a hand to lighten the load, a hand she could reach for when it got too dark, too hard. She needed Thana.

The two older Fae Thana had entered with joined us then, carrying nothing but the clothes on their backs. Thana quickly wiped her cheeks and replaced her sadness with a mask that even I could barely see through. She smiled, and I found myself second-guessing if we'd had the conversation we had.

"Hi, Mama. This is Ara, daughter of Vaelor and mate of Rogue." Turning, she gestured to them. "And Ara, this is my mother, Mya, and father, Augustus."

Augustus dipped his head in greeting, smiling as he watched Mya step forward.

"It's a pleasure to meet you, Ara. I've heard many things about you," she said. "But don't worry—only good things."

Augustus nodded and took his daughter's hand, kissing the back of it.

"Are we free to reside in our old chambers?" Mya asked, glancing back and forth between Thana and me.

My brows furrowed, and before I could answer, Thana replied, "Yes. I've been keeping them warm for you."

With that, they took their leave, and we stared after them as they strolled up the entryway steps hand in hand.

"They lived here before?" I asked.

"Many, many years ago."

I didn't pry, even though there was one particular question on my tongue. Thankfully, Thana answered it anyway without me having to ask.

"They knew Vaelor," Thana whispered. "They adored him, as did everyone."

Taking a deep breath, I nodded slowly, once again reminded of his positive impact on those around him and how badly I wished I could've experienced it. He was the kind of person who left an impression on everyone he met, because he was so genuinely good, and I wanted that impression. I wanted my own memories of his altruism and kindness and warmth.

A wisp of jealousy grew in my chest. It was ridiculous, but I couldn't help it. I was jealous of all these people—an innumerable amount of people—who got to know him. Everyone but me, and I never would.

"That seems to be most of the Fae," Thana said, snapping me from my sinking thoughts as the influx of people dwindled. No one entered the gates for a few moments, but Thana looked on as if she was waiting for someone. "But there were a few humans as well, and they walk *much* slower."

Another person came around the corner, a female shrouded in a blue-gray cloak.

My breathing stopped.

That cloak.

Her face peeked up as she looked straight at me, her eyes bright and blue.

Mother.

Chapter Three

Ara

My hand dropped as I hesitantly stepped around Thana, unable to believe my eyes. "Are you…" Tears spilled down my cheeks without delay.

She took a slow step toward me and nodded. "Ara."

I shook my head. I couldn't believe it, couldn't let myself, for if she dissipated like a vision, I would break all over again. This was fate's cruel joke. It had to be.

"My mother is dead," I whispered, staggering back.

"No, Ara. I am not." It was her voice—my mother's sweet voice, tainted with hurt.

My eyes darted to Thana to see if she also saw her, to make sure I wasn't dreaming or hallucinating. Thana's mouth hung open, her eyes glued to my mother.

My gaze shifted back to my mother slowly, cautiously. Her face was the same, only more hollow, starved. Her eyes were the same, the freckles still speckled over her cheeks, her long auburn hair hanging beneath the hood.

"But how…? The letter didn't burn." My voice cracked, my lip quivering.

CHAPTER THREE

"I was locked in a cell." She stepped closer.

"So, you… You weren't safe."

She shook her head. "There was nowhere for it to go."

I shattered. The sobs escaped me in a strangled cry as I sank to my knees. She sprinted to me, dropping to my side as she threw her arms around me.

"Mother, I-I thought I lost you. I thought you were dead." The words tumbled from my mouth, nearly unintelligible, as I wrapped my arms around her in return. "I thought I'd never see you again, never hear your voice again."

She sat back on her heels and pushed the sweat-soaked hair from my face.

"I thought I killed you," I barely managed before another cry escaped me.

"Oh, my love, no." She pulled me back into her, holding my head on her shoulder. "No."

"With that letter, I thought Evander…"

"He did find it, but that wasn't your fault. It was my own. I should've burned it right away." She released me again. "He found it and locked me in the dungeon along with…" She peeked over her shoulder and extended a hand. A tall, curvy blonde took her hand, dropping to her knees beside us.

A strangled, confused laugh escaped me. "Livvy? What? Why did he…"

She rolled her eyes, throwing her hands up. "Goddess if I know. I didn't even know you were"—she gestured up and down as her eyes snagged on my ears—"Fae. Much less where you were or what happened to you."

"I'm so sorry."

"Don't be. I don't want to…dwell. How are you? How is it here?" she asked as her eyes shifted to the castle wearily.

"Well, it's a lot to explain." I brought my eyes back to my mother, and it suddenly occurred to me that she probably didn't know what happened to Evander. "Mother, Evander… he died during the battle."

Her brows furrowed before she nodded, clearing her throat.

"And you should know—you should both know that King Adon is not human. He's actually Rogue's brother. He's Fae. A manipulator, actually."

The blood drained from their faces, and they spoke simultaneously.

"A manipulator?"

"Rogue Draki? The King of Ravaryn?"

Turning to my mother, I answered her first. "Yes, a manipulator. We're assuming that's why the previous king handed over his crown to him rather than his own daughter."

She nodded, her throat bobbing as she swallowed hard.

"And yes, the King of Ravaryn. He…" I peeked at my mother, who eyed me curiously. Her gaze locked on the exposed marks on my neck, and her eyes widened slightly, her chest rising and falling quickly. "He's my mate."

My mother's lips parted in a small gasp, and my heart sank. *The son of her lover's murderer.* Every ounce of guilt I'd felt during the past few weeks came crashing back as the blood drained from her face.

"Mate? So you…" Livvy's tone turned teasing as she wiggled her brows.

I tore my eyes from Mother's face and held a hand up to Livvy. "Yes, but he's not here. Let's go inside. It's a lot to explain."

Livvy nodded and followed as I stood, but Mother hesi-

CHAPTER THREE

tated, meeting my gaze.

"Please," I whispered as I held a hand down to her.

She stared at it for a moment and swallowed hard before cautiously sliding her hand into mine. I pulled her up, and we walked to Thana.

"I don't know if you got a chance to speak with them yet," I said, "but this is my friend, Livvy, and my mother, Elora."

Her eyes widened in understanding, an awed grin on her lips. "Vaelor's Elora?"

The ghost of a smile pulled at Mother's lips. "Vaelor," she breathed as if saying it for the first time. "It's been so long, too long, since I've heard his name. Yes, I am Vaelor's Elora." Her eyes brimmed with tears.

Thana nodded with misty eyes before turning to me. "I'm sure you three have a lot to catch up on."

"There's something you need to hear as well," I said before leading them inside.

As we entered through the front doors, we found Iaso sitting on the stairs, her head in her hands, and Ewan seated next to her with his hand on her back. He noticed us first and froze, sitting straighter. His head tilted to the side as he studied Mother's face, as if unsure he was really seeing her.

"Elora?" he whispered, barely loud enough for us to hear.

"What?" Iaso glanced up at him and followed his line of sight.

"It...It's Elora," he replied.

She stood slowly, gripping the handrail as if for dear life.

"Iaso," Mother said with a cracked voice.

That snapped Iaso from her disbelief. She ran to Mother and threw her arms around her. Tears rolled down Iaso's cheeks, soaking my mother's cloak as Mother wrapped her arms around Iaso in return.

"Oh, how I have missed you, old friend." Iaso's voice shook, and she tightened her grip on Mother.

Pulling back, Mother placed her hands on Iaso's face, nodding, her own cheeks soaked with happy tears. "And I you. *Greatly.*"

Iaso's eyes glowed golden as they roamed over Mother's form.

"Oh, none of that right now," Mother said, waving a hand.

"Well, I see some things never change," Iaso said, chuckling through her tears.

Turning to Ewan, Mother smiled, wiping her cheeks as she laughed. "I knew you wouldn't be able to stay away for long."

Ewan rolled his eyes, but his smile was endearing as he slid an arm over Mother's shoulders and pulled her into a hug. "It's so good to have you back, El. We've missed you."

Iaso met my gaze. "I guess there's a lot to discuss, hmm? Should we go to the library?"

"The library," Mother said wistfully. "Is Alden still there?"

My own cheeks ached from smiling so long and hard when I slid my hand into Mother's. "He's still there."

"Then yes, I would like that very much."

* * *

Alden was seated in a large chair by the fireplace when we entered, his nose in an old book per usual.

Without looking up, he said, "How may I—"

"Alden," Mother breathed.

Alden stilled, his chest rising and falling quickly. Slowly, he pulled his reading glasses off and raised his face to us. For the first time since I'd met him, his expression was unreadable.

He hesitantly rose to his feet and stepped toward us. Standing directly in front of Mother, his lip quivered, and a small, hitched breath escaped him before he threw his arms around her, holding her tightly. She wrapped her arms around him in return, and his form shook with cries as he rested his cheek on top of her head.

"Elora."

They stood this way for a few moments in silence before he cleared his throat and turned away to wipe his face.

"But how did this…How are you here? The letter didn't burn. We thought…" He shook his head.

"I was being held in a cell. I can only assume the letter didn't send, because…" She dropped her eyes for a breath before raising them back to meet his. "Because I didn't feel safe, and I didn't know if I ever would. I had no home anymore, no family, save you and Ara. There was no other place for it to go."

Alden nodded slowly. "Well, I'm so happy to have you back here. We all are. This is a day I never thought I'd live to see, but I am thankful for it. To have you both here is…more than I could ever ask for." His eyes glanced over to the others, snagging on Livvy. "And who is this?"

I turned to Livvy as she studied his face without hesitation. She stared at him for a moment before glancing at me and back to him.

"You two are related, aren't you?" She pointed a finger between the two of us.

Alden chuckled as a grin broke out on my face.

"It's the eyes," she said. "Identical."

"Those are Vaelor's eyes—her father's," Mother said

proudly, gazing at me. "I've always adored them."

"Ah," Livvy said before sticking a hand out to Alden. "I'm Livvy, Ara's friend."

Alden took her hand, giving it a firm shake. "It's very nice to meet you, Livvy. Any friend of Ara's is a friend of mine. I'm her grandfather, Alden."

I grinned at the interaction. Livvy wasn't afraid of him, or any of the Fae for that matter, not that I could tell. I wasn't surprised; she was brave, far braver than I had ever been. She would fit right in.

"I'm Iaso," she interjected, giving Livvy a warm smile. "The castle healer."

Livvy turned to her, extending a hand. "And you are *stunning*," she said, lifting her eyebrows.

Iaso laughed—a warm, genuine laugh. "Thank you, child."

Her eyes lit as she briefly examined her, and Livvy pulled back before leaning in and squinting.

"Is that magic?"

"Yes. It's how I survey someone's well-being," Iaso said, and her face fell. She took a deep breath, cupping her other hand around Livvy's. "Remind me to bring you tea later."

The smile slid from Livvy's face, but she nodded as she pulled her hand from Iaso's.

"Yes, well, I'm assuming you're all here to share the news of Rogue, then?" Alden asked, turning to me.

I nodded and he motioned to the circle of chairs behind him. As we sat, everyone turned to me, and my cheeks tinted pink.

"Rogue is… Well, he…" I sighed, lifting my eyes to Thana. "He shifted."

Her mouth fell open as she leaned forward in shock.

CHAPTER THREE

"He shifted. Fully shifted? Are you sure?" The words tumbled from her mouth as she sat back, her eyes wide.

"Um, yes. There's no denying that. When I claimed him, it had the same effect as his claim had on me. It broke whatever remnant was left of the curse. It happened just last night, and"—my eyes darted to my mother—"we are leaving tonight to find him."

She nodded slightly, her brows creased. "The curse."

Her eyes landed on my pointed ears before shifting to Iaso, whose face was equally as solemn.

"It was broken when Rogue claimed her. She has access to every bit of his power now," Iaso answered.

Mother paused. "Rogue, the son of Adrastus."

It wasn't a question but a statement. A heavy statement that weighed over me, crushing me. *But I-I—*

I didn't want to feel guilty, not for this. Not over Rogue. *He doesn't deserve that.*

Alden reached out to place a hand over hers. His eyes gleamed with the remainder of his tears as he whispered only to her, "He is not like Adrastus."

Mother stared at his face as her throat bobbed. "How… How do you—"

"He was abused, just as the rest of us. Just…wait until you can meet him. I promise you'll see," Alden said with a tight nod. He squeezed her hand once more and sat back in his chair.

She turned to me and I held her misty gaze. "He is good," I said, barely above a whisper. "He is."

She bit her lip as her brows pulled together. "So, you have Vaelor's magic now?"

I nodded as my mouth ticked up in a small smile. Holding

my hand up, a small ball of blue lightning appeared in my palm, shimmering and crackling. I glanced up at her, and her eyes were locked on my arm, a pained expression on her face.

The ball disappeared instantly as I dropped my arm. Hesitantly, she reached out and gently grabbed my hand, turning it over to see the scar. Her fingers shook as she touched it.

"Is this a scar? What happened?" Her voice cracked. "Are you all right? How did this happen?"

Her eyes darted from me to Iaso and back.

"It's a long story. Can I tell you in your chambers? Where we can speak alone?"

"Yes, okay." She cleared her throat, sitting up straighter. "And you're leaving tonight?"

With a deep breath, I attempted to settle myself. "Yes. When he shifted, he lost control and flew north. Farther north than anyone has ever been. We gave him the night and day to return, but…" I shook my head. "I have to find him. I have to bring him home. He has no one else to go after him. We"—I motioned around the group—"are his family."

Her expression was unreadable as she listened, but when I finished, she nodded slowly. "All right. Are you two going as well?" Her gaze shifted to Alden and Iaso. "Whose ship will you be taking?"

"Mine," Ewan answered.

Mother nodded. "Are you sailing with them when they leave?" she asked Iaso.

"I am. Rogue, he… He may not be my blood, but he's my son, and he needs me."

Mother's lips fell slack. "Your son? You'll have to tell me

about that when you return," she whispered.

Iaso smiled. "I would love nothing more. We have so much to catch up on."

"And you?" Mother said, turning to Alden.

His gaze shifted to me, and he hesitated as if the words wouldn't leave his mouth.

"Alden, would you mind staying with Mother and Livvy? I think it would be best if they had a friend around while they settle in."

Alden's face relaxed, relieved before he turned back to Mother. "Yes, I'll stay."

Turning to Ewan, I asked, "Is this ship still on track to arrive by sundown?"

"Yes."

"All right." I peeked through the window—mid-afternoon. "And we're boarding as soon as it arrives?"

"I would assume so, yes," Ewan said.

"I would like to leave as soon as we can," Iaso said. "I'm anxious to find Rogue. I don't like how far north he is. He's in uncharted territory."

"I know, Iaso. Me too," I said. There weren't words to express the amount of anxiety building in my chest—if that was even the term for what gnawed at me. Panic felt more accurate. "Well, Mother, can I escort you to your room?" I stood, holding an elbow out for her. "Liv, would it be okay if Alden escorted you?"

She faced him and shrugged her shoulders. "Sure."

He stood and held an elbow out for her that she took without hesitation.

While I may not know every room in the castle, I knew mine would be free from now on, so that's where I led my mother. As we crested the top step into my old chambers, the fire lit.

She glanced around the room as she slowly walked to the bed and ran a hand over the smooth, wooden bed frame. "Were these your chambers?" she asked, her voice low.

"Yes, but I'm not going to stay here anymore."

She nodded in silence. "I stayed here, too, before I moved into Vaelor's rooms."

My breath hitched. "You stayed here?"

She turned to me, her eyes glistening with tears. "Yes, so long ago. It's odd how fate aligns things. She never misses a detail, does she?"

I shook my head, swallowing against the lump forming in my throat.

"Ara, I'm so sorry this happened the way it did. Everything. I wish I could've been here for you. I should've been here for you. I should've *told* you."

"No, don't apologize. Please." I couldn't bear to hear her apologize when she did everything to save us, spending twenty-six years living a lie with a man she didn't love. She'd sacrificed enough.

"I would do *anything* to protect you, Ara, and Vaelor would have, too." She closed her eyes as she took a shaky breath. "I wish he could see you now. You are so…strong. You've always been *so* strong."

My lip quivered. "Strong," I repeated, nodding once.

Would that be the word I'd have used to describe myself? Had it ever been?

A strangled sound escaped me. "Strong," I said again, if only to convince myself, nodding frantically. "Strong," I said for a final time before shattering.

CHAPTER THREE

My head shook as I crumpled in on myself. She ran to me, catching me as we fell to our knees.

"Oh, my love." Her voice shook, just as mine did.

"I am *not* strong. I am not. I've just weathered the storm as it came—what choice did I have?" The thoughts tumbled from my mouth. "I have been here *alone*. Yes, Alden is my blood. Yes, Iaso is kind, and yes, Rogue has been—has become everything to me, but I was new here. I had no one who was *mine* as everything just piled on, crushing me, killing me. I-I—"

Her grip tightened on me, pulling me closer as the sobs wracked me.

Strong. The word echoed in my skull and cracked the shield I held up constantly. It was all a facade, a necessary front that held in every devastating emotion that threatened to consume me. This emotion—this chaotic, overwhelming emotion—was an ocean, building, thrashing, crashing against the seawall I'd built to protect myself from this exact moment.

But that single word cracked it, and the ocean of torment took its chance, shattering it and pouring from me wave after wave in every sob.

No, strong was not the word I'd use. Afraid. Traumatized. Hurt. Those were the words that built the shield I carried.

But it was not strong.

Chapter Four

Ara

After I gathered myself, we moved to the two chairs by the fireplace, and I told her everything in great detail—why I was kidnapped, meeting Alden, Iaso, and Thana, the attempted murder, Rogue saving me, King Adon, the battle, the scar. All of it.

It left me nearly breathless by the time I'd finished, but I hadn't realized how badly I needed to say it aloud for the weight of it to leave my shoulders. And as much as I needed to say it, Mother needed to hear it to understand everything.

"And that's how I got this scar. I had to save him, just as he had me. After that, Evander… He shot me. Iaso saved me, but she couldn't save our friend Doran, Delphia's brother. He died, and Delphia disappeared with him."

She had let me tell the entire tale uninterrupted. After I'd finished, I pulled my eyes from the fire to face her. Her trembling hand covered her mouth as she sat in the chair, slouched at the shoulders.

"Mother?" I whispered.

"I-I never thought Evander… When I agreed to marry him,

CHAPTER FOUR

I thought he would be the safest option for us. I had no idea. I never thought—"

"Hey." I placed a hand on her arm. "It wasn't him. It was Adon. He had no control, no choice."

"Either way, I can't help but feel like I failed you," she said. "The man I placed in your life because I *thought* he would be safe tried to kill you—not once, but twice. Ara... I am so sorry."

"No, Mother, please. You did *not* fail me, in any way. Please don't apologize for anything, especially something out of your control." I dropped my head to my hands, rubbing my swollen eyes. "I am so tired of apologies, so tired of apologizing."

I lifted my eyes to meet hers and took her hands in mine.

"Let's just...Let's move forward if we can. I want us to build a life here, just as we were meant to. You have been weighed down, suffering through this in silence for so long. I want you to be happy, to live freely. You *deserve* that."

A tear slipped from her eye.

"Ara, when did you become so...grown?" She laughed as another tear fell, and she quickly wiped it away.

I laughed with her before the descending sun caught my attention. The smile slid from my face, and she turned, following my line of sight to see the sun kissing the horizon.

She tilted her head to the side. "So you love him, then? He's kind to you? Genuinely kind?"

"Yeah." A smile pulled at one side of my mouth. "Yeah, he is."

She nodded, swallowing hard. "You know his father... I mean, I'm sure you know he killed Vaelor."

My gut twisted. "Yes, Alden told me, but he is *not* like him,

I promise. While Rogue is his son, he suffered his abuse all the same. Adrastus tried to kill Rogue when he was thirteen because he couldn't shift. Iaso saved him, and that's when she took him under her wing."

Her brows pulled together.

"It's a miracle he hasn't become as hard and merciless as his father, solely because of him," I said. "Despite all odds, he has remained good."

She didn't respond, and I held my breath as the anticipation built in my chest.

"Then I am excited to meet him, your mate. I know that is a wonderful feeling."

"Yes, it…" I stopped as her words took root in my mind. "You know? You *know* it's a wonderful feeling?"

My heart raced as her mouth curved up.

"Yes, you know, they say humans are lost—disgusting, even—because we can't feel our mates." Her smile was sad, nostalgic. "That does not mean we do not have them. You are extremely powerful, are you not?"

My head spun as another piece of my world tilted on its axis.

"The mate bond is truly remarkable in that way," she said.

"You and Vaelor? How did you know? You were mates?"

"Yes, my love. He told me. I couldn't feel it necessarily, but I knew. In the back of my mind, in the depths of my heart, in my soul, I knew. I mean, you know how it can—"

I held up my hands. "Oh, no. I know what the bond does, and I do *not* need to hear the details of you and Vaelor in *that* regard," I said in a rush.

She laughed again.

"Well, yes, we were, and it made the love all the sweeter, I

CHAPTER FOUR

think, knowing we would have you someday. Although, we did wait for a bit. Iaso has that tea." Her eyes dropped to my belly, and my eyes went wide as my hands covered it. "As I'm sure you know."

My cheeks flamed. "Yes, Mother, I know."

The rays of sunset peeked through the window, illuminating her burnt auburn hair and pulling us from our conversation.

Grabbing my hands, she took a deep breath. "It's almost time, my love. I know you must go, but please, *please* be safe. I need you to come back and bring your mate with you."

My throat constricted as I nodded. She had only just arrived, and I was already leaving her.

"We'll be back soon. I promise."

She stood and stuck an elbow out to me just as she always had.

"I would like to walk you down to the ship, at least. Maybe give Ewan a good scare." She laughed, wiping another tear as it fell.

* * *

Ewan's ship was visible in the distance as we exited through the front gates.

The sails were blue—a deep navy that nearly blended in with the sea as the setting sun cast its glow upon it. On the bow was a carved, wooden syren holding a lit torch in her hand, her long tail reaching far below the water.

"She's a beaut, eh?" Ewan said, strolling past Mother and me as we stared in awe.

She looped her arm through mine, tugging me after Ewan.

We followed him down the rocky path lined with tall, swaying grasses. I peeked over my shoulder to see Liv and Iaso, but not Thana or Alden. I knew Thana was staying behind to tend to her family, but Alden's absence surprised me a bit. My brows furrowed as I turned forward again.

Lee was on the dock, ready to assist in the ship's docking when we arrived, all already soaked with sweat after the trek. The breeze, while nearly constant, did nothing to cool the sticky, summer heat.

Ewan clapped a hand on Lee's shoulder before they moved to catch the ropes being thrown overboard, looping them around the posts until the ship was anchored to the dock.

When they turned back to us, Lee's eyes fell on Livvy. He slid around Ewan with ease and stepped towards her. "And who might you be?"

Her eyes widened as he took another step closer. She tilted her face up at him, as she was short—not an inch over five foot—and Lee was every bit as tall as Rogue.

"My name is Livvy."

"Livvy," he purred. "And where did you come from, Livvy?"

She tucked her hair behind her ear to reveal the shell of her ear, her chin high. "Auryna."

"Ah, I see. A friend of Ara's, then?"

Livvy squinted at him—in irritation or interest, I couldn't tell. He released a low laugh.

"But I'm guessing you're staying here now." He gestured to Draig Hearth.

Livvy rolled her eyes. "Don't tell me you stay here as well."

"Ah, it seems we'll be roommates. Maybe I'll see you in passing." The corner of his mouth ticked up. "My name is Correnyk Lee, by the way."

CHAPTER FOUR

He stuck a hand out to her. Her eyes flicked down to it and back up before she cautiously slid hers into it. He lifted her hand to kiss the back of it, keeping his eyes on Livvy the entire time. My lips pressed into a tight line as I held back a laugh; I could nearly feel her snide remark bubbling below the surface.

"Most everyone calls me Lee, but you? You can call me Ren."

"Yeah, sure." She pulled her hand away and patted him on the bicep as she walked around him. "Ren."

"Sounds much better from your lips," he whispered.

Her eyes cut back to him. If looks could kill, he'd be on the ground already. They held each other's gaze for a moment before her eyes did an up-down, and she turned to me without another word.

Throwing her arms around my neck, she gave me a tight hug as she whispered, "I can't believe you're leaving me here. You better come back. *Soon.*"

I wrapped my arms around her in return. "They will treat you well, I promise. I think you might enjoy the company here more than you did in Auryna."

She scoffed and I chuckled, giving her a quick squeeze.

"I'll return as soon as I can."

"Wait!" A voice rang out from the distance.

We all jerked in its direction, and I covered my mouth before I burst into laughter. Running down the hill as fast as he could was Alden, holding his gray robes up to his knees, revealing skinny, pale legs. His long, white braid bounced from shoulder to shoulder as he dodged the stones and brush.

I never understood why he favored those long robes, but at this moment, I was grateful for them. This was a sight I would never forget.

"Don't…leave…yet!" His voice was breathless and cracked as he shouted.

While I attempted to hold back my laughter, Mother and Iaso did not. They were practically wheezing.

"Alden! What are you doing?" Iaso shouted as she wiped her eyes.

He raised a hand to show a small, black book, and my heart leaped at the sight.

When he finally reached the dock, he was out of breath and drenched. "I was…" He braced his hands on his knees. "I found…" Another desperate breath. "I have this."

He held up the book. It was bound in black leather with a small, red crystal in the middle.

I took it slowly and flipped it open to the first page, gasping at the name. "This is Stryath's."

"Yes." Alden stood again, resting his hands on his hips. He cleared his throat and wiped his forehead with the back of his hand as he stepped closer to examine the page with me. "Yes. I read most of it and lost track of time."

Hope bloomed in my chest, and I clung to it desperately. "Does he talk about the first transition?"

"He doesn't say *how* to bring them back, but he does describe some telltale signs of *if* they're back. This journal is around the time of Drakyth's thirteenth birthday."

"His first shift," I murmured.

He nodded, taking another deep breath. "It's all in the eyes. No matter what form he takes, dragon or Fae, his eyes will tell you if it's truly him or his beast. When he becomes conscious again, his eyes will return to normal. Until then, don't believe a word he says or any action he takes. He may be…beastly, for a lack of a better word."

"That's useful," Iaso said. I handed her the journal, and she flipped through a few pages.

"Thank you, Alden," I said before throwing my arms around him. "For everything."

He wound his arms around me in return. "You're so welcome, Ara." He squeezed, and I chuckled as he sucked the breath from my chest. "May the Goddess be with you."

As he released me, Mother threw her arm around my shoulders and pulled me into a tight embrace, finishing the traditional farewell. "And may she strike down any who wish you harm. May she bathe you in triumph."

I felt her take a long, shaky inhale before she stepped back, smiling even though her eyes sparkled with fresh tears.

Ewan stepped forward then, clearing his throat as he extended an arm out to his ship. "Well, without further ado, welcome aboard."

My heart leaped as I stared at the long plank leading onto the ship.

I swiveled to Lee, and before I could say anything, he cut in. "I'll watch for correspondence and let you all know *immediately* of any impending threat. As of now, the armies have retreated from the border."

I nodded, and with a deep sigh, I stepped onto the plank. It creaked under my weight as I continued up onto the deck. Ewan and Iaso followed, leaving the rest of our small family on the dock below. I leaned my elbows onto the rail as Iaso joined me, and Alden and Lee untied the ropes, tossing them back to the crew members aboard the ship.

My eyes misted as the water around the ship began to move, pushing us away from the dock. My throat tightened as Mother smiled, wiping her cheek with one hand as she waved with the other. Livvy stepped into her and slid an arm around Mother's shoulders as Iaso placed a hand on mine.

We'll return with Rogue, and then I'll have everyone in one place. Safe.

I swallowed hard.

For now.

We continued away from the dock, farther and farther, until I could no longer make out their faces. They became nothing more than black silhouettes against a vibrant sunset until it sank below the horizon and their forms disappeared with it.

I gazed after them long after they were gone from my sight, knowing they would be staring in return.

Dropping my head to my hands, I took a slow, deep breath. Between Rogue, Thana, and my mother, the last twenty-four hours had been a whirlwind of emotion, and it left me exhausted. My eyes were still swollen from the countless tears I had shed—and would no doubt shed again very soon.

I rubbed my face before dropping my hands, revealing the dark ocean below. My eyes followed the flow of the water, and I sank into its spell as the sight and sound of the waves entranced me, distracting me from my thoughts.

The sea misted my face as I took another deep breath, inhaling the sea's brine and warmth. Even after dark, the air was warm and humid. As the seasons had shifted from spring to summer, I had exchanged my normal tunic for a sleeveless one, opting for fewer layers, but it was for naught. No matter what we wore, our clothes were soaked and clinging to our skin by the end of the day.

I lifted my hand to my mouth and mindlessly bit my nails.

CHAPTER FOUR

The clothing we wore these days was in stark contrast to those the dresser had given me—sleeves, thick pants, fur-lined coats.

A knot of dread reformed in my gut.

Where could we be going that was so far north, the weather would be so drastically different?

"Did you notice how the water is moving forward rather than towards the back of the ship?" Iaso whispered. There was a light smile in her tone, but there was also hesitation as if she was carefully breaking me from my trance, afraid I might shatter at any moment.

No, I hadn't noticed. I squinted at the water, barely visible by the light of Ewan's lit lanterns. My mouth fell open. "It's pushing us?"

She nodded. "Ewan's magic is related to the sea, like most from Nautia. Rather than waiting for the wind to push us forward, he commands the sea to do it instead." The pride in her voice was clear. "It makes it easier for his crew, not having to adjust the sails as much—the ideal Captain."

My mouth tilted up in a smile. "That's incredible."

"Aye, it is." Ewan joined me on my other side as he patted me on the back. "If I don't say so myself."

We laughed and fell into silence as we stared at the horizon ahead.

"So, the dresser gave you winter clothing, eh?" Ewan asked.

"Yep. Deep winter clothing."

"No one has ever been that far north," Iaso said, leaning onto her elbows.

"Not until now," Ewan whispered.

The silence crept back over us as the full moon ascended, casting us and the sea in its silver light, bouncing from the crest of each wave. The same moon over the same horizon that only a day prior had carried Rogue as he disappeared—a full day ago now with no sign of his return.

My chest tightened. I pulled my eyes away and turned around, reclining onto the rail to face the ship instead.

"We will find him." My voice was low but sounded much stronger than I felt.

Ewan and Iaso nodded in agreement, and the ship groaned as it picked up speed, racing toward the edge of the world.

Chapter Five

Ara

A week had come and gone—seven painfully slow days, each one longer than the last, literally and figuratively, as the sun seemed to set later and later. The nights, while short, had garnered something beautifully entrancing over the past two days. After the sun sank below the horizon, the sky lit with more than just moonlight. Iaso called it the Northern Lights, but the interesting part was that everyone saw different colors. We had argued incessantly, hilariously, the first night it happened before coming to that conclusion. Iaso saw green in every shade imaginable, while Ewan saw a rolling blue, like an ocean in the sky.

For me, a deep fiery orange and red flickered against the black expanse. I had never seen anything like it, so utterly breathtaking, and while I knew it had nothing to do with Rogue, I couldn't help but see it as his fire consuming the darkness.

It gave me hope on this seemingly endless journey. It also made me wonder what Rogue saw; if perhaps what he gazed at each freezing night, even in his current state, also gave him comfort. I hoped so.

We had been steadily sailing north, moving slower while Ewan slept but moving at record speed when he was awake.

The air had cooled from the sticky heat of Ravaryn. It wasn't quite cold enough for the winter gear yet, but the days were crisp and the nights biting—getting more so with each passing day. Thankfully, Ewan had small heating lanterns bought from craftsmen in Blackburn, lit with a never-ending fire that would warm any room, no matter the size or temperature. While they were incredibly helpful, they only worked in enclosed spaces; they wouldn't protect us from the icy weather on deck in the open air.

As the last rays of sunlight extinguished, the temperature dropped with it. I rubbed my hands together and breathed into them, my breath a puff of white steam.

We would need our coats tomorrow at this rate.

Everyone aboard the ship had been warned about the possible weather and packed accordingly, but we still didn't know exactly what we were sailing into.

The weather was one thing, but what of the rest of nature? The sea, the sea life. If Rogue was out here, he had to be hunkered down somewhere, which would mean land. Were there creatures on that land other than him?

With a sigh, I gave one last glance at the horizon before climbing down the ladder to go below deck. The instant warmth soothed my frigid muscles, and I shook out my tense shoulders, breathing in the heated air.

The main hallway was lit the brightest, but even it was dim during the night. Running my hand along the wall, I continued forward until I heard Ewan's hushed voice.

CHAPTER FIVE

"You don't believe in the legend?" he asked.

The sound of movement and a glass bottle being set on a table trickled out from the cracked door, along with the light of a heating lantern.

"No, I don't believe they exist *anymore*. Maybe centuries ago, but I've been alive for a very long time and have never come across a single person who has seen one," Iaso said. Another clang sounded from the room.

"Maybe that's because no sailor has lived to tell the tale," Ewan replied, his voice low, barely above a whisper.

The room went silent, nothing but the sounds of the sea and the ship's groans audible—not even the sound of my own breathing.

Saw what? What could kill every sailor who has laid eyes on it?

The rational part of me wanted to go in and ask, but the tired, overwhelmed part couldn't take the remaining few steps into the room. Not yet.

The answers to those questions could at least wait until morning.

I made a beeline for the room down the hall. Opening the door, I slid in and silently closed it behind me. The smell of Fae rum filled my nose as the heating lantern lit, illuminating the barrels and bottles. Other than lanterns and winter clothing, rum was the next best thing—for both warmth and distraction.

Grabbing a small wooden stool, I dragged it closer to the lantern and picked a random bottle from the shelf. I plopped down on the stool as I popped the cork and took a large gulp. Flinching at the taste, I swallowed and took one more for good measure before turning my eyes to the small fire within the lantern.

Losing myself to the flames, my thoughts returned to Rogue as they often did. I took another swig and sputtered a little as it burned its way down my throat.

His beacon was still just as bright, calling me ever farther north, but…

I sat up straighter, dropping my eyes to the floor as I focused on the feel of him. I set the bottle down.

He was no farther north than he was the day before. Was he stationary?

Between the whirlwind of the last few days, I hadn't noticed he hadn't truly moved in the last day. He was on the same land, and we were inching ever so slowly closer rather than just trying to match his pace northward.

My heart leaped into my throat as my eyes darted to the porthole.

We're coming, Rogue.

The small, rusted circle was frosted with ice but perfectly framed the moon. I gazed at her, just as she watched me in return—just as she watched over Rogue.

It felt like reassurance, like the moon was offering her sympathy with the promise that *this* wouldn't last forever.

For the first time since we boarded, a small beam of hope ignited in my chest. He didn't seem so impossibly far away anymore. We *were* gaining ground. I sucked in a deep breath as my heart fluttered and took another swig, cringing and wiping my mouth with the back of my sleeve.

We're coming.

* * *

CHAPTER FIVE

I couldn't tell if the room was swaying around me or if I was swaying within it.

An involuntary groan escaped me as my vision spun again, nearly knocking me from my feet as I edged my way down the hallway, leaning on the wall as I went.

I was working my way to Iaso. She would have a tea that would soothe this before it became a hangover, and as the ship swayed with another swell of the sea, I was desperate for it.

It was late, but I hadn't slept yet. Not that I thought I would. After sleeping most of the first day away, sleep had been just as elusive as Rogue. Although, if I was being completely truthful with myself, the issue started way before this journey.

The last few months had been…a lot, this and the resurrection of my mother taking the cake. Not that I wasn't happy—I was. My mother being alive…That was a twist of fate I would thank the Goddess for every day for the rest of my life.

And I was glad Rogue had finally, *finally* shifted. I knew it was something his soul had needed, but the way it unfolded left me stunned, worried, and…scared.

Is that selfish? Am I allowed to be scared? It's not me who's been subjected to such pain and forced to lose himself.

Oh, but I was. I was so damned scared. Maybe we wouldn't find him. Maybe I would spend the rest of my days trying to catch him, because I knew, in my heart of hearts, I would never stop looking. Maybe I wouldn't be able to bring him back like I promised.

What would happen to Ravaryn without their king? What would happen to Rogue…to me?

Would I survive never seeing him again, never touching him, or speaking with him? Could I survive chasing his ghost?

My breath hitched as my drunken heart physically cracked.

My hand was flat on my chest, holding the pieces of my heart together, when I reached Iaso's door. I gave a quick knock and waited, inhaling another shaky breath as the ship gave way again. She opened the door within a minute, the look of concern pressed into her features barely visible in the dim, flickering light.

"Ara? What happened?" Her golden eyes roamed over my body. "Have you been poisoned?"

"No, it's just rum. Do you have tea?" I closed my eyes and leaned my forehead on the door frame, searching for the coolness I hoped it would bring.

She pressed a hand to my cheek, whispering, "Are you all right, Ara?"

I cracked my eyes open to her. The circles under her eyes had deepened with lack of sleep—haunted, just like I was.

"Are you?" I whispered back.

She dropped her eyes, giving a quick nod as she stepped aside. I stumbled inside and sat on her bed, resting an elbow on the bed frame as she quickly poured water into a metal kettle and placed it over the small flame.

She turned the chair from her table to face me and sat. "Rum, hmm?" she asked, pulling me from my stupor.

"Right now, my head is quiet," I replied without opening my eyes.

The sound of movement nearly pried my eyes open, but not quite.

"I know you've been through a lot. You've endured more in the past few months than most do in their entire lives, but just like Rogue, you are s—"

CHAPTER FIVE

"Strong," I finished for her and snorted, even as tears pricked behind my lids. "So very strong."

"Ara…"

"No, Iaso. If anyone is strong, it's *you*." I opened my eyes to find she had moved to sit on the bed next to me. Her brows pulled together as she tilted her head to the side, listening. "It is my mother. It's…It's Rogue and Alden and Delphia. No, if I'm strong, I'm strong like a roach that refuses to…refuses to…die." A sad chuckle escaped me, followed by a shaky sigh. "Just a sturdy, little roach that refuses to die."

These were drunken words, steeped in self-pity, alcohol, and doubt, but it made them no less true.

"Well then, if you are a roach, then I am as well. As are your mother and Rogue and Alden and Delphia. Against *all* odds, we are still here. Enduring, surviving. We are all *here*, just as you are. Whatever fate has in store for us, it matters not because we are survivors. As we always have been. As we always will be."

My eyes watered as they lifted back to hers.

"This is just another thing we *will* survive," she whispered and slid an arm around my shoulders.

I laid my head on her shoulder, letting the tears fall freely. They dripped from my cheeks, wetting her shirt, but she did nothing to stop me.

"I'm already so tired," I croaked. "And there's so much more to come. That battle…We were so outnumbered. That's not even a fraction of his army, is it?"

She lifted a hand to my head and slowly smoothed my hair.

"No…No, it's not." Her voice was solemn as her body stilled. "But we must continue because people need us. Ravaryn needs us. They've placed their last hope in us, so you *will* continue. We all will. And one day, the sun will peek over the horizon and shine so brightly, you'll forget it was ever dark at all. And then… Then, you will *live.*"

The word struck a chord—*live*—but I knew she wasn't speaking solely for me.

"That includes you, too."

She was silent for a moment before responding. "Yes."

I waited for her to continue, but she didn't, and I didn't push. We sat in silence, my head on her shoulder and her arm wrapped around me, swaying with the ship for Goddess knows how long.

Minutes, hours, days later for all I knew, the kettle whistled, snapping me awake. Iaso carefully slid out from under me and walked to the table. After mixing the herbs, she placed them in a tin mug and poured the heated water over top before returning to the bed.

She blew on the cup as her eyes lit, strengthening the tea.

"Here. This will help," she said, handing me the steaming cup.

I took a tentative sip, testing my stomach. The first swallow instantly soothed the nausea, and I gulped the rest without another thought.

"Can I stay here tonight?" My words slurred as I fell back, already slipping into unconsciousness.

"Of course." She patted my hair once more before she slid in beside me, pulling the thick, wool covers up to our shoulders. "Goodnight, child."

* * *

I stirred awake a few hours later. Glancing at Iaso, I carefully

CHAPTER FIVE

slid out from beneath the covers, found the last bit of tea, and brewed another cup.

Once it was done, I grabbed the mug and snuck from the room, careful not to wake her. Back in my own room, I pulled on fur-lined leggings, boots, and my thickest coat before heading for the deck with the tea, climbing the ladder and cracking the door open.

The air hit me in the face like pure ice, sucking the breath from my chest. I quickly climbed onto the deck and shut the door behind me.

The tea steamed as the temperature rapidly cooled it, and I gulped it down before it could freeze over. After I finished it, I turned, finally taking in our surroundings.

My lips parted in a gasp.

Everything sparkled—the pale sunrise in the distance, the chunks of floating ice in the relatively calm sea, the frost that coated every surface of the ship. The soft rays of yellow did nothing to warm the air around us, but they ignited every surface. It was magnificent, even as my lashes started to freeze.

The cold had created a world of beauty that thrived in its harshness.

Tears pricked my eyes as chills erupted over my covered skin—not from the temperature but from the view. I knew in my bones this wasn't a sight seen by many, if any at all.

Slowly and carefully, I walked to the rail. In the distance, large icebergs bobbed in the open waters, bumping into those around them, creating small waves in an otherwise calm sea. Dropping my gaze to the waters below us, I watched as they pushed us forward, the bow of the ship plowing forward through the ice.

I was mesmerized and lost in thought, my attention glued to the wooden syren's tail as it cut through the frozen ocean when I noticed a thick layer of ice creeping its way up the bow. It slowly climbed over her tail, spreading out as it continued upwards.

My heart skipped a beat, and I leaned over the rail to get a better view. It continued, consuming the ship quicker than was natural. The ice crept along the entire bottom of the ship, rising from the water on all sides, casting the wood in a solid sheet.

The door behind me opened and shut.

"The ship is slowing," Ewan shouted. "What—"

"Ara?" Iaso asked behind me, but I didn't pull my eyes away from the rapidly growing sheet of ice as I waved them over.

"Come here. Look."

They joined me, leaning over the edge as I pointed to the ice. Ewan's eyes followed, but when I looked at Iaso, her gaze was straightforward, her face pale and eyes wide.

"Oh, my…" she breathed.

"Iaso." Ewan's voice was tight fear as his eyes darted to hers. "It's…"

"Syrens," she finished. "We're in the Sorrowed Sea."

The blood drained from Ewan's face.

Turning, I followed Iaso's line of sight. My breath shallowed as I locked eyes with a creature I hadn't noticed. She nearly blended in with the frozen ocean around her. With pale blue skin and white hair, she was the personification of winter herself. Ice dripped from her hair, her bare breasts, her skin. Her eyes were as white as her hair with no pupil, but they were still clearly locked on us, her gaze heavy and chilling.

CHAPTER FIVE

The ship came to an abrupt halt, tossing us forward. Everyone aboard the deck staggered forward as the ice crept over the handrail. My breath hitched as I watched it inch closer and closer to my glove.

I didn't pull my hand away. It was almost mesmerizing—the beauty of it, shimmering in the sunlight, even beneath its hidden promise of death.

A choked scream snapped me out of it, and I jerked my hand back.

My head whipped toward the sound.

The entire stern of the ship was frozen—men included. At least half a dozen, icebound. Another man, oblivious to the impending icy doom, climbed up from another hatch.

Ewan shouted, "Don't touch the ice!"

He didn't listen as his eyes locked on his comrades. He sprinted toward one—an old friend by the sound of his cries—and the second the bare skin of his fingertips touched the ice, he stilled. He was frozen in motion, his momentum carrying him overboard, long before the ice consumed him. His muffled screams reached our ears as he hit the water. Then he bobbed, as solid as any other iceberg.

My breath shook as we staggered back from the rail, watching the frost rapidly devour the ship.

Hundreds of Syrens pulled themselves from the water and sat on the floating chunks, the droplets of water freezing along their skin, creating crystalline diamonds.

"These are the creatures of legend you were speaking of last night," I whispered.

"Yes," Ewan answered before doing a double take at me. "How—"

"Doesn't matter," Iaso said.

"What do we do?" I asked, clenching my fists.

"I-I don't exactly know," Ewan whispered.

Fear twisted my gut. My throat tightened, and I swallowed against it.

A few of their scaled tails slapped against the water, the sound echoing over the sea like a warning.

"What are they?" I asked.

"I didn't even think they existed anymore... According to legend, they were women once, hurt or scorned by men," Iaso said, her voice barely above a whisper. "When they are....ready, they offer their lives to the Goddess by throwing themselves from the Northern Cliffs. Their human forms die in those waters, but their souls are turned into these lethal creatures—the Syrens. In exchange for an eternity safely away from men, they are sworn to protect..." She swayed and gripped the rail tightly. "Oh, dear Goddess."

My heart pounded.

"They *will* sink this ship," she said, her voice raspy. Her eyes shot to the climbing ice as it cracked audibly, racing upwards. "They—"

She paused and without looking at him, she whispered, "I love you, Ewan."

"Are you serious? *Now* is the time you wish to tell me?" he whispered forcibly without looking away from our soon-to-be murderers.

"Well, I couldn't let you go to your watery grave without hearing it, and I couldn't go without saying it."

Ewan turned to her then, his face torn. Iaso peeked at him, and the second their gazes locked, Ewan closed the distance between them. One hand wound in her hair, and the other found her lower back as he pulled her into him.

CHAPTER FIVE

He kissed her deeply and thoroughly—long overdue.

Pulling back, he whispered, "If I am to go to my 'watery grave,' then I'll be damned if I don't taste you first. You have always been my northern star, Iaso, and I would follow you to the ends of the world. In this life and the next."

A choked sound escaped her as she threw her arms around him.

"I love you, too, Iaso," he whispered, wrapping a hand around the back of her head, holding her against his chest as he watched the ice.

We were backed up as far as we could go when I felt the heaviness of the Syrens' gazes land on me. A disturbing chill spread over my skin as if their eyes were probing me, invading me.

Turning from them, I found hundreds of eyes locked on my face, and my heart sank.

They wanted something. *She* wanted something, the first Syren to have revealed herself to us. There was no way to know what, but it clearly had something to do with me. Whether she wanted a martyr or a sacrifice or even just her next meal, I would be it. If it would save Iaso and Ewan, then I would do what was required.

As I met her gaze, I inhaled a shaky breath and took a step forward. The ice crunched under my boot, shooting cracks in every direction.

"Ara, no!" Ewan shouted and jerked forward.

I whipped my head back to him and held a hand up as I dropped my eyes—his boot narrowly missed the ice by half an inch. Iaso snatched him back with her eyes glued to me, tears freezing on her cheeks as they fell.

"I love you, too, you know," she whispered, and I nodded,

holding back tears of my own.

We held each other's gazes—both panicked and terrified—as we waited for the ice to embrace me, but to my *immense* relief, nothing happened. So I nodded, turned back to the Syren, and took another step, then another and another. She slowly tilted her head to the side as I made my way to the handrail.

As soon as my gloved hands hit the rail, bright blue pupils appeared and entrapped me in her stare.

Panic swarmed in my chest as I realized I *couldn't* look away.

Chapter Six

Ara

My grip tightened on the rail. My entire body tensed, but I couldn't move, couldn't look away.

"Ara?" Ewan asked.

I wanted to answer. I wanted to scream and run back to them, but I could do neither. I was locked in place, unable to move or be moved—not by the wind that my magic stirred, not the sway of choppy seas, not even by the shock of energy I released. A bolt flew through the ice as if carried by a current, and she flinched, her eyes wide, but her grasp remained.

"Ara," Iaso cried.

I winced at the brokenness in her voice, but I couldn't turn to soothe her.

They thought I was going to die here—just as I did.

Who are you? The voice slithered into my mind, deep and smooth. Dark. Endless, like the bottom of the sea.

My lips parted, but I couldn't speak.

Why do you smell like him, but not? You are connected to the Draig, yes?

The Draig? Rogue! You've seen Rogue? You— My thoughts were frantic, spiraling. I jerked against her restraint to no avail.

But you smell different. You smell like... Her chest rose as she inhaled deeply, and her eyes roamed over my face. *Your magic smells of...her. The Goddess has blessed you as well, has she not?*

Yes, I replied.

Her brows furrowed, her eyes flitting to the men aboard the ship. She glanced at each one with apprehension, but her gaze paused on Iaso. Pain flashed across her pale features for a split second before they smoothed into frosty indifference.

Her cerulean eyes met mine again. *The Goddess saves all.*

The Syrens silently returned to the sea, one by one, until just she remained.

With one more quick glance at Iaso, she dipped her chin in farewell and her pupils disappeared along with her trance. Gasping, I stumbled back, clutching at my temples. A splitting headache erupted across my skull as the remnants of her tentacles released me.

Iaso sprinted toward me and caught me as I stumbled, warmth flowing from her palms in strong waves.

The ice thawed in seconds, melting into cold puddles, but the men who had been attacked didn't recover or wake. I winced at the sound of their bodies falling to the deck. Ewan whispered to his next in command, the man's face grave as he listened. When Ewan finished, the man nodded once and gathered men for what I could only assume was to dispose of the dead.

My stomach twisted, threatening to expel its contents. I dropped to my knees and clutched my abdomen as Iaso

CHAPTER SIX

mumbled unintelligible words at my side.

"Ara, hey." Ewan placed a hand on my shoulder.

Iaso dropped in front of me and gripped my cheeks, pulling my attention to her as her eyes glowed. The ache dulled as she studied me but refused to yield entirely.

"What was that?"

"She was in my mind. She spoke to me," I said, my entire body trembling.

"I've never heard of that." She glanced at Ewan.

He shook his head. "I haven't either." Ewan released a shaky breath, creating a puff of white vapor. "But we may be the first ship to ever be granted the Syrens' mercy. Thanks to you, Ara."

Iaso nodded before facing me. "How?"

Walking past them, I gestured to the hatch. "Let's go inside first. I need tea, I think." I knelt down to grab the handle before pausing. "And rum. I need rum. Anything to make the knives in my skull dull."

"Rum? Yes, rum. I need that as well." He chuckled, but there was no humor in it.

Iaso hesitated, glancing over her shoulder. She stared into the distance and surveyed the horizon.

"What is it?" I asked.

She didn't respond. Instead, her hand covered her mouth as her brows pulled together.

"Iaso?"

She turned to us, her eyes wide but not with fear. If I had to guess, I would say it was…hope, which in turn fanned my own. My heart leaped into my throat. Releasing the latch, I stood on shaky legs, swaying as my head throbbed with the motion.

"Ewan, do you remember what the Syrens protect?" she asked.

"They protect..." He trailed off. "Is that where you think Rogue is?"

I glanced in every direction, looking for something, anything. "Where? Where do you think he is?"

Iaso lifted her face again, searching our surroundings. "If we are in the Sorrowed Sea, then—"

Her words stopped abruptly as a small black dot came into view on the horizon, and I felt him. He was an irresistible call, a demand yanking me forward.

"He's there," I voiced with a sureness I didn't quite understand but felt in every inch of my body. Just his nearness set me aflame, the *almost* sight of him tugging at my own lifeline.

But he wasn't the only one. There was something else—*many* somethings. An uncountable number of massive, moving beasts that dwarfed even the creature of night, and it had been monstrous. I could feel their heartbeats, their life threads, each and every one calling to me, tickling the feelers of my magic.

They were, by far, the strongest and oldest creatures I had ever encountered—alarmingly so.

"But...what is there with him?" I asked. "What animals live on this island?"

"This is the Hearth," Iaso said. "The birthplace of the wyverns. *His* wyverns."

"Wyverns?"

My eyes locked onto the tiny island in the distance as the word ricocheted through me, dislodging every fact I knew about them—which wasn't much, considering the limited books in Auryna. The only bits of information I knew were common knowledge, basic facts about the creatures.

Historically, wyverns were infinitely connected to the draigs, their bloodline somehow intertwined. It allowed the wyverns to choose their master, but there hadn't been a sighting in hundreds of years. Their history was thought to be just that—history, left to be written and spoken about, but not... seen. Lived. Still living.

"Wyverns?" I asked again when they didn't respond. "I didn't think those still existed."

I edged my way back to the rail.

"Apparently so. Although, I think most of us believed they died off years ago since they've been silent for so long." Iaso's voice was nearly a whisper, dripping with awe and disbelief as she joined me at the rail.

Even from this distance, the isle stood out from everything around it, every bit its name—the Hearth. It was jet black against the icy, white sea with waves of heat rolling off it, blurring its surroundings. The ocean immediately surrounding it was thawed, calmly lapping on the black sand beaches that hemmed half the isle, the other half ending in jutting cliffs. Plumes of steam and smoke wafted from the island, drifting over the sea.

"Why would Rogue come here, though?" I asked.

"It's... Well, it's..."

I glanced at Iaso. The gears were turning behind her eyes as she processed what it meant. She stood straighter, a smile curving her lips.

"They—the Wyverns of Old..." She let out a breathy sound, halfway between a cry and a laugh. "Of course, they would choose him. They would be fools not to. If he knew their location, then they've chosen Rogue as their king, deemed him worthy of ruling, of wearing the Obsidian Crown. Their ruler is always a draig, you see, but not every draig rules. They only choose one in each lifetime, but no one has worn the crown since Stryath. He was chosen a thousand years ago. This is"—she shook her head with another awed laugh—"the highest of honors. The ultimate sign of indisputable power."

Goosebumps erupted over my skin as pride swelled in my chest. While I was surprised by their existence, I wasn't shocked in the slightest that they chose Rogue.

I would choose him, too. In every fight, in every dream, in every choice.

A smile tugged at my own lips.

"The Hearth is their home, their breeding grounds," Ewan added, "and no one has ever laid eyes on it other than their chosen. The fact that you were able to lead us here is a miracle."

"It's never been done before," Iaso said. "Even those who get too close by happenstance are warded off by the Syrens."

The smile slid from my face. "Will they allow us to go ashore?"

A heartbeat of silence passed, louder than any words.

"I hope so," Ewan finally answered.

* * *

My fingers tapped mindlessly as we neared the island. I was ready to go, nearly chomping at the bit, with several daggers strapped to various locations and a bag of clothes for him.

Rogue's call was unbearable. My body was tense, restraining the urge to jump ship and swim to shore if that would get me there faster.

CHAPTER SIX

It felt like the bond but immensely stronger. With every passing second, my nerves frayed further. It wasn't just the bond *leading* me to him—it dragged me by my life thread, *demanding* I get closer.

Closer.

Closer...

"How much longer?"

"Just a few minutes. I think the north shore would be our best option. It seems to be the least rocky."

Jagged black stones, glistening like polished glass, were shattered in massive chunks along the beach. They also sat across the sea floor, gleaming just under the water's surface, but the northern tip seemed to be mostly clear with just one boulder near the water's edge.

"We'll have to take the dinghies the rest of the way."

With one last glance at the island, I took a deep breath and followed after Ewan, anxiously tapping my fingers on my thigh.

We were so close to finding him, but that wasn't all we had to do. We—*I* had to bring Rogue back, return his consciousness which I had no idea how to do. *Would our presence be enough? Would talking to him be enough?*

Without an elder draig, we were flying blind, and I didn't like it. Not one bit.

A small thought returned in the back of my mind, flaming my anxiety. *What if I can't? What if...What if we lose him entirely, alive but gone?*

I rubbed at my chest, inhaling a deep breath with closed eyes.

It's not an option. He will *come back.*

Ewan climbed over the rail and stepped into the boat. It

swayed under his weight before he steadied it and held out a hand to Iaso. With a deep breath of her own, she glanced at the island, took his hand, and climbed over. I followed behind her, taking the seat at the front.

Ewan shouted to his crew, and the boat lowered painstakingly slowly.

Everything seemed to be happening in slow motion, purposely teasing my already frayed nerves, moving entirely too slowly for the anxiety coursing through my veins.

The temperature around us dropped a few degrees as we dipped into the water, the bottom of the boat already cold enough to seep into our shoes.

Untying the rope, Ewan pushed against the ship with the oar. Silence hung in the air as he replaced the oar, and the water caressed the boat at his command, sending us toward shore.

My heart thundered my ears with each diminishing foot that brought us closer, and I could barely stand it—the restlessness, my churning stomach, the tightness in my chest.

Just looking at the foreign shore we would soon be stepping upon sent wave after wave of unease through me, so I dropped my eyes to the water. Even it seemed to be calmer than me—although, at this point, I would think most things were.

It was crystal clear between each white-capped wave, revealing thin fish swimming between the glinting black stones, schooling and creating flashes of silver. The rocks became smaller and less frequent until the sea floor became nothing but black sand, rolling with each wave.

My chest constricted with fear but also hopefulness as I dragged my eyes forward to the beach.

CHAPTER SIX

We were getting closer—closer to shore, to Rogue, to going home.

Something shifted near the massive boulder on the shore. My eyes darted in the direction but saw nothing out of the ordinary. I stared, waiting for movement when I noticed...

The boulder was breathing.

"Oh, no," I whispered.

A second passed, and it shifted again. We froze, the boat no longer moving.

A head rose from the boulder—no, not a boulder.

The entire body moved. Wings of the blackest skin unfolded from its back, stretching as it rolled its shoulders.

My eyes widened to saucers as it stood, its long, serpentine neck unwinding from around its body.

We remained motionless, not even daring to breathe.

Its head snapped in our direction regardless, its glowing yellow eyes boring into our boat. They lit with confusion quickly followed by anger. With lightning speed, it ran on the knuckles of its massive wings and hind legs, sliding into the water and disappearing against the back sand.

"Oh—" One of them shouted behind me, but the words were caught off as the boat lurched backward. Ewan's magic acted on instinct, the water pushing us back at full speed, too suddenly.

We were thrown forward as the boat jerked back, and a scream tore from my throat as I was thrown over the edge, falling into the water head-first.

The waves rolled under the surface, and I rolled with them as the currents yanked me in every direction. Ice consumed me as I tumbled end over end, losing all sense of direction.

Seconds passed. Minutes. My lungs burned while my

extremities numbed. I flailed, kicking and grabbing for anything to gain ground.

My entire body hit something solid, bumping me upwards, and my head broke through the water's surface, just for a moment. I sucked in a ragged breath, vaguely hearing my name called as another wave crashed into me, throwing me under again.

I rolled end over end, ramming into the sea floor before being picked up and slammed again. There was nothing to grab—no rocks, no limbs, nothing, but the sand that gave way under my desperate attempts as stars danced behind my eyelids.

I'm going to die here. Liquid fire filled my lungs as they screamed for air. *This close to Rogue...and I'm going to die before I see him.*

Blinding white panic tore through me. I couldn't see. I couldn't feel. I was frozen, locked in a never-ending spiral as I was beaten into submission by the sea who demanded her price.

I kicked and sprawled and reached for anything until my muscles were weak. I could barely clench my fingers, much less fight the sea. Exhaustion, lack of air, defeat, whatever it was weighed me down as I stilled. I sank lower, relenting to the thrashing current.

I nearly wanted to give in. I started to, my mind blackening, calming... and it almost felt like peace. Like rest.

I almost wanted it.

I started to reach for it.

After everything, the chaos and pain and guilt... Rest was just out of reach.

Something sliced through my shoulder. The remaining

CHAPTER SIX

air tore from my lungs in a muffled scream, and my hand clutched at it as warm blood seeped between my fingers.

Suddenly, I crashed into something hard, stopping the incessant spiraling. My hands frantically grabbed at whatever it was as my eyes popped open, burning with sea salt.

Two distinct, glowing yellow eyes stared back at me.

Another silent scream caught in my throat, but I latched onto the spines along its back.

It stared for a brief second before its eyes darted to my hands. I tightened my grip on each spine as my vision tunneled.

My skin was numb with ice while my chest was engulfed in flames.

It was torture.

Agony.

Go. The thought frantically echoed in my mind as I jerked my hands, pleading with a beast that could kill me just as easily.

It glanced back at me before shooting forward faster than I could've imagined. It took everything I had to hold on as we slithered through the water. The second we climbed onto the shore, I fell onto the black sand, clutching at my chest as I coughed and gagged.

After expelling the water from my lungs, I wretched over and over, emptying the contents of my stomach until only hollowness remained. My arms and legs gave way beneath me, and I collapsed onto my back, shaking and exhausted.

But not freezing.

A sob escaped me as my hands dug into the sand on either side of me. It was warm.

Opening my eyes, I again looked straight into two yellow

orbs. He studied me, leaning closer to sniff.

I attempted to move, to escape, but my body refused, lying limp against my every command—too exhausted to obey. *Traitor.*

Resigned, I closed my eyes as silent tears slid down either side of my face.

I lay there, waiting for the pain of death that never came. Instead, I heard the sound of gravel and sand crunching under its heavy weight. I peeked an eye open as it returned to its perch, lying down with its long neck wrapped around its body once again.

After a few minutes, I tested my limbs, wincing as my thighs ached with the slightest movement. Bracing myself, I forced my body to roll over onto all fours, suppressing a cry as pain stabbed every muscle.

My eyes shot to the wyvern. His eyes were still closed, uninterested.

I took another breath, clenching my jaw before standing. A whimper escaped me as I took a step, stumbling and falling to the ground.

A cry tore from my shredded throat as my knees hit the ground, and my hands flew to my neck. The air burned all the way down, but making a sound was like trying to speak with a white-hot dagger stuck in my throat.

Traitor, I thought to my body again as a fresh wave of tears slid down my cheeks. *We don't have time to waste. Yet, here I am, weak and useless, stuck on the shore of this Goddess-forsaken island.*

Inhaling another deep breath, I stood again, covering my mouth with my hand as a sharp pain raced through my body, nearly knocking me back down.

CHAPTER SIX

I paused, studying my surroundings as I adjusted. When I steadied, I looked to the water and found Iaso and Ewan. They were still in the boat, hovering offshore. I lifted a hand, and they waved back.

With that, I turned in the direction of Rogue, and a choked sound escaped me. Straight ahead was a path of sorts—a black sand hill that led inland. One I would have to climb to find Rogue.

The sight nearly defeated me.

Closing my eyes, I allowed a brief second of respite before bracing myself and taking a slow step forward, then another and another.

Each step was agony—knives in my feet, my thighs, my lungs. My head pounded. Blood leaked from the wound on my shoulder, dripping from my fingers.

Tears poured down my cheeks, and I let them fall, not bothering to wipe them. *If all I'm destined to do is cry these days, why even bother?* The thought scraped at my nerves, cultivating a rage that fed on the havoc already wrecking me.

I pushed forward, gritting my teeth as I slowly gained momentum, but my feet felt so *heavy.* There might as well have been stones in each boot. Lifting them was exhausting, but climbing the hill… It was excruciating.

With a roar of frustration, I shucked off my heavy, water-soaked fur coat. It fell to the sand behind me with a squelch, and I continued, screaming with each step.

I made it nearly a fourth of the way up when the sound of a boat sliding onto shore broke the silence.

Whipping my head around, I found Iaso stepping onto the shore as Ewan stood in the shallow water, holding onto the edge of the small dinghy.

Chapter Seven

Ara

The wyvern snapped awake and quickly leaped from his perch. It closed the distance to Iaso, its throat reverberating with a deep, unnerving growl—a warning—as it bared its teeth, lowering its head to eye level with her.

Her eyes shifted to me, and I shook my head. With silent understanding, she looked back to the wyvern, holding her hands up in surrender. She started to back away but paused.

Slowly, she reached a hand into her coat pocket and pulled out a vial. My eyes narrowed in on it. Whatever it was, Iaso knew I needed it.

The wyvern growled again, closer this time. She froze, scrunching her eyes as its breath blew the strands of her hair.

My heart raced, but I was helpless to do anything but watch.

With another steady step back, she dropped the vial into the sand, her eyes flicking to me.

I gave a quick nod as she took the final few steps to the boat, rejoining Ewan. He slowly slid his arms around her waist, pulling her back into him with his eyes locked on me, wrinkled with worry.

"Go," I mouthed to him.

He hesitated but dipped his chin. Grabbing her hand, he led her back onto the boat and the waves pushed them away. Once they were far enough from shore, the wyvern returned to his perch without another glance in my direction.

It had to be Rogue. The Syren said I smelled of him. The wyvern must sense it, too—attaching me to him in some way, permitting me on the island but not the others.

As the wyvern closed its eyes again, I staggered to the vial she dropped, falling to my knees in gratitude as I unscrewed the cap and downed its contents. The ache in my muscles dulled within seconds. The wound on my arm scabbed over. The daggers and salt in my lungs dissipated, allowing me to breathe again.

"Thank you," I sobbed, pulling my knees to my chest and burying my face in them.

I gave myself five minutes. Just five minutes.

My eyes were swollen when I raised my face to the sea again. The dinghy was already at the ship with a rope attached, and from this distance, I could barely make out the two figures standing on the small boat, watching, waiting to see me rise.

With another deep breath, I stood, bracing for the pain that never came.

A shaky breath of relief escaped me.

Giving them a quick wave, I turned and began the trek back up the hill.

As I crested the top, my mouth went slack.

The island was large, speckled with steaming, blue pools and slabs of black stone. The sun shone rays through the steam, glinting off the sand and gravel. In the distance were the remains of a castle, abandoned and crumbling. Built atop a steep incline, it was undeniably the island's highest point, just like Draig Hearth.

I wondered briefly if it too dropped off into the ocean on the other side, but I didn't have time to truly consider it.

Wyverns were everywhere—hundreds sleeping, walking, swimming. Existing.

My presence did not go unnoticed.

Their heads turned to me one by one as they stilled with caution. My heart leaped into my throat, but I descended the hill with my eyes locked on the obsidian ruins.

As I neared the first group of wyverns, my breaths shallowed. I tensed, but they didn't move as I walked past, and neither did the next group or the next.

They were allowing me by, allowing me free reign of their home.

Temporary relief flooded me before the anxiety returned.

He was here. He was near. I knew it. I felt it in my bones, and his call was more than just that. It sucked the very breath from my lungs with the promise that he would return it.

With each step, my pace quickened until I was sprinting toward the castle.

Rogue.

His name echoed through me, claiming me, reminding me who I belonged to, who belonged to me.

Rogue.

I raced across the island, feeling thousands of eyes on me, but I didn't care. It didn't matter. Nothing mattered.

Nothing but him.

Him.

My heart pounded.

CHAPTER SEVEN

So close.

Sweat dripped down my spine.

So close.

My lungs burned once again. My muscles burned. Everything burned.

So close.

Just a few more steps.

My feet came to a screeching halt at the base of a massive staircase—wide enough to accommodate the Draigs it was built for. It was cracked, but solid and inky like the rest of the ruins.

"Rogue," I breathed.

A moment passed, and my heart thundered in my ears.

The sound of movement echoed from inside—a thump and then another.

Heavy footsteps.

Anxiety pulsed through me. Standing still was unbearable. *Waiting* was unbearable.

As he crested the staircase, I was frozen in place, unable to move even if I wanted to. He was the largest creature on the isle by far, triple the size he was the last time I had seen him. With the same blood-colored scales, he stood out against the dark stone in exactly the right way—as if he belonged there. As if it were built solely for him.

He rolled his shoulders and stretched out his wings between the two obsidian columns marking the entrance of his castle, casting a shadow across his kingdom.

He was magnificent. Breathtaking. "Beautiful."

His slitted eyes immediately found me, glowing like molten lava.

I stood straighter as heat flooded me, rolling through my

veins like liquid desire before pooling between my thighs. My cheeks flushed as a gasp escaped my parted lips.

His throat lit with sparks as he lowered his head, his nostrils flaring with an inhale.

He invaded me in every sense, my every inch, and he *knew* it.

Still, he didn't move. He waited like the undeniable king he was.

He waited for *me* to go to *him*.

With an uneven breath, I began the climb on shaky knees.

His gaze never left me during my ascent, but when I was within mere steps of him, he backed out of sight.

Swallowing hard, I took the final step, cresting the staircase to find Rogue standing before me. It was actually him, in his Fae form—naked and covered in a layer of grime. His massive, blood-red wings hung behind strong shoulders as he stood tall, his chin tilted down.

While everything else seemed to return to normal, his eyes had not. They were still slitted, glowing, and firmly locked on me.

A feline smile ticked at one corner of his mouth, and my breath hitched. He took a slow step forward as his head cocked to the side, studying me. On instinct, I took a step back.

He released a low, breathy laugh. "Do not run from me," he commanded, his voice sending a chill down my spine.

The air heated as the smell of smoke and evergreen spice surrounded me, *flaming* me.

"And what if I did?"

He took another step closer. "I *will* chase you, prey."

A thrill shot through me at his promise.

CHAPTER SEVEN

"Like I've been chasing you this past week?"

I took another step back, and his eyes dropped to my feet before crawling back up my body, taking in every inch.

"Hmm, based on the way you smell, I'm sure the past week without your mate has been..." He took another step closer, his chest rising with another inhale. "Torturous."

I almost said yes, because it was—for more reasons than his clouded mind could conjure, but that was a conversation for another time.

Right now, I just needed to remind him who he was.

I stifled a smile and took another step back. What better way than to remind him of our first time?

"Don't," he warned.

I bit my lip, grinning as I turned and ran, giving his dragon the hunt he so desperately craved.

A deep, thundering laugh echoed behind me. "You can run, but it will do you no good."

Those words. My heart skipped a beat, and I urged my feet faster, bracing for the chase I knew would follow.

Dipping behind the farthest crumbling wall, I darted down what seemed to be a hallway with no ceiling. I followed it to the end, took a sharp left, and kept sprinting.

It was at a steady incline, with each turn I took climbing higher.

My heart thundered in my chest as I reached the top and the floor leveled out.

The room—if it could be called that—was magnificent. While the rest of the castle was made of obsidian, these walls were dark glass that allowed sunlight to filter through and bounce off every surface. Dark, maroon vines bloomed along the wall, filling the air with a floral scent. The same vines that adorned the exterior walls of Draig Hearth.

Along the back wall, centered in the middle, was a throne made from the same black stone, massive and perfectly untouched by the elements.

I took a cautious step toward it when Rogue landed with a loud thud behind me.

A scream escaped me as my heart jolted, returning me back to the task at hand. I bolted for the throne, but he quickly wrapped an arm around my waist, snatching me back into his chest.

"Oh, no, you don't," he purred into my ear.

I almost melted into him. *Almost.* Instead, I jerked and kicked against him before reaching down to snatch the dagger from my boot. Before I could stab it into his calf, he grabbed my wrist.

His chest vibrated with a low chuckle. "Not again. Drop it."

I hesitated, my breaths shallow.

"Drop. It."

The dagger clattered to the ground, the sound echoing through the empty room.

"That's my good girl," he said, releasing my wrist to run an extended claw up my arm. Goosebumps erupted in his wake as a shiver ran down my spine.

His tongue slid along the marks on my neck—*his* mark—and I moaned involuntarily.

"I want to taste every single inch of you." His hand grazed along my breast, circling over a nipple before sliding down to skim along the top of my trousers. His fingers dipped down beneath them, barely above where I wanted them—*needed* them. "Especially between these pretty little thighs."

CHAPTER SEVEN

"Oh, Goddess," I breathed.

My body was burning, and he was the fire. The match. The air. He was everything that set me aflame.

A hand gripped my throat, choking off my breath.

"You moan *my* name when you feel like this," he whispered into my ear, sending sparks over my skin before lessening his grip, returning the air to my lungs.

Focus.

I took a deep breath, but his scent was the only thing I inhaled. His fingers slid lower, and my cheeks flushed, knowing he could feel the slickness.

"So ready," he murmured, sliding a finger into me. "So..."

"Yours?"

"Mine," he growled.

My head fell back on his chest as he pulled out before dipping two fingers back in, another moan escaping me.

Focus.

Grinning, I slid my hands down my thighs, pushing my hips into his groin.

He released a dark laugh, gripping my hip with one hand and sliding his other up my spine to grip the back of my neck, holding me in place as he ground into me.

My grin curved into a triumphant smile as I reached my calves and snatched the dagger from my other boot, stabbing it into his calf as I twisted out of his grip.

With a laugh, I took off in a sprint toward the throne.

The sound he released stole the smile from my face—a powerful growl that shook me to my bones. Of anger or lust, I didn't know, but it propelled me forward as adrenaline shot through my veins.

I darted behind the throne, breathing heavily with my back

pressed into it.

The thundering in my ears drowned out the sounds of his heavy footsteps as he neared.

As my eyes adjusted to the darkness, an overly large door appeared.

"Ara." The voice was Rogue's, but not—lower, possessive. Feral.

My heart lurched.

I jerked forward and turned the knob. The door creaked with age but gave way slightly. Shoving it open with my shoulder, I glanced back and locked eyes with Rogue as he stepped around the corner.

The door swung open.

He stopped, smirking. My brows furrowed at the look on his face as my foot took another step…but connected with nothing.

My eyes snapped forward just in time to see the open ocean churning beneath me.

A scream tore from my throat, and then, I was free-falling.

I tumbled end over end as the roaring wind whipped my hair around my face, slicing my cheeks. I scrunched my eyes as I frantically pulled at the strands.

I had been falling for too long. I had to be—

Holding my hair back, I cracked my eyes open to see the rocky water rushing toward me. The waves thrashed, capped with white as they foamed at the mouth to devour their falling prey.

My breath left me in a whoosh as the wind stole the remaining air in my lungs. My hands covered my head on instinct.

About to die. My fists balled. *Again.*

CHAPTER SEVEN

Overwhelming anger pulsed through me.

Death is fucking following me.

The sea spray coated my skin moments before a dark shadow caught me mid-fall. We hovered for a split second, breathing heavily as the ends of my hair swayed in the water below.

My arms wrapped around his neck in a vice grip as I gasped for air.

And he let me fucking fall.

Chapter Eight

Rogue

The taste of her fear and desperation alone would have driven me forward in the hunt if nothing else, but that wasn't exactly what happened.

Another scent danced along her breath, something I recognized but couldn't place—warm and rich, whispering of...

The scent filled my lungs, clouding my thoughts before narrowing in on her.

Need.

This delectable little creature was in need of me.

It was irresistible, leaving me entirely at her mercy, even as her fists pounded my chest.

"What is wrong with you? Who are you?" she screamed.

I flew back to the doorway and stepped smoothly onto the stone. Once we were back onto solid ground, she fought my hold, kicking and screaming, but I only tightened my grip.

"What is wrong with you?" she repeated. "You *let* me fall!"

Stopping in front of the throne, I set her on her feet, towering over her as her face twisted in anger.

It was amusing—such a small creature raging at one so

much larger than her. *Brave.*

A smile tipped one corner of my mouth, and she stood straighter, her cheeks flushing. A heartbeat passed before her hand reached back and cracked across my cheek.

The amusement dissipated in a burning flash—immediately replaced with something much darker.

She shoved at my chest as she shouted, "I came all the way here for you. I nearly died for *you*. Twice, might I add."

I gripped her wrists as they hit my chest again. She tried to jerk back, but I didn't release her. She screamed in frustration.

"I told you not to run."

Her mouth fell open before snapping shut. "Wake up, you fucking flying lizard! Wake up before I kill you because this"—she shook her hands again, reinforcing my hold—"is insufferable."

Flying lizard. I almost broke out into laughter, but the rage on her face and in her words was very real.

"You disobeyed me."

"Oh, I disobeyed you?" She was smiling, but her tone was far less than happy. "Disobeyed," she repeated, shaking her head and chuckling to herself.

"Yes, disobeyed. Had you listened, maybe you wouldn't have nearly fallen to your death."

Simple logic.

Her eyes were wide, her chest rising and falling quickly. "You *watched* me step off the ledge with that ridiculous smirk on your face. You wanted me to fall."

The sparkle of rage in her eyes was intriguing, something I wanted to provoke if only to see her explode.

"Perhaps I wanted to teach you a lesson. Disobeying your

king has consequences."

That did it.

Her eyes flashed a second before I was flung back several feet by two matching bolts of lightning from her palms. I landed on my back with a thud and a satisfied smile that only flamed her anger as she stalked over.

Leaning over me, she snarled, "Perhaps my *king* needs a reminder that his mate takes orders from no one. *Perhaps* he needs to learn to bow to her instead of shoving his foot so far in his mouth that he can no longer breathe. A lesson I thought he would've learned already when he knelt before me again and again and *again.*"

I sat up, rising to one knee as I cocked a brow. "Perhaps my *mate* requires me on my knees once again."

The warm, spicy scent of her arousal met my nose again. *Delicious creature.*

She stood straighter. "Perhaps you should beg for my forgiveness before I grant you such a pleasure."

I dropped my eyes, chuckling as I rose to my feet. "Beg? You wish for me to beg?"

She locked eyes with me, the heat turning her gray irises to molten silver.

Mesmerizing.

"I won't beg." I took a step forward.

She mirrored me, walking back a step with each step I took toward her until her back was pressed against the wall.

"And I'm not sorry for letting you fall."

Her hand snapped back to slap me again, and I caught her wrist before she had the chance. I raised it to the wall above her head. Her other hand clawed at my hold, and I captured it, too.

CHAPTER EIGHT

"I won't apologize for chasing such a...*willing* prey," I whispered over the skin of her neck as I inhaled her scent. Her breath hitched. "I caught you, didn't I? You didn't die. You weren't hurt—well, maybe your pride." She jerked against my hold as I laughed, and my free hand moved to her waist, holding her still. "I just like the taste of desperation in my hunt."

She was still as stone then, listening to my words as the scent of her arousal deepened with each breath. My knee slid between her legs, widening her stance, and I could nearly hear her stifled moan.

"I want to *taste* the desperation on you when I feast," I purred into her ear, and her throat bobbed. "Are you desperate, little prey?"

She didn't answer.

"I think you're so desperate for my tongue between your thighs that you've already soaked through your undergarments."

Again, she didn't answer.

My hand slid lower along her waist and teased along the hem of her trousers, directly under her navel. She was tense, her mind fighting me every step of the way.

"Ever the fighter. Tell me, if my fingers sank lower, what would they find?"

She lifted her chin. "They'd find me so slick, your mouth would water."

She swirled her hips, pressing into my thigh, and my mouth ticked up in a one-sided grin, momentarily stunned. She took the opportunity to slide one of her hands free and plunged it beneath her trousers. My eyes were glued to the movement, heat pulsing through me, as she dipped her fingers into herself and pulled them back out, glistening.

To my surprise, she slid them along my lips. I licked the taste of her from them, groaning as she filled my mouth.

My hand flew to her throat, locking her against the wall as my mouth dipped to hers, but before I could devour her, her palm found my chest.

We were so close, I could feel her breath.

Her lips—red and swollen—smirked. "Beg."

I shook my head, releasing a breathy laugh. "You wicked little thing."

"Beg, and I will grant you whatever part of me you wish. Don't, and well…have nothing," she said with a voice that could've brought any man to his knees.

But I wasn't any man.

"It seems we're at a stalemate," I said as I kissed the curve of her neck.

She was breathless as she tilted her head, granting me access. "It would seem so."

"And what should we do about that?"

"We can't do anything." She slid her other hand free from my grip. "Not until you wake up."

"What—"

She shoved at my chest hard, and I staggered back a few steps as she caught me by surprise. Without missing a beat, she flung herself at me and wrapped her legs around my waist. My hand wrapped around her in return, holding her to me.

I started to smile, but her palms found my face, holding my gaze on her. Her eyes flicked back and forth between mine, searching for something, but clearly not finding what she'd hoped for.

"Come back to me, Rogue. *Please.* Wake up. We need you.

CHAPTER EIGHT

I need you."

My brows furrowed. I tried to listen to her, to understand her, because her voice was desperate—not in the way I had wanted only moments ago—but my thoughts were muddled. Her words nagged at something deep within the recesses of my mind, but it felt as though I was tugging a small thread that refused to unwind.

I shook my head, unsure of what to say or how to give her what she wanted. I didn't know *what* she wanted.

A small, defeated breath escaped her as a tear fell from the corner of her eye, and I followed it as it rolled down her cheek.

She wrapped her arms around my neck and reclined her head on my shoulder. "I don't know what else to do. I don't know what I'm doing. This wasn't a job meant for me, and I-I'm sorry, Ro. I just..." She stilled, her face buried in my neck.

I had no idea what she was talking about, but her pain burrowed into my chest—worse than any pain of my own, begging me to resolve it.

"I love you," she whispered and sank her dull teeth into my neck.

My eyes shot wide as I tensed. Searing bolts of lightning pierced my skin, pulsing through my entire body and reiterating a claim I had seemingly forgotten she held over me.

Another bolt of her energy shot through me, and I gasped, sucking in the icy air as if breathing for the first time. Her scent filled my very being—rain and wildflowers.

My own form of coming home.

She had grabbed the string I couldn't seem to unwind, wrapped it around her fist, and yanked it from the shadows.

My arms tightened around her as I finally truly *recognized* who I was holding.

"Little storm."

A sob wracked her, and she pulled back. My blood still coated her lips, and I laughed, wiping it away along with a fresh tear.

I looked around the throne room, still holding on tightly to Ara—the only steady thing in my life at the moment. It was like waking from a dream, only to discover it wasn't a dream at all, but a reality I had no control over. I knew exactly where we were; I recognized this place, but *I* didn't bring myself here.

"Are you...?"

"I'm me," I whispered.

She smiled and surrendered, crashing her lips to mine with a fervent hunger, and a satisfied groan reverberated through my chest at the feeling.

"You are *not* leaving me. Not with this shift. Not ever," she muttered in between kisses. "You're mine, just as I am yours."

"Mine," I snarled with an intense possessiveness I had truly never known before now. It was a tidal wave that would've knocked me to my knees if not for the overwhelming need to take her here and now. To claim her. Protect her. Have her.

I pulled back, my eyes grazing over her. There was a faint haze surrounding her form, a gleam to her skin as the sun washed over her. Her eyes seemed to glow with their own light, an entrancing silver I couldn't look away from.

Treasure, a deep voice growled from the recesses of my mind. *My treasure.*

My eyes flickered as the beastly part of me fell in love with her. While other Draigs chose their trinkets, mine chose something much more exceptional. I felt it, the growing affection—nearly infatuation. The flames in my irises glowed bright enough to illuminate her face as my eyes reflected in hers.

Mine.

She lifted a hand to my cheek.

"Yours," she whispered, nodding.

Setting her down, I grabbed her wrist, holding her gaze as I moved her hand to my mouth, kissing her palm. Her breaths quickened as I kissed her wrist, the scar on her forearm, the crook of her elbow, continuing upwards until I reached the hollow of her throat.

"You *are* mine." The words left me of their own volition, pulled from my throat by the fierce need to claim her again and again and *again.*

"Yes," she moaned—a deliciously breathless sound I wanted to swallow while buried inside her.

Lifting her arms, I pulled her blouse over her head and tossed it to the side. She unbuttoned her trousers, letting them fall to the ground before stepping out of them and into me.

My hands grazed over her waist, her back, her breasts—desperately needing to feel every inch of her.

She yelped as I nipped at her skin and slid my hands down to lift her. Her legs wound around my waist, lining me up with her clothed entrance, already soaked with need.

My grip tightened with a groan.

At this moment, that small scrap of fabric preventing me from sliding into her was the bane of my existence.

But one that was easily rectified.

My lips never left her skin as I climbed the stairs and sat her on the throne. Dropping to my knees before her, I placed a hand on each of her thighs, slowly pulling them apart. One hand slid higher, closer, and her breath hitched as I hooked a finger in her underwear, teasing along the edge.

"I meant what I said. I will taste every inch of you, Ara." With a smirk, I ripped the fabric from her skin and tossed it to the floor below. "Don't wear these again," I ordered, meeting her gaze.

She nodded breathlessly as her legs spread before me, baring herself on my throne—a feast fit for a king.

Her hips hiked, a moan sliding from her parted lips as I bent and ran my tongue over her, groaning at the taste—ambrosia fit for a god.

I nipped at her sensitive spot and sucked away the pain, smiling as she wound her hands into my hair with another broken cry—the sounds of her prayer as she worshiped her god, one *so* willing to be on his knees for her whenever she needed it.

Her fingers knotted in my hair and pulled my head up. "Please, Rogue. I need more. I need *you*."

I resisted her pull, barring my arm over her waist as I dipped back down between her thighs, dragging my tongue over her slowly. I wanted her on edge, provoked until she could no longer stand it, until she was writhing beneath me with no restraint. I wanted her to *beg* for mercy.

My pursuit of her ecstasy was ruthless. I swirled my tongue, plunging my fingers into her until her screams were the only sounds I could hear. She came once—a beautiful shattering—but I didn't stop.

She ripped at my hair, her breath hitching as I swiped over

CHAPTER EIGHT

her hypersensitive clit, but I needed it, needed to hear her, taste her as she fell apart on my tongue again.

"Rogue, I can't…" Her words fell into unintelligible gasps, and satisfaction rolled through me.

I moved faster, harder, as she wound tighter, her body arching ethereally—the kind of beauty painted by artists, preserved for history as she was too glorious for this world to not be shared.

But this one—this magnificent storm—was mine, and mine alone.

Nothing had ever filled me with more pride.

"Beg for me, little storm. Beg for release, for mercy."

"No." The word floated from her in a pant.

My fingers curled inside her as I pulled back an inch, clicking my tongue. "Stubborn."

Her gaze met mine, heated and desperate, and her mouth ticked up in a grin as she ground her hips with the movement of my fingers. "Would you have me any other way?"

"Never," I purred. *Fuck mercy.* The way she moved against me, watching me with such delicious depravity offered none.

My gaze remained fixed on hers as she watched me devour her until she came on my fingers again, her mouth falling open in a silent cry as her fingers pulled at my hair. I was soaked with her release when I rose to her, breathing in her moans as I kissed her. My tongue pushed into her mouth, making her taste herself as her hand reached down to wrap around me.

I slid my hands beneath her and lifted her as I turned and sat on the throne. With her legs on either side of me, she lined me up at her entrance and let her head fall back as she sank onto me. I reclined with a hand behind my head as she lifted herself and dropped down again, chasing her own pleasure.

She placed a palm on either side of my face, raising my eyes from our conjoined bodies to her face. She kissed me once, and then again, and again. She kissed my lips, my cheeks, my forehead as she rode, her hips rising and falling with each peck.

My hands moved to her hips, over her waist to her breasts, exploring, touching, savoring. One hand slid to the back of her head, knotting in her hair.

My fingers dug into her hip as I lifted her, pounding into her with a burning need, satisfied only by her screams as they echoed through the empty throne room.

Music to my ears.

Minutes, hours, days could have passed.

We were lost to time in the throes of euphoria with no desire to return.

* * *

"I shifted." It was more than a statement: a realization.

She was curled in my lap, my fingers drawing circles over her lower back as her head rested on my chest.

"I know," she whispered. "Are you all right?"

I hesitated, unsure how to answer. Everything felt physically fine, but the memory of that first shift had me scrunching my brows. The pain had been excruciating, unlike anything I had ever experienced. Broken bone after broken bone, dislocated joints pulled and stretched larger, the tearing of flesh and skin…

Her ear was pressed to my chest, and she peeked at me with

concern. "I can hear your heart racing."

"I was just...It was painful, I can't deny that. More so than I have ever felt, but it's something every Draig before me has gone through, and every single one conquered it in the end."

I had shifted, and I would shift again, by choice. I would put myself through it over and over again until one day, it would be as simple as breathing.

It was the way of Draigs, and I was relieved to even be able to do so, to be part of my family's long-standing traditional magic, to feel the connection to my ancestors.

Everyone but my father.

I chuckled as a small wave of satisfaction rolled through me. I hope he's watching from whatever hell he resides in. This shift has allowed me to be everything he tried to force me to become—the first fire-wielding dragon. Everything he desperately wanted to control and then nearly killed me for, all just beyond his reach from the other side of the veil.

I hoped he was watching so I could conquer every bit, every ounce of my magic, as a massive vulgar gesture to him if nothing else.

Even beyond the unreasonable and ridiculous satisfaction, though, there was something else, another sensation, that had awoken.

I felt...different. I felt proud—a refreshing feeling I had never felt about myself. Why would I have? I was the Draig without a shift—the ultimate disappointment.

Now, I felt...whole, as if the world around us had become a little less dark, a little less lackluster.

There wasn't a way to explain it, but I knew, without her saying a word, it was exactly the whirlwind of emotion she had gone through when her tied magic was freed.

I hadn't even realized there had been a piece missing until it was filled, but now, I saw it clear as day.

"You saved me," I murmured, releasing her to raise a hand to my neck, to the mark *she* created to free my shift, the one she had re-created today to save me once again.

She claimed me—not once but twice—devoted herself to *me,* and in the process, gave me the other half of myself.

"I, too, must be blessed by the Goddess," I said with an uncontainable smile, winding my arms around her waist again as I kissed the top of her head.

She released a laugh that warmed my chest. "Why do you say that?"

"To be claimed by you, the mighty Storm Bringer? I cannot fathom another reason I would be so lucky." She started to protest, but I tightened my hold on her and continued. "I don't deserve that. I don't deserve you, but I will spend every single day of the rest of our very long lives earning it, earning *you,* my kind, brave, and unfathomably *strong* force of nature."

She had shocked me with a force I hadn't felt before, knocking me across the throne room on an angry whim. I couldn't imagine the damage she could do with real rage and intent.

"Strong." She chuckled, wiping her cheek. "For some reason, that sounds better coming from your mouth." She tightened her hold around me. "Goddess, I missed you."

"I missed you too. More than I can put into words."

We sat this way for a long minute before our situation started to dawn on me.

"Wait, if I flew here, how did you get here? Where are we—" My eyes widened to saucers. "No…No, that's not…"

CHAPTER EIGHT

She pulled back, meeting my gaze with a slight smile. "Yes. Whatever is going through your mind, yes."

Shock settled over me for more reasons than I could count.

"The wyverns? They're still alive?" As the words left my mouth, my thoughts raced. "The wyverns, they—"

"They chose *you*, my chosen one. They have deemed you worthy of finding them, of wearing their crown, of being their king." She placed a hand over my heart. "You"—she tapped my chest—"because you are *worthy*."

I had no words.

"Maybe it is I who is not worthy of you," she whispered and stood, grabbing my hand to pull me up. "Come on."

I followed her in silence, refusing to give a voice to the never-ending war of self-doubt that tore at me.

I had never been worthy. Not of my title. Not of my people's trust. Not in my father's eyes. Not in my own eyes.

But I could be.

I took a deep breath.

I could be worthy. For her. For them.

For me.

We stepped onto the ledge above the staircase and stood between the two massive obsidian columns, and my breath caught.

The eyes of every wyvern swiveled to us, locking on me. My skin pricked with awareness as I was laid bare before them—my darkest thoughts, my greatest fears, every insecurity—but while I was vulnerable, I wasn't uncomfortable.

A heartbeat passed and they *knew* me, through and through.

Another heartbeat passed and each head lowered ever so slightly, their wings stretching out to either side. A feeling of certainty filled me, pulling my spine straighter as they bowed in acknowledgment.

The wyvern on the distant shore—long and serpent-like—rose slowly and rumbled, the sound low but familiar, an ancient, soul-binding pledge that struck me to my very core.

The rest of the wyverns echoed the sound, rising in unison. It continued, spreading and growing until the entire island nearly vibrated with resonance.

My own wings ruffled, stretching out to their full length before the same sound rumbled through my chest. My pupils slitted, my throat sparking with fire as the sound was thrown over the island—my acceptance of their pledge.

With my reply, they riled, flapping their wings, leaping from ledges, roaring into the sky. Their excitement was nearly as palpable as my own. My heart felt lighter, uplifted by every wyvern's approval.

Ara looped her hand in mine, pride shining in her eyes, reflecting in the tears that threatened to fall. My own smile returned with awe as I wound my fingers in hers, and my gaze turned back to the wyverns.

My wyverns.

"I can't wait to tell Doran about—" The words stuck in my throat.

My jaw clenched with my chest, both nearly tight enough to crack bone. I could feel Ara's eyes on me, the empathy rolling off her in waves as she tightened her grip on my hand but didn't breathe a word.

Clearing my throat, I uttered, "Doran *firmly* believed the wyverns were still alive. There were several drunken nights lost to the back and forth over facts, legends, and clues. He would've loved to see this."

CHAPTER EIGHT

I released a small chuckle. He definitely would have given me a vulgar gesture seconds before clapping me on the back with congratulations in the midst of his *I-told-you-so's*.

"I miss him, too," she whispered. "I'm sorry, Ro. I wish he could have seen all this."

"Me too," I sighed. Just a week too late—his death decades too early.

If the wyverns were here, that would mean this was the Hearth: an impossibly lost island, protected by the elements and Syrens. The bond could have led her, but we were at least a week from Draig Hearth, over open water, including the Sorrowed Sea.

My chest clenched at the thought of another person I loved risking their life, but I took a deep breath against it, rubbing my knuckles on my sternum.

"If we're on the Hearth, then...how did you get here?"

"Well"—she lifted a hand to my neck and delicately touched the mark she left—"I just followed you."

Her touch on the mate mark returned a lightness to my chest. It didn't banish the heavy grief, but it allowed me to breathe. It was an irresistible feeling, a drug undoubtedly as addictive as the rest of her. I grabbed her wrist lightly and pulled her hand to my mouth, kissing her silver scar.

"No." I kissed it again with a chuckle. "I meant, how did you travel here?"

"Oh." Her face fell slightly as her cheeks flushed. Pulling her hand from mine, she gestured to the shore. "We sailed."

"We?" Turning, my eyes followed hers and spotted the ship hovering just offshore.

"Yes, Iaso, Ewan, and me."

I swallowed hard. Several people I cared for risked their

lives for me.

"Come on. I know someone will be *very* relieved to see you intact and conscious." She smiled but it didn't quite reach her eyes as she tugged me down the stairs.

"Iaso?"

"She…blamed herself," she whispered, peeking back at me. "For what happened when you were thirteen, because it was my curse that blocked your shift."

Rage rushed through my veins like liquid fire. *Fucking Adrastus.*

"No. It wasn't her fault. I don't want her taking the blame for anything that bastard did."

"I know. I told her that, but I believe she'll listen to the words more when they come from your mouth."

Chapter Nine

Ara

His hand never left mine as we headed back to the shore, now fully clothed. As we crested the hill to the beach, the dinghy hovering off the coast jerked toward us, moving at an unnatural speed.

Just as we stepped onto level ground, Iaso stepped out of the boat into the water, wading waist-deep as fast as she could. Shedding her fur coat, she continued forward, the sun glinting off her golden rings and beads. Ewan jumped in and followed after her.

The wyvern along the coast lifted his head to her but didn't move as his eyes shifted to Rogue, waiting.

"My son. My son." Her cries echoed across the beach, her voice cracking with each word. "My son."

Rogue released my hand to run to her, catching her as she stumbled from the waves. The second her arms wrapped around him, words tumbled from her mouth, drowned by her sobs.

"I am so sorry. So sorry. I never meant… I cannot believe…"

Rogue's brows furrowed as he pulled back, holding her at

arm's length.

Her cheeks glistened with tears as she gestured to the scar hidden beneath his tunic. "That spell. That *curse*. It was the curse that prevented you—"

"Iaso." She stopped, breathing heavily. "Do not ever apologize for what you did to save Ara. You saved her, my *mate*, Iaso. Remember all those conversations you had with me? The ones where I rolled my eyes and pretended to ignore you? You said over and over again that you wished I could find love and a mate, could find happiness. That would have never happened without that spell. You gave her a chance, gave *us* a chance, to do just that. That is all you are responsible for. That is it. Nothing else."

I nodded at his words, at the honesty in them. Everything he said was true: Iaso had saved me and given my mother the chance to hide until it was safe again.

She had saved us all—me, my mother, and Rogue.

"If I had never placed the spell, your father would've never—"

He shook his head before interrupting her. "If you had never placed that spell, Ara would be dead. I do not blame you for what he did. I never could, because I *know* you saved me—in more ways than one. Do not ever carry the weight of anything he did, Iaso. Please. I could not stand it knowing you did."

She stared for a moment before nodding slightly and placing her hands on his cheeks. "No matter how you look at it, it was my spell that prevented your shift, and for that, I am sorry, but I appreciate your forgiveness nonetheless, even if you don't consider it that. You may not be my blood, but you will always be my son, and I will always, *always* protect

CHAPTER NINE

you." She released a shaky laugh as another tear slipped from her eye. Quickly wiping it away, her eyes darted back to the growing number of wyverns along the shore. "Although, it would seem you may no longer need my protection."

Rogue laughed, hugging her tighter with one arm as they turned to face his growing ranks.

"I am so proud of you, Rogue, but to be truthful, the wyverns would have been *fools* to not have chosen you."

"Aye, that they would have been," Ewan added, throwing his arm around my shoulders in a quick squeeze. "And you— good job, lass. I don't know how you did it, but thank the Goddess, you did. I am glad to see you are well, Rogue."

Rogue gave me a sly smile that had my cheeks flushing. "Yes, I'm quite well. Now, we just need to find the crown."

His eyes shifted inland, and our eyes followed. My heart stopped for a split second as we were met with hundreds of eyes watching, waiting.

"I'll need it to be able to communicate with them."

"Is that what the crown does?" I asked. "Allows you to speak with them?"

"Yes, it'll give him the ability to speak with the wyverns, to understand them," Iaso answered. "To command them."

"Command?" I eyed the wyverns. There were hundreds, larger and mightier than any creature I knew of on the mainland. In a war where we were greatly outnumbered, that could be...

"Yes, command," Iaso said. "That's why the wearer of the crown has historically been the undeniable ruler. What army could face this?"

It didn't need to be said, but hearing it renewed a sense of hope.

Maybe this would turn the tide. Maybe this would be what persuaded Adonis to end the war and withdraw from Ravaryn.

A chill ran up my spine.

Rogue stepped forward as the guardian wyvern stepped down from his perch, lowering his head to Rogue. He placed a hand on his snout and the wyvern closed his eyes, lowering farther.

"I'll be back, I promise." The wyvern's yellow eyes flicked to me, and Rogue followed his line of sight with a faint smile. "As will she."

Rogue's gaze shifted to each of his wyverns, acknowledging them before he joined us again and slid his hand back into mine.

"We—" Iaso started to speak but stopped, dropping her eyes. Nudging its nose against one of Iaso's golden rings was a tiny golden wyvern—tarnished and filthy, but golden nonetheless. It was young, barely bigger than a large dog.

Iaso froze as the wyvern's pitch-black eyes roamed over her jewelry, snagging on the golden beads in her braided hair, the golden armband snug on her bicep, and the rings adorning her fingers.

The breeze blew, and the scent of infection wafted from it. The small wyvern shifted and released a sound that could only be described as a pained whimper as its right wing drug along the ground.

"Ah," Iaso said, dropping to her knees. She eyed it carefully as her hand slowly reached out to touch the injured wing. It whipped its head to her, snarling as she lifted it. "Hey now," she scolded.

It shifted its head forward again, letting her probe the

CHAPTER NINE

injury. In the soft membrane of its wing, near the meat of his shoulder, was a wound, blistered and festering with pus.

"Oh, poor child. I see." The wyvern's metallic skin reflected the light of her glowing eyes as her fingers delicately grazed along the site. "It's boiling with fever."

The wyvern shifted, crouching away from her touch as another whimper escaped.

"How did you know I was the healer?" she whispered. Its inky eyes turned to her, blinking once before the wyvern nuzzled its snout into her golden rings once again. She chuckled. "Or were you just curious to see someone as golden as yourself?"

She ran a hand along its stocky neck, and it leaned into her, closing its eyes. With a sigh, she stood, wiping her hands on her trousers. "All right, well, we have to bring him. He won't survive otherwise."

Without a word, Rogue nodded and scooped the wyvern into his arms, grunting at the weight. The wyvern slumped against him as Rogue carried him onto the dinghy. Iaso started to follow but did a double take at the vegetation growing along the steaming rocks.

Her head tilted as she stepped closer, sliding her hand beneath a leaf to study it. She nodded and dropped to her knees. Carefully, she scooped the sandy dirt and pulled the plant up, roots and all.

"Wildfyre," she said with a shrug. "It only grows in warm places. Very hard to find."

* * *

Leaving the wyvern in a spare room with Iaso, Rogue joined

me on the deck and leaned on the rail next to me.

The sun kissed the horizon behind the island, turning the frozen sea a brilliant orange as the ship groaned and moved forward. We stood in silence, watching the wyverns stare at us in return. As we drifted farther away, a few leaped into the air, circling the island before following behind us of their own accord.

My head whipped around as the slender wyvern I had deemed their guardian soared overhead, his shadow swallowing the ship. He flapped his wings, the force creating a wind that blew my hair back. Two more followed suit, continuing ahead of us, and then another and another. Five wyverns in total followed their king's lead, even without the crown.

I wrapped my arms around myself as chills erupted over my skin—not from the stinging cold that permeated the air away from the isle, but from the pure power radiating from these creatures, from Rogue.

He threw an arm over my shoulder and pulled me into him.

As the sun dipped below the horizon, it disappeared in a flash of green before casting the world in darkness. I glanced up as the stars twinkled to life, calling to the moon as it rose, illuminating us in a silver haze.

Rogue's hand slid under my chin to tilt my face to his. "I love you, little storm," he whispered, leaning closer to slide his lips along mine in a delicate, tender kiss. "Thank you."

"As if I would ever let you leave me so easily."

He laughed against my lips, filling me with a warmth that chased away any remaining chill. His grip tightened on my chin as he deepened the kiss, shifting from heartwarming to ravenous. His other hand knotted in the hair at the base

CHAPTER NINE

of my neck as my hands found his cheeks, and I pulled him down to me, needing him closer.

I was nearly lost to the feel of him when an icy breeze blew over us, sucking a gasp from my lungs. Snow swirled in the wind, growing thicker with each passing second.

"It's *much* colder away from the island," he murmured, blinking rapidly as his lashes started to ice.

Shielding my eyes with one hand, I took his with my other and led him to the hatch. As soon as we climbed in, he closed the door, and heat enveloped us. I stifled a smile as he closed his eyes and sighed briefly, reveling in the warmth.

When he opened his eyes again, they swirled with the same molten desire as before, reflecting the flickering lantern light. I held his gaze, slowly backing into the wall and he followed my lead, leaning over me with one hand braced above my head.

The ship swayed, bringing him close enough for me to feel his breath on my cheek.

"My savior," he whispered with a smirk, taking my chin lightly between his thumb and forefinger.

"I was just returning the favor," I whispered back.

He grinned as his eyes sank to my mouth. A heartbeat passed and he lowered to me, gliding his lips along mine.

"What a pair we are." He tilted my chin up, kissing my lips one more time before moving along my jaw, down my neck, meeting his mark.

His words were reminiscent of another time, another conversation.

We were still the same people with the same past but... entirely different.

Everything felt different.

He nipped at the mark, sending sparks along my vision as my moan drifted down the empty hallway.

Better, I corrected myself. Everything felt better.

"Not so broken after all," I replied breathlessly, arching into him.

"No." He smiled against my skin. "Not so broken after all."

I wound a hand in his hair, pulling him deeper into me. The tips of his wings slid along my calves as his free hand roamed over my waist, his scent filling my lungs. He was everywhere around me.

He was here.

Here.

Overwhelming relief flooded me as the realization sank in. He was here. With me. Safe.

Tears welled in my eyes, and I quickly wiped my cheeks as my breath hitched. He pulled back, furrowing his brows.

"Hey," he said, concern pressing into his features. "What's wrong?"

"That scared me. I was…" My breath hitched again as a fresh wave of tears welled. "Terrified, Rogue. I was so terrified. Terrified that I would never see you again, that we lost you to your shift, and I would spend the rest of my days chasing you across the world—and mind you, I would have. I never would've given up on you. And I was worried you would be angry with me or upset that I—"

He moved a hand to either side of my face, stopping the words tumbling from my mouth uncontrollably. He shook his head and laughed under his breath.

"Let me make one thing *abundantly* clear: there is not a single force in this entire realm that could keep me from you. Not the shift. Not Adonis. Not even the chains of death.

CHAPTER NINE

I would claw my way from the grave, defying the Goddess herself, before I ever let you shed a tear for me. You are not just my mate, Ara—you are my *home*. Even if you hadn't come to my rescue, I would have returned eventually. I would have found a way. I will always return to you."

I bit my lip, nodding with blurred eyes.

"You're stuck with me. Whether you like it or not, I'm yours." His smirk returned. "All right?"

I couldn't help but mirror his smile. It was infectious. *He* was infectious—a disease I welcomed with open arms, and he certainly took his chance, worming his way into every fiber of my being.

"Okay." I chuckled, sniffling as I wiped my cheeks with my sleeve.

"As for being angry with you, what do I possibly have to be angry about? For you claiming me? For freeing my shift? Ara..." His thumbs swiped across my cheeks. "You are single-handedly the best thing that has ever happened to me. I would've always been yours, and gladly so, but to know you are mine because you *want* to be? Because you *gave* yourself to me? That is a gift I didn't expect to see in this lifetime."

Another tear slipped from my eye, but not for sadness or fear.

I inhaled a shaky breath through my smile and cupped his cheek with my palm. "When I spent my entire life wishing for freedom and adventure and...love, never once did I expect it to come in the form of a six-foot-five Fae with wings, but Goddess, am I glad it did."

Rogue chuckled, lowering his forehead to mine. That was exactly what Rogue had offered when I needed it most—freedom. The freedom to hope and want and actually take what I want without guilt or fear or restraint. To be free of any shackles other than his, and his were shackles I adorned myself with willingly, wholeheartedly.

He didn't give me my voice, but he sure did coax it out of me—even if it was in the most infuriating ways.

He pressed his lips to my forehead in a soft kiss before stepping back.

"Now," he said, extending an arm, "show me where our room is. I would say we both need about a week's worth of sleep."

A laugh escaped me, deepening his smile as I grabbed his hand and started down the hallway. Peeking up at him, I added, "A week at the very least."

Chapter Ten

Ara

We had all stripped back down to our typical summer clothing as we approached Ravaryn, the air hot and sticky. The heating lanterns had been turned off, but nothing could lessen the heat on deck. I swore I could nearly see heat waves sometimes.

I hate the summer season, I groaned to myself as we sat on a wooden bench that creaked under our weight as we did so. Leaning back on the rail, Rogue threw an arm around my shoulders and pulled me close, kissing the top of my head.

The journey home had been uneventful, the days quick.

Iaso's golden wyvern was faring much better already. While his wing was still pained, the deep infection had healed, the fever gone. She had spent day and night with him, keeping a close eye for fear that the fever would boil him. At some point, their relationship had become less like the healer and the healing, and more like mother and child. She had taken to him just as much as he had her. By the third day of our return trip, she had already claimed him as her "second child," and he played the part, following her about like a lost puppy.

She had named him Aurum, claiming it meant "shining dawn" in the ancient language, "gold" in others. I couldn't think of a better name. With the loss of infection and a good scrubbing, his golden metallic skin had regained its luster, shining as brightly as her golden eyes and rings.

They were made for each other. There wasn't a doubt in my mind.

"We'll reach Draig Hearth by sundown tonight," Ewan shouted from near the bow. Iaso and Aurum played behind him, her laughter echoing over the wind as she ran and jumped, the tiny wyvern leaping about behind her. Ewan watched them fondly, grinning from ear to ear.

Rogue lowered his face to mine. "Want to have some fun today?"

"Depends. What did you have in mind?" I asked.

"Come on." He turned and dropped an arm under the backs of my knees, scooping me off my feet. I yelped as he leaped into the air, hovering a few feet above the deck. "We'll catch up with you guys in a few hours," he yelled down to Iaso and Ewan.

They nodded and waved, all smiles and laughter as they preoccupied themselves with their small wyvern.

I couldn't take my eyes off Iaso as we flew higher, even as the crystal-clear water grew larger and she grew smaller. Iaso's brown skin had bronzed in the sun, her green and gold attire complimenting her perfectly. It was as if the gold she adorned herself with was created solely to grace her skin, as if the world was created around her, for her, rather than the other way around.

When I could no longer make out their forms, I turned forward. "So, where to?"

CHAPTER TEN

"I thought we could go for a swim and have a nice summer day to ourselves before we return," Rogue said, smiling sheepishly.

"Sounds good to me. Let's get lost."

His chest shook with laughter as we flew over the water toward an island in the distance. The water was shallower here than it was at Draig Hearth, calmer and a light turquoise color that matched my mother's eyes.

I had already spoken to Rogue about her and Livvy's arrival and while he was excited to meet them, I could see the nervousness in his eyes, even if he didn't voice it. It wasn't unfounded. My mother had every reason to be skeptical and afraid—and we both understood that. I just hoped that, with time, she could get to know him and see the differences between Rogue and his father because there were many. In fact, blood was the only thing they shared.

"Look," Rogue whispered, pointing down.

I leaned over, gasping as my eyes landed on the largest turtle I had ever seen. It swam slowly with a school of fish, casting its massive shadow over the rainbow corals beneath it.

We were so absorbed by the graceful creature, we didn't see the wyverns coming.

They plowed into the sea, spraying us with salt water. I squealed as we were soaked, Rogue's booming laughter the only thing I could hear.

They scared the living daylights out of the sea life which scattered in every direction as the five wyverns barreled through the crystal water before bursting through the surface and shooting straight up into the sky.

They chirped back and forth, dipping and diving.

"Well…" Rogue shrugged with a mischievous grin. "We *were* here for a swim."

I wiggled my brows at him and tightened my arms around his neck. "I believe they're waiting on you, your majesty."

A wink was my only warning before he dove into the water. He released me as we went under, and I held my breath, swimming along the bottom until my lungs burned—a nice contrast to the burn I had felt under the surface just days ago. The water was warm and smooth, the sand soft beneath me.

I wanted to remember the ocean like this, rather than the death trap I had spiraled in.

Peeking my eyes open, they burned before adjusting to see the sun's rays shining through the water, illuminating the flashy fish and shells. As I swam near, the fish darted away, and I chuckled to myself.

I turned back to Rogue to find the guardian wyvern between him and me, his pitch-black scales tinted blue under the sea. A slight moment of fear took hold before I stood and scooped my hair back, letting the water run down my back. The sun kissed my skin, the breeze blowing the salty air around us.

The wyvern swam past me, letting his hardened skin run along my leg. I gasped and stilled, but he circled back, doing it again. I reached a hand out cautiously and glided it over a wing as he swam past.

"He likes you, it seems," Rogue said when he broke the surface beside me.

I turned to him, and my lips parted. Water droplets rolled down his tanned skin, his wings hanging relaxed behind him. His hair was long past his shoulders, several small braids dispersed through it, all soaked and slicked back.

CHAPTER TEN

My eyes dipped lower, following his scar down his bare chest, but I stopped as they met the waistband of his trousers and rose back to his eyes.

"Like what you see?" He tilted his head to the side, wading toward me.

"It's all right." I shrugged. "Could be better."

"Better? In what way?"

I hooked my fingers in his trousers. "The sight would be better bare."

"Would it now?"

"I'm sure of it," I hummed and stepped into him, letting my hands run over his torso.

When he was close enough, I peeked up at him, biting my lip as I smiled, and his eyes didn't miss a single movement. He watched intently, his gaze heated.

Too easy. He was all too distracted as I swiped my leg behind him and knocked him off his feet with a shove. He fell back into the water with a shout and a splash as I took off in the other direction, running as fast as I could through the water as laughter bubbled in my chest.

I didn't get far.

A scream escaped me as he scooped me from behind and tossed me into the water.

I jerked to my feet, staggering as my hair plastered to my face. Pushing it back, I giggled and said, "Okay, truce?"

"Never," he replied, closer than I realized.

I didn't have time to open my eyes before he scooped me again and leapt into the air, shooting into the sky.

"I haven't smiled and laughed like I have with you since… ever. I don't think I ever have."

His words were light and full of mirth, but they tugged at

my heartstrings. I slid my soaked tresses back and wrapped an arm around his neck, pulling myself up to kiss him on the cheek. He chuckled, peeking down at me as we flew.

"Well, you better get used to it. I plan to have a *very* long life of smiles and laughter with you." It sounded sappy, but I meant it—every word. He had suffered enough, given enough.

"You'll get no argument here," he replied.

Lifting me higher, he kissed me on the forehead, grinned, and winked. Again, my only warning. I screamed as he barrel-rolled us back into the water.

* * *

The sun was setting, casting us in brilliant orange, as we sat on the sandy beach of some lost island.

Rogue tossed me an apple from a nearby tree and the water flask he'd brought as he plopped down beside me and rested his elbows on his knees. We were exhausted after spending the day swimming and baking in the sun, but it was a satisfying exhaustion—the kind that filled your heart and made you want nothing more than to bathe, cuddle up in bed, and sleep a deep, dreamless sleep in the arms of your lover.

Rogue sighed, and I peeked over at him as I took another bite of the sweet fruit.

"Doran didn't know how to swim," he said, resting his chin on his arm. "I was supposed to teach him after this damned war was over."

I pulled my eyes back to the ocean, dropping the apple to my side.

"I still forget he's gone sometimes—well, you saw. It makes

me feel like the worst person alive and definitely the worst friend. Who forgets their one friend is dead? I find myself wanting to tell him things, and I—"

"No," I interjected. "No, you're not. For so long, it was just you, him, and Iaso. I think...I think it would be sad if your soul just cut him off or disregarded him as a friend, as someone to talk to. No, I think it shows how much he meant to you, how much he *still* means to you."

He nodded without tearing his eyes from the waves lapping at the shore. "He was my only friend for so long. I had Iaso, but she was my mother, you know? There are some things you just can't tell your mother." He laughed, running a hand through his salty hair. "Sometimes, you just need a friend who will listen to every real, raw thing you have to say and then throw a bottle of rum at you and tell you to stop whining. He was that for me, and I for him. We had each other—brothers against the world."

A lump formed in my throat, and I swallowed hard.

"I'm sorry, Ro. I know he was a great friend to you," I whispered, glancing over. "I'm sure he's just on the other side of the veil, telling you to stop whining as he takes another shot of rum for having to listen."

His form shook as he laughed and looked to the sky. "I'm sure you are, you bastard."

Chapter Eleven

Rogue

We waited with the plank as the ship neared shore. People were filing down the path that led to the dock. Alden, Lee, Thana, and...

A flash of white hair caught my attention, and I stood straighter, gripping the rail. "Is that..."

"Delphia." Ara's voice was as hopeful as I felt.

Relief flooded me, a grin stretching across my face. *Thank Goddess.*

Behind Delphia were two more women—one with auburn hair and one with blonde.

Nerves ate at my insides at the sight of the two women I had yet to meet—both very near and dear to Ara.

I had never been a well-liked person, but these two had personal reasons to despise me. Ara had told me Livvy was a good friend to her, the one who encouraged her to chase me out of the tavern. I can only hope she doesn't harbor any resentment, or Goddess forbid, guilt over what *I* did. But her mother... Her mother had every reason in the world to hate me, solely because of my father.

CHAPTER ELEVEN

I couldn't imagine how I would ever win her approval, and I wasn't even sure I deserved it, but I'd be damned if I didn't try, because I meant every word I'd said to Ara; she was my home. I would always find my way back to her. *Always.* Nothing would stand in my way.

I would fight tooth and nail to gain their trust, but most importantly, their forgiveness. Ara needed that. *I* needed that. It would be an honor to be accepted by her family—one I would earn.

The ship swayed and stopped as it docked, and Ara peeked up at me with an excited smile, giving my hand a quick squeeze.

The plank lowered, connecting the ship to land, and we walked down, hand in hand. Dozens of eyes landed on us instantly.

Both women looked at Ara expectantly. I thought she would release my hand to run to them, but she did the opposite, tightening her grip as if she needed my strength and reassurance.

Then, Ara inhaled deeply and tugged me toward them.

"Rogue, this is Livvy," Ara said, motioning to the blonde. "Livvy, Rogue."

Her eyes did an up-down before shooting to Ara. She smirked at her and glanced back at me, sticking a hand out. I took it, shaking her hand. "Nice to finally meet you, Rogue," she said with an unwavering confidence that brought a shocked smile to my lips.

"You too," I said before swallowing hard, waiting for the introduction I knew would hurt the most.

Hesitantly, my eyes shifted to Elora's, finding hers already on me, brimming with tears. Her lip quivered while her chest rose and fell quickly. A mixture of panic and pain swam in her eyes, and my heart sank.

I opened my mouth to speak, to apologize, to say anything to lessen her hurt, but she spoke first.

"Rogue Draki," she breathed, her voice shaking. "You are… You are undeniably his son." Her breath hitched, a tear falling from her eye that she quickly wiped. She closed her eyes, shaking her head before attempting to gather herself. "I'm sorry. I'm… You are the spitting image of your father."

I closed my mouth, nodding as my heart broke for her, the guilt heavy. "I know, and I'm sorry—for so, *so* many things, but right now, I am most sorry for that."

Her eyes found mine again as she studied me. I wanted to avert my gaze, to walk away and give her space, to never dredge up the painful memories that clearly still haunted her, but instead, I stood, clutching Ara's hand as if she could somehow change this. The guilt swarmed me; I knew I had to remain here if only to show her I was not him, that I could be worthy of Ara, but doing so would require me being near her, rubbing salt in her unhealed wounds.

My entire life, I had tried to heal the scars Adrastus left behind, mend the things he broke, and this was another reminder I would never outrun him. Even his face mirrored through mine, reminding everyone of his atrocities.

I was a walking, living, breathing reminder of the pain he caused.

My eyes lowered.

No.

Ara squeezed my hand. Rubbing my jaw, I inhaled slowly.

No, I'm not. I'm a reminder that we survived him.

I lifted my eyes back to Elora, releasing Ara's hand to

cautiously step towards her. Her gaze dropped to my feet before shooting back to my face with wariness, but she didn't falter. As slowly as I could, I knelt to a knee and bowed my head.

"You saved Ara's life, and for that, I will be forever grateful." I raised my eyes to find her brows furrowed, hands clasped together at her chest as if she were protecting her broken heart. "I know I cannot make up for what my father did, but please know that I am *deeply* sorry. He was a monstrosity among the Fae, and I will spend the rest of my days proving I am nothing like him, if you will allow me to. I love your daughter, Elora. While I don't know what I ever did to warrant such a blessing, she is the best thing that has ever happened to me, and I swear before the Goddess herself, I would never harm her, or you, or Livvy, or anyone in our family."

She stared into my eyes for several moments before nodding and slowly lowering to her knees with me. "You suffered at his hand, too. I know it was not you who…who murdered Vaelor. You may share his blood, but you are not him. That much is clear."

"Thank you," I said, a light smile of relief pulling my lips. "And you…" My eyes shifted to Delphia as I rose to my feet. "We missed you."

Her hair was just as white as it had always been, but messier, less kempt. Her eyes were hollowed underneath, lined with dark circles. Even her cheeks had sunken slightly and lost the blush she usually held. Every part of the warm disposition she shared with Doran was gone, replaced with something much colder, draining the color from her already pale skin.

It was as if her soul was determined to die with Doran,

sucking the life from her day by day. In the mere couple of weeks he'd been gone, she had already deteriorated so much, consumed by grief.

My heart sank and I closed the remaining few feet between us. I lifted my arms to hug her, but she took a step back, her face tight as her throat bobbed. That had hurt; I took a step away from her to give her the space she clearly wanted.

"I just…I needed to bury my brother."

"I would've helped you, Delphia," I said. "We could've been there for you. You didn't—"

"No," she interrupted. "No, it was something I wanted to do alone. He was *my* brother."

"I understand," I said with a nod, even as her words caught me by surprise, stinging slightly. They had taken me in as family years ago, but she was right, of course; he was her brother. She had every right to bury him by herself if she so chose. "Where did you bury him?"

"Home, Rogue. I took him home."

Their home village was small, tucked away in the southeastern corner of Ravaryn, down below Nautia. Doran had taken me a few times; even though their childhoods had been harsh, the town had held a special place in his heart.

"We were just worried about you," I said. "I'm so sorry, D. So sorry. I wish I could've helped him, saved him. Hell, I would've traded places with him if I could. He didn't deserve his fate, but I promise you this—Adonis will receive his punishment. We will burn him to the ground so he can watch from the afterlife as we dance over his ashes and toast to every fallen Fae, especially Doran."

Delphia's face was laced with restraint, her mouth pressed into a flat line. She inhaled a shaky breath, her lower lip

CHAPTER ELEVEN

trembling. "The worst death imaginable. I want all those responsible to suffer because it is *deserved*. I will make sure they writhe in agony before they die, just so they can have a taste of what this is like to live without my brother. My *twin*. I-I—" Her voice choked as angry tears spilled from her eyes. "I will do whatever it takes."

"As will we, Delphia," Ara added, stepping closer.

Delphia's eyes shot to her—icy and hard—before softening to accept Ara's words. Thana, who had been hovering at Delphia's side, as if she were scared to get too close but unable to stay away, stepped closer and took Delphia's hand in hers.

"Yes, we will all do whatever it takes," Thana said. "He deserves retribution. Doran was kind and gentle and a damn good friend."

"Aye, that he was," Ewan said, joining the group with Iaso at his side.

Alden nodded. "Taking Doran's life—any Fae life—will be his biggest regret. When he is inevitably struck down by one of this very group, it will be well deserved. When he faces the Goddess, may she show him no mercy."

Delphia took Alden's hand with her free one as she nodded in acknowledgment. Her eyes shifted around the group, slowly but surely, before stopping on mine.

"May she show him no mercy," I echoed, the words reigniting my rage.

It was a wildfire catching in my chest as my fingers itched for blood. *His* blood.

My fists clenched.

He deserved no mercy, not now and certainly not in the afterlife. He had already taken so much—too much—and it was his turn to feel the brunt of war. His turn to choke on his own blood as we nailed him to the decrepit remains of whatever hell he crawled out of, just as he and his general had done to so many of our kind when they nailed them to their homes.

Everyone here deserved to end his miserable life, but a deep, sick, feral part of me smiled at the prospect, hoping it would be my hand that delivered the final blow.

"Rogue?" Ara asked carefully.

Her face was illuminated by a flickering, orange glow, and my brows furrowed in confusion before I felt it. Glancing down, flames licked up my arms from my palms, worse than any slip had been before. They ceased immediately, but something still felt off.

I lifted my eyes back to Ara and stilled. She had a halo of delicate light around her, an aura I desperately loved and wanted to wallow in. I stared for a beat, entranced by her.

She was a treasure in a world of darkness—a light I was meant to chase until the end of my days.

I would tear apart the entire realm just to sit her atop the ruins. I would do *anything* to ensure she was safe.

Protected.

Protect.

Protect what is mine.

Adonis was a threat to *her.* The fierce need to incinerate him and everything he held dear swept through me.

Burn for her.

She swallowed hard as my hand raised to her cheek. She leaned into it, but there was concealed concern still pressed into her features. Lifting my hand, I smoothed the crease between her brows with my thumb.

"For my beautiful treasure, I will burn."

CHAPTER ELEVEN

The words echoed in my ears before I realized they were mine.

Stepping back, I dropped my hand, blinking rapidly as the light disappeared from around her.

"Your eyes..." Delphia breathed, her eyes darting to Ara. "He really did shift, then," she said, shocked but convinced as her gaze shot back to me.

Everyone's eyes were on me.

Ara nodded, biting her lip as she leaned into me. "Are you all right? Your eyes...They were your dragon's."

The angry heat coursing through my veins cooled in an instant.

I had lost control—so soon, and over nothing of consequence—and worse still, I hadn't even realized it until they told me so.

"Yes, I'm fine," I said, rubbing my forehead before dropping my hand. "I'm fine," I repeated. For whose reassurance, I didn't know, because even as the words left me, I only partially believed them.

* * *

I let Ara lead me back to my room, her hand a comforting warmth that kept me grounded.

Once we reached the door, however, apprehension prevented me from turning the knob. What would we find inside? I knew what I had done when I'd left, the spell I'd broken, the wall I'd left in pieces.

The room would be an echo of that night—a reminder of my lacking self-control, of what I forced her to endure.

I dropped my hand to my side. "Maybe we should stay in

your chambers tonight."

"These are my chambers now," she said before flushing, "if you're all right with that."

A smile pulled at the corner of my lips. "Staying down the hall too far for you, little storm?"

"Ah, yes. That's exactly it." She edged closer, her silver eyes glinting with amusement. "Although, I would consider it more for your benefit." She reclined her head back onto the door, tilting her face to mine.

"My benefit?" I asked, resting a hand against the door frame above her.

She nodded. "If you're going to find my bed every night regardless of where I stay, I figured this might be easier for you. Truly, I had your best interest in mind."

Her hand found the doorknob and turned it slowly until it clicked.

Smirking, she backed into the room, and I followed her lead without a second thought. "Honestly, you should be thanking me," she added.

"Is that right?"

Our faces were mere inches from each other as I swung the door shut behind us.

"Yes," she breathed. "Now, you'll have me here"—her hand rested on my abdomen, slowly sliding up and under the opened buttons along my chest as she stepped to my side—"in your chambers"—her hand grazed over my shoulder, down to the base of one wing—"in your bed."

Her exploration was cut short as I knotted my fist in her hair. My lips touched hers as she gasped, smiling against my mouth.

"Thank you," I whispered. She pulled back and lifted a

CHAPTER ELEVEN

brow. "Thank you for hand delivering my own personal salvation." I tilted her head, kissing her jaw. "Thank you for forgiving me. For rescuing me. For loving me. For existing." A trail of kisses dappled her neck as I moved lower. "I will spend every single night showing you exactly how grateful I am."

My teeth sank into the scar at the base of her neck, the metallic taste of broken skin filling my mouth as she screamed a moan that would reach well beyond the confines of this room.

I kissed the wound, licking the taste of her from my lips before rising to whisper into her ear. "In *every* way I can imagine."

Chapter Twelve

Ara

We lay in the mussed bed, an exhausted entanglement of limbs. My head rested on his shoulder, my hand drawing lazy circles on his chest as the sun peeked through the window, already repaired from the damage.

Rogue's head tilted toward the light.

"They fixed that rather quickly," he said before chuckling. "Was that your attempt at distracting me?"

He had looked so stressed as we neared the door, I had done the only thing I could think of to calm him.

Rolling onto my side, I propped my head on my hand. "Was I that obvious?"

"Maybe a little, but I appreciate it nonetheless. That was a…*nice* distraction." A devilish grin spread across his face.

"Nice?" I cocked a brow at him. His form shook with laughter, and I rolled onto my back with a laugh of my own.

"I'd say that was better than nice." He snaked his arm around my waist and pulled me into his side. "Much better than nice," he whispered, running his fingers through my

CHAPTER TWELVE

hair. "So…what was the real reason you decided to move in here?"

I paused, meeting his gaze. "I gave my room to my mother," I answered, carefully leaving out that I had stayed here the night before I even knew she was alive. "She actually…" I let out a soft laugh. "Well, it was hers first, when she lived here with Vaelor."

"Huh. What are the odds of that?" he asked.

I rolled onto my stomach and propped my chin on my hands. "She and Vaelor were mates, too."

His eyes widened. "She told you that?"

I nodded. "Mhmm. She couldn't feel the bond in its entirety like a Fae, but he could. He told her after they fell in love, and she said she already knew there was something more between them."

"Fate always finds a way, I suppose." He sighed. "I'm sorry they didn't have more time."

Even as my heart ached for him and the genuine regret in his voice, all I said was, "Me too," as I laid back down and snuggled into his side.

We lay in near silence after that, the only sounds that of our breathing, the bristling of curtains in the breeze, and the steady crash of waves from the sea below—a calming melody that lulled me into a sleepy haze, broken only when Rogue sighed.

"I'm glad she came here, though, for you. I imagine it was a terrifying decision for her to make, returning to where she witnessed her mate…murdered." His grip tightened around my waist ever so slightly. "She's brave, just like her daughter."

"That she is," I whispered.

Rogue slid his arm from beneath me and sat up, throwing

his legs over the side. He sat on the edge, running his hands down his face with a heavy sigh. "I'm not going to be able to rest until I get briefed. I'm going to go find Lee, all right?"

He turned and leaned over to kiss my forehead slowly. I lifted my hand to his cheek and pulled his face down, bringing his lips to mine.

"Sleep, little storm," he whispered.

* * *

I slept—truly slept without interruption or worry or the constant creaking and groaning sounds that accompanied Ewan's ship—but as I roused, my stomach felt this was the perfect opportunity to remind me I missed dinner, gnawing and growling.

Stretching, I yawned and cracked my eyes open to see it was dark. Rogue had joined me in bed, now asleep with a wing thrown over my legs, his dark hair mussed and splayed over the pillow.

The night was quiet, the moon high, shining a soft light through our window as the thin, sheer curtains billowed in the breeze. The sky was clear as the waves softly lapped at the cliff, and the fire in the corner was lit, crackling and swaying.

The protection spell cast over his window must be different this time. They didn't usually let in the wind, but I felt it now, kissing my skin as it drifted through, bringing with it the scent of summer and brine.

I prefer it this way, I think.

Peeking at Rogue, I lightly kissed his shoulder before sliding out from under his wing. I glanced around, finding one of his black tunics, and I lifted it from the back of the chair to pull it overhead. It hung down far below my hips, swaying around my bare thighs as it swallowed me.

Wrapping my arms around myself, I tip-toed to the door and peeked back at Rogue. The thin blanket covered him from the hips down, but it left his upper half exposed to me and the moon.

My eyes roamed over him, stopping at his black locks—the same dark, endless color of the night sky that he and his wyverns touched each night. The same black as the Obsidian Crown he would soon wear.

His lashes and brows were just as dark, surrounding his maroon eyes, the same deep red as his wings, as the vines that hung along Draig Hearth, as the vines that grew along the ruins at the Wyvern's Hearth.

His tanned skin was taut over his massive form—all muscle and strength and resilience, only reiterated by the deep, jagged scar. The moonlight illuminated him on one side, a silver light that haloed him in a way that almost didn't seem natural, as he so clearly belonged to the sun, to warmth. The firelight on his other side highlighted him, the flickering orange dancing along his skin in all the right ways, a beautiful reflection of his own magic.

It was as if he was specifically created to wear the crown, created to be the physical embodiment of everything the Draigs were.

He was magnificent.

I swallowed hard. Even if profound power didn't radiate from him, if the wyverns hadn't chosen him, if he wasn't born into the crown, he would have never been average.

Beyond *what* he was, it was who he was. Beneath his powerful exterior was an even more powerful soul who just longed for peace, and that was…breathtaking.

"Rogue Draki, you are worthy of so much more than you think," I whispered under my breath before slipping out the door and closing it silently behind me.

I strolled down the empty, dimly lit hallways in search of food, unaware of where the kitchen might be as I had never gone looking before. I headed for the breakfast room, hoping the kitchen would be somewhere near it.

As I neared, the faint sound of giggling reached my ears and I paused. The sound trickled from the room a few feet ahead of me, the door ajar.

"What did you say this was?" Livvy mumbled through a full mouth.

My lips fell open in an amused smile as I darted forward, cracking the door open to peek my head in.

"What are you doing in here?" I asked, cocking an eyebrow.

They all jumped, my mother and Thana clutching at their chests as they gasped. Iaso was perched on the counter, grinning over her shoulder with a pastry halfway in her mouth while Thana's mother, Mya, stood beside her, reclining on her elbows, a glass of wine in her hands.

"Good Goddess, Ara," Livvy said, bracing herself on the counter.

"You scared the daylights out of me," Thana breathed, giggling. "What are *you* doing in here?"

I didn't get a chance to answer before my stomach answered for me with a loud grumble. A split second passed, and we all burst into laughter as I quickly shut the door behind me.

"It seems I'm not the only one who needed a late-night snack," Mother said breathlessly, wiping her eyes. "Come,

CHAPTER TWELVE

have a seat."

She gestured to the counter by Livvy. A tray of berry pastries iced with a sugary white frosting sat beside her, already half gone, along with a few empty bottles of wine. Several glasses were scattered about the counter.

"All right. Scoot over."

Livvy shimmied to the side with a squeal as I braced my hands on the counter, leaping up to sit beside her. Mother grabbed a plate and placed a pastry on it as Livvy poured a glass of sparkling wine.

As I took a bite, the flavors burst across my tongue in an array of sugary bliss, countered perfectly with the buttery crust. I moaned, savoring it before taking another bite.

"Good Goddess, who made this?"

They all turned to Mother, and she shrugged her shoulders sheepishly.

"You bake? Why didn't I know that?" I asked, stunned.

She took a sip from her glass. "I used to bake all the time. I loved it—I still do—but I didn't get much of a chance in Evander's manor. 'The kitchen is no place for a lady,' they would say." She rolled her eyes, taking another sip. "You know who loved my baking? Vaelor. That man had an insatiable sweet tooth."

She laughed a true laugh I wasn't sure I'd ever heard, but it was beautiful to see her let go. Even her hair, which she used to wear pinned up, hung in loose, free spirals around her freckled face, pink with a bit of sunburn.

"From what I recall, we *all* enjoyed your sweets," Iaso said, snatching another pastry from the tray. As she took a bite, she rolled her eyes back with an exaggerated moan. "I probably missed that about you most. Best baker I've ever known."

"Yep, me too," Livvy added.

"These are quite delicious. You are remarkably talented," Mya said. "Goddess knows I can't bake."

"No, you cannot," Thana said, raising her eyebrows dramatically as Mya swatted her arm.

"Don't make me beat you, child," she teased. "I seem to remember you rather enjoying my cooking growing up."

Thana laughed, eyeing her mother. "Yes, Mama, I did." She looped her arm around her mother's shoulders, giving her a quick kiss on the cheek.

Seeing them reunited was beyond heartwarming. They were clearly close.

"I can't believe you never told me you loved to bake," I said, washing down the treat with a big gulp of wine.

"There were a lot of things I didn't get a chance to tell you, love." She placed a hand on my knee. "But we have all the time in the world now, and I can't wait to tell you everything."

My eyes stung as I nodded. "I can't wait."

It was like getting to know my mother for the first time all over again. This was a side I had never seen before, but it lightened my heart to see her so…free, so unburdened, if only for these fleeting moments.

"That's beautiful," Iaso said, her eyes misty as she clutched her wine glass to her chest.

I couldn't stop the giggle that escaped me. "Iaso… Are you drunk?"

She feigned offense at my question. "No, child, of course not. I've only had this much—" Her eyes shifted to her empty glass as she lifted it, and her brows scrunched. "Well, I may be."

A cacophony of bubbling laughter, easy words, and sweetness filled the night as we sat and enjoyed each other's company.

It was so unlike anything I had ever experienced. I had never had friends, much less friends like this, who just enjoyed being near each other. It filled my chest with a warmth that lifted my mouth into a smile until my cheeks ached and my belly burned from laughter.

The hours slipped by like seconds as the moon steadily rose and then began to sink back down on the horizon. Before I knew it, we had finished the last of the wine, said our goodnights, and gone our separate ways, but the happiness carried me back to Rogue's room. When I slipped inside and crawled into bed beside him, I was blissfully content, wanting for nothing other than his closeness and the warm embrace of sleep.

* * *

Pale sunshine washed over the breakfast room as Rogue and I entered the next morning.

The long table, lined with pots of coffee and tea, pastries, cheeses, and a dozen different fruits, had most of our makeshift family around it—Alden, Iaso, Ewan, Mother, Thana, her mother and father, Livvy, and Lee, all patiently waiting for our arrival as they sipped from their mugs. Even Aurum sat in the corner, feasting on his own large chunk of meat still attached to the bone. Everyone was here…but Delphia.

"Good morning," Rogue said as we took our seats. His eyes scanned the table, lingering on Thana for a beat, and I knew he was searching for Delphia. Thana shrugged slightly, shaking her head.

"I hope you all slept well," he added with a sigh.

"Aye," Lee said, smiling over his mug as his eyes cut to Livvy. She suppressed a grin, jerking her face away from him as she turned to me. I eyed her suspiciously, dampening my own smirk. "I slept like a rock after all the wine we had last night," she said.

"So did I," Iaso agreed, rubbing her forehead, and Thana nudged her with her elbow as Ewan peeked over, chuckling.

"Wine?" Rogue asked, cocking an eyebrow at me.

"We had a bit of a girls' night last night while the rest of you slept," I said before popping a grape in my mouth.

"It was quite nice," Mya said. "I rather enjoyed it. A respite we all truly needed."

Augustus' eyes twinkled as he smiled lightly at his wife, lifting his hand to hers.

"So," Alden started, refilling his mug with steaming black coffee. "We need to find the crown as soon as possible."

"Yes." Rogue took a long gulp of coffee. "I learned last night from Lee that there are several platoons stationed in various locations, gathered and placed over the last week or so."

I sat straighter as he spoke, dropping my fork to the table. He hadn't told me any of this yet—granted, he had only learned the night before, but this felt like news to wake a person for.

His free hand slid beneath the table and rested on my thigh, giving it a light squeeze.

"Two groups, small and organized," Lee added. "One has made camp in an abandoned village on the west coast, and one has set up camp at the Marsh."

"Why the Marsh?" I asked. "What do they hope to gain

CHAPTER TWELVE

there?"

From what Rogue had told me, the Marsh was not an easy access point into Ravaryn due to the mountain range separating us from Auryna. It was particularly impassible north of the Marsh; it was steep, intersected with hidden canyons and cliff sides, and packed tight with a dense forest. It would take them days, maybe weeks, to come through—if they made it through at all.

Rogue and Lee both shook their heads, but it was Lee who answered. "We're not sure, but the Flies are keeping a very close eye on them."

"Flies?" Livvy and I asked simultaneously.

Lee grinned, wiggling his brows. "I dubbed our spy ring the Flies, as in flies on a wall: silent, forgotten, and listening."

My brows rose as I nodded slowly, stifling a smile.

Livvy paused and covered her mouth as she snickered. "Do the spies like that name?"

Mother and I burst into laughter, Alden cracking a smile, and Iaso sputtered as she choked on her bite of toast.

Lee's face fell in mock hurt as his gaze shifted around the table and landed on Livvy, his hand clutching his heart. "You wound me."

"Oh, stop, you big baby." Livvy swatted his shoulder. "It is clever, I suppose. No one would ever guess that."

Rogue cleared his throat as his own mouth curved up in a suppressed smile. "Send two more...Flies per encampment." Rogue pressed his lips into a flat line as he fought his laughter. "I want them surrounded at all times, so we can be alerted to any movement as soon as it happens."

"Will do," Lee replied and took another bite before wiping his mouth and standing.

Then he leaned over and gave Livvy a quick kiss. Her cheeks flamed, her blue eyes wide as he exited the room with a smug grin of his own. She smiled faintly as she lifted her hand to her mouth, touching her lips gently.

Her eyes found mine, and I didn't dare bring attention to it by saying anything. Instead, I just grinned and sipped my coffee.

"So, where is the crown?" I asked. "Where do we find it?"

"My grandfather, Drakyth, took it with him as the only remaining Draki blood when he abdicated," Rogue said as he piled his plate high. "It was never seen again."

I gawked at him. When Rogue had said we needed to find the crown, I thought maybe it was packed away, tucked off in one of the forgotten rooms of the castle—not alarmingly lost. "Okay. Where is Drakyth?"

"We don't know," Thana uttered, shaking her head. "No one does."

"We should send him a letter," I said, turning to Rogue.

"Won't that take…awhile?" Livvy asked. "How will he receive a letter if you don't even know where to send it?"

"There's an incantation," Mother answered. "It uses the magic of the realm, activated by the words themselves. Anyone can do it with the right phrase. They don't even have to be said aloud."

"Even a human?" Livvy leaned forward slightly, her lips parted.

"Yes," Rogue replied—to me, not them.

"I'll grab some paper and a quill," Alden said before dashing from the room. He returned moments later, handing the supplies to Rogue.

He scribbled a note down, folded it, and turned to the

fireplace. The note burned away in a flash as soon as he tossed it in, and a smile ticked at the corner of my mouth.

"Now wha—" Livvy asked but stopped.

A letter sizzled and floated into the room. Rogue snatched it out of the air and unfolded it, his brows furrowed. He held it up. "This is mine. It sent it back?"

Alden shook his head and turned to Iaso, who shrugged, leaning forward to take the note. She glanced it over, but it looked the same as when he had sent it.

"I don't know." She handed the note back to Rogue.

"That's odd, right? Does that ever happen?" I asked.

"I've never seen it," Iaso replied. "I'm not sure how or why that would happen. Could we try again?"

Rogue nodded, folding it before he tossed it into the fire and waited. It spat it right back out, untouched.

Groaning, he crumbled it and tossed it onto the middle of the table.

"We'll just have to track him down. Alden and Iaso, you two would have been the last to have seen him here before he disappeared. Any idea where he may have gone?"

Iaso shook her head, chewing on her lip as she tossed a chunk of cheese to Aurum. "No."

"Neither do I," Alden sighed. "I'll search the library; although, I'm unsure where to begin. Maybe their ancestral lands?"

"I..." Mother started, sitting her mug down on the table. "I may be able to help." She glanced at Alden. "Have you ever seen Vaelor's nook?"

"His nook?" Alden rubbed his chin. "No, I haven't."

They both turned to Iaso, and she shook her head.

"All right, then. When we finish up here, I can take you

there." Mother released a deep breath, her eyes dropping to the table.

She remained silent for the duration of the meal, only speaking again when everyone was finished.

Rogue, Alden, Mother, and I stepped into the hallway as the others remained seated, looks of concern pressed into their features. We thought it might be…easier for her if the room wasn't crowded when Mother returned to the special space that had been her and Vaelor's secret—one she was now graciously sharing with us.

Rogue gave her a soft look, extending his arm. "Lead the way."

Her throat bobbed as she nodded and took a slow step down the hallway that only led to one room.

My heart ached as my eyes shot to Alden's to find his on me as well. We shared a pained look before reluctantly following after her.

Chapter Thirteen

Ara

We rounded the corner. At the end of the hallway was Vaelor's door, no longer covered in cobwebs but shrouded in the same shadows. Just on the other side was where my mother watched Vaelor take his last breath, where she held him until the light left his eyes, where her love left this realm.

My eyes darted to Mother. Her hands shook, her rapid breathing nearly audible as she started to take a step forward.

"Stop," Rogue said, his voice tight. He shook his head, running a hand through his hair. "Stop. You don't have to do this. Just tell us where to look."

"Thank you, Rogue, but no…" She sighed, glancing back at the solitary door. "No, it has to be me."

Rogue's brows furrowed as he dipped his chin. "Are you sure? We can find another way to find the crown."

She smiled faintly, sadly. "Yes, I'm sure." She faced the door and slowly edged toward it.

Stopping in front of the door, she lifted her hand to the knob, inhaling deeply and exhaling slowly before hesitantly turning it.

It clicked and her breath hitched, her body tensing. A heartbeat passed before she pushed the door open. The fire lit in the corner, crackling and glowing for its guests.

Her eyes trailed over the room, taking in every single detail. She strolled to the bed and placed a hand on the age-worn blankets for a brief moment. Her eyes closed as a tear dripped onto the fabric, leaving a single wet freckle in the dust. She quickly wiped her cheek and walked by the window, letting her finger trail along the windowsill before her eyes stopped on the fireplace.

Her face was laced with restraint. It seemed she had to force her eyes to raise, her face lifting to the painting before her gaze. When it finally landed on their faces, she froze, the only movement that of her rising and falling chest.

We didn't dare break her silence; we waited patiently as she took in the room for the first time in over twenty-six years.

I would've given her all the time in the world, given her anything she needed to dampen the grief that rolled off her in waves, but within a few measly minutes, she cleared her throat. I turned back to her, my heart physically hurting.

Her eyes were swollen, her cheeks red and damp, but she held her chin high as we all faced her.

"The nook is in there." She pointed without shifting her eyes.

My lips parted as I slowly turned, already knowing where it would be.

The closet.

I scrunched my eyes as my face dropped to the floor.

Rogue's voice broke the heavy silence. "Elora, no. There

CHAPTER THIRTEEN

will be another way." He stepped toward her, tilting his head down. "I cannot—will not ask you to go in there where you... where you watched it all unfold."

"You didn't ask," she whispered, hesitantly reaching for his hand. She gave it a light squeeze and dropped it, facing the door.

With one unsure step after another, she made her way to the closet and lifted a trembling hand to quietly open one of the double doors.

Clothes hung inside, heavy with dust but otherwise in perfect condition. Her breath hitched again, a choked sound coming from her as she lifted a hand and lightly touched the fabrics.

My hand covered my mouth. The pain we must be causing her was unimaginable. I swallowed hard, biting back tears of my own as one of hers dripped to the floor.

"Mother, please," I whispered, stepping up to her.

She turned to me, her expression one of agony and bravery. Her lower lip trembled, but her strength was clear in the way she clenched her jaw, turning back to the darkness within the closet as she refused to yield to the sorrow.

I grabbed her free hand, and she glanced back at me. I gave her a quick nod—a small form of reassurance that I would be here with her every step of the way—and her mouth ticked up in a small smile.

Turning forward, she lifted her other hand and pushed the hangers apart. My lips fell open as everyone but Mother leaned forward to look.

On the wall was a delicate carving. *V + E.*

Her hand rose, hovering over the V that belonged to Vaelor. She carefully traced the letter before flattening her palm over it. "Every day, my love. Every day," she whispered under her breath.

Without turning back, she held a hand out. "I need a dagger."

My eyes widened. "A dagger?"

She didn't answer as Alden silently set a small knife in her hand.

My heart raced as I watched her touch the point of the blade to the tip of her finger. She grimaced as it pierced her skin, and a dot of red formed.

Careful to not let it drip, she raised her hand and traced the E, leaving a trail of blood that quickly sizzled and disappeared. The outline of a door suddenly appeared, closed with no handle.

She gently pushed it, and it groaned as it swung open.

A small window let in light along the back wall, and lanterns lit every corner, ridding the shadows where the sun couldn't.

I glanced over my shoulder at Alden to find his face stunned, his mouth hanging open.

"I had no idea," he breathed, stepping around my mother and me as he entered.

I followed behind him, taking in the entire room with awe. On one side, there were rows upon rows of books—all bound in the same brown leather. Candles were placed generously around the room, sitting on small, brass plates.

I inspected each one around me. Something about the way they remained, some barely burned at all, snagged on my heartstrings. They were all here with the intention of being burned, but Vaelor never got the chance, and now, here they sat, untouched and unused.

CHAPTER THIRTEEN

One had been burned down nearly to the bottom, and I couldn't stop myself from wondering what it had seen, what Vaelor had used its light for.

With a deep breath, I turned away to find Alden in the opposite corner of the room, sifting through the multitude of canvases reclining on the wall. Behind him was a tall easel with a half-painted canvas resting on it.

It was an orchard—or the beginnings of one. Unfinished apple trees and the silhouette of a woman were the only markings on it. On the stool in front of it was a dirtied rag and a dried pan of paint, cracked and faded.

So much left unfinished.

Mother followed me closer to it, stopping short when she saw what it depicted. She hesitated, dropping her eyes to the stool, where she carefully reached for the crumpled rag. Her fingers grazed it, and she closed her eyes again.

I thought she would pick it up, but she didn't. She pulled her hand away, leaving it lying where Vaelor had left it all those years ago.

Shaking her head, she cleared her throat and turned away.

"These are journals," she said. "He journaled everything, so I just…I thought there may be useful information here."

"Wow, yes, I'm sure there is," Alden whispered, stepping beside her with a small canvas tucked under his arm, the painted side hidden against his body.

"It starts left to right so the earlier ones would be up there." She pointed to the top left corner of the bookshelf.

Alden nodded and reached up to grab the first journal. Setting the canvas down, he flipped the book open to the first page, his eyes darting across it before turning to the next with a deep breath.

"I believe this was right after he traveled to Draig Hearth for the first time." Alden closed the book, picked up the painting, and turned back to us. "I can scan through the journals until I find what we're looking for if there is anything to be found."

Mother nodded. "We can prop the door open so you can come and go as you need." She scanned the room one final time, a deep longing reflected in her eyes. "I think I'll retire to my chambers if you don't mind."

"Of course," I said without hesitation, extending an elbow to her. "I'll walk you there."

As we stepped back into Vaelor's bed chamber, Rogue's voice reached us. "Thank you, Elora."

"Yes, thank you," Alden said, his voice choked. "Thank you *so* very much for sharing this."

She stopped before peeking over her shoulder, letting her eyes fall on his unfinished painting. "You're welcome."

We walked in unbroken silence until we crested the top step into her keep.

"What…" Mother's eyes bounced around the room.

Iaso and Livvy sat in the two chairs, with a kettle and teacups between them on the small table. Thana was on the other side, pouring a floral oil into a steaming bath. Mya turned to face us as she set a vase of blue flowers on the nightstand.

Iaso stood as Mother stepped into the room. "We know that was extremely difficult, and we wanted to show our gratitude. For you to have returned to that place, there must have been something truly useful in his nook." She took one of Mother's hands in both of hers. "You are so strong, my friend, and I am so damn proud of you."

"Thank you, Iaso. Thank you all." Her throat bobbed as

CHAPTER THIRTEEN

her misty eyes shifted to each person.

Iaso gave a quick peck to Mother's hand before letting it go.

"I've brought some tea—just a calming one—which we can share, or we can give you your privacy, whichever you prefer."

"I appreciate this so much. It has been so long since I've had friends. True friends." She took Iaso's hand again, laughing softly. "But I do think I would like to be alone for a bit."

I nodded, as did Iaso. "Of course."

Leaning in, I gave her a kiss on the cheek and backed away to the door. Iaso wrapped her arms around her in a tight hug before joining me, as did the others.

"I placed a few books, towels, and bars of soap by the tub," Thana said, resting a hand on Mother's shoulder as she leaned in. "As well as some wine if the tea isn't enough."

Mother chuckled, placing her hand on top of Thana's. "Thank you."

"Anytime," Thana replied with a soft smile.

As we descended the stairs, the cracked sound of a sob echoed down the stairwell, followed by another. I slowed, aching as I glanced back, and Iaso placed a hand on my shoulder.

"Let her get it out, child. Give her time," she whispered, continuing down.

I stared at the light emanating from her room for a moment before reluctantly following the others down.

Rogue met me in the hallway as I strolled back to our chambers, already exhausted.

"Alden believes those journals will be really helpful," he said, opening the door and motioning me in. "The few pages he scanned over while I was in there with him were highly detailed entries of Vaelor's visit to Draig Hearth, so if he can just read forward to when he was crowned, *hopefully*, he will have mentioned where Drakyth might have gone, or at least a general direction."

"I hope so. That was hard for her."

"I know," he said, his voice low. He wrapped an arm around my shoulders, pulling me into him.

My head fell to his chest, and I took a deep breath as his scent calmed me. After a moment, I pulled back, meeting his eyes. "What is the plan when we have the crown? You just put it on your head and what? You can talk to the wyverns?"

"We'll have a coronation—an official coronation." A faint grin graced his lips. "Our people will be invited with the promise of food and drink and dancing. The Obsidian Crowning is a bit of a big deal, a once-every-few-centuries event, so it's always a special celebration."

He stepped toward his desk, turning the chair so it faced me as he sat in it.

"That sounds like fun," I said, stepping between his spread legs as my hands rested on his shoulders.

His hands slid along my hips, resting on my waist as he tilted his face to me. "It's where you'll be crowned as well."

I jerked back ever so slightly. "What do you mean? I'm not—"

"Marry me." The words tumbled from his mouth but there was no uncertainty, no hesitation. "Marry me and take the throne by my side. Wear the crown you so rightfully deserve and rule Ravaryn as my equal in all ways."

No words would come. My mouth hung open as I stared at him, unsure.

"We're already mated, but I want you in every way I can

CHAPTER THIRTEEN

have you," he whispered, lifting my left hand to his mouth to kiss my ring finger. "Marry me, before our family, our people, the Goddess herself."

I swallowed hard, processing his words. We hadn't spoken of this before, and I was stunned. Torn. In Auryna, I had sworn I would never marry. We were mated, yes, but marriage almost felt like a betrayal to who I used to be.

"Rogue, I—"

His eyes slammed back to me, and my words stopped in my throat. He stood, sliding a hand to the back of my neck, and tilted my face to him.

"Don't say no. If you can't say yes, don't say anything." His mouth grazed along my jaw, down my neck. "I will wait for you, Ara, as long as you need, but I will have you in every way, in every lifetime. You are my mate, and you will be my wife."

I started to pull back, but he held me firmly in place as he kissed the mate mark. My breathing stopped at the feeling, and I suppressed the moan that threatened to escape.

"When you're ready," he whispered. "Not a moment before. I won't force you."

He turned us and edged me backward until I was seated in the chair. He dropped to his knees and spread my thighs, a smirk ticking up the corner of his mouth. "But I'll be damned if I don't try to persuade you."

His eyes followed his hand as it slid up my thigh, over my hip, along my waist, between my breasts. It paused over the mate mark before sliding up my throat to cup my cheek as he met my gaze.

"I am so in love with you, Ara." He whispered the words as if they were not truly meant for me, just his thoughts escaping him.

They were genuine and raw and nearly pulled a yes from my mouth right then and there, but he stopped me when his mouth landed on mine in a delicate kiss.

My hands slid into his hair as I pulled him closer to me. While I was wracked with trepidation, his words softened me, beckoned to me. I wanted to give in and give him everything he wanted.

I wanted to see him overwhelmingly happy, as I knew he would be if I said yes. I wanted to give him everything.

I wanted him.

As his hands devoured my body and his mouth pressed farther into me, as his scent filled my lungs and his presence swelled in my chest, I wanted him and him alone.

But marriage was something I promised myself I would never fall into…

Would it really matter? We were already mated, eternally linked and devoted to each other. Would marriage really, truly matter—to him or even me? It was just a title, a word, that essentially meant the same thing that we already were.

Still, fear bit at me, and he seemed to notice as he broke the kiss, pulling back to meet my eyes.

"You are everything to me, little storm." He tilted his chin down, his grip tightening on my cheek. *"Everything."*

His free hand braced on the desk behind me as he leaned in to press his lips to my forehead, but he paused. His brows furrowed as he sat back with the folded piece of paper his palm had landed on.

"This was not here before."

My heart raced.

"I didn't put it there."

CHAPTER THIRTEEN

Anxiety pulsed through me as he unfolded it. His eyes scanned the page at lightning speed before his jaw clenched. Black smoke rolled from him in heavy waves as his magic carefully avoided burning the sheet.

"Who?" I asked.

His eyes lifted to me, his gaze terrifyingly enraged, liquid fire swirling in his pupils.

"Adonis. It's from Adonis."

Chapter Fourteen

Rogue

Little brother,
I was rather generous, was I not? I let you take your precious Fae—they were a waste of space and near death anyhow, long past any use to me. However, it seems you have taken something of <u>mine</u>.
Enjoy while you still can, thief, because you won't for much longer.
- Adonis Draki, First of His Name, King of Auryna, & True Heir to the Throne of Ravaryn

"He's declared himself the true heir to the throne. *My* throne," I growled. "And he's accused us of taking something other than just our people. Something that belonged to him."

"What?" Ara snapped, jerking to her feet. "There's no way. Even if Delphia and Thana would do that—which they wouldn't—how would they have even reached anything of his? They rescued them from the dungeons, which are far, *far* below Adonis' chambers. Surely he's not talking about

CHAPTER FOURTEEN

Livvy and my mother. They're humans, yes, but they are *my* people."

The fierceness in her tone caught my attention, and my eyes grazed over her face. With narrowed eyes, a tight jaw, and flushed cheeks, her expression was one that could've been set in stone—the look of unyielding loyalty, of merciless protection. A true force of nature. One to be feared.

A proud grin ticked up the corner of my mouth as I turned back to the letter and read through it one more time.

"I don't know. This could be a ploy of some sort, but what reason would he have to lie? He's already started a war. Surely, his broken, mangled conscience doesn't need more justification for the tragedy he's already caused."

"That man—that *monster*—doesn't have a conscience at all," she spat as she paced the room. "Maybe he's delusional… He's absolutely delusional, but this seems like an awfully random thing to be confused about, or even lie about. What could he hope to gain? What does he want?"

I shook my head, wracking my brain. "I have no clue, but either way, we need to speak with Delphia and Thana *immediately.*"

I rose to my feet as she nodded.

"I haven't seen Delphia since the day we returned." Her eyes met mine, concern creasing between her brows as it always did.

"Neither have I."

She sighed deeply, and I slid my hand into hers, tugging her to the door.

"We'll check Thana's chambers first and hope that Delphia happens to be there, too," I said.

We reached Thana's chambers fairly quickly, and I gave a

quick knock as we arrived.

Thana's voice sounded from inside. "Come in."

We opened the door to find Delphia, as well as Thana's parents, lounging about her room, relaxed and seemingly content.

Violet curtains swayed in the breeze, and the scent of lavender permeated the room. Potted wisteria grew along the window, the periwinkle blooms dangling from the vines as they consumed the wall.

The air shifted as they took in our expressions, the smiles sliding from their faces. Delphia's spine straightened as her gaze bounced from Ara to me.

"What is it?" she asked, rising to her feet to go to Thana's side.

"We need to talk." I stepped into the room and sat in the chair closest to the door.

"Mama, Papa, would you mind giving us a moment?" Thana asked.

"Of course, dear," Mya said. Her husband, Augustus, stood before her, holding a hand to her. She took it, and they slid past us out the door.

"What is it?" Delphia repeated more firmly.

I pulled the letter from my pocket and handed it to them, their eyes scanning over it before jerking back up to us.

"We did no such thing," Thana practically yelled her denial.

"That dirty fucking liar," Delphia seethed.

Thana paced her room, arms waving as she spoke. "What does he think we took? We didn't have time to steal anything, even if we wanted to. We barely had enough time to get out with our people."

"My blind was waning within minutes covering that many

people," Delphia said. "I was stumbling into the treeline when we finally made it to cover, and it took me days to recover. There's no possible way we could have gone back in to steal anything."

"We didn't think either of you would," Ara reassured them, reaching out to grab Thana's hand. "We just need to figure out what the hell he's referring to."

"And what he's planning," I added.

"We should speak to the others who returned," Delphia said.

"Well, the majority of them have returned to their own homes. They've scattered over Ravaryn." Thana ran a hand through her hair. "We can round up those who have remained, though, ask if they have any clue what this is about."

Frustration boiled in my gut, but it was Delphia who audibly groaned.

"It's just one thing after another," she grumbled, turning away from us.

Thana's eyes shifted to her as Delphia ran her hands down her face with a forced sigh and swiveled back to us, stalking toward the door.

"Fine, let's go then. Meet us in the library in an hour."

My gaze met Thana's, and we hesitated. This was so unlike the Delphia we had known all these years that I could hardly believe she was even the same person.

"Well?" Delphia turned back to us.

Thana cleared her throat. "Yeah, all right. We'll see you two in an hour."

She slid past us, giving another weary look as she did. Once they were out of sight, Ara leaned in.

"Delphia is hurting." she whispered, her voice consumed with sympathy. "Bad."

We strolled into the hallway, closing the door behind us.

"Her energy…" Ara shook her head. "I can feel that it's changed. She used to feel so light, so warm, and now, it's as if there's a darkness clinging to her, swallowing her bit by bit. Grief is consuming her."

"I can see it on her too, in the way she's deteriorating before our eyes."

The dark circles beneath her eyes hadn't diminished in her time back at Draig Hearth. If anything, they had deepened while she continued to waste away.

"I'm not even sure I've seen her truly smile once since she's returned," she whispered. "Not in our presence, anyway."

I ran my hand over my jaw as it clenched and unclenched. Neither had I.

A slow, whispering thought crept in at that moment. If it was our presence that stole her smile and soured her mood—*my* presence—then maybe…perhaps she blamed me for his death.

My gut sank.

She wouldn't be wrong.

I was not only his king. I was his friend, his brother, as he was mine, and I was the reason he was on that battlefield. I should've watched his back. I should've paid closer attention. I should've done *anything* to protect him.

In the deep recesses of my mind, pushed down and locked in a box, was the truth. I blamed myself, and realizing that Delphia probably felt the same way broke the box entirely, the pieces shattering and ricocheting through me.

I dropped my eyes to see faint wisps of smoke drifting from

CHAPTER FOURTEEN

my palms.

It may have been Evander's blade that cut him down, but Doran's blood was on my hands, and Delphia knew it.

"After this meeting, I'm going to distance myself from her for a bit. I fear my presence is just a reminder of his death." It wasn't a lie, but it wasn't the entire truth either.

Ara peeked up at me. "Rogue, she's your friend. She wouldn't want that. She needs you now more than ever."

"I just want to give her the space to heal without pouring salt in her wounds."

Ara's gaze was heavy as she studied my face, searching for what I assumed was the truth in my words. I lifted her hand and kissed the scar along her wrist.

"Come on. Let's go find Iaso."

Her eyes lingered for a moment before she nodded, turning her gaze forward again, and I released a silent breath.

* * *

The sun was setting when we had finished speaking to each and every Fae who remained at Draig Hearth.

I dropped my head to my palm with my elbow resting on the armrest of the chair as Delphia and Thana walked the last person out. Ara sat to my right, seeming just as wiped and frustrated as I was. With a sigh, she bent over and tied her hair into a loose bun atop her head.

"We've received word from Adonis," Iaso said.

My face tilted up to find her and Ewan's eyes pinned on someone behind us. I turned, peeking over my shoulder as Elora and Livvy walked in.

Concern pressed into their features as Livvy's face

blanched, Elora's steps slowing.

"What did he say?" Elora asked hesitantly.

Livvy tugged Elora's arm, and they joined us around the fireplace, taking their seats.

"He's accused us of taking something that belongs to him," I said.

"Which is completely absurd," Ara added, throwing her arms up before collapsing back into her chair. "As if prisoners could've stolen anything."

Elora shook her head. "We absolutely did no such thing."

"Neither did we," Thana said as they rejoined us. "No one did that we can tell."

"We were doing our best to survive that wretched place. Stealing would not have furthered our cause," Elora seethed, irritation pricking her voice.

Livvy shook her head as she whispered, "No, it wouldn't have."

"We just wanted to let you both know, because at this point…" Ara sighed. "We don't exactly know what to do. How do we prepare for something like this? We don't even know what he's referring to."

"Prepare for what?" Alden asked as he strolled in, clutching several journals. "Sorry, I was reading on the beach. It's quite nice…" His words trailed off as he took in everyone's expressions.

I held up the letter, and Alden took it cautiously and read it over.

"What in the—"

"We don't know," I said.

"I'm assuming you've already spoken to the rescued Fae?" Alden asked.

CHAPTER FOURTEEN

"Yep," Ara said, glancing up at him. "Nothing. Nobody knows anything."

"If we believe everything they say," Delphia said.

"You believe someone is lying?"

"Well, someone has to be, right?" She stepped to the closest chair and sat, leaning forward on her elbows. "Why would Adonis lie? What would he gain from that? No, I believe he's telling the truth—at least about this. Someone has to be lying."

"They seemed genuine to me," Thana said. "They were prisoners, D. I don't think they had anything on their mind other than solely surviving." Her eyes darted to Elora and Livvy.

"Maybe," Delphia grumbled, sinking back in the chair. "Either way, he intends to take whatever it is back, whether we have or not, and everything considered, he seems fully capable of infiltrating this castle." Her gaze found Thana again, hovering for a moment too long.

Thana jerked back slightly, her face crumpling at the unnecessary and hurtful reminder of what Thana had done to protect her family.

"Delphia," Ara and I snapped simultaneously.

Her eyes flicked to us, cold and hard as ice.

Thana cleared her throat as she slid an unreadable mask back over her face. "Yes, well, I suppose that is true, but believe me when I say this—no betrayal will ever come from me again. My family is safe, and that includes all of you. I would die before I let harm befall you again." Her gaze fell on Ara, bleeding with remorse.

Ara shook her head. "No, Thana. Don't explain yourself. I trust you."

Thana nodded and sat in a chair of her own.

"We'll figure it out. In the meantime, try not to let him divide us," I commanded, my eyes solely on Delphia.

She dipped her chin once in acknowledgment and rose to her feet. "Sorry," was all she said to Thana before exiting the room.

"There has to be more to her agony than just grief," Thana whispered to Iaso. "I'm worried about her."

"As am I, but alas, I cannot heal wounds of the heart. Only the physical," Iaso replied.

"I'm worried too, but we have to focus on Adonis right now." The words were bitter on my tongue as I disregarded Delphia's pain. "I need to find Commander Lee. We need more guards posted, especially in front of our chambers, including those who were rescued. I will not let that bastard harm them again, nor any of you."

"Good, yes, and I will hurry through the journals," Alden said. "Vaelor was thorough in his writing so it's taking me a bit longer than I anticipated to get through his timeline."

"Let me know when you find something of use," I said as I stood and stepped closer to Ara. She closed her eyes as I kissed the top of her head. "I'll see you in our rooms later tonight, all right?"

She nodded, sinking into her chair as she crossed her legs and grabbed her cup of tea.

"I'll join you," Ewan said as I gave a grim nod.

Chapter Fifteen

Ara

Alden dipped into his office, Thana excused herself for the night, and I turned to Iaso, Mother, and Livvy, defeated.

"Adonis is manipulative and frustratingly clever. I'm worried about what he'll do next, or what he's already done that we just haven't discovered. What could he have lost that is crucial enough to send a message to Rogue? It was their first contact, and *that* was what he had to say? It doesn't make sense."

Mother shook her head. "I haven't a clue. All those years, we welcomed him into our home, shared our food and drink, had trivial, meaningless conversations. For Goddess' sake, he came to your eighteenth birthday dinner. All that time, and I had no idea a monster lurked beneath the surface…watching, waiting." She shivered. "That's terrifying."

"Horrifying," Iaso breathed.

Mother turned to her, crossing her legs in her lap. "We never would have known. He hid it so *well*. Be it glamour or manipulation, he did it well. It never waned."

My eyes shifted to Livvy. Her knees were pulled to her chest, her face abnormally pale and eyes unfocused.

Iaso and Mother continued to talk as I leaned toward Livvy. "You won't go back to the dungeon. I promise." I placed a hand on her knee.

She jumped, her face jerking up to mine as if I had jolted her from her thoughts.

I pulled my hand back hesitantly. "Livvy?"

"I'm sorry," she mumbled, sliding her feet back down to the floor. "I just…" She swallowed hard. "I cannot…will not go back to that dungeon, Ara."

"You won't, Livvy. I swear on it."

"I don't want to go back to Auryna at all," she muttered. "You know my dad—if that's what you want to call him. He may have needed me, but I certainly don't need him. I don't want to go back to that life."

Livvy's father became the stereotypical alcoholic after Livvy's mother passed when Livvy was only a child—useless, aggressive, and utterly ignorant of everything his daughter did to support him. When Livvy became old enough, she worked every night at that tavern just to keep food on their table, while he drank away every penny that remained. After we'd first met, I had tried incessantly to give her coin, a better-paying job, anything that could help, but she refused each time. She wanted to pave her way and earn her place, but it didn't stop me from dropping off meat or grain at their home when I could. She would accept it, but we never spoke about it. We didn't need to. I knew she appreciated it, even if she didn't want to need help.

"This"—she waved her hands—"may be a kingdom full of magic and strangers. It may be frightening and I'm not

CHAPTER FIFTEEN

welcome in most places, but it's nothing compared to his... drunken rage." She flinched, closing her eyes.

"Did he... Did he hurt you?" I asked as shock and fury rolled through my veins. I sat up straighter. "Did he lay his hands on you?"

Her gaze darted to mine before dropping to her feet. She bit her lip and nodded once.

"You will *never* go back. You can stay here with us, Livvy. Let Ravaryn be your home, as she will treat you better than Auryna ever did. That I can promise." I reached forward to wrap her hands in mine. "And know this—if I ever see that worthless piece of shit again, I'll remove his hands from his body. He clearly doesn't deserve them."

She laughed and leaned closer. "No, Ara. Bring him to me so I may remove them myself."

"Even better," I chuckled.

"Thank you, Ara," she whispered.

"Of course." Livvy had been my only true friend in Auryna. She had actually seen me as my own person when everyone else just saw me as someone's daughter, and I would forever be grateful for that. "You kept me afloat when I needed it most, and now, it's my turn. You deserve to actually live, to *rest.* You deserve a chance."

Her breath choked as she swallowed hard, her hand splayed on her chest. "I hope to do just that."

I peeked at the others. They were lost in a conversation that had drifted from talk of Adonis and the impending war.

A sly grin pulled at my lips as I turned back to Livvy. "Starting now."

She cocked a brow, smiling. I jerked my head toward the door, and we both stood before exiting the room. We strolled down to the front door, nodding to the staff as we passed, arm in arm.

It gave me a certain amount of pride that Livvy didn't have to hide who she was. There was a time when rounded ears would've been cut from their human bodies at Draig Hearth, but that wasn't the case any longer.

With my arrival and eventual acceptance, things had mellowed a bit. The burning hatred had dimmed, now reserved for those who deserved it, and that was certainly not Livvy.

I cracked the massive door open, and we slipped out, descending the entryway stairs into the bailey. The moon was high tonight, kissed by wispy clouds on either side.

"Which way?" I asked, pointing in either direction.

There was nothing to the left but sparring gear and a stone wall. To the right was the incline that led to the ledge, overlooking the sea. It held a special place in my heart, but I wanted it to be her choice for the night, as I had already seen most of the surrounding grounds. Forward was the front gate that opened to the solitary road into Draig Hearth.

She glanced in all directions with her mouth tilted to the side and her hand on her jaw, feigning indecision. I laughed, swatting her arm.

"You better decide before I decide for you," I teased.

"Okay, okay." She held a up defensive hand before pointing forward.

"Out it is," I said and tugged her forward.

The guards eyed us as we left—not in disdain, but concern. Their glances bounced to each other as if unsure, but we didn't give them a chance to stop us before we kicked up our heels and sprinted from the gate. The guards darted into the gate's opening as they shouted to each other, their words drowned out by our own rapid footsteps.

We ran until we were out of breath from both running and laughing so hard that our bellies burned, and Livvy doubled over with a hand on her chest.

"I haven't run like that since...ever," she breathed, rising back to her feet. "I have never run that far, but it felt good. Now where?"

I glanced around. We were in the forest, dark but peaceful. The distant sound of waves lapping on shore was barely audible, and I cracked a grin.

"Come on," I said as I took off toward the beach.

"More running?" she groaned before pushing off dramatically to join me.

Within minutes, we broke through the tree line and froze.

It was a little oasis, entirely shielded by the trees and a stone ledge, creating a small circle of quiet, secluded beach. The calm waves licked along the sand as the clouds freed the moon and cast a silver light over us.

We both glanced at each other, paused, and quickly started undressing without another word. We pulled everything off except our undergarments and corsets and darted for the water.

As the first wave hit our feet, we moaned simultaneously. It was a warm embrace over tired souls, soothing us if only for this moment.

Wiggling my toes in the sand, I let one more wave caress my calves before jogging forward and diving into the water.

I swam until my lungs burned for air before planting my feet and breaking the surface. Dipping my head back, I ran my fingers through my hair, letting the water run down my back as a gentle breeze kissed my skin.

"This feels incredible," I murmured, opening my eyes to Livvy.

She was still on the shore, mesmerized by the sea.

"Livvy, what are you doing? Come on." I waved her forward.

She smiled, wading forward slowly, taking her time as if she were savoring it. "I've never seen the ocean before."

"It's amazing." I turned to stare at the horizon. "It seems to go on forever."

"Yes, it does. I didn't expect it to touch the sky like that," she said as she joined me.

"I know. I didn't either when I saw it for the first time."

"It's funny, isn't it? How much bigger the world is outside our small village? How odd is it that I was so consumed with such a minuscule life as if that was all the realm had to offer? I couldn't see beyond what I already had. I didn't have it in me to want for more, but I get it now, you know? Your hunger for *more* and your unwillingness to settle for less. I didn't… I didn't know there was *this much* more." She chuckled, but it didn't reach her eyes. "I can't believe I would've wasted my life away in that bar, taking care of that ungrateful degenerate. What a waste of life that would have been."

My heart ached for her, but I didn't say a word as she spoke. They were words that needed to be said to lift the burden she had carried for so long. When she was finished, a single tear slid down her cheek and dripped into the ocean—a goodbye for the life she had decided to leave behind.

Good riddance.

I slid my arm around her, and she let her head fall onto my shoulder. There we remained for Goddess knows how

CHAPTER FIFTEEN

long, hidden in the darkness and secluded from the rest of the world.

Or so we thought.

Without warning, we were both tackled into the water, a terrifying shock that left my heart pounding, but the hands that held me were large and rough and familiar.

My head broke through the surface, and I screamed with mock rage. "Rogue!"

He scooped me up with a roar of laughter as Livvy broke through the surface, her face excited as she turned to Lee and pushed his head back under the water. She took off toward us before she was scooped up, tossed into the air, and landed with a huge splash.

Her head popped up as she sputtered and laughed, pushing the hair from her eyes. Once they were clear, her gaze locked on him with determination as a grin tugged at her mouth.

"Okay, okay. Truce?" Lee held his hands up.

She tilted her head to the side, crossing her arms over her chest, which only accentuated her breasts. "Beg," she commanded, her voice lowering a few octaves.

Lee stiffened, stalking closer to her, and I quickly averted my gaze as I slid my palm on Rogue's cheek to pull his face away.

"That is not something we need to see," I said, snaking my arm around his neck.

"No, I would suppose not." He waded through the water to distance us from them.

"How did the conversation go with him?"

"About how you would expect. There will be more guards on duty from now on." He sighed. "But let's not talk about it right now. It seemed like you two were enjoying yourselves, and I don't want to ruin that."

"Your presence could never ruin anything for me," I whispered, pulling his face down to mine. "Ever. You are always a welcomed distraction"—I kissed the hollow of his throat—"from anything I'm doing."

I kissed along his neck as he hummed in approval, letting his head fall to the side.

"Is that right?" His voice was low and husky, one that was reserved solely for me.

"Mhmm. Always."

His palm slid under my chin to tilt my face to him and force my gaze to his.

"I am more than happy to provide your *distractions* anytime you please, little storm. Just say the word." His lips whispered across mine, and my eyes slid closed. "We both know I am completely incapable of denying you anything."

He deepened the kiss like a starved man as he groaned into me, knotting his hand into my hair.

I could've stayed here for eternity, lost in him, in this moment. It was blissful—the waves, the moon, the taste of him, his scent mixed with that of summer. The pleasure was nearly excessive, bubbling in my chest with a warmth that stole my breath.

But the sounds of Livvy and Lee pulled me from his trance, and I gently shoved him back as I broke the kiss.

"They're right there," I said, gesturing to them without tearing my gaze away from him.

"I don't care," he growled, immediately closing the distance. His hand wrapped around the back of my head and pulled me against him again.

I moaned and sank into him as my hands found their way

CHAPTER FIFTEEN

into his soaked hair.

It was insatiable, the hunger that ravaged us. I believed we could live in his bed chambers forever if the rest of the world would allow it.

"Do you two need us to leave, or…?"

Livvy's tone was joking, but Rogue's was not as he answered, "Yes."

"No." My eyes shot to him with a shocked laugh.

Livvy's mouth fell open as Lee cocked a grin. "Come on. Let's give the man what he wants."

He extended an elbow to her, and Livvy wound her arm through it as they waded back to shore. The water rolled down her nearly bare body as they stepped onto the beach, and Lee didn't miss a single drop as his gaze scorched down her. She winked at him and tugged him forward, snatching her clothes as they disappeared into the trees.

"Was that necessary?"

I turned back to Rogue, but he didn't respond. The second I faced him, his mouth was on me again. His hands roamed every inch of my body before sliding under my behind and lifting me. I wrapped my legs around his waist, and he groaned, breaking the kiss. He cocked his head to the side, lifting one brow as his fingers slipped below my underwear.

"I thought I told you not to wear these again?"

"You cannot be serious."

I started to laugh, but the smile slid from my face as he said, "Perhaps I should teach you a lesson," with complete seriousness.

My cheeks flushed furiously as I lost all train of thought. "A lesson?" My voice sounded as breathless as I felt. "And how do you plan on doing that?"

Chapter Sixteen

Ara

Rogue had me backed against the rock wall on shore, my feet still submerged as waves lapped softly at my calves.

"How do I plan on teaching my sweet, deviant little storm a lesson?" he whispered along my neck as his hand looped one wrist then the other, lifting them above my head.

My breaths were uneven as he pulled a dagger from his sheath and held the blade between his teeth. He ripped his belt from his trousers, tossing the sheaths to the sand, and my heart skipped a beat as he tied the belt around my wrists. My shoulders stretched when he lifted my hands and pulled me to my tiptoes as he hooked them on a small stone ledge.

He grabbed the dagger from his mouth. "Keep them there."

He paused, waiting, and I nodded breathlessly. Grinning, he dropped his eyes as he slid the flat side of the blade along the bare skin exposed below my corset. I gasped at the feel, chills erupting in its wake. Without a word, he held my corset and sliced the strings upward. It split in two, exposing my breasts to him. I gasped, chills spreading over my exposed

CHAPTER SIXTEEN

torso as a cool breeze whispered across my skin, but I didn't dare break away from his heated gaze. His dark maroon irises lit with fiery sparks as he held a tight leash on his beast.

He slid the tip of the blade down between my breasts to the waistband of my undergarment and cut them from me, too, with expert precision so as not to nick my skin in the process.

He stepped back, admiring his handy work, clicking his tongue. "You're too beautiful for your own good."

He strolled to where my clothes sat along the beach and lifted my shirt, tearing a strip off before walking back. Leaning forward, he tilted his head to the side as he studied me. "Your lesson," he said, holding up the fabric before he carefully laid it over my eyes and tied it around my head.

Between the fabric and the dark sky, I could see nothing, not even the outline of his form. It made my other senses hyper-aware. My heart raced, my breaths quick.

I couldn't see him but I felt him all around me, heard him moving, and when he placed a gentle hand on my waist, I jumped.

"Easy," he chuckled. "It's just me, little storm. Do you trust me?"

I nodded, swallowing hard.

"I need to hear the words."

"Yes, Rogue. I trust you."

His finger trailed over my waist and circled around a breast before sliding up to my shoulder. It burned a trail along the curve of my neck, brushing my hair back and exposing his mate mark.

His mouth was on me then, warm and biting at the mark hard enough to bruise, but it sent sparks in my vision—a quick pain chased away by euphoria. I arched into him, my core burning. His other hand wound around my waist, holding me closer to him.

His canines lengthened along my skin, and I gasped, waiting for him to puncture, but he didn't. He kissed the mark instead before moving up to my jaw.

A hand slid between my thighs, and they spread on instinct, granting him access. He groaned in approval as he continued working his way to my mouth along my jawline.

He plunged a finger inside me as his lips met mine. I moaned into his mouth as he moved faster, deeper, before pulling his finger from me and using my own slickness to rub circles around my sensitive bud. My hips writhed against his hand, and he stilled, letting me chase my pleasure.

I wound tighter, my breaths shallow, as I rode his hand. I could feel the blood rushing to my core as the sensation built, but right when I was about to explode, he pulled his hand away with a chuckle.

I gasped in frustration, jerking at my hands. The rock ledge was too high for me to free myself. "Rogue—"

He slid his soaked fingers along my lips, and I opened obediently. He sank them into my mouth with a satisfied groan.

"Not yet," he hummed, pulling his fingers from me.

A moment passed, and I gasped again, arching as he poured salt water over my hypersensitive nipples. The water cascaded over me, creating a new sensation. It caressed me, but it wasn't enough.

He poured another scoop of water over my right breast, and the second the water left, his mouth was on me. He sucked me into his warm mouth—a stark contrast to the cool

CHAPTER SIXTEEN

water.

I moaned, pushing up on my toes, arching into his mouth. His tongue swirled around it before nipping and pulling back, and I whimpered at the loss.

He repeated the same thing on the other side. My entire body was edge—my core soaked, my clit and nipples aching for friction.

"Rogue, please," I moaned.

"Oh, little storm…" He slid a finger between my breasts and down between my thighs. He slid it through the slickness, dipping it into me. "Are you finally ready to beg for mercy?"

I scoffed. "No." *Yes.*

He released a breathy laugh as he sank to his knees, letting his hands trail lower down my sides before he lifted one leg over his shoulder and then the other until I was seated on him. His tongue ran over my swollen clit, and a scream tore from me.

It was *too* good—the way his tongue swirled and licked, the way his fingers plunged into me at exactly the right rhythm, hitting exactly the right place.

My breaths quickened with his increased pace. He knew my body better than I did. He knew my every move, my every want and need, my breaths, my moans.

I was on the precipice of orgasm when he pulled away again, kissing my inner thigh.

Frustration boiled through me. This was deliciously tortuous, and I wanted to scream. I wanted release. I wanted him. I wanted *more.* "Rogue!"

"Yes, Ara?" His voice whispered over my slit, teasing right where I needed him.

"Is this supposed to make me want to marry you? Because—

"

He dropped my legs instantly and jerked to his feet, his hand wrapping around my throat. His face was close enough to mine that I could feel his breath on my neck as he choked off my words.

He hooked my leg around his waist and lined up at my entrance.

Please. My hips hitched, but he didn't move. *Please, for the love of...*

"Tell me you don't enjoy this. *Lie* to me, little storm. Let me taste the lies as they leave that sweet little mouth." He ran his thumb along my lower lip before thrusting into me. A loud moan escaped, and he chuckled, skimming his lips over the delicate skin of my throat as he whispered, "Lie for me, sweet girl."

He pulled out and slammed back in, setting a brutal pace. I needed it, and he knew it as he pounded into me. I didn't want gentle. I wanted him to be brutal. Rough. Primal. Take what he wanted and satiate the overwhelming burn in my core that only he ignited.

He grabbed the belt, lifted me from the ledge, and spun me so I was pressed into the wall. He placed my tied hands on the wall so I could brace myself as he slid his hands over my backside. One hand grabbed my waist and the other slid higher, knotting in my hair.

He lined up and slammed into me again, satisfyingly deep, using his hold to move me on him. A scream tore from my lips as I took everything he had to offer, and he worked every ounce of attitude from my body.

If he asked me to beg right now, I would, but something told me he wouldn't. He didn't need me to as my body yielded

CHAPTER SIXTEEN

to his every touch, his every whim.

"So perfect," he growled, releasing my hair to brace himself on the wall above my head.

His other hand moved between my thighs. He slowed his hips, and I gasped as he dipped a finger alongside his length. I was so full—deliciously full. Then, he slid it back out, soaked, and shifted to my clit, moving in circles as his pace quickened.

I melted into scream after scream, a wanton mess of pleasure and chaos and desperation. My back arched to grant him more access, meeting his hips with each thrust.

"I love you, Ara," he whispered into my ear.

"I love you," I sobbed, turning my head toward him.

He gripped my chin and kissed me deeply, sending new spirals of pleasure through me as he captured me from both ends, breaking the kiss only to whisper, "Come for me."

And I did—blinded by the sparks of a long drawn-out orgasm. He pounded faster as I clenched around him, driving his tongue into my mouth as he spilled inside me with his own finish.

"So fucking perfect," he whispered as I collapsed into his arms with exhaustion.

My eyes slid closed as he scooped me up, kissing the top of my head.

* * *

Rogue and I both jerked awake to someone pounding on the door.

As we climbed from the bed, he grabbed his dagger before stalking across the room.

"Oh, come on. What intruder would knock?" I rolled my

eyes as I threw a robe around my bare shoulders. "In front of the guards you posted, no less."

Rogue glanced at me and ran a hand through his hair, but he didn't drop the dagger as another heavy knock sounded.

"What is it?" Rogue's voice was tight as he jerked the door open.

I leaned around him to see Lee, his eyes wide and nostrils flared. He was breathing heavily like he'd run the entire way as he braced a hand on either side of the door frame. "Adonis' army... The Marsh... It's burning."

My stomach bottomed out. "Let's go." The words left me before Rogue had a chance to reply.

Rogue held Lee's erratic gaze before shaking his head.

"Yes. You fly us there, and I will drown the fire with rain."

Rogue turned to me then. "Magic cannot be used within the borders of the Marsh."

Realization flooded me like ice water. "Then...how do..."

Lee let out a heavy breath, running a hand through his sweaty hair. "We can't let it burn. We can't. It's the *Marsh*, Rogue, the Goddess' birthplace. It's sacred."

"I know." He inhaled slowly. "Ewan. Get Ewan and meet me back here. I'll get dressed."

Lee nodded forcefully and took off in a dead sprint, disappearing down the dark hallway.

"What is Ewan going to do that I can't?" I asked as I ripped my robe off and grabbed clothing from the dresser.

"I'm not sure he can do anything." He pinched the bridge of his nose, inhaling slowly. "But the Marsh is near the coast, and the ocean isn't within its confines, so if he can lift the water enough to surround the Marsh and then just release it all inwards, the water should fall naturally without the help

CHAPTER SIXTEEN

of magic, right?"

As much as I wanted it to be possible, it seemed far-fetched. That kind of power would require an immense amount of strength and control. "Can he do that? Move that much water?"

Rogue shook his head, pulling on his trousers before plopping into the chair by the desk and dropping his head into his hands. "I don't know, but if he can't, the Marsh is going to be decimated."

Lee and Ewan burst into the room, Ewan in nothing but loose sleeping pants. Iaso entered behind them, her eyes wide with fear, her steps frantic as Rogue shot to his feet.

Iaso's voice was pained, cracking as she asked, "Why the Marsh?"

I hadn't considered their why—hadn't had time to—but there was only one reason why they would. There were no people or villages there. It wasn't even in Ravaryn's borders, but they knew it was sacred ground to the Fae. They knew we would rush to douse the flames.

"A distraction," Rogue said as he came to the same conclusion.

"Or a trap," Iaso breathed.

My blood chilled, remembering the last time Rogue left for the Marsh. My hand absentmindedly went to my abdomen, feeling where a scar would have been without Iaso's healing salve.

Rogue swore under his breath. "I don't think we have a choice. Even if it is, we have to save the Marsh. If people were to find out it burned, they would be..."

"Devastated," Iaso finished for him. Her eyes brimmed with tears as she covered her mouth, and I realized the Marsh meant more to Iaso than she had ever told me.

"We'll just have to take every precaution." Rogue ran a hand through his hair. "Ewan, how much water can you move?"

Iaso's gaze darted to Ewan, her hands on his shoulder.

He held Rogue's gaze until understanding dawned on him. With a hard swallow, he nodded. "As much as is necessary."

"What?" Iaso whispered. "What are you…"

"We're going to surround the fire with water on the outside of the anti-magic borders and then release it."

"If I give it all a shove inward, it should flood the area," Ewan said.

Iaso's face jerked back slightly. "What? That would be *way* too much power. That would drain him." She turned to Ewan, and his arm slid around her waist. "No, you can't…"

He lowered his face to her as he whispered, "I am, love."

Her lip quivered. "It will kill you."

"No, it won't." He placed a hand on her cheek, pushing the curls back from her face as a soft smile graced his lips. "My sweet healer would never allow that."

She blinked rapidly before nodding and taking a shaky breath. "I'm coming. I can… I can find a tonic to revitalize you afterward." She paused, her mouth downturned as her brows knitted. "But I can't guarantee it will fill your magic's well again—if it will ever fill again. Ewan, this could drain you…permanently."

My heart dropped. I opened my mouth but snapped it shut, my hand raising to cover my lips.

"I know, but this ground is sacred, especially to you, and I will not let it burn if there's anything I can do to prevent it. I won't allow that kind of hurt to reach you." He slid his hand along her hair again, and she leaned into it.

CHAPTER SIXTEEN

Iaso took another deep breath, and her face hardened as she exhaled, a mask of determination settling over her. "How are we getting there?"

"Me," Rogue said. "But Iaso..." Her eyes found him, glistening with unshed tears. "I don't think I can carry two yet."

Her mouth fell open slightly as her breath left her like it'd been knocked from her chest. A single tear slipped from her eye, and Ewan slid a hand on her cheek and turned her gaze back to him.

"It'll be all right, love," Ewan whispered.

If Rogue can only carry one, then... The thought lingered in the back of my mind, but that wasn't the most alarming part of that statement. The sounds of screams and crunching bones reverberated through my skull, and I flinched. "Rogue. The shift..."

He held up a hand. "I can do it. Meet me in the shifting room in twenty minutes."

They all nodded and left to prepare themselves, Lee giving one last pained glance to Rogue before closing the door behind him.

Rogue fell back into the chair again. He slid his hand into mine and pulled me toward him so that I was standing between his knees, kissing my scar before shifting his hands to my cheeks and tugging me down to his lips. The panic settled in my chest—only slightly—as my lips molded to his. With a sigh, he released me, and I stepped over his lap to straddle him, leaning my head on his chest. He wrapped a warm arm around my waist, holding me tight as his other hand found the back of my head.

"If you can only carry one..." I started but couldn't finish the sentence.

"It must be Ewan, little storm."

I nodded against his chest, wrapping my arms around him. "I know. I don't like it, but I know."

His chest shook with a chuckle, and my brows furrowed. I pulled back to look at him, my hands resting on his waist.

"What?"

"Nothing." His mouth ticked up in a grin as he pulled me forward for another quick kiss. "I just expected more… arguing."

I scoffed, and he tapped my hip in an indication to move. I slid from his lap, and he stood. After pulling his tunic overhead, he grabbed my hand and walked to the door.

"I guess I may not need these," he muttered, motioning to his clothes.

As he held the door open, his eyes on to the floor, I stepped into the hallway. "Hmm, you're right. We could just give everyone a show and have you walk naked to the shifting room."

I yelped as a hard smack landed on my ass. I swiveled on my heel, my mouth hanging open as my hand rubbed my stinging cheek. "Was that necessary?"

He walked past me, chuckling. "The only person who would enjoy seeing me naked is you, Ara. I promise."

"The same goes for me," I said, rolling my eyes as I jogged to his side.

"I—" He stopped, and I glanced up at him. With a devious gleam in his eyes, he nearly smirked as his head cocked to the side. "I'm not sure that's true."

He smacked my ass again and walked ahead of me.

Chapter Seventeen

Ara

The shifting room was still empty when we arrived, and Rogue released a subtle breath.

I waited at the threshold of the door as he entered. He strode forward with his face downcast, not bothering to examine the room. When he noticed I didn't follow behind him, he turned back to me. His face was tight, his spine rod straight, but I saw through it, the mask of bravery hiding his fear. I closed the distance between us and stood on my toes as I threw my arms around his neck. He let out an audible exhale, relaxing a bit as he wrapped his arms around me in return, resting his cheek atop my head.

"I'm scared," he whispered so low, I wasn't sure the words were meant for me. I tightened my grip around him, and he sighed. "Will you wait in the library? I don't want you to see this."

My eyes scrunched at the memory, my heart pounding. I nodded and released him, turning to the door. I took one step and then another before a small wave of panic washed over me as I realized he was really, truly leaving. I spun and stepped back into him, hugging him one more time.

"You better be careful and stay safe, or I swear to the Goddess, I will hunt you down." I tried to make the words sound teasing, but my voice shook too much. My breath hitched as I held back the tears burning behind my eyes. "You better come back. You both better come back."

"We will." He pulled back and placed a palm on each of my cheeks, leaning down to look me in the eyes. "I promise you."

"That's a heavy promise to make," I whispered as a tear rolled down my cheek.

He wiped it with his thumb. "One I intend to keep."

I left him then, against every screaming instinct. It took every ounce of restraint to close the door behind me and leave him, to let him face this alone, but he needed to. This was his beast to conquer, his mountain to climb, and I wouldn't intrude where he wanted privacy.

I walked around the corner to the rest of the library and found Iaso, Ewan, and Lee.

Alden stepped out of his office then, a red handprint imprinted on his cheek as if he had fallen asleep at his desk. He cleared his throat, pushing his glasses up his nose. "What's going on?"

Lee explained everything, followed by Ewan explaining his role and then Iaso's. When they were finished, Alden's gaze landed on me, his head tilted to the side, his brows pinched.

"I'm staying behind," I said flatly.

Iaso stepped forward, gesturing to the hallway that led to the shifting room. "Is he…"

I nodded and strode around them to the other side of the large library, finding an ancient wooden table lined with stacks of books. The chair screeched as I pulled it out and

CHAPTER SEVENTEEN

plopped down, leaning forward with my elbows on my knees. I dropped my face to my hands as the others joined me around the table, sitting in chairs of their own.

"He didn't want me in there with him," I said. "He didn't want us to hear."

"Understandable," Lee whispered.

"Has anyone told the others? Delphia? Thana?" I asked.

No one answered as my gaze bounced from one face to the next. Nodding, I sighed. "I'll do that after you leave."

It was torturous, waiting with tensions so high. My foot bounced under the table as I bit at my nails, thinking through every horrible scenario, wondering what part of him was transitioning now and if he was okay—if any of this would be okay.

He shouldn't be forced to shift this soon. He had only just returned. Then to carry Ewan that far across Ravaryn?

I dropped my hands to the table. "How do we know my storms won't work?"

Iaso reached a hand over to cover mine. "People have tried all kinds of magic through the millennia. Not even air magic works, which means that its border reaches into the sky, well above us. A storm created by magic would not pass over the Marsh."

My jaw clenched so tightly, I thought my teeth might crack.

"I'm sorry, Ara," Alden said. "The land is devoid of all magic—in itself, but also any belonging to the Fae. A magical wasteland, if you will."

"Not a wasteland." Iaso's eyes narrowed at him.

He chuckled, clapping a hand on her shoulder. "No, not a true wasteland as there are animals and such, but in terms of magic? It kind of is."

She huffed, rolling her eyes. "The Marsh is special, with or without magic."

"Yes, well, this *special* place"—Alden winked at Iaso—"is somewhere Vaelor used to frequent quite often, and his magic couldn't find a way in either."

"He did?" I asked with renewed interest, thankful for a distraction.

He nodded, a soft smile pulling at his lips. "Well, by boat, the Marsh isn't far from Nautia. He used to love camping there. He said it made him feel…normal, average when he could live without magic, if only for a few days."

While I hadn't had my magic very long, I had melded with it; it was a part of me, like a leg or an arm or a heart—a vital piece of me I had grown to rely on. I couldn't imagine what it would be like not to feel the magic running through my veins or the thump of every beating heart around me, to not hear the call of storms or the crack of lightning. I don't think I would like it. I imagined it would be too…quiet. I had come to find comfort in the steady thrum of life.

"He met Elora near there, actually," Alden said.

"I didn't know that." Iaso leaned forward on her elbows.

Alden quirked a brow. "She never told you?"

Iaso shook her head. "I guess we never really talked about how they met."

I opened my mouth to speak, but a bone-rattling roar stopped the words in my throat. They all froze, but I jerked to my feet, the chair falling to the floor behind me. I sprinted to the room and threw the door open, only for Rogue's burning gaze to wrench toward me—a flickering fiery orange split by slitted pupils. I hesitated, waiting to see if he would still recognize us.

CHAPTER SEVENTEEN

He lowered his face to mine, his eyes taking in every inch of me.

"Are you…?"

He answered with a subtle nod, and I let out a breath of relief. The others rushed in then, their faces falling slack at Rogue. None of them had seen him in his dragon form, save Iaso, but that was from a distance. Seeing him up close and personal was an awe-inspiring experience, and it showed on each of their faces.

Iaso's wide eyes glowed golden as they roamed over him. She stepped forward without hesitation and placed a hand on his massive wing. "You are magnificent, my son."

"Aye," Ewan breathed, walking around Rogue's form. "I've never seen a Draig in their shifted form. It's terrifying, to be truthful. Remind me to never get on your bad side."

"Well…" Iaso said before swallowing hard. She eyed Rogue, and he tossed his head toward his back. Her breath shook as she turned to Ewan and pulled her cross-body bag of potions and salves over her head, handing it to him. He slid it on, and Iaso tightened it around his body before flattening her palm on his chest over his heart. "I love you."

Ewan placed a palm on her cheek and kissed her lips gently. "I love you, too."

Turning to Rogue, she leaned in toward his massive head. "There's a tonic in the bag that will revitalize him long enough to make it back to the castle. Make sure he takes it, no matter what. Shove it down his throat if you must. Just…" Her next words trembled as she spoke them, barely louder than a whisper. "Bring him back to me, Rogue, please. Bring *both* of you back."

He nodded, and all eyes turned to Ewan, his face paler than

it was a minute ago. Iaso grabbed his hand, clutching it to her heart for a moment as a tear fell. She quickly wiped it away and kissed the back of his hand.

"I'll come back, my love. I always do." He wrapped a hand around the back of her head and pulled her into his chest before kissing the top of her head. Reluctantly, he released her and turned to Rogue with a slow inhale. Shaking his head, he muttered, "This seems like a horrible idea."

Rogue gave slightly as Ewan climbed onto his back and settled. Only then did Rogue's eyes shift back to me.

"I love you," I whispered. Stepping closer, I lifted a hand to his face, chuckling through the rising tears as I kissed his snout. His eyes glowed brighter, and I smiled. "Be safe."

With that, he turned to the open wall and stepped forward.

"Oh, Goddess," Ewan shouted, reaching to grip the spikes along Rogue's neck. "Go as fast as you can, big fellow, but *please* do not drop me."

A grumbling sound nearly resembling laughter escaped Rogue before he leaped into the air, Ewan's scream carrying over the wind to us as they disappeared below the ledge. Alden chuckled, throwing his arm around my shoulders.

"I hope they make it in time," Lee said, his brows still pinched with worry.

"Me too," Iaso and I said in unison, watching as our loves coasted over the sea.

* * *

As the sun dipped below the horizon, I bit the inside of my cheek, sitting in the chair beneath Rogue's window. The entire day had come and gone with no word from Rogue,

CHAPTER SEVENTEEN

Ewan, or Iaso.

I had spent the morning relaying the message to everyone I could think of, but by lunch, I was talked out with nothing left to occupy my mind, so I waited—possibly the worst thing to do as the growing tension in my chest became more and more unbearable.

I couldn't imagine what they found when they arrived. Would it be just a fire, or would there be an army lying in wait? If there was an army, they wouldn't be expecting a dragon, that was for certain. If this wasn't a trap, however, but a distraction…what were Adonis' true intentions? What did he want to distract us from? Another attack? Another village?

With a deep sigh, I stood, stretching my arms up, joints aching from sitting still for so long. I turned, and my gaze landed on Rogue's desk. Papers, quills, and books were scattered over its surface, but one page drew my attention more than the others. The flickering firelight illuminated the letter from Adonis, the black words reduced to scribbles from this distance. A chill settled in my bones.

Fools. We are fucking fools.

I sprinted down the hallway, looking for Lee. Assuming he was still in the courtyard with his men, I headed toward the entryway, my muscles screaming as I pushed my legs harder. Reaching a staircase, I hooked my hand around the banister, swinging myself around the corner and down the stairs. My chest burned, and I made a mental note to train more, harder.

The entryway was down the hall on the right, lit with torches. The large wooden door was propped open, and the sounds of clashing swords flooded from the bailey. My heart lurched, but at the sound of Lee's commands to stop and trade partners, I settled some. I was close. My pace slowed slightly, but as I jogged past Livvy's room, my feet came to a halt.

My head tilted to the side, listening. I didn't hear another sound like I thought I had, but I still backpedaled a few feet until I was directly in front of her door. I pressed my ear to the solid wood, and the sound of metal clicked, followed by a soft thud—not just metal. A window latch.

I threw the door open to find the room dark, and a sleeping Livvy sprawled across her bed. I squinted into the darkness toward the window, and a man's face came into focus. I didn't have time to scream before he came at me, the moonlight glinting off a blade in his hand.

Adrenaline flooded me. His form lit with a silver haze as my irises crackled, and he stilled, his face falling. In shock or fear, it didn't matter; I relished the look either way, grinning as I sprinted at him. The movement snapped him from his stupor, and he ducked as I swung, my entire fist wrapped in a sizzling energy. He swiped his blade, narrowly missing my face. With not one single ounce of shame in my body, I kicked as hard as I could, straight at his groin. He dropped with a loud groan, coughing and sputtering.

I wrapped my hand around his throat with a satisfied grin as his face jerked to mine. With my hand close to his heart, the thumping radiated into my fingertips, the delicate energy tempting. It was practically offering itself to me, and I *wanted* to take it.

The energy crawled from his heart and into my hand like beaming veins of white beneath my skin. His heart beat slower as the energy wound itself into my hand, climbing my arm. The light emanating from my irises glowed brighter,

CHAPTER SEVENTEEN

and as his life ended, I pushed his chest, sending him falling back.

He hit the ground with a thud at the same moment a hard fist connected to my jaw, sending a sharp wave of pain and nausea through me. My head jerked to the side as I stumbled back a few feet before falling over a chair. I fell straight on my back, knocking the breath from my lungs. Another man had stepped from the shadows and stood over me as I gasped for air, clutching at my chest. Baring his teeth, he reared a leg back and kicked me in the ribs with his boot, a sickening crack echoing in my ears as a strangled cry tore from my throat.

"Livvy," I groaned. She had always been a deep sleeper, but she couldn't be tonight. She couldn't. "Livvy!" The sound was broken and choked, muffled by pain.

He didn't waste a second before kicking again, and I wheezed, my face twisted in a silent scream. He leaned over me and grabbed my chin to force my eyes on him. He studied my face before a vile grin stretched across his face, his eyes dipping to my covered breasts. I screamed, rage numbing the pain for a moment, and grabbed his head. My crackling silver reflected in his dark eyes before I head-butted him as hard as I could. A deep ache ricocheted through my skull, and I clutched my forehead with a groan.

He stumbled back a few steps, clutching his nose as blood poured between his fingers. "You bitch."

He took a step forward, and I scrambled back across the floor. A squelch sounded through the nearly silent room. He didn't have a chance to take a second step as a small blade protruded from his throat. A gargling sound left his bloodied lips, and his hands fumbled at the tip of the dagger before he fell to his knees, then to his face, a pool of blood forming around him.

Livvy stood where he had, pale and shaking, her white shift flowing gently in the breeze. We stared at each other, breathing heavily.

I grabbed the arm of a chair next to me, wincing as I pulled myself to my feet. "You took whatever it was, didn't you?"

Her breath choked off as her eyes watered. She wrapped her arms around herself and nodded.

"Livvy... What did you take?" I asked.

She fidgeted with the sleeve of her shirt. "I-I was scared that if I said anything, you would give me back. Well, not you, but Rogue—understandably so. I'm scared, Ara. I'm so scared." She lifted her hands covering the bottom half of her face as her brows scrunched.

"It's not just your dad you're scared of, is it?"

"No." She slowly shook her hand. "No, it's not."

"If it is Adonis—Adon, I mean—if it is him you fear, I can promise on my life that you will never fall into his hands again. Ever."

The weight of my words seemed to settle something in her. With a deep, slow inhale, she sat in the chair next to me, pulling her legs up and crossing them. I sat in the chair I had braced myself on and turned it to face her directly.

"All right..." She fidgeted with her hands in her lap. "Yes, it is me he's looking for. Although, I didn't *take* anything. It's just...me. He wants me." She cringed as the words left her and rubbed her wrists again absentmindedly.

"You?" My blood chilled. If she meant what I thought she meant... *No, I can't be right...*

"I can't feel it, you know. When I look at him, I feel as

CHAPTER SEVENTEEN

though I'm looking at a random stranger on the street. I didn't feel—I *don't* feel…"

"The mate bond," I whispered, finishing for her.

Her eyes snapped to me as she nodded. "Yes. The mate bond. But he says he does."

My hand covered my mouth as my eyes burned. Adonis was as cruel and merciless as his father, and my heart broke, shattering at the thought of sweet Livvy in his malicious grasp.

I sat up, leaning forward with my elbows on my knees. "Livvy, did he… I mean, he didn't…"

"No, he didn't…force himself on me, if that's what you were going to ask," she replied quietly.

I released a breath I hadn't realized I'd been holding.

"I'm all right," she said, and I sat back in my chair. "Mostly."

"Mostly?"

* * *

The sky was pitch black, shrouded in dense clouds, sparse lightning striking the ocean miles away as Livvy sat on Iaso's table. For the first time since she'd saved me from her attempted kidnapper, she was completely still.

I had grabbed Lee from his training at Livvy's request, and he rushed to Iaso's surgery, worry marring his face. His jaw was tight even now, his brows pinched.

"Are you sure?" I whispered, reaching for Livvy's hand.

"I've never been *more* sure of anything, Ara. I have to remove it."

She may not be nervously fidgeting, but I was. The procedure she was about to endure was painful—an excruciating experience that may or may not remove the scar he left to plague her.

Iaso came from her chamber with Aurum on her heels, already larger and meatier than when she'd rescued him. Iaso's hair was tousled and thrown atop her head, the usual gold beads missing. Her hands were full of vials, bottles, and herbs, but as she laid them on the table, my eyes landed on the glint of metal, the silver sparkle of sharpened blades saved solely for surgery.

"Well…" Iaso said with hesitation. Her brows were creased, her hands smoothing out the apron that covered her green, silk pajamas. "Show me."

With a deep breath, Livvy stood slowly, but her hands hesitated on the waistband of her pants. Closing her eyes, she slid them down along with her undergarment. My breath hitched. Horror filled me, immediately chased away by rage as my mouth pressed into a tight line.

Below the hem of her undergarments, carved into the skin above her womb, were the letters A.D.—Adonis Draki. The scar was jagged and deep, the kind cut with malice and the intent to scar.

His failed attempt at claiming ownership of her womb, her body.

My stomach twisted, bile rising in my throat.

"He does not own me," Livvy declared. "He never will. I would cut my womb from my body before I ever allowed him to take what he wanted from me. My body is *mine*, and mine alone."

Iaso nodded. "Yes, it is. We will remove his last mark from your body this night, and he will never touch you again. He does not own you, Livvy. No man ever will."

CHAPTER SEVENTEEN

Livvy's face was tight with determination. She gripped Lee's hand with one of hers and mine with her other as she lay back on the table.

Iaso pulled a carved piece of wood from her apron pocket and reluctantly placed it between Livvy's lips. "Bite this. When I begin...it will hurt, child, but the pain will not last. I'll heal it as soon as I finish cutting away the old tissue."

Livvy's teeth clenched around the soft wood as she nodded fiercely, her eyes wide. Iaso grabbed a blade, and her glowing golden eyes set fire to the silver as she leaned over Livvy's abdomen.

The first cut lit Livvy from the inside. She screamed around the wood as her jaw clenched and her body bowed from the table.

"Do you wish for me to continue?" Iaso whispered softly.

Livvy nodded, swallowing hard.

Iaso's eyes flitted to Lee with empathy. "Hold her down."

Reluctance crossed his features before his eyes lowered to Livvy. A tear slid down the side of her face as she nodded in agreement.

His arm barred against her abdomen, and Iaso turned back to her work, meticulously cutting the letters from Livvy's skin.

The seconds passed by like hours as Livvy writhed against Lee's hold in agony, even as she attempted to remain still. Her skin was soaked with a sheen of sweat, her breathing ragged, when Iaso finally finished.

"All right," Iaso said, setting the bloodied knife to the side and picking up a small glass container. "This is a healing salve. It will rid you of any scar if applied fast enough, but...it burns."

Like fire, I thought but didn't dare say aloud. I gripped Livvy's hand a little tighter as my gaze darted to Lee. We locked eyes in understanding, and his hold tightened as well.

Livvy's eyes flicked back and forth between us, but she didn't have time to utter a sound before Iaso's fingers spread the ointment across her raw skin. Livvy's body bowed against Lee's hold as her tortured scream ripped through the room with a vengeance.

"Okay, done." Iaso stepped back with her hands up.

Lee removed his arm immediately, and Livvy rolled onto her side, curling in on herself, her face twisted in a silent sob. The wood fell from her mouth to the floor with a brief clatter.

I leaned over her, cocooning her in a tight hug as my own tears fell. "It's done. It's over. You did it, Liv. You did it."

She nodded helplessly as she wrapped her arms around me in return so tightly, I almost couldn't breathe. "I will never let him see me again. Never touch me again. Never even breathe the same air as me again, Ara. I swear it before the very Goddess herself."

"I would slit his throat if he even dared," I vowed, and I meant every single word.

For everything he'd done to the Fae, to the people around him, to Evander, my mother, Doran, Rogue, me, and now Livvy—for his atrocities, he would die. At my hands or another's, it didn't matter. Whoever got there first.

Lightning cracked outside, striking again and again and again, the storm echoing my rage as it ravaged the ocean.

It didn't stop until we had walked Livvy to her room and laid her to bed with Iaso's sleeping tea. Her breaths still hiccuped from the force of her cries as we clicked the door shut behind us.

"He *will* die," I said through the heavy silence.

"Soon," Lee added, his knuckles cracking as he clenched his fists.

The sun peeked over the horizon as the clouds dissipated when I finally made it back to our chambers and crawled into bed. Exhaustion had long since settled in my bones after several nights of disrupted sleep and the outpouring of emotions in the last few hours.

I had taken the sleep tea as well, with orders not to disturb me for the next few hours—the only exception being Rogue's return. Even as a bit of anxiety pulsed through me at what my vivid, tea-induced dreams would bring, nothing could have prevented the heavy weight of sleep as the tea kicked in. My eyelids might have weighed ten pounds at that moment.

The second I slipped under, however, wispy black tendrils of magic twisted and grew in the distance, accompanied by an army of silent minds and soundless screams. The gut-wrenching nightmare of Adonis dug its grimy claws in and refused to release me.

Chapter Eighteen

Rogue

The sun was at its peak when we finally landed—nearly crashed—into the shifting room.

We were covered in soot, but the Marsh had been saved, minus a few burned trunks. The fire hadn't seemed too large at first, but it fought to stay lit. When Ewan vanquished one area, two more popped up. It was relentless, but so was Ewan in his fight.

It took hours, several attempts, and every bit of Ewan's magic, but he finally managed to diminish it for good before falling unconscious. I shoved that damned tonic down his throat in a panic and then another. Three tonics down his throat, but he didn't wake.

I grew increasingly panicked with each passing minute, and after five *very* slow minutes, neither Ewan nor the fire had woken again, so I resolved to carry Ewan back in my front claws.

Carrying a person by dragon back had been *much* more draining than I anticipated—perhaps it was because I wasn't used to this form or the fact that my nerves were shot, but

CHAPTER EIGHTEEN

carrying his limp form in my claws was harder. My arms screamed, my grip shaking and loosening with each passing mile; I did it, but just barely. By the time I touched down in the shifting chamber, my muscles were barely functioning.

Ewan was still unconscious when I landed, and I carefully laid him on the cold stone. I shifted back as quickly as I could before grabbing the clothes I'd left and throwing them on. Swallowing hard, I strode over to him, leaned down, and scooped my arms under his shoulders and knees. Against every screaming muscle, I lifted him slowly, wincing and grunting as we rose.

Once I was standing fully, I inhaled deeply and turned toward the door, walking as fast as I possibly could to Iaso's chamber. I kicked the door as there was no way I could knock without dropping him entirely, and not even a few seconds later, she jerked the ancient wooden door open, her face distraught as her eyes fell on Ewan's lifeless body in my arms. She stepped from the doorway, and I strode in.

Her room was a reflection of her—dried herbs and flowers hanging from the ceilings, the bedspread as green as the vines that grew over her massive windows overlooking her greenhouse.

I laid him down gently on the bed, doing my best not to fall over him as my muscles gave under the weight. I braced a hand on the bed frame, closing my eyes as I breathed, allowing the worst of the ache to pass.

"The tonic? Did he take it?" Iaso smoothed Ewan's hair back away from his forehead—the gentle movement in stark contrast to her strained voice. She gasped as a tear fell on his cheek and wiped it away, whispering, "Sorry."

"Three." Her face whipped to me, pure panic on her

features. "I gave him three."

Her bottom lip quivered as she slowly turned back to Ewan, her golden eyes casting him in her light. "He seems okay… mostly. No lasting damage from what I can tell. Perhaps his body just needed the rest."

I didn't know if she was saying the words for me or herself—I wasn't even sure she truly believed them—but I answered them regardless. "He'll be okay, Iaso. He's strong, and I knew for a fact, there's not a single force in this realm that could keep him from you. He will return."

Just as nothing could keep me from Ara.

A sob escaped her, and she turned to me, burying her face in my chest."I do believe he'll wake again, but his magic? His well is…tapped. Even after three doses, I can still feel his emptiness."

Another cry left her, wracking her body. I wrapped my arms around her, holding her as long as she needed without saying a word. There was nothing I could say; she was right. There was a high possibility it wouldn't come back, not with how much he'd used. He'd tapped his magic's well and dug deeper—far deeper than any Fae should go.

As she took a slow, deep breath and released me, she turned back to Ewan. "Do you…Do you think he'll still look at me the same if it doesn't come back?"

My head jerked back slightly in surprise. "What? Iaso, this isn't your fault in the slightest."

She turned back to me, her brows pinched. "I promised I would heal him, and he nearly killed himself because he knew what the Marsh meant to me."

"He made his choice." My head was nearly swimming with exhaustion as I leaned on the bed rail again. "He would never

CHAPTER EIGHTEEN

put that on you."

Nodding, she swallowed hard. "Perhaps."

She took his hand and brought it to her lips, kissing it as she sat at his side. She peeked over her shoulder, opening her mouth to say something, but she stopped when she saw my state. Her eyes roamed over my form, down to my tightening grip on the rail.

"Are you all right?" she asked, her eyes glowing as they continued their assessment.

"Just…tired." That was the understatement of the century. I was completely depleted; even my eyes burned to rest.

"Oh, of course. I'm so sorry." She stood and walked to her table of vials. The glass clinked as she grazed through them with her back to me. "This will help you recover."

"I don't think I need anything," I said, but she returned with a vial regardless.

"Just in case." She closed her hands around mine as she handed me the vial.

I chuckled, nodding as I slid it into my pocket. "Thank you, Iaso."

She glanced at Ewan, the worry returning to her eyes. "Thank *you*, Rogue, for helping save the Marsh."

I wanted to ask about her attachment to the place, why it was particularly special to her, but I was too tired. No matter how intriguing, I didn't have it in me to start another conversation. Instead, I hugged her once more, kissed the top of her head, and left, shutting her door silently behind me.

I practically staggered my way back to our chambers and groaned when I saw Lee striding toward my door.

His eyes found me then, his jaw tight. "A lady's maid told

me you were back. How did it go? Is it still standing?"

Taking a slow breath, I pinched the bridge of my nose. "Yes. After an excruciatingly long night, Ewan managed to put it out. The trunks of several trees were burned, but no long-lasting damage."

"Good," Lee said. "And Ewan? Is he…?"

"He's alive. Unconscious, but alive."

His face relaxed for a moment before tightening again. "Have you spoken to anyone since you've been back?"

His tone, as cautious as it was serious, caught my attention, and I already knew. My jaw clenched and unclenched as smoke wafted around me. "What happened?"

Lee's eyes followed the black haze for a moment before he swallowed hard and brought his gaze back to mine. "Don't panic—"

I stepped into him. "What. Happened?"

"Two men broke in and attempted to kidnap Livvy."

My brows furrowed, my face pulling back a few inches.

"And Ara is the one who found them as they climbed in the window."

"What?" I practically yelled as rage consumed my fatigue, adrenaline rolling through my veins like liquid fire. "Where is she?"

I jerked toward our door when Lee grabbed my arm, and I swiveled back to him. Orange light flickered across his face in the dark hallway, reflecting in his green eyes as my pupils burned. My skin heated beneath his palm, smoke rolling over his arm.

He hissed and released me, shaking his hand in an attempt to cool it. "Ara's okay, just bruised. She and Livvy killed them both."

CHAPTER EIGHTEEN

"And where were you?" I seethed. The light reflecting on his face glowed brighter. He stepped back, and I stepped forward. "Why was my mate the one to kill the intruder?"

He dropped his eyes. "I was training my men in the bailey. The intruders came in through Livvy's window and would have gone seemingly unnoticed had Ara not saved her." His gaze flitted back to me, his hand rubbing his chest absentmindedly. "I'm extremely grateful to her. I don't know what I would have done."

I inhaled deeply and ran a hand through my hair as I stepped back. "Sorry."

"It's all right. She's your mate. I get it. Iaso gave her sleeping tea a few hours ago. That's why I stopped you. I figured she needed—deserved the rest."

Nodding, I glanced back at the door. "Why did they come for Livvy?"

"She's his mate, Rogue. Adonis' mate."

"Oh," was the only word that escaped me as shock rocked through me, closely followed by a small wave of pity.

My gaze flitted back to Lee, my brows drawing together as I truly looked at him. I had been so tired and preoccupied that I hadn't noticed his unease. Worry had settled in his eyes, deepening the dark circles beneath them.

"She doesn't want to go back." He held his chin high, his spine rod straight.

I shifted back a step, shaking my head. His words, his body language… It was as if he were scared I would hand her over, but there wasn't a single reason under the sun or stars I would ever force her to return. Not to that monster. Not to any man.

Regardless, I admired his willingness to fight for her. It

spurred a newfound respect for Lee.

"I would never make her," was all I said.

His face and shoulders relaxed as he exhaled. "I actually had something else I needed to talk to you about—or rather, show you."

I nodded cautiously, and he led me down to the bottom floor of the castle. There was only one place we could be going. As we stepped into the dungeon, straw crunched underfoot, the scent of filth and mildew wafting from the cells ahead.

The guards at the door jerked from their chairs as they greeted us in passing. We dipped our heads and continued, strolling past the empty cells—not much use for them lately, I supposed.

"I had my men on high alert, searching the grounds and surrounding land for any suspicious activity as soon as Ara told me what happened," Lee explained as he stopped in front of the last cell. The sounds of mumbling and pleading drifted from inside. "We found him running for dear life. They shot him in the leg with an arrow to stop him."

Lee unlocked the cell door and slid it open. The prisoner's face jerked toward us and paled. I had never seen him before, that much I was certain of. His gaze darted around the room, hovering over one corner as he cowered, crying, his lip already busted and bruised.

Lee's face was a solid mask of anger as he stepped into the cell. "We think he told Adonis' men where to find Livvy's chambers."

The prisoner's eyes darted back to him, wide and watery as he shook his head fervently. "No, not I. No, no, 'twas not me, Your Majesty."

CHAPTER EIGHTEEN

My eyes narrowed at him. His fear was genuine, but I couldn't decipher if his words were as well. He was too terrified, his voice and body trembling from our presence. If there was truth in his words, it was highly concealed behind panic.

"Then why were you running like your life depended on it?" Lee asked.

"I only—I didn't—" His eyes darted to the corners of the cell. They roamed across the stone in one smooth motion as he pressed himself back into the wall, shaking his head. "She... No!"

His gaze jerked toward mine, and his head slammed back into the stone behind him. Lee lunged for him, but it was too late. The prisoner slammed his head again, and blood seeped down the wall as he slumped forward, the back of his skull crushed, his limp body hanging from the chains at his wrists.

Lee and I were frozen, our mouths hanging open as we slowly looked at each other.

"What just happened?" I asked.

Lee shook his head before he stepped forward and slid a hand under the man's chin, pressing two fingers to his throat. After a moment, he dropped his hand. "No pulse. He's dead."

Too stunned to conjure anything else, I asked again, "What just happened?"

"It seemed our traitor was also a coward."

I raised my brows, tilting my head to the side as I gave the dead man one more glance before turning to the door. I couldn't blame him. When he finally admitted it was him who tipped Adonis off, his death would have been slow and painful—compensation for Ara's bruises, the ones I had yet to see. It didn't matter how bad they were. If he were the underlying cause for a single hair out of place on her head, he would be dead.

In fact, if it was he who put Ara and Livvy in danger, his death should have been slower. I ground my teeth, suddenly irritated he got off so easily. I'd already decided on our way down here that he was to lose his tongue and hands first, as one of them—either his mouth or his letters—was his way of sharing intel. Not that it mattered now; he wouldn't be doing much jabbering to anyone from the other side of the veil.

Shaking my head, I took a deep breath and strode out of the cell. After saying farewell to Lee, I made my way back to my chambers, the exhaustion returning with each step closer to relief. My body ached as I finally stepped into our room and silently closed the door behind me.

Ara was asleep, spread across the middle of the bed with the covers down to her waist. Stripping my clothes, I left myself in nothing but my underwear as I made it to the edge of the bed.

I knew to expect some damage from their fight, but I stopped dead in my tracks as I took a closer look at Ara. She was covered in a sheen of sweat, and her face was mottled with bruises, the deepest on her jaw and forehead. I leaned forward, my heart pounding as my finger skimmed along the purpling skin. She flinched, and her shirt moved with her, revealing blackened ribs.

My breath left me in a whoosh as I slid her shirt farther up. Her entire abdomen was covered in purple and black blotches, her breathing shallower than normal. Her ribs had to be fractured.

This was much worse than I expected. My jaw clenched as

CHAPTER EIGHTEEN

flames rushed through my veins. I wanted to wake her and ask if she was okay, to see her eyes open and hear her sweet, sleepy voice so I *knew* she was okay as guilt pricked at me for leaving her here. She was deeply asleep, though, and I imagined being unconscious was far less painful than being awake right now, especially at the sight of those broken ribs.

She jerked and moaned at the movement, her breath hitching. I waited, and she did it again, her brows furrowing and lips frowning. Mumbling words started to flow from her, increasing in intensity. Within seconds, she was nearly screaming.

It had to be a nightmare. Carefully, I leaned over her and shook her shoulders.

"Ara, hey." I shook her shoulders again, a bit harder.

She thrashed against whatever took hold of her in her nightmare, sweat dripping from her as she muttered unintelligible words.

Fear crept in as I shook her again, but she still didn't wake. She was clearly terrified but stuck within the claws of whatever held her.

With a deep sigh, I lit a spark at my fingertips. "I'm sorry," I whispered, cringing as I lowered it to her skin. The small flame licked at her fingertip—not enough to burn, but hot enough to feel, to startle.

She jerked awake, sitting straight up. She gasped painfully and clutched at her abdomen with one hand as she shook her other one and brought it to her mouth. She sucked on the hot finger with confused shock in her eyes.

As she woke, her eyes widened, and she dropped her hands. She attempted to crawl to me but hissed, grabbing her ribs again. "Ow."

"I'm sorry," I whispered. Reaching around her, I propped a pillow behind her on the headboard and helped her scoot back to rest on it. "Lee told me what happened."

"Two men tried to kidnap Livvy," she muttered, rubbing her forehead but wincing as her fingers touched the bruise. "*She* was what he was referring to in that damned letter like she were an object." Ara rolled her eyes.

Exhaustion settled over me again, thick and heavy, bending me to its will as I climbed into bed beside her. She scooted closer, and I tucked her hair behind her ear. Grabbing her chin, I tilted her face up to get a better look, and she closed her eyes as my fingers delicately skimmed over the contuse. "I'm sorry, little storm."

"Not your fault," she whispered.

"Lee's men captured a man moments after the attempted attack. He was brought to the dungeons last night."

Her eyes widened before her brows furrowed. "What? Well, let's go."

She started to move, and I rested a hand on her thigh. "He's dead."

Her face jerked back to mine. "How?"

"He…" I shook my head. "He killed himself."

She sank back into the pillow, her breath leaving her in a whoosh. "Well, hopefully, that cuts off Adonis' ties to Draig Hearth."

"Hopefully." I was too drained to think about that right now; even my brain ached. I slid beneath the covers and reclined on the pillow. "What was your nightmare about?"

She paused before whispering, "Adonis."

My jaw clenched. Even in dreams, he haunted us.

"Are you all right?" I asked, propping an elbow behind my

CHAPTER EIGHTEEN

head.

"Yeah, it was just a nightmare, but you know that tea...It always feels so real," she said, scrunching her eyes as she rubbed her forehead again. "I don't believe I'll take that again."

I chuckled. "They're not always so bad, hmm?" My finger ran lower, grazing the mate mark as the memory of the first time she dreamed of my mouth between her thighs flashed through my mind.

She tilted her head to the side, granting me more access.

"Not always," she hummed before her eyes fell back to me. "But this one was enough."

"What was it about?" My hand moved over her shoulder to her back. She turned away from me, sliding her hair over her shoulder as my fingers slid down her spine and back up.

"His magic, mostly, the hold he has over people. I could see the magic, working its way from one person to the next until everyone was nothing but...controlled husks. Their minds were entirely empty of their own free will. It was horrifying." She flinched. "I watched him force a man to kill his family."

"It was just a nightmare."

"This was a nightmare, yes, but Evander wasn't." My hand paused on her back. "He was real and everything he was forced to do was real. The manipulation is real. This is happening."

My gut wrenched with guilt at not making the connection. *Thoughtless.* An apology was on the tip of my tongue when she sighed and sank back into me, reclining her head on my chest.

"I'm so ready for this to be over, but it feels like it's barely begun."

"Me too." I kissed the top of her head. "And you're right. It *is* happening, but I'm sorry you had to watch it nonetheless, even if only in a nightmare."

She sighed, nuzzling even further into my lap. I laced my fingers through hers and raised her hand to my lips, kissing the silver scar along her wrist. We sat in silence for a moment, the only movement that of our chests rising and falling.

"You need to sleep. I know you need a few dozen hours to recover." She sat up again, a pained sound leaving her with her breath. She scooted to the edge of the bed slowly and paused, bracing a hand on her ribs before she stood with a grunt. "I don't know why I didn't expect to be this sore. I should have asked Iaso for something."

"Are you up for the day, or were you planning to come back to bed?" I asked.

"Yeah, I'm up." She plucked a pair of trousers from the dresser and slowly, painfully, bent over to pull them on.

"Go to Iaso first before you do anything else."

She chuckled, her eyes lifting to mine. "Bossy."

"Concerned," I corrected.

She smiled lightly, her eyes warm, as she strolled back to the bed and leaned over to kiss my lips gently. "Yes sir," she whispered with a wink.

I groaned at the words and wrapped my hand around the back of her head to pull her down for a deeper, hungrier kiss. She smiled against my lips as I released her.

She strolled to the mirror, and I watched her in her reflection as she ran a brush through her hair before braiding it back.

"I think I'll help Alden with his search today," she said, her smile faltering. "We need to find the crown. With magic like that…Adonis is too powerful. His army is too powerful. We

CHAPTER EIGHTEEN

need something, anything, to gain ground and the wyverns... They'd change everything."

She was right, of course. He was powerful. He had an endless, hypnotized army, but that wasn't my biggest concern. I wouldn't dare breathe the words aloud because no one else had yet. It hadn't seemed like anyone else had considered what may truly happen if he were to come in close contact with one of us.

If that magic of his touched one of us.

Chapter Nineteen

Rogue

It was the next morning by the time I rose. I had faint memories of Ara crawling back into bed at some point and leaving again before I had roused. She left a note on the pillow next to mine that read:

Gone with Alden. Come find us if you need me. I love you.
    Ara

In turn, I left a note for her detailing my plans for the day.

After dressing and eating a light breakfast, I headed straight for the library, silently hoping I wouldn't see any of our family. I wanted solitude—certainly not their concern, or Goddess forbid, pity when I inevitably told them what I was setting out to do today.

I needed to shift again. I needed practice. The last one was as painful as the first, and the thought of doing it again left me nauseous if I let it linger for too long. I was going to change that; I couldn't allow myself to be afraid. We didn't

CHAPTER NINETEEN

have time. With war looming on the horizon, I needed to master it, but more than that, I *wanted* to.

I wanted to shift without fear or pain. I wanted to embrace every part of who I was and thrive in it because it was mine. This shift, this familial magic, the Draki name was mine, and I wanted to claim it with pride because I deserved it—with my blood, sweat, and tears, I had earned it.

To do that, I needed to shift again…and again and again.

I swallowed hard, turning the back corner of the library to find the door to the shifting room, shrouded in shadows. It was once a grand entrance, lined with lit torches, carved wyvern bones, and other ceremonial extravagance—before the decimation of the Draki line.

The shifting bloodline had come to an abrupt halt with me, or so we thought. After the death of Adrastus and the final remaining descendant was left without a shift, the room was deemed useless, just another sad reminder of what could have been for our family—for me. So, it was left to rot, abandoned in a forgotten corner.

Until now.

I had never entered the room before two days ago—saw no need—but standing before it now, I felt nerves swirling in my gut, as if I was somehow still unwelcome and undeserving. I knew that was merely my own insecurities pricking at me after a lifetime of hanging my head in shame, so I shoved the feeling down. I had shifted, my father was an awful, worm-eaten memory, and I was chosen by the wyverns for my heart and soul, my being.

If nothing else, I was worthy of stepping inside, of standing where my grandfather had once stood, and his father before him. I had already been in there once; I didn't understand why it felt wrong now, or why I was standing here attempting to convince myself that I deserved to enter.

I lifted my hand and slid a finger over the ancient carvings, leaving a trail through the dust that had accumulated over the decades.

Before we left for the Marsh, I hadn't taken the time to look around. In fact, I kept my eyes down. I hadn't wanted to see it. We were under too much pressure with such little time, and when I finally saw this room, the one so sacred to my family, I wanted it to be on my terms.

That was why I was here—to take in every detail, every inch of history, to take my time before shifting at my own pace, slowly and steadily as my ancestors would have. I wanted to experience being a dragon and flying for the leisure and beauty of it, not solely for necessity.

My hand stopped and flattened onto the smooth wood as I lowered my forehead to it, closing my eyes. "Skin for scale, nails for talons, blood for blood, flight for freedom—with this shift, I am released."

Those words had been uttered before this door hundreds of times—thousands of times before this room was even a wisp of thought—and I could feel the thrum of history echoing behind them, sending a direct line to every ancestor before me.

Chills erupted over my skin as I dropped my hand, standing tall. Taking a deep breath, I reached for the doorknob and twisted until it clicked. I pushed the door, letting it swing open before me.

The wall along the back revealed the morning sky, lined by the sea beneath it. The opening was large—large enough to accommodate even my dragon form, just as it was built to be. My grandfather, Drakyth, and his father before him, Stryath, would have shifted and soared from this very room over and over through the centuries, free from the burden of the ground-bound. As a dragon shifting for no other reason than the pleasure of it, our only concern was where the fish were, the feeling of wind beneath our wings, and the sun along our scales. That was one thing I distinctly remembered from my time at the Hearth—the freedom.

It was glorious in a way the rest of the Fae would never understand, and it made me feel infinitely more connected to my family than anything I had ever known.

A faint smile crept across my face. It was an otherworldly feeling—more than just blood and name, but to *know* how they felt, to soar alongside their memory.

For the first time in my life, I was proud of the Draki name.

Pulling my eyes from the sky, I lifted my face to see the ceiling. It was entirely covered in detailed carvings of dragons, each one related to me in some way. I took my time, studying each one, before I noticed the freshly carved wood, oiled but distinctly newer by decades. Confusion wracked me for half a second before I noticed the dark red stain and delicate flames.

My faint smile broke into a shocked grin as I realized it was me. Someone in our family had commissioned a carving of my dragon form, and they had done so quickly.

Running my hand along the back of my neck, my cheeks burned as I dropped my eyes, letting them fall on the lit fireplace lined with obsidian. The flames flowed with the breeze, dancing to their own crackling song.

What surrounded me now was so, *so* different from what surrounded me as a child. Our new situation, the family and friendships we had built, was foreign, and at times, a bit frightening, but it more than made up for anything I had ever suffered. To have Ara was a blessing I never thought I would have the pleasure of experiencing but to have her *and* a family? Not of blood and obligation, but of…loyalty? Love, even?

A dream. It was a dream, one I would protect with everything I had.

I turned to the shelves along the right wall. There were several trinkets lined up, and I knew, without a doubt, that these were the claimed treasures of previous Draigs. Their claim still remained, a distinct hum over each object attempting to ward me away.

As I grazed over the objects, a chuckle escaped me. My dragon had chosen Ara, I knew that. I could feel the thrum hovering over her whenever I partially shifted, the aura that surrounded her as my dragon so lovingly viewed her with rose-tinted glasses. We were both unconditionally in love with her.

The thought of her placed atop these shelves amused me. She would never be an object, a trophy to be viewed and appreciated. No, she had the heart of a ruler, a lover, and a warrior, and that was exactly what made her so exceptional.

She was truly the daughter of Vaelor—born to wear the crown. She would rule Ravaryn with as much compassion as he did, and she would thrive.

My thoughts of Ara atop the throne—deliciously so—came to a halt when my hand stopped on an object on the third shelf from the bottom.

A dented golden ball, tarnished with age and brine.

The scent accompanying it was sickening, a vile combina-

CHAPTER NINETEEN

tion that was distinctly Adrastus.

Gritting my teeth, I picked it up, inspecting it closer. Rage swelled in my chest as I stared at it; knowing he lived among this room sent another spike of anger through me. My heart pounded in my chest, nearly audible as the molten light from my pupils lit the ball, reflecting off the metallic surface. It infuriated me even further to see my own reflection in the same way he would have seen his.

He didn't deserve any of this—not the shift, the kingdom, the crown, a mate, not even his own claimed.

I marched toward the open wall and launched the ball. It sailed over the sea for a distance far greater than any other living Fae could have thrown before crashing into the water. It disappeared from sight as it sank below the waves, never to be seen again.

Running my hand over the scruff along my jaw, I sighed.

I guess now is better than never.

This would be the third time I'd shifted, but the thought still sent a rush of fresh fear through me, adrenaline pouring through my veins. Both times, it had been quick but excruciating. It was fast taste of pure hell as my skin melted away, my bones broke and rebuilt in new shapes, talons tore through my nail beds, and sharp, dagger-like teeth ripped through my gums. Every small detail of the shift was a unique form of torture, but one that would lessen with each shift.

Goddess, I wish you were here, Doran. At least then you could make some snide remark about me being a coward.

Sighing deeply, I looked up, as if that would somehow make him hear me.

You better be up there with the Goddess laughing down at me.

Dropping my gaze, I ran a hand through my hair, standing

straighter.

It needed to be done. Everyone was occupied, and I could fully devote myself to this hell for the next day or two without prying eyes or worried words. There was no excuse.

My heart raced as I slowly peeled my clothes from my body, folded them, and stacked them neatly on one of the chairs by the fireplace.

According to the book I skimmed, the pain would lessen around the tenth shift and decimate from there. Just ten times.

Nausea rolled in my gut, and I bit my fist as breakfast threatened to return. Ten times I must break every bone in my body.

Ten times.

I took a deep breath.

I had done it twice already. I could do this again…eight more times.

My stomach lurched.

Closing my eyes, I took a slow breath and urged it forward. My femurs snapped simultaneously, and a scream shredded my throat, but I didn't stop. Smoke clouded the room instantly, leaving only enough clarity for me to see the sky—clear and blue and bright. Calm.

The sky was calm. No rain. No sadness. No fear.

Snap.

I bit back another scream of agony. The sea was smooth and calm. My eyes watered.

My skin burned away in my own fire.

Snap. *Agony.*

The breeze kissed my raw skin like the kiss of death. Even its gentle touch was excruciating. It sent me over the edge,

CHAPTER NINETEEN

and I lost all control. My knees buckled, and I fell to my hands with another crack. My nails bit into the stone beneath me as a roar tore from my chest, the broken sound becoming thunderous as it shifted from Fae to dragon.

Bones crunched faster than I had allowed. Shattering faster, cracking faster, moving within my body of their own volition.

My vision darkened, my mind a swirling mass of black and red, lost entirely to the shift.

My wings stretched, as if horses pulled at each end, ripping the joints from their socket just to replace them.

Talons tore from my extremities as each of my nails shredded.

Darkness surrounded me on all fronts while I struggled to remain conscious.

Nothing but agony until...

The pain paused. I inhaled sharply as if I hadn't taken a breath since I'd started.

It stopped. Assessing myself, I moved my long, scaled tail. It swiped across the open floor as my talons scraped the stone. My wings lifted effortlessly, painlessly, as my tongue swept along razor-sharp teeth.

It was done. I did it. A brief wave of relief and satisfaction filled me as I opened my eyes. The smoke had cleared from the room, and everything was sharper—my vision, scent, taste.

I had intended to shift back and forth repeatedly, but the sight of the open sky before me was too tempting.

I leaped from the edge and soared down the castle wall until I reached the water and leveled out, the sun gracing my scales with warmth as the sea spray misted me from beneath.

Bliss.

With a flap of my wings, I sailed forward, reveling in the flight when two shadows fell over me. Within seconds, two wyverns joined me, dragging their hind claws through the water as they swayed side to side.

They chirped, tossing their heads at me. I let out a sound that could best be described as a gruff laugh and shot to the sky with them right below me.

We soared straight up at lightning speed until we broke through the few wispy clouds. Sunlight refracted off the cloud's cool mist, creating a rainbow of iridescence.

I paused to take in the view when the black, serpentine wyvern Ara had deemed the Hearth's guardian joined us with a roar, quickly followed by the last two. Mist swirled around us as we hovered, locking eyes for a brief moment.

A small, amethyst-colored wyvern broke through to nip at the guardian's foot, and he chased after her, pulling another laughing sound from me.

I had my family on the ground—Ara and Iaso and Alden and every new member we had accrued over the months—but this was my family of the sky.

As they all joined in the game, I sank back to the water's surface and glided over the gentle waves with a new-found lightness rising in my chest.

Chapter Twenty

Ara

My chest was so full of pride, I could hardly breathe through it.

Rogue was beautiful—terrifyingly massive, much larger than the wyverns that trailed after him, but beautiful, nonetheless.

I covered my mouth, suppressing a giggle as the wyverns shadowed him, occasionally tapping him with their wings or chirping to get his attention. All five of the grown wyverns that had followed us back joined him in his flight.

As far as I knew, this was the first time he had flown with them since our return, but they clearly enjoyed his company.

I peeked my head through the window frame, the gold-lined glass creaking as I pushed it open farther.

"What are you looking at?" Alden asked, ducking as he stepped through the door of Vaelor's nook.

"It's Rogue." I smiled back and waved him over. "He shifted, and he's flying with the wyverns."

He joined me at the window with a grin of his own. "It's about damn time he's gotten to fly with them. Won't be long until he won't feel a thing when he shifts. It'll come as naturally as breathing air." He stepped back from the window and sat in a chair. "I believe your father may have been excessive when it comes to journaling."

I laughed without turning away from Rogue, watching as he rose into the air before diving into the water. My mouth fell open as he broke through the surface—a glistening image of strength and grace—with a large fish. He tossed it in the air before catching it in his mouth again.

"I believe so too," I replied.

"I wish I had a way to scan forward without missing anything. This is a bit.….much." I peeked over my shoulder, chuckling as he lifted a thick book with crinkling, worn pages shoved in alongside the pages it already held. He dropped it in his lap with an exaggerated sigh and pushed his glasses up his nose. "I don't particularly care to read about him and Elora."

Another laugh escaped me. "Not much for love stories, huh?"

"Not in regards to my own child," he uttered. "You know, he could have at least dated the pages."

"That would have been helpful."

Glancing back at Rogue one last time, a glint of gold caught my attention. I squinted, shielding my eyes with my hand.

"Alden! Look. It's Aurum. He's joining them," I said with awe. This was the first time he had flown since Iaso had healed his wing.

Leaning over the windowsill, I looked straight down. Standing on the ledge below was Iaso, her golden beads glinting in the warm sunlight, her green gown flowing with the breeze. Both of her hands were on her mouth as she watched with motherly worry as her two children flew over the waves.

Chills erupted over my skin as my eyes pricked. It was beautiful. *They* were beautiful.

Rogue's head turned back to us as Aurum joined him. Rogue dwarfed Aurum, shielding him completely from view as the small wyvern dipped below Rogue's massive wing. Iaso waved at him, and Rogue dipped his head before continuing forward on the horizon.

As they distanced themselves from us, I turned back to Alden. His legs were crossed, his long silver hair tied back in a braid, as per usual. He cracked open the thick journal, and the loose pages slid out, scattering about the floor. He looked at them and blinked once. Twice. With a sigh, he gave me a flat look and bent over to gather the pages.

I suppressed a laugh as I crouched down to pick them up for him and stacked them in a messy pile on the desk beside him.

The last page, however, caught my attention.

To Vaelor,

It was addressed *to* him, not written by him. My heart lurched, and I stood to flip through the stack.

To Vaelor,

To Vaelor,

To Vaelor,

All addressed to Vaelor, and signed at the bottom of every page was the same name.

I held them up to Alden, my heart pounding. "These aren't journal entries, Alden. These are letters."

His eyes widened with hope. "From?"

"Drakyth." My eyes dropped to pages, a thick wave of hope

flushing me. "They're from Drakyth."

* * *

"We know where Drakyth is," I exclaimed as I stepped through the open door of Iaso's nursery.

It was a wonderland of green, the air thick with humidity as the scent of soil and flora permeated it. Condensation blurred the glass and allowed the sun to shine through in beams.

Iaso stood from behind a particularly happy flowering bush as she dusted her hands on her apron.

She was breathtaking in every scenario, but Iaso in her garden was otherworldly. Her dark skin, glistening with a sheen of sweat, was highlighted perfectly by her green dress that hung in strips of varying length, wrapping around her shoulders and waist before falling around her bare feet. Her hair was voluptuous—curled and free around her face, with shining, golden beads tied in randomly.

Sometimes, I wondered if she was meant for this world... Or if we were invaders living in hers.

"How? Where?" She strode toward me, snapping me from the trance.

"It turns out Vaelor and Drakyth were in correspondence. It seems they were nearly...friends, actually. Acquaintances, at the very least. They wrote to each other over the decades. At some point, Drakyth settled in a town called Rainsmyre."

She nodded quickly, gears turning behind her eyes. "I know where that is. How long ago was that? Is he still there?"

"We don't know. I left as soon as we found his location, but Alden is still reading through them. It shouldn't take him long, and I told him to come find me when he finishes."

We climbed the steps back into her surgery, and she motioned me to the table and chairs by the window as she gathered tea and cups.

"And Rogue doesn't know yet, I presume?"

"No, not yet. We found the letters stuffed in a journal right after a certain golden wyvern joined Rogue in flight."

She smiled to herself as she poured the steaming liquid. "You saw that, huh?"

"Yes, I did. He looked strong. No weakness or uncertainty, at least from what I could tell." Looping my fingers through the handle, I lifted the cup and took a long sip.

"Oh, yes. He should be back to full health now. The wound healed mere days after our arrival, but I have to admit, I've grown rather attached to him, so I was a bit nervous to let him go."

"Nervous?"

"Well, we never truly know, do we? Perhaps he would still have pain, or maybe the wound would reopen during flight, or hunters would hunt him down out of ignorant fear should he wander too close to their camp, or…"

My eyes flicked to her, as uncertainty was not usually a trait of Iaso's. Her brows were creased as she watched the tea swirl in her cup.

"Or maybe he wouldn't come back?" I whispered.

"It's silly, really. He's a wyvern." She chuckled sadly. "He's meant to be free and—"

"It's not silly, Iaso," I interjected. "It's not silly at all. I understand the love for our animal companions—have experienced it myself with my wolfhound when I was a child. There's a special kind of soul bond that forms between animal and person. It's a powerful thing, and I know without a shadow of a doubt that Aurum loves you, too. Besides, *he* chose *you* on the island, did he not?"

"He did, I suppose, but just for reference, I would let him go should he choose to leave." She smiled into her cup before she lowered it slightly, and her eyes flitted to mine. "I just wouldn't be happy about it." She took another sip. "And I'm not above bribing. Should it require an entire stag a day to keep him here, I would offer him two, just to spoil him too rotten to ever want for more."

"What more could he ever require?" I asked sarcastically.

"Exactly. He would grow fat and happy here with me. We would be quite the team, I believe."

"That you would. The golden healer and her golden wyvern."

Her eyes—truly golden as the evening sun shone through the window to light them from every angle—crinkled at the edges as she laughed.

Peeking over my shoulder to the open window behind us, I closed my eyes and basked in the warmth for a moment. The sky was clear most days now that I had learned to control my magic a bit—that, and the fact that my mind wasn't clouded in chaos and despair.

I was nearly hopeful. Things had taken a turn for the better lately—Rogue's shift, our mating, my mother, Livvy, the wyverns. It was like fate rooted for us, turning the tides in our favor…

Still, too many good things in a row always had a way of leading to something unfathomably bad, and that undercurrent of doubt haunted me even in dreams. *Especially* in dreams.

CHAPTER TWENTY

He was one man, alone in his hatred, but he was one man who could take anyone from us at any given moment—in death, or worse, in mind.

No one else had spoken about it yet—the fact that he could…alter one of us. No one had even mentioned it, but I knew without a doubt, Doran would have if he were here. As the master battle strategist, he would've considered every single outcome. He would've already voiced his concerns *and* found a solution.

I hope you're enjoying your rest, Doran, but we could really use that beautiful mind of yours right about now.

Without so much as a mention, I was starting to think that maybe the fear didn't taunt others in the same way.

Maybe it was a foolish fear of mine. Would we ever even be close enough to him for that to happen? If we were, if we had him surrounded and were within his reach, he couldn't possibly work on every single one of us quickly enough before one of us delivered his final blow.

Someone would end his miserable life, and his control would snap the second his soul left his body, taking every wisp of magic with it.

A sharp bite of pain snapped me from my thoughts as my teeth broke through the skin of my lip. I cursed silently, licking the blood away as I turned back to Iaso.

Yes, it was just an inexperienced, foolish fear from a worrier, and a worrier I was.

Iaso didn't notice my break in focus as she said, "They should be returning soon, I would think."

"Yeah, I think so too. The sun will be setting soon."

"What do you think our next steps will be?" she asked, and it caught me off guard.

It always did when people asked anything of me. The fact that I had any say in matters such as this was still mind-boggling. I knew I was no longer a prisoner, but this was more than that. My words held weight, which was a strange and unfamiliar feeling...even before Rogue's proposal.

The reminder of it wrenched the nerves in my stomach. If we were to marry, the responsibility would be *much* greater than a simple question of what-ifs.

Would the weight of it crush me as someone so unworthy of ruling a kingdom I had only lived in for a few months? The weight of a crown, a title, the Draki name, an entire kingdom...

And...

I am human-born.

The thought halted me.

Goddess, I had not even considered the fact that I was half-human to be a deciding factor in Ravaryn's acceptance. Nautia only extended their loyalty in honor of my father. Draig Hearth had softened to me because Rogue would tolerate nothing less; to disrespect me was to offer their head to him.

I didn't believe the rest of Ravaryn would be so kind. Close to no one knew Vaelor was mated to a human, and the word had only started to spread when my identity was revealed.

My stomach flipped, and my hand rose to cover my mouth. I swallowed hard as a newly rooted uncertainty settled in. Another reason I couldn't marry Rogue—his people would not approve.

I could be his mate, and nothing more.

"I guess we'll go hunt Drakyth down," I sighed.

I'd never wanted more than what we had, and I definitely

CHAPTER TWENTY

never wanted to marry, but now…

"I figured so," Iaso said. "Should we go let the others know while we await their return?"

I nodded in response, and she stood, extending an elbow. *Now, knowing that we* can't *almost hurts worse than just deciding we shouldn't.*

* * *

We told them one by one as they were scattered across the castle.

As my mother registered I would once again be leaving, I expected she'd be upset, but instead of sadness, the only thing that shone through her gaze was pride. She cupped my cheeks with misty eyes. "You remind me more and more of your father every day, in all the best ways."

She hadn't wiped the flour from her hands, though, so we had a good laugh at the lingering powdery hand prints on my face before we said our goodbyes.

She gave me a quick peck on the cheek and leaned in to whisper, "He won't know what's hit him."

With that, she winked and turned back to folding dough.

Moving on to find Delphia and Thana, Iaso and I passed Lee in the hallway. His training leathers were soaked with sweat and holding a surprising amount of weapons—two swords on his hips, one along his spine, and a chest strap with small throwing knives of varying sizes.

We both stopped in our tracks, eyeing him.

He held his hands out to the sides, giving us full view with a cocky grin. "Need to see the back, too? I'm sure it'd give the best view," he teased with a wink, but his facade faltered when Iaso nodded with raised brows, spinning her finger.

A deep laugh echoed down the hallway as he turned slowly.

"Okay, okay. Show's over, pretty boy," Livvy said as she stepped through the front door, wiping sweat from her forehead. She was dressed in her own black training leathers—clearly made for her, as they molded to her curves. Her long, blonde hair was braided back away from her face, and her cheeks were pink from exertion.

My mouth ticked up in a smile. "Livvy, are you training?"

"Yep," she said, holding her chin high. "I figured I should learn to defend myself, everything considered. Starting with daggers for now." Her eyes flicked to Lee as she pointed the small blade at him. "But I'll master a sword soon enough, and then I'll have *you* on your ass."

"Keep dreaming, blondie," Lee said.

"Well, we actually have good news," I said, cocking an eyebrow.

Their gazes snapped to me.

"You found him?" Livvy asked as if she didn't need an answer. Excitement rose in her voice as she climbed the entryway stairs to join us.

I nodded and told them everything.

"Good thing you and Alden read faster than anyone I know. Good work, guys," Lee said, clapping me on the back. "Brilliant," he uttered, shaking his head as he and Livvy left to bathe. She nodded and peeked over her shoulder at me, giving a thumbs up with an excited smile.

The sun was beginning to set as we searched for Thana and Delphia.

"Where else could they be?" I asked.

Iaso shook her head, shrugging her shoulders. "I'm not

sure, to be truthful. We checked their chambers, the kitchen, the library…" Her words trailed off. "Come on. There's one more place to look."

We strode to a part of the castle I had never seen before, another endless hallway made of the same gray stone as the rest. Iaso stopped before a small door, thinner and shorter than usual. It looked inconspicuous—old and very well-used, as the wood around the handle was faded and scraped by decades of use.

She carefully opened the door and motioned me into the darkness.

"What in the world?" I peeked my head in, glancing left to right. It was a passageway. "Why would they come here?"

"It leads to the south side of the castle and spits out just a mile or two from the local village."

"The village where they met?"

She nodded and lifted her skirts as she stepped over the threshold. I followed behind her, shivering as the cool air enveloped me. The torches on the wall closest to us lit for a brief second before the fire jumped to the left. Torches lit one at a time down the passage, creating an illuminated path to follow, beckoning us in that direction.

"That way," Iaso pointed, following the light.

"Is that the way to the exit?"

"That's the way to who we're looking for. The torches will always lead you to what you're looking for. As long as it's with good intentions, of course."

"Oh, yeah. Of course," I said nonchalantly as if anything about magic was matter-of-fact.

We heard their voices long before we actually saw them.

"…go. A war is coming, Thana, one that we don't need to

be involved in. Please, let's just go."

"What? H-How could you say these things? These people are our family."

"Doran was my family."

A heavy silence flowed down the hallway.

"I know... I know, and I'm so sorry he died, but how does abandoning our family honor his death? Do you think that's what he would want?"

"He can't *want* anything, Thana. He's *dead*. Why don't you get that? It's like I'm the only one still mourning him. Everyone is moving on without him, but I can't. I won't. I won't forget him."

"No one has forgotten him, D. No one ever could. We're all just trying to survive right now. As you said, there's a war coming, and all of Ravaryn hangs in the balance. They depend on the people in this castle to save them, and that includes you."

Another prolonged silence.

"Not me. Not anymore."

Iaso and I slowly backed away, unwilling to interrupt their conversation, but the torches revealed us as they lit the way forward.

"Who's there?" Delphia snapped.

We stepped from the darkness, and her face hardened. Thana's eyes were downcast, red, and swollen.

"Adding eavesdropping to your never-ending list of hobbies, hmm?" Delphia's mouth pressed into a hard line when we didn't respond fast enough. She stormed past us, shoving me with her shoulder.

"We found Drakyth," I said.

She stopped with her back to us.

CHAPTER TWENTY

"In Rainsmyre."

Her abdomen heaved with a deep breath before she turned back to us. "Does Rogue know yet?"

"No, he's not here, but we're planning to tell him as soon as he gets back."

"Good. I assume we'll be leaving as soon as possible?"

"We? I mean, yes, I would think so—"

"All right. Fetch me when it's time to go. I'm ready to get out of this hell hole." She turned on her heel and strode silently down the hall out of sight.

I turned to Thana.

"I... I don't know," she said, shaking her head, defeated.

"Healing takes time, child. She'll return to us," Iaso said, winding an arm around Thana's shoulders and pulling her into a hug.

Thana collapsed on her shoulder with a sob. "She wants to leave, and I just can't go with her. My conscience won't allow me to leave you all in the face of everything, no matter how much I...love her. I love her, Iaso, I love her. She has always been my person, and now she wants to leave."

I swallowed hard as my eyes burned.

"Well, maybe, she *needs* to go," Iaso whispered, rubbing Thana's back. Thana froze as Iaso spoke. "Sometimes, people just need space to find clarity, to heal, but she wouldn't stay away forever, that I can promise you. Anyone can see the love you two share. That feeling is clearly mutual." She pulled back, cupping Thana's cheeks to meet her gaze. "She will return to you."

Another sob wracked Thana, a wave of fresh tears descending down her cheeks. "I don't want her to go." Her words were broken with forced breaths.

"I know, child. I know," Iaso whispered.

I stepped closer and wrapped my arms around them. Thana moved to me, sliding her arm around my waist as she took a deep breath. We embraced for a long moment before she sighed, pulling back and wiping her cheeks.

"So, we found Drakyth. That is good news, at least."

My head tilted to the side as I nodded. With that, we sauntered back down the hall to their doorway. As we stepped over the threshold, the lack of daylight caught my attention.

"Oh, the sun has already set. I'm going to go check the shifting room and see if Rogue has returned. Meet us in the library later?"

Thana nodded with a sigh, and Iaso wrapped an arm around her shoulders, giving her a quick squeeze.

"Yes, we'll be there. I think I'll take Thana back to my chambers for tea"—her eyes shifted to Thana—"if you're up for that?"

Thana chuckled, nodding. "Always."

Waving to them, I made my way back to the library. It was empty and dark, lit only by moonlight and a few small candles. The fireplace hadn't lit yet, which left the library a bit ghostly.

The door to the shifting room was already open when I rounded the corner. Peeking my head in, I glanced around but didn't see him. "Hello? Anyone home?"

"Yeah, over here," Rogue said.

His voice rang out from the other side of the treasure shelves but when I walked around, he wasn't there.

My brows pulled together. I glanced around, but I was entirely alone. "Rogue? Is this a joke?"

CHAPTER TWENTY

"I'm right here?"

Then, without hesitation, he stepped out from the wall, a look of confusion on his face—a solid stone wall.

Chapter Twenty One

Rogue

Ara blinked before stepping around me. "What just happened?"

"What are you talking about? I was in there." I gestured to the room behind me.

It was Stryath's office—that much I was certain of from the shredded paintings and papers, but it had been destroyed with a vengeance. Everything was mangled and broken, even down to the torn rug along the floor.

Her eyes bounced from the room to me and back. "There's nothing there."

"Yes, there is. Just look—"

"I can't see anything." She reached out to the room, but her hand hit an invisible wall. She patted along it, but the wall stopped her from entering.

"Ah," I breathed. Not a wall. "A spell."

I had only returned from my flight half an hour before she arrived. We swam and hunted, feasted on the creatures of the sea beneath the warm sun until we had satisfied every need. Upon my return, the room was just…there. I thought I

CHAPTER TWENTY ONE

had missed it on my way out, but now, I wasn't so sure.

"What does it look like?" Ara asked.

"It's an office, but it's been destroyed."

Leaving her at the threshold, I stepped back into the small room. It was ancient—as old as the castle itself. The desk was made of a cracking oak, oiled as black as the chunk of obsidian that sat atop it. Directly behind it was a massive, empty bronze frame that had at one point held the mirror laying in pieces at its base.

I crouched down and lifted a piece. I started to put it back down when I realized I wasn't staring at my own reflection.

There was something else in the glass. Something blue and gray, swirling.

"There's a broken mirror in here, but it's showing me something other than my own reflection."

Organizing the pieces, I laid them out on the desk. The shape was complete save for one piece. I ducked under the table, searching the floor, under the rug, everywhere, but to no avail. A small corner chunk was missing.

It didn't matter, though. As the mirror's pieces connected, the image became sharp.

I looked out over the Hearth, and the attention of every wyvern that lounged about snapped to me as well. They saw me just as I saw them.

"The mirror is like…a portal of some sort. I can see the Hearth."

"What?" she asked. "Can you bring it out?"

"Well, it's broken, but…" I grabbed a large piece and held it up. In this section, I could make out the entire form of one wyvern. "Yeah, here," I said, stepping back into the shifting room.

I handed it to her, and she squinted at the glass. Her head cocked to the side, and she held it to the light.

"I don't see them." She shrugged as her eyes shifted back to the room she couldn't see.

"Huh," I grunted as she handed the piece back. Glancing down, I could still see the wyvern staring back at me. "The room must be protected by a blood spell."

"Interesting...but I came with news." She cocked an eyebrow at me, a smirk curving her lips.

"Happy news?" My hand slithered around her waist as she stepped into me.

"We found Drakyth."

My heart stopped. "Where?"

"Rainsmyre. We found letters between him and Vaelor, and in them, he told Vaelor he bought an estate there."

"And he took the crown with him," I said. It wasn't a question, but she confirmed it regardless.

"Yes. They never referred to it as the crown directly, but they spoke of something of great importance. They just kept saying 'it.' He brought 'it' with him to his new estate and placed it somewhere 'safe.'"

"Good." I paced the floor, running a hand over the scruff on my jaw. "Good. That's a start. At least we know where to look first."

She reached a hand out to loop it in mine, spinning me back to her. The grin that spread over her face was infectious. "A damn good start."

My thumb grazed over her lower lip before I slid my hand lower and gripped her chin. Tilting her head back, I lightly kissed her lips—soft and malleable under my own.

So delicate, I could not even fathom how someone as hard

CHAPTER TWENTY ONE

as me could ever belong to her by her own choice.

Her hands found my chest and pushed me away.

"So my *King*, when do we leave? Tonight? In the morning?"

I paused. "In two days."

Her brows pulled together. "Two days? Why?"

"Because, little storm, things must be done. Assignments given. Plans made. I don't intend on going alone, so I have to give those orders as well."

Bullshit. Utter bullshit. I fed her the meaningless words as I carefully kept my true plans hidden, but she disregarded the reasoning completely, snagging only on the ending.

"Alone," she repeated, nodding. "You don't intend on going alone, so you need soldiers, because I'm not going?"

"Ara, you've only just returned from saving me. You risked your life to sail on unknown seas only hours after Livvy and your mother's arrival. They are *here*." Her face twisted with indignation, and I couldn't help but feel like I was digging my own grave. "I would never ask you to leave them again so soon. Not for this."

Her spine was rod straight as she seethed at my explanation, one she clearly wasn't buying.

"Not to mention, we don't know if he'll even be there. This may only be the beginning of a long search. It could be days, weeks, months even, if we even have that much time—"

She stepped up to me with a fiery look in her eyes that nearly lit me from the inside. A fiery passion that could've pulled a smile to my lips had I allowed it—but I definitely did *not* as that would have only flamed her further.

Fucking hell, I'm lost to her. In love with even her anger.

"And they will still be *here* upon our return." She jabbed me in the chest with two fingers. "*With* the crown *and* the wyverns." Another jab. "*After* we tip the scales in our favor."

Pride swelled in my chest. She clenched her jaw as I wound my hand into her hair, and I lowered to run my lips along her jaw as I whispered, "That is exactly why you will wear the crown of Ravaryn, my *Queen*."

I could feel her breath hitch, but she didn't stutter in her response.

"I would chase that Goddess-forsaken man across the entire realm to find that damned crown. You doubted me once in Nautia—"

"And I swore to myself I never would again."

With a single hand, she pushed me back again. My hand slid from her hair as she held me at arm's length.

"Not only does Ravaryn need the crown—deserve it just as it deserves the peace you ache to offer it—but it is yours to wear, and yours alone. We will bring it home to its king, and with it, we will end this war before it ever truly starts. *No one* needs another Ten Year War, and there's no way Adonis would think he'd stand a chance against an army of wyverns. He will lay down arms in the face of them." A sly smile cocked at the corner of her mouth. "And you, our mighty flying lizard."

I dropped my mouth open in mock offense. "Flying lizard? Is that what you call me when I'm not around?"

"Only when there are listening ears," she teased as I slowly walked her backward.

She gasped as the exposed skin along her back hit the cold stone wall, and my mouth was on her in an instant, swallowing the sound. My hand looped around her wrists, holding them above her head.

"To be truthful, I don't care what you refer to me as," I

CHAPTER TWENTY ONE

whispered against her breathless lips. "Only that you do."

Her lips enveloped me in warmth, a give-and-take I would chase until the end of my days. My tongue teased along the seam of her lips, and she opened for me without hesitation, my free hand gripping her hip as she ground against my hardened length.

"We have people to see," she muttered without breaking contact.

"Do we?" My lips moved to her jaw and down her neck as she moaned, arching her back to give me access.

I moved lower, kissing my way down her chest. A claw extended and I met her gaze, smirking as I sliced through her blouse, revealing her breasts to me.

"Rogue!" She attempted to free a hand to cover herself, but I tightened my grip and held her wrists against the wall. "We really do have to meet the others literally right out there." Her eyes shifted to the open door that led to the library.

Rising to my feet, I released her hands, and her face fell slightly as I stepped away from her and strode to the door.

"I'll need to get a new shirt before we—"

Her words stopped abruptly as I shut the door, holding her gaze as I turned the lock. The click rang through the silence.

"Don't deny me what is *mine*, little storm." I stalked back to her slowly, drinking in her every reaction—every hitched breath, the chills spreading across her bare breasts, the flush of her cheeks. She backed into the wall again as I neared her. "Don't deny yourself what you *crave*."

Her eyes darted to the door, hesitating, and when she turned back to me, my heart leaped, my cock twitching. There was a devious glint in her gaze that made me want to do horribly wicked things to her. Her swollen lips curved up in a smirk as she grabbed my shirt and jerked me forward. She wrapped her arms around my neck as she pulled me down to her. Her mouth found mine, molding to my lips with a desperate hunger that had me groaning into her.

My hand dove between her legs and dipped beneath her trousers. No undergarments.

Pride and satisfaction rolled through me, and I broke the kiss long enough to whisper, "Such a good fucking girl."

She smiled against my mouth, a small whimper escaping her, shattering any restraint I had left. I ripped her pants down, and she kicked them off without taking her arms from around my neck. As soon as my own trousers were unbuttoned and tugged down, she wrapped her legs around my waist.

I slammed her into the wall and thrust into her with no hesitation. She gasped, moaning as she knotted her hands in my hair. I covered her mouth with one hand to stifle the sounds, even though I hated doing so.

My pace was brutal; I knew it was as her screams grew louder against my palm. This was quick and rough, satisfying the deep burn that consumed us both so thoroughly. She was a wanton mess, scream after scream, with her head reclined on the wall, and I *loved* it. I loved watching her, the way her body reacted to my cock buried deep inside her. Her brows were furrowed, her eyes rolling back. If I could see her mouth—her delicious little mouth—I knew it would be open in desperate pants.

I needed to see it. I needed to see her writhe.

As I slowed my pace, her eyes found me again. I smiled and slid my hand from her mouth before gliding it over her cheek to the back of her head. I knotted my hand in the hair at the base of her skull and pulled her head back, exposing her neck.

Dipping my face to her throat, I kissed along her skin, whispering between each peck. "Try not to be loud when you come on my cock, little storm. Those cries are just for my ears."

Her throat bobbed as I started to move inside her again, and she clamped her lips shut, whimpering against them. Removing my hand from her hair, I braced a hand on the wall above her head, the other on her ass. I pulled back enough to look her in the eyes. A smirk curved my lips, a faint orange haze glowing over her face. I saw my glowing irises and slitted pupils reflected in her eyes as they widened—her only warning.

I pounded into her, the sounds of her slick and stifled moans the only things I could hear. Her cries were growing louder, and she slapped her own hand over her mouth. I gripped her wrist and yanked it overhead, clicking my tongue.

I wouldn't allow her to conceal a single part of herself in this moment. I had removed her clothing, leaving her bare, because I wanted to see her, every beautiful inch of my mate as she fell apart for me. Those lips, those moans, were *mine*, and not even she would hide them from me now.

She buried her face in my neck and clamped her teeth around my mark to smother the sounds. With each quickening thrust, she bit harder until she broke the skin, and sparks licked beneath it.

Fucking hell. If there was anything better than watching her, it was feeling her.

I gripped her chin and jerked her face toward mine. My

blood coated her lips, painting them red, and I groaned, reclaiming her mouth. My canines extended as I bit her lip. The sharp tips pricked her skin, and she sucked in a breath as her own blood leaked, mingling with mine. I took the opportunity, thrusting my tongue into her warm mouth, reveling in the way we tasted together.

Perfection. Utter perfection.

"Rogue, please, I need...I need..." She whimpered and writhed.

"I know what you need," I replied, sliding my hands under her ass and moving her to the floor, turning her on her hands and knees. She arched her back and looked over her shoulder at me, her gaze heated and smile delirious. My eyes rolled back at the sight as I groaned; she was so fucking beautiful.

I grabbed her hips and thrust into her in a single smooth motion. She threw her head back, and I wrapped a hand around her throat, pulling her up against me. I held her against my chest, choking her as I snaked my other hand between her pretty little thighs.

It took maybe ten seconds of circling my fingers over her clit before she exploded. This time, I did cover her mouth—for her—as the sounds tearing from her throat were loud enough for Auryna to hear. I finished with her, spilling into her slickness before we fell forward.

I caught us and rolled so she was lying on top of me. We sat there, breathing heavily as she rested her head on my chest. She was so small atop my large frame, so delicate, that it was a wonder I didn't break her with how rough I was. I slid my hand down her spine and back up to the back of her head, holding her close.

It was odd how a man in love could hold his entire world

CHAPTER TWENTY ONE

in his arms.

* * *

Thank the Goddess I had stashed an extra set of clothes in the shifting room because Ara's poor blouse wasn't salvageable. She pulled on my shirt, and it swallowed her. She cringed, holding her arms out to the side, the sleeves covering her hands.

"They're going to know," she said.

I laughed and stepped closer to grab her wrist. I rolled her sleeve up before switching to the other one. "You're my mate, Ara. Would it really be so strange for you to wear one of my shirts?"

She watched me intently as I finished rolling her sleeve and lifted her hand to kiss the lightning scar along her wrist.

"I suppose not," she whispered.

"Besides, I think it looks rather…good," I said, my chest warm.

She chuckled, glancing down and quickly tucking the bottom into her trousers as she sighed. "I guess this will just have to do."

I laced my fingers through hers and guided her to the door. As I unlocked it, she put her hand over mine on the handle. Pausing, I grinned and looked at her expectantly, lifting a brow.

"Are you sure they won't know?" she asked.

Laughing, I dipped down and kissed her forehead. "Only I can smell your desire, little storm."

She took a deep breath. "All right." She nodded once and stood straighter, holding her shoulders back. "Good."

I opened the door and moved to the side, motioning her forward. She walked past me, and I stepped up behind her, winding my arm around her waist. Leaning down to her ear, I whispered, "Although, the mussed hair and flushed cheeks *may* give it away."

She gasped and swiveled on her heel to face me, but I glided around her.

"Rogue," she whispered forcibly.

I peeked over my shoulder and tipped my head toward the library, grinning. "Come on. We have people to see."

She groaned, rolling her eyes before smoothing her hair. "Better?"

"Better," I said, sliding my hand back into hers and leading her around the corner.

Everyone was already seated around the table when we arrived. All eyes snapped to us, and I nearly felt the blush tinting Ara's cheeks.

I placed my hand on her lower back as I guided her to the seat next to mine.

"We're leaving in two days."

"Two—" Delphia started to argue, but my eyes cut to her, and her mouth snapped shut.

"Two days," I said with a tone that offered no room for question.

She dipped her chin once, her expression tight.

"Who will be joining us?" My eyes shifted across the table from person to person before landing on Livvy and Elora. "I assume you two will be staying, correct?"

They glanced at each other. "Yes, we'll stay. I fear we would be more of a hindrance than anything," Elora said as Livvy nodded.

CHAPTER TWENTY ONE

"I'll go, of course," Ewan said from his seat, Iaso standing behind him with Aurum at her heels. She slid a hand onto Ewan's shoulder.

Ara nodded. "Thank you, Ewan."

"As will I," Lee voiced.

Livvy peeked over at him with an unreadable expression. His arm flexed as it extended to her beneath the table, either holding her hand or resting on her thigh. She swallowed and returned the soft smile to her face.

"Good." I nodded once. "You'll be a great pair of hands to have along."

"Hands, muscle, brains…" Lee smirked, but it didn't quite reach his eyes as his gaze dropped to where he was touching Livvy.

"And me," Alden said. "I knew Drakyth, and I know I would recognize him even now."

"Oh, I didn't even consider that you might have known him," Ara said.

"When Vaelor took the throne, Drakyth was there to abdicate, so we met several times in the weeks leading up to the ceremony and at the coronation."

"Good. We'll be glad to have you," I said.

He dipped his head in acknowledgment.

"Iaso?" My eyes shifted to her, and her brows pulled together.

Her gaze dropped as Aurum ran the length of his body along her leg before tucking his wings and curling at her feet. "I do believe I should stay with him…" Her eyes lifted back to me conflicted. "If you don't mind. I'll still send some salves and tonics. Anything you may need."

"Of course. That little guy needs you more than us right

now, anyway. We're just going on a manhunt," I said.

Iaso had done more than anyone for me over the years, and she deserved a respite. I would not force her, or even allow her, to feel an ounce of guilt for her decision. She had earned it tenfold.

"And I'll go too," Delphia said.

Thana's face was down-turned, her gaze glued to the table with her lips pressed into a flat line. "I'll stay."

Delphia didn't so much as glance at her, and my eyes cut between them before lowering to Ara. She shook her head, mouthing the word "later," but the tension was thick enough to cut with a knife. Worrisome. These two never fought, not in the fifteen years they had known each other—at least, not to my knowledge.

"Thank you," I said to Delphia, shoving the confusion down.

She nodded. "So, two days from now. Sunrise departure?"

"Maybe a little later, as some of us do enjoy sleeping," Alden chuckled, glancing at me.

"Midday," I answered.

Delphia sighed dramatically, and I clenched my jaw. She was grieving the loss of Doran—I knew that—but I couldn't deny that she was grinding my nerves.

I wanted to give her time and grace, but she was making it unbelievably difficult.

"All right, then. Lee, Delphia, Alden, and us"—I gestured between Ara and myself—"will leave at midday, two days from now."

"And may I suggest you pack lightly," Iaso added. "Rainsmyre may have rain in the name, but it is a rather hot place."

Alden nodded. "Very humid. Very warm."

"Where is it?" Ara asked.

CHAPTER TWENTY ONE

"It's in the southwest corner of Ravaryn, on the opposite coast from us," Alden said.

"Is it like Nautia, then, since it's on the sea?" Ara glanced between Alden and Ewan.

Alden snorted and covered his mouth. "No, not quite."

"No, Rainsmyre is not nearly as beautiful as Nautia," Iaso added.

"Not many places are." Alden leaned forward on his elbows.

"Rainsmyre is a fishing town," Ewan chimed in. "It's a bit…"

"Filthy," Lee interjected. "The majority of it is filthy, but it has its charms."

Ara perked up, a smile stretching across her face. "Great. I can't wait."

While our travel wasn't under the best circumstances, I was still excited to show her the sides of Ravaryn she hadn't gotten a chance to explore. I wanted to offer her that—traveling and adventure and discovery—and I would one day, when we finally had the chance to breathe without the threat of Adonis looming on the horizon.

"Before we go anywhere, I should say…" Alden sighed. "I finished their letters. They end abruptly after several letters of Adrastus growing more concerning by the day. Drakyth was worried that…that he would do something."

I dropped my head to my hand with a groan.

* * *

It was getting late by the time the group dispersed.

As we strolled the empty hallways in silence, Ara's hand looped through mine, the moonlight drifting in through the scattered windows. The only sounds were the waves crashing below and our own footsteps.

It was rather nice actually, the silence. I had hated it once, as it was all I knew—constant silence, other than the maids and servants. As a child, I would scream in frustration just to break the monotony, but it never did any good. It was my pathetic attempt to claw at the chains of silence I was shackled in, but I never held the key to release them. My father saw to that, destroying any hope of one when he cast me aside as a hated disgrace. No friends. No trips outside of his estate—outside my own chambers, truly.

Silence was my only companion until Doran. He broke the never-ending isolation, risking his own head to speak with me.

I had met him before my father even took the crown. We were just boys, then, maybe eighteen or nineteen, but he was much braver than me. Smarter, too. He always had been.

My heart sank, and I sighed, rubbing my knuckles over my sternum. His absence was a hollow ache that echoed with loss every time I was reminded he was gone.

He had saved me, and yet, I couldn't do the same.

The truth still weighed on me. It would crush me if I allowed it, but like every other time, I shoved it down, ignoring the deep hurt in my chest until it dissipated for the time being.

They say time heals all wounds, but I was beginning to lose faith in that statement. How does anything heal wounds that don't bleed? That aren't severed or cut? They don't scab or close. There was no healing salve or stitch or tea to mend the areas afflicted.

How could one heal a wound that reopened with every mention or memory? Would that not lead to a scar more

CHAPTER TWENTY ONE

permanent than a wound of grief? A scar of nostalgia, a constant reminder of something or someone irretrievably gone.

My chest clenched.

Could the soul heal? That was what felt damaged: something so deep and intangible and unreachable that no healer could possibly hope to mend it.

No... Wounds of this caliber were left entirely to the injured to heal, and that was the most terrifying part.

"I wanted to speak with you about something," Ara whispered, glancing up at me.

I cleared my throat. "What's that?"

"Well, I overheard Delphia speaking to Thana today. Iaso and I were searching for them, and we didn't mean to eavesdrop, but... We should do something to honor Doran. He deserves it, but also so Delphia knows she's not alone in her grief. I think she's feeling a bit...lost. Left behind."

Can you read my mind? I peeked at her, but she didn't respond—for obvious reasons.

"What did you have in mind?"

"Oh, I don't know," she sighed. "I've been wracking my brain all day, but I'm not familiar with the customs here, the traditions. How do you normally honor the dead?"

"Ah, we should have a burial. A king's burial, actually. He deserves that."

"Without his body?" she asked hesitantly.

"I don't think it would matter really. We could do the ceremony regardless." I ran a hand over my chin in thought. "I can't believe we didn't think of this sooner. If anyone deserves it, it's him." Sighing, I dropped my hand back to my side. "Poor Delphia. I hate that she had to bury him herself."

"I know," Ara whispered, running her hand over my forearm lightly.

"I understand she had every right to do it herself as his last living blood, but damn, I would have done just about anything to be there when he was laid to rest."

"You're right. She did, but I think he would have appreciated having you there as well. I'm sure he knows that you would've been if you had the chance." She glanced up. "He was a great friend. Even the very first time I met him, through all that icy hair and cold blue eyes, he radiated warmth. I knew I could trust him. He was just that kind of person—the one you wanted on your team."

"That he is." My breathing stopped, and her hand stilled on my arm. "Was. That he was."

Chapter Twenty Two

Ara

Rogue and I stood on the beach before the endless expanse of darkness, mere minutes before sunrise. We had spent the entire night preparing for the burial ceremony. According to Rogue, a king's burial had to be done at sunrise.

They leave us at sunrise to drift home to the Goddess at sunset.

Just as Rogue finished weaving the final bits of driftwood and vines onto the arch that now graced the small boat, the others started to arrive, still half asleep. Alden led the way, still in the gray robes he liked to sleep in. Delphia and Thana were right behind him, close but not touching.

"Why are we—" Delphia started as she rubbed her eyes, stumbling down the hill, but her words stopped as she opened her eyes to see the boat.

Her chest rose and fell quickly.

"Is this… Did you…" She shook her head as the words refused to leave her. She cleared her throat and stood at the boat's edge.

Leaning over, Delphia examined the contents inside. Doran's nicest clothing—a silver tunic with impeccable leather trousers—sat beneath an embellished dagger. It was old with twisting vines of bronze that resembled flames along the hilt. Her gaze followed the wooden archway up, catching on the small greenery at the top lit with tiny glowing orbs. They were a special type of seed that, when imbued with fire magic, glowed like stars. Rogue had placed them generously along the branches, spending hours positioning each one to create a night sky against the foliage.

Her eyes brimmed with tears. "This is a king's burial."

Rogue's eyes roamed over the arch. "He deserved it."

A tear slipped as Delphia's breath hitched, and she quickly wiped it away as her gaze fell back to the boat. "And that blade…" She peeked up at Rogue with pinched brows, her expression confused. "That was your mother's."

"The family always places one of their most valued possessions in the boat, so the honored can take it with them in the afterlife," Rogue said.

Delphia's face hardened at his words, and she dropped her eyes again. "In remembrance of their past life. They take pieces of us."

She placed a hand on the vines, closing her eyes as she lowered her forehead to it. "Thank you."

"Don't thank us. We should have done this weeks ago," I said, resting a hand on her shoulder.

She peeked up at me, her eyes already red. My eyes stung as she threw her arms around me in a tight hug—one she hadn't offered since her return. I wrapped my arms around her, holding her as a sob broke her.

Thana joined us then. "Delphia."

Releasing me, she shifted to Thana and whispered only

loud enough for Thana and me to hear. "I...I don't know if I'm ready. He needs this, deserves it, but I can't let him go. I don't know how I ever will."

"You don't have to let him go." I leaned closer to them to whisper. "Keep him in your heart and memories, but let go of the sadness. He would scold you for carrying it even this long."

She laughed, and the sound brought a breath of relief to me. Releasing Thana, she took a step back and wiped her soaked cheeks.

"All right." She turned back to the boat and unfastened the necklace from around her neck. "You better take damn good care of this, D. I swear to the Goddess, if you lose it, I will hunt you down when I join you in the afterlife."

Rogue and I laughed as she gently lowered the necklace onto the folded clothing.

Alden patted Rogue's arm. "A king's burial for Doran. I could think of no one who deserves it more."

At the sound of footsteps, I turned to find Iaso with a steaming pot and Ewan carrying a platter of teacups.

Iaso lifted the pot. "We brought coffee."

Delphia smiled faintly. Thana laced her fingers through Delphia's and glanced into the boat, pausing for a moment. She slid her hand from Delphia's, pulled a bracelet off her wrist, and laid it gently by the necklace.

Delphia slid her hand back into Thana's, and they stepped away from the boat. One by one, they all placed items in the boat until his entire family had contributed to the burial.

"He'll be a rich man in the afterlife," Iaso joked.

"He certainly will," Alden said. "Rich in love, just as he was in life."

Delphia snorted. "That's a bit cheesy."

"Doesn't make it any less true." Rogue clapped a hand on her shoulder—just as he used to do to Doran—and she didn't move away from him.

I smiled to myself, wishing I had anything of importance to give, but I had nothing. The dagger I once held so close to my heart was lost in the pond when Rogue kidnapped me. The ring my mother gave me was either stolen or lost that same night.

I had nothing to give.

The smile slid from my face just a fraction, and I glanced around the ground. Just on the edge of the forest were iridescent flowers—green but throwing a reflection of a rainbow, a type I never would have seen in Auryna. They radiated beauty and magic.

A beautiful reflection of Ravaryn.

As the others chatted, I jogged over and plucked a bouquet of them. I took my time walking back, and when I made it to the boat, the flowers were no longer just stems, but a woven crown. I laid it in the boat beside his other offerings and placed a hand on the warm, smooth wood. "I'm sorry I couldn't give more, Doran. You... You deserve so much more, but please know, you are and always have been so well-loved, even in death. Your people will never forget you, just as I know you would never forget them, even without the gifts."

When I stood and turned to the group, they all stared at me.

"That was beautiful," Iaso said as she looped an arm through mine, tugging me to her side.

The sun's first rays peeked over the horizon then, lighting the horizon with beams of orange and yellow.

CHAPTER TWENTY TWO

"It's time," Rogue breathed as his eyes met Delphia's.

She nodded, swallowing hard. She and Rogue stepped onto the sand and pushed the boat into the shallow water. They waded out knee-deep with it, but the waves lapped at it, working against them.

"I could help to push it out if you would like," Ewan said.

"Has your magic come back?" I whispered.

Ewan nodded once, and a smile pulled at my lips.

Delphia sighed deeply, glancing back between the boat and Ewan. Her brows furrowed in defeat before she nodded and stepped from the water. Rogue followed her, but they halted at the edge, letting the small waves lap at their feet.

We all watched as Ewan's magic pushed the boat slowly. Once it was past the breaking waves, Ewan handed a bow to Rogue—Doran's bow.

Rogue stared at it for a moment before passing it to Delphia. A choked sound escaped her as she studied it. She closed her eyes, taking a deep breath, and when she opened them again, her face was a solid mask of stone and focus.

She docked the arrow, lifted the bow, and pulled the string back with expert precision. Her eyes shifted to Rogue, and he dipped his chin as the arrowhead lit with fire. She inhaled slowly and released.

I held my breath as the arrow sailed over the waves with a slight hiss. It disappeared from sight as it struck the boat directly in the middle, exactly where Doran's things would have been.

A second passed and flames appeared, rising along the arch, licking their way across the dried wood.

Rogue urged it to burn hotter and hotter. When the temperatures reached high enough to melt the metals and meld them with the ashes of everything else, the flames burned a brilliant blue—the same shade as Doran's eyes.

* * *

After a few hours of sleep, I met Livvy and Lee at the front gates. The afternoon sun was especially warm today, the air thick and sticky, and sweat rolled down my spine as we strolled down the path.

"So, where are we going?" I asked.

"Well," Livvy drawled. "I wanted to find a trade for myself, or at least a hobby. Since I spent so many years serving at the bar, I thought it might be interesting to learn to brew my own alcohol." She looped her arm through mine. "As it turns out, Lee's friend owns a brewery."

"Training, brewing... So multi-talented." I smiled at her, lifting my brows as I downplayed the happiness bubbling in my chest at her making a life for herself here. She was settling in beautifully.

And a brewery would be a nice reprieve from the heaviness of the burial this morning, I thought but would never say aloud.

The burial was beautiful and so deserved, but I couldn't deny it took a heavy emotional toll. I could still feel the ache behind my eyes from the tears shed on the beach and back in the room—for Doran and everyone who had lost him.

I only wished Rogue was coming with us, but he had returned to the shifting chamber. My heart hurt to know the pain he endured with each shift, but he said it would lessen over time, and the only way for that to happen was to do it. Repeatedly.

I had offered to accompany him, but he declined, claiming

he wanted me to go with Livvy, as we had already made the plans. *Go and enjoy the day with your friend before we leave yet again,* he said, but I wondered if it was truly because he didn't want me to see the pain it caused him. Or worse, because of some misplaced guilt he harbored for what happened during his first shift—which would be preposterous, of course. He had suffered a great deal more than I did, and I would tell him such.

However, I knew there were some battles of the mind that could only be conquered alone, so I left him and Draig Hearth to give him as much space and privacy as I could.

"It's been really interesting to learn the process," Livvy said. "We've started with mead."

"My favorite. When will it be ready?"

She laughed. "Oh, my batch won't be for a long time. It takes time to ferment, you know," she said in a matter-of-fact tone.

"Rys says you're a natural at it, though," Lee said with a smirk.

"Of course, he would. I believe he only encourages me because he loves to watch me work, all sweaty and focused—" She paused, peeking at me.

"Oh, does he?" I cocked an eyebrow at her.

"We both do," Lee said smoothly.

My eyes widened as I suppressed a smile, keeping my gaze on the path ahead. "They both do," I repeated, nodding.

"Well"—Livvy shrugged—"honestly, Ara, can you blame them? Men are simple creatures, Ren and Rys included. I believe I could do anything and they would applaud."

"I feel like I should argue that, but I won't," Lee hummed.

"Because I'm right," Livvy said, winking at me, and I

laughed into my hand.

"If you say so." Lee glanced down at her with amusement in his eyes.

"I do. I do say so."

"Ah, all right. I guess that settles it, then, hmm?" He slid hand around her waist and pulled her into him to kiss the top of her head.

She closed her eyes, a light laugh spilling from her lips. She looked so genuinely happy, sinking into his side without a second thought. She felt safe with him, that much was clear, and it warmed my heart to see someone—potentially even two people, I suppose—worshiping her.

We neared the small village within half an hour. I slowed, taking in the sights. I had never been here before, or any of the villages near Draig Hearth for that matter, but they were exactly how I would imagine them.

A cobblestone road ran through the center of town, lined on both sides with wooden buildings of various sizes and full to the brim with people—merchants and their carts, buyers, children, a few horses, and another animal I couldn't place. A smile curved my lips as we entered the crowd, squeezing by people here and there, and no one noticed. We blended straight in and melded with the overflow of people just living their lives.

What amazed me the most, though, was how they treated Livvy. Even with her hair braided back, revealing her curved ears, the majority didn't pay her any mind, and those who did notice didn't seem to care.

My brows furrowed. *They didn't care?*

I was lost in thought when Livvy smiled back at me and tugged my hand, leading us toward a stone building.

CHAPTER TWENTY TWO

As we stepped across the threshold, the noise from the streets died down, replaced with the familiar sounds of a tavern.

My eyes adjusted to the dimmer light, and my mouth fell open. It was magnificent.

Stone archways swooped across the ceiling, intersecting with each other in various locations. At each connection hung a chandelier, made of bone with melted candles along each point, casting a soft glow over the several round tables.

But what caught my attention the most were the massive barrels along the back wall, larger than any I had ever seen. They were easily ten feet wide and laid on their side with several pouring spouts lining the bottom curve of each.

The top of the barrels met a railing that stood along a balcony, and standing there, resting on his elbows with a wicked grin was who I assumed was—

"Hello, Rys," Livvy said.

"Well, hello there, darling," he said. "And hi to you, too... Ara?"

I smiled as I replied, "Yes."

He dipped his chin, bowing his head. "Welcome to the Black-Eyed Brewery, my Queen."

"Oh dear Goddess, please don't call me that."

His face lifted back to mine with curious amusement.

"Just Ara." My cheeks burned.

"Understood." His eyes flicked back to Livvy, hovering for a moment. "Want to show her where we work?"

She held an elbow out to me with a proud grin. "Of course. Please, will you join us, my *Queen*?"

I squinted my eyes at her, and she giggled. "I suppose I could grace you with a few spare moments of my precious time..."

She and Lee both burst into laughter as I slid my arm into hers, and we ascended the spiral staircase in the corner of the room.

Rys was waiting for us as we crested the top step. He stepped toward me first, extending a hand. "It's very nice to finally meet you, Ara. My name is Orrys but, as you can tell, everyone just calls me Rys."

I took his hand, and we shook. "Nice to meet you, Rys."

His hands were rough and calloused, signaling a lifetime of work, and up close, I noticed how large he was. He wasn't as tall as Lee, but he was much wider. His olive skin stretched over a massive muscular form, hiding only behind his thin, linen tunic. From the collar, however, peeked dark marks— tattoos, I realized—that reached up and around his throat. They almost appeared to be vines or branches, but his black hair covered half of what was exposed.

Handsome, I thought at Livvy as I tilted my head to the side with raised brows. Livvy grinned as if the thoughts were written on my forehead.

"I've heard many great things about you from these two. This one in particular," he said, nudging Livvy with his elbow.

"Hey, now. Let's remember I only have one friend. Who else was I supposed to talk about?" she joked.

"That's hurtful, you know, to hear you don't consider us friends," Lee teased as we strolled along the balcony overlooking the tavern below.

"No, Ren, I don't think it's hurtful." Rys' dark eyes flicked to Lee. "I'm not sure it's her friends we want to be."

Livvy's lips parted, her cheeks flushed before she regained composure. "Oh, hush, you love drunk fools. Or should I say,

CHAPTER TWENTY TWO

lust drunk?" She cocked an eyebrow at them before tugging me in front of the group to begin her tour.

Lee hummed dramatically as if he were truly thinking it over. "I would say both are applicable. Do you agree, Rys?"

"Love drunk? Perhaps. Lust drunk? Absolutely. We're completely inebriated."

It was a good thing they couldn't see Livvy's face as we walked ahead of them, because her eyes were wide and her cheeks beet red.

I squeezed her arm, and she glanced at me. "Good Goddess, you best be careful, or you'll start a tavern brawl. It seems the men of Ravaryn are infatuated with you."

She rolled her eyes. "No, just these two fools."

"Well, they couldn't have chosen a more deserving woman to fawn over," I whispered. Peeking over my shoulder, I asked Rys, "So, why the Black-Eyed Brewery? Do you have a lot of fights here or something?"

Lee grinned as Rys blinked. When he opened his eyes again, they were entirely black, consumed with a swirling darkness that created an unnerving depth in each socket.

Movement along his neck caught my attention then. His tattoos were...moving. They weren't vines or branches.

No, they were snakes.

As his own eyes peered at me, so did the slithering beings along his throat. They climbed around him, peeking from his shirt. I couldn't see their eyes, but I felt them, looking at me—*seeing* me.

"I'm a seer. Although, not a very good one." He stepped closer, extending a hand to me. More snakes slithered from beneath his shirt sleeve onto his palm. "My magic is very limited, confined to only the people I personally know."

Mesmerized, I reached a hand out and gently touched a snake, but I jerked it back as a tongue flicked out.

Rys laughed. "They can't hurt you."

"That's incredible," I whispered. "I've never heard of a seer before."

"Thank you," he chuckled. With another blink, his eyes returned to normal. "There aren't many left, but still, most are better than me, hence, why I run a brewery and tavern."

"Still the most impressive magic I've ever seen," Livvy said, placing a hand on his forearm. "Never doubt that."

"Hey—" I started to tease but stopped short, cocking my head to the side in thought. "You… You know I have magic, right?"

It struck me then that I hadn't actually shown her. I wasn't even sure it had ever been explicitly said around her as the past few weeks blurred together.

She swatted my arm, rolling her eyes. "Of course I do. Although, we've never talked about it. I want to *see* it."

"I guess it just…slipped my mind." *What is the world coming to that* me *developing magic slipped my mind? What the fuck—*

"You still have to show me one day," she said, looping her arm back through mine. "I was waiting on you to bring it up, though. I know there are more consequential things than showing me a magic trick or two."

"It'll be *much* more than a magic trick," Lee chimed in. "That I can assure you."

Livvy rose an eyebrow at me, impressed, as she led me to the room at the end of the balcony hallway. We stepped onto another stone staircase that led down into a brewing room. The scent of alcohol permeated the air, undercut by the scent of butterscotch and warm sugar.

CHAPTER TWENTY TWO

I moaned dramatically as I inhaled. "That smells delicious."

Rys clapped a hand on my shoulder. "That's our most recent batch—a caramel mead."

My brain halted as my head snapped back to him. "Did you say caramel?" My eyes shot to Livvy. "I *love* caramel and mead."

"I know," she said. "Why do you think I brought you today of all days? It finished a day or two ago."

"Can we try it?" I asked both Rys and Livvy.

"Of course. I've already pulled a bottle and some glasses for us," he said, extending a hand toward an old table. Atop it sat a corked glass jug and several mugs carved from bone.

"I can see why you like him," I whispered to Livvy.

Chapter Twenty Three

Ara

I stumbled into our chambers well after sunset, covering my mouth as I suppressed a giggle. A warm fuzziness had settled over me hours ago and remained for the night as we sampled different mead, wines, and whiskeys.

It was a nice night. Just friends and happiness and…alcohol.

My eyes scrunched as I laughed into my hand and tiptoed around the dark room to the bedside as silently as I could. The only light was from the moon outside the open window and the fire in the corner—neither making a sound, for which I cursed them both. I didn't want to wake Rogue after his shift; he needed the rest.

As I neared the bed, I accidentally kicked the frame, sending an unimaginably annoying pain through my toes.

I suppressed a groan and hissed at the fireplace, "I wish you were louder."

"Me?" The sound came from the chair next to it, nearly scaring the daylights out of me.

My hand flew to my racing heart. "What in the—"

I squinted, taking a step closer to see Rogue's face appear

from the darkness, grinning as if he was holding back laughter. My head whipped back to the bed. Empty.

Idiot.

"Well, how was the shift?" I drawled, placing a hand on my hip. I stood straighter and pretended the room wasn't swaying under my feet.

Perfectly sober.

"Good." He hummed, nodding as he pushed off the armrests and rose to his feet. "Incredible, even."

He edged closer, and I did my best to keep my eyes on him, but he could've been moving at lightning speed for all I knew. He was right in front of me now, his lopsided grin peering down at me as he slid his hand under my chin. My eyes closed on instinct; he was so warm and steady. My body ached for his touch constantly, and now was no different.

He provided the stillness I desperately needed—tonight and every night.

Cheesy, I thought to myself with another giggle. *When did I become so cheesy?*

His thumb ran along my lower lip. "What are you laughing at?"

I opened my eyes to his warm red ones. How odd was it that the gaze that was once so calloused was now the softest I had ever seen?

"Myself, it seems," I whispered. "Have I always been so…"

"Sweet? Mostly."

"No," I laughed, shaking my head.

"Ravishing? Since the day I met you. Feisty? More so than anyone I have ever met. Kind…? No." He laughed, a deep genuine laugh that distracted me from a single word he had just said. "No, you haven't always been kind, but I think I like you more for it."

His lips slid along mine, stealing the breath from my lungs.

"Have I ever told you I love you?" I asked against his mouth as he walked me backward. The backs of my thighs hit the bed, and he lifted me to sit atop it.

"Tell me again."

I pulled back, smiling at him like he was the only light in my very dark world. Perhaps he was, or perhaps I was no longer interested in the light. Perhaps all I needed was darkness—dark hair and dark eyes and dark nights spent in the coziness of his hold. Perhaps all I needed was right in this room.

"Rogue Draki, I love you, with every bone in my body—and yours." I giggled and placed a palm on each of his cheeks, holding him close enough to feel his breath. "I love you."

The smile slid from his face just a fraction, and mine followed.

"What? Did I say something wrong?"

"No… No, you said the rightest words I've ever heard." He kissed my lips and then my forehead before turning away to grab a cup I hadn't noticed from the nightstand. "Here. Before we lay down."

With a sigh, I tipped the cup to my lips, and the scent met my nose—Iaso's hangover cure. I chugged the rest before handing the cup back to him.

He kissed the scar along my wrist before scooping me up and lying me down with my head on the pillow. My eyelids felt heavy the second I was horizontal, and I moaned as I snuggled under the covers. With closed eyes, I reached a hand back and grabbed his shirt, pulling him down behind me. His laugh echoed through the room as he laid a wing over us and wrapped an arm around my waist.

CHAPTER TWENTY THREE

He molded to me so perfectly, it would be an insult to fate to ever say we weren't made for each other.

* * *

It was even warmer the next day.

"This has to be the hottest day of the year," I said, lounging back on the bench in the training yard.

I didn't do well in the heat. My body seemed to reject the hotter temperatures as the sun greedily sucked the life from me and laziness crept into my bones. An overwhelming need to wallow surpassed any motivation nearly every time. Unfortunate timing considering—

"I know. I love it," Thana said, turning to the sun. "The sun. The heat. I could sunbathe all day if the world allowed it." She flipped her dagger by the hilt and caught it by the blade with her fingertips. "Maybe I was a lizard in another life."

She flung the blade, and I rolled out of the way last second. "Was that necessary?"

"You need to work in the heat and get used to it. You're about to travel across Ravaryn in the dead of summer," Livvy said as she grabbed a flask and tossed it to me.

I opened and sniffed it before chugging the water gratefully.

"Is that not what we've been doing for the last two hours?" I grit out as I ripped the dagger from the wood it had embedded in. I flicked it straight down, where it landed in the dirt, rocking back and forth as I snatched a sword from the rack—long and heavy, made of dark steel.

Wrong choice.

I swung at Thana and, with a wicked grin, she spun and blocked. The clang of metal rang out across the bailey, pulling a quick cheer from Livvy as she stepped back out of the sparring circle.

"To be honest, I didn't even know you trained," I said to Thana, turning to replace the sword. "I think I'm going to be done for the—"

"Based on how you fight and lounge about like a cat on her deathbed, I wouldn't believe you trained either."

My eyes shot back to her as the smile slid from my face, already aggravated by the heat. "I didn't realize you were looking for a fight."

"Not that you have much of one to offer." She pointed her blade at Livvy, throat level. "Maybe I should try her instead."

"Do you typically go for the easier fight?" I dropped my eyes to watch as I spun the sword in my hand. "Can't say I'm surprised."

Her amethyst eyes flicked back to me as a grin spread across her face. "There she is."

We went round after round for well over half an hour until sweat soaked through our clothes, her violet hair now a deep wine color. My muscles screamed as I lifted the massive sword, taking my stance once again—a rewarding pain, one I knew would pay off tenfold when my muscles were no longer sore.

I matched her moves with an expertise that had been ingrained in me a decade ago, mirroring her every move. It was second nature now, but the weight of the sword definitely impacted my swing time, and as she lunged, I moved to block a second too late.

Her sword—smoothed by the protection spell—struck my shoulder, knocking the blade from my hand. I clutched at it as pain radiated down my arm.

CHAPTER TWENTY THREE

Dropping to my knees, I bit my lip, suppressing a pained cry. "Good Goddess, that fucking hurt, Thana," I hissed through clenched teeth.

"I am so sorry," she said, covering her mouth as she held back a laugh. "You moved a bit slower than I anticipated."

My eyes shot to her for a moment before a laugh of my own slipped through. "That Goddess-forsaken sword weighs too damn much. It's making me slow."

"Well, that's Rogue's training sword. What else would you expect? It was made for a six-foot-five dragon shifter." I examined the sword closer, but there was nothing special other than its size. I hadn't known it was Rogue's; there were dozens of blades along the rack. Thana scooped the sword up, and her eyes widened as she felt it out. "Respect. I can't believe you were even able to wield it at all."

"Oh, let me see," Livvy said, extending a hand.

Thana cocked a brow as she handed it to Livvy who gasped and immediately fell to one side the moment she held the entire weight. She gripped the hilt with both hands and lifted it from the ground, moving awkwardly as she stumbled.

"For the safety of everyone here, please put that down," I mumbled and rose to my feet.

"Yeah…" Livvy said, dragging it back to Thana. "That's not for me."

"I'm definitely wiped out now." I took the sword from Thana to replace it along the rack. "I need food, water, and a nap. What about you guys?"

"I'm in," Livvy said, quickly followed by Thana.

We made our way to the kitchen. It was mid-afternoon—past lunch hours—but I partially expected my mother to be hiding in there, lost in her art of flour and sugar.

I smiled as we pushed the door open; I wasn't wrong. The scent of chocolate drifted from the kitchen, beckoning us in. My mother was stirring a pot of simmering chocolate, Iaso covered in flour from her hands to her elbows.

"Is Mother giving you a lesson, Iaso?" I teased.

"One dearly needed," Mother said.

Iaso's mouth fell open in mock offense. "I wouldn't say *dearly* needed, but it has been fun, nonetheless."

Along the counter was a grazing tray filled with fruits and small pastries. Thana, Livvy, and I descended on it in an instant, moaning as we filled our empty bellies.

Cautiously, as if we may bite the hand that fed us, Mother slid over a pitcher. "Lemonade."

I poured three cups, one for each of us, and Thana's eyes rolled back dramatically as she sipped it.

We ate and drank our fill, making idle conversation with Mother and Iaso as they worked on their dessert.

"Can we come back for some when it's done?" I asked.

"Sure," Mother said. Iaso's eyes found Mother's, and they shared a suspicious smile.

I started to ask, but Livvy looped her arm through mine, tugging me to the door. "How about that nap now? I know I desperately need one, and I didn't swing an obnoxiously large sword around."

Livvy led me through the doorway as I glanced over my shoulder at them. They waved before Thana leaned over to Mother and whispered a few unintelligible words.

I couldn't deny Livvy, though. I was exhausted; the farther we walked down the hallway, the heavier my eyelids got. By the time we reached my chambers, my muscles begged me to lie down, but as we entered, Rogue was seated near a

CHAPTER TWENTY THREE

steaming bath. His hair was tied atop his head, and the only thing he wore was a pair of black leather trousers.

My eyes dipped down his torso, following along his scar. He was carved by the Goddess herself, and that fact was confirmed every time I saw him bare.

His eyes flared, and the room warmed—not from the summer heat or the steam rising from the water.

"All right…" Livvy said. I nearly jumped, forgetting she was there for a brief moment. "Have a nice bath." Her eyes shifted to Rogue. "Make sure she naps. It's been a long day already."

She kissed me on the cheek before disappearing, closing the door behind her.

"What is this for?" I asked, walking over to him.

He rose and stepped into me. Grabbing the hem of my shirt, he paused, waiting for me to lift my arms. I did so dutifully, and he pulled the shirt overhead and tossed it to the side.

"A bath?" He cocked an eyebrow. "Do you not bathe often?"

I swatted his arm. "Of course I do, but why are *you* here preparing a bath?"

His hand slid along my bare waist, leaving a trail of goosebumps in his wake. "Would you prefer someone else?"

"No," I whispered.

"Good," he whispered back as his fingers explored lower, grazing along the waistband of my trousers until he reached the buttons. He unbuttoned them slowly, dropping to his knees before me. Lifting one foot, he slid one side off and then the other.

My breaths came fast as his hands rested on each of my ankles and grazed higher. He rose to his feet as his hands met my hips and continued to rise higher—over my waist, around my breasts, up to my neck. Finally, he tilted my face up to him and kissed my lips.

"Are you joining me, then?" I asked.

"That was my plan."

My heart lurched. We had shared everything—secrets, flesh, bonds—yet this still felt so intimate. A newfound intimacy I hadn't realized I needed.

He kicked off his trousers, and we sank into the water slowly. I sat between his legs and reclined on his chest with a sigh, the scent of lavender mixing with evergreens in the oil that coated our skin and rose with the steam.

He moved beneath me, but I couldn't be bothered to open my eyes as the warmth caressed my sore muscles. Between his hold, the bath, and my full belly, I could've fallen asleep right here.

His hand dipped below the water and rose with a washcloth. He squeezed it above my shoulder, letting the water cascade over my bare breasts.

A moan escaped my lips, pulling a satisfied groan from him that vibrated his chest beneath me. He slid the cloth along my neck and down my shoulders, moving it lower between my breasts and along my stomach only to stop just above the apex of my thighs.

"Why stop now?" My voice was breathier than I intended, but I didn't care as he moved lower, doing exactly as I'd hoped. I melted into him, letting my legs fall open as he used the cloth against me—for me—working in small circles at the apex of my thighs.

His other hand slid along my waist, rising higher until he reached my throat. He squeezed enough to cut off my air supply, and I didn't stop him. It accelerated everything—my heart, the building pressure, the lust—everything but my thoughts, which ebbed and flowed exclusively toward him.

He held my very life in his hands, and I was safer now than I had ever been.

The pressure built and built, my hips jerking toward his hand, begging for more friction as my mind started to cloud. My lungs burned, but so did my core, burning in twin flames, vying for attention.

His hand moved a fraction faster, and I was there, tumbling from the cliff he had placed me on. Sparks exploded in my vision at the same second that air flooded my lungs.

It was an overwhelming euphoria that only he could offer me, and he knew it, but it was one he would never deny me.

He was my vice, just as I was his—wicked, addictive, and always leaving us craving *more.*

"I'll never have enough of you," I whispered as I turned to straddle his hips.

"I know." His hands explored my every curve while his gaze remained on mine. "It's a curse and a blessing, isn't it? To be so starved yet satisfied at all times?"

"Starved…" I hummed, kissing along the hollow of his throat. "Are you starved now, Rogue?"

His grip tightened on my hips as his breaths deepened. I moved higher, nibbling at his earlobe.

"Do you ache to be inside me? To fill that hunger that gnaws at you?"

A growl ripped through his chest, not Fae but dragon. A hint of orange flickered over me, and I smiled against his skin as a thrill of satisfaction shot through me.

His hand knotted in my hair, and he jerked me back. His

eyes were glowing, slitted as his control slipped, his fire encapsulated in his pupils.

A magnificent display of power—his own *and* the one I held over him.

"Do you doubt that I would burn the realm for you, little storm? Or did you need a demonstration?" he whispered as his hardened length ground against my bare core.

A moan threatened to escape me when a light outside the window caught my attention. My gaze shot past him, landing on the ocean, and my breath hitched.

The sea was on fire. Waves of rolling flame licked toward shore.

My mouth ticked up in a smirk as my gaze drifted back to him.

"I don't doubt you for a second"—my palm slid along his jaw and onto his cheek—"but you seem to have forgotten who I am."

Clouds consumed the afternoon sky, and within seconds, rain pelted the ocean. Lightning struck the sea, mixing with his fire in an explosion of steam and smoke before the rain extinguished it all.

"Beautiful." His thumb slid along my cheekbone beneath my eye. "As silver as the moon."

I knew my eyes would be a crackling silver, just as his were a burning orange-red.

"As bright as the sun," I whispered.

"Perfectly matched." His eyes softened, returning to his normal maroon.

My hands were on his cheeks as I smiled at him and slid my lips along his in the gentlest kiss we had ever shared—a stark contrast to the breathtaking feeling that swelled in my

CHAPTER TWENTY THREE

chest.

"I love you," I said, just as I would a hundred more times. A thousand.

"I love you, too," he mumbled against my lips as he lined himself up at my entrance.

As he eased inside, his grip held the back of my head, forcing me to moan into his mouth. He groaned in approval before pulling out and thrusting back in.

***

I woke several hours later to the sun lowering on the horizon and the fireplace lit, along with several candles around the room.

My hand reached out to find an empty bed, and I sat up, glancing around. Rogue was nowhere to be found. The bath was gone, too.

"What…"

I threw the covers back to get out of bed, but something heavier than the linen blanket moved with it. Red peeked out from beneath the black fabric.

Smiling, I crawled out of bed to walk to the end. I gently pulled the cover back, revealing a thin, brilliant red gown and a note lying on top.

> *Send for me when you wake up and put this on. We have somewhere to be.*
> *-Thana*

My smile grew into an elated grin as I scribbled a note to

Thana, tossed it in the fire, and turned back to the gown.

I lifted it to get a good look before pulling it on. It was surprisingly light and soft—although I shouldn't be surprised, considering how light every dress I'd worn in Ravaryn had been.

I spun back to the mirror and stilled.

The fabric looked nearly liquid, pouring over my form like a shimmering, strawberry wine before pooling on the floor. It cascaded over my curves and revealed both thighs with slits that reached high above the creases of each hip.

A stiff wind would reveal every part of me if not for the dainty gold chains holding it all together. They wrapped around my waist like delicate vines before crawling over my shoulders.

I turned, eyeing my backside in the mirror. The silk dipped to just above my behind, revealing my entire back. The golden chains dangled from my shoulders in varying lengths, each tipped with a ruby teardrop.

Facing forward again, I noticed the chains along my hips. Three swooped over each side, but the left had a charm hanging from it. I glanced down and lifted it.

A laugh bubbled in my chest.

Not just a charm, but an R.

A knock sounded on the door then, and I turned to find Thana and Livvy entering with excited smiles and red dresses of their own.

"I brought the goods," Livvy said, holding a glass bottle above her head.

"What in the world are we doing?" I asked.

They both laughed but refused to answer. Thana sat three shot glasses on the bedside table, and Livvy popped the cork

CHAPTER TWENTY THREE

to fill them.

"Don't ask questions we're not allowed to answer, yet."

Livvy handed me a glass, and all of us clinked them together before downing the burning liquid.

Thana did a little shimmy and set her glass back on the table. "Now, let me have a look."

They both stepped back to examine the dress as Thana motioned for me to spin, and I did so happily.

"Where did this come from?" I asked. "I didn't ask the dresser for this."

"No, it didn't come from the dresser," Thana said. "It came from Rogue. He had it made at the modiste in the village."

My cheeks burned. For some unfathomable reason, the thought of him going somewhere like that for me, choosing something specifically for me…

"It's perfect," Livvy said, holding her hands over her mouth. "I've never seen anything like it."

"Neither have I," I mumbled. "It's beautiful."

"Well, my Queen," Livvy teased with a wink, "ready to see your knight in shining armor?"

I smiled to myself, glancing back in the mirror one last time. There was once a time that wearing something like this would have made me want to crawl back into my shell and hide, but tonight, I wanted nothing more than to see Rogue's reaction. This gown would stop him in his tracks, perhaps even bring him to his knees.

My eyes tracked over the slits on each side—easy access if he *were* to drop to his knees.

I suppressed a grin as I turned to them. "Yeah, let's go."

Chapter Twenty Four

Ara

The others were gathered outside the village, all garbed in various shades of red, and Livvy and Delphia left my side as my eyes fell on Rogue.

He had on his usual black trousers, but his maroon eyes and wings were highlighted by his blood-red shirt. It was different than what he normally wore—thin, with long sleeves and a V-shaped collar, the drawstring left untied to reveal his chest. His long hair was tousled with small braids wound through it and tied half back.

He extended a hand, and I took it with a smile. Lifting it, he spun me around, pulling a laugh from my lips.

"You could bring the realm to its knees."

"It's only you I wish to have kneel before me," I whispered, and his eyes flared.

"I would happily oblige." His gaze sank to my hips before crawling back up to my eyes. "It would be all too easy."

I grabbed his chin and pulled him down to kiss him. "Maybe another time."

"Later," he promised with a wink before turning to the

CHAPTER TWENTY FOUR

others.

Mother smiled deeply as we locked eyes. She was in a glorious gown made of long, flowing, ruby silk. Her auburn hair hung in its natural loose curls, her freckled cheeks tinted with sunburn.

She was a completely different person compared to the tightly sealed, well-manicured woman I knew only months ago. She looked…free. Wild. Happy. In her element.

She looked like she was home.

"I've never seen you look so beautiful," I said as I took her hand.

"I dressed for the occasion."

"And what is the occasion?" I asked with a raised brow.

She pressed her lips flat and locked them with an imaginary key as her eyes flitted to Rogue with a twinkle. "You'll have to ask him."

I spun to ask him when Iaso looped her arm through mine. She was missing her normal green, but she was just as golden. Her entire form twinkled with jewelry; even her gown—as red as the deepest sunset—gleamed with tiny, golden beads.

"Have you seen anything more adorable?"

She pointed to Alden who sat a few feet away in a circle of children, closer to the village—which I just noticed was entirely decorated. Red banners were strung across every building, and the streets were decorated with a rainbow of flowers. Strings of flickering light hung over the cobblestone streets, illuminating the elated faces below as the sun set above us.

"What is going on?" I whispered under my breath as I lowered my gaze to Alden.

He sat cross-legged on the ground, his gray robes replaced

with vermilion ones. His smile was infectious as children smoothed a floral, scarlet liquid through his hair, dying his white locks a bright red.

He waved me over, and as I neared, he reached a hand out and pulled me down with him. The children eyed me hesitantly, but I nodded, and their hands found my hair instantly. They weaved it into a circlet braid atop my head. When they were finished, two little girls ran to the field beside us, plucked flowers, and gently placed them into the braid.

My cheeks ached when they finally finished, as my smile hadn't faltered once. I couldn't even be bothered to care what it looked like, because it felt so good to be a part of something so carefree and heartwarming. Children were masters at that—bringing us grown folk back to the present, to the ground.

There was a beautiful simplicity in their joy.

My spirits were unimaginably light as I rose to my feet, noticing they had braided and flowered Alden's hair as well. Turning to Rogue, I motioned to my hair. He smiled and mouthed, "Beautiful," as music drifted from the village streets, an upbeat tune that urged me to move.

Grabbing my skirts, I sank into a deep bow. I paused, grinning as his feet stepped into view. When I rose again, he bent at the waist before extending a hand.

I slid my hand into his, and he kissed the scar along my wrist.

"What a queen you will be," he whispered.

"So, care to tell me what this is?"

"You really don't know?"

My brows pulled together as I looked over my shoulder at the village, painted in red. He snaked his arms around my

CHAPTER TWENTY FOUR

waist and pulled my back into his chest.

He kissed the top of my head and said, "Summer solstice, little storm, which just so happens to be—"

"My birthday." I whipped my face back to him with an open mouth. I hadn't told anyone, but—my eyes shot to Mother who stood by with a satisfied grin.

"What better way to celebrate than with the solstice festival?" Rogue asked.

"I couldn't think of a single thing I'd rather do more." My eyes stung, and I laughed, gently sliding a finger beneath my darkened lashes. "Why red, though?" I asked, motioning at our clothes.

"Tonight, when the moon is at its highest, our most sacred flowers will bloom," he said.

"Fire's breath," Ewan said. "The brightest red you'll ever see." He patted me on the shoulder as he dipped his chin in greeting.

"Wearing red is how Ravaryn honors the flowers. It's tradition," Alden added.

"Amazing," I breathed.

"I can't wait to see. We don't have anything like this in Auryna," Livvy said, peeking over her shoulder as Lee grabbed her hand.

"You are a vision." He lifted her hand to kiss it as Rys looped an arm around her waist from the other side.

"A vision if I've ever seen one," Rys said.

"Tonight will be full of food and drink and dancing," Delphia said, surprisingly…happy. Not her normal level of warmth but much more than I had seen since her return.

Thana slid her hand into Delphia's. "It will be glorious, a great celebration before everyone heads out tomorrow."

We leave tomorrow. The thought threatened my mood, but I shoved the anxiety down.

"Well, then, we must make the best of tonight," I said, giving Rogue's hand a quick squeeze. "Ready to show us what we've been missing all these years?"

He led the way into the crowded streets, the air lit with excitement and anticipation. The breeze carried the sounds of music and the scents of bread and mead.

It was an amazing mix, one that lifted my heart by the second. The farther we made it into the village, the more my chest swelled. I could've drifted along in the breeze with how light I felt if it weren't for Rogue's touch anchoring me to the ground.

We stepped into what appeared to be the town square. The string lights created a circle around the center, and inside were women dancing, all dressed in red. They barely touched as they spun, holding their skirts up to reveal bare feet. Their giggles echoed through the square, blending perfectly with the lively tune as if the laughter itself was a vital instrument in the song.

Their smiles never faltered as the music spun faster and faster, their feet moving quicker to match the pace, their skirts spreading like trumpet flowers as they released them to hold each other's hands. They hopped and leaped and flowed along the tune, their faces a vision of happiness.

When the music finally stopped, the crowd clapped and cheered as the women ran into a group hug, stumbling and laughing as they caught their breath.

"I want to do that," Livvy said with as much awe as I felt.

"You will," Thana replied. "We all will, but first…."

Her eyes flitted to Rogue and me with a devious grin.

CHAPTER TWENTY FOUR

"We have to kick off the festivities." Rogue took my hand and pulled me to the center before I had a chance to ask what he meant.

My cheeks flamed as I gazed forward past the dancing circle.

There was a throne, made of an ancient wood, smoothed by time and use. It wasn't carved from a large piece of wood, but braided with smaller branches and vines, fresh flowers weaved into every crevice. It sat atop a small platform, high enough for the surrounding crowd to see whoever sat on it.

As we neared, I tried to slip my hand from Rogue's, but he tightened his grip as he peeked over his shoulder at me, a devilish excitement gleaming in his eyes.

The flush in my cheeks deepened as he pulled me up the steps, and our faces became visible to every person in the crowd.

"Rogue," I whispered, lightly pulling my hand. "There's only one seat."

He turned and sat on the throne, his entire demeanor changing. He was no longer just Rogue. He was regal, his spine straight and his chin high, as if an invisible crown sat on his head. There wasn't a single fleck of insecurity or doubt on his face as he slid on the mask of King Rogue Draki.

Power emanated from him, forcibly snapping my mouth shut as he met my gaze with fiery eyes.

"Sit," he commanded, patting his thigh.

I couldn't deny him if I wanted. Turning, I sat on his thigh as he snaked an arm around my waist and down to my hip, where his fingers found the R-shaped charm on my bare thigh.

I felt his smile before he kissed my neck lightly, now

exposed by the braided crown.

"Tonight, we welcome the summer season with open arms"—his voice thundered over the crowd—"and open casks." The crowd erupted in cheers and laughter. "While we celebrate the blooming of summer and our dear fire's breath, may we also welcome my mate, Ara. Born from the blood of Vaelor Wrynwood and his *human* mate, blessed by the Goddess herself, and the Bringer of Storms, I could think of no one more my equal than she."

The crowd's silence was deafening as they hung onto his every word. Their eyes flashed to me and stayed as they truly took me in for the first time. I held my composure, preventing the panic from showing on my face, even as a deepening blush betrayed me.

He just revealed my human half.

Anxious questions bombarded me all at once as I prepared for their reaction. Would they riot? Would they rage? Would they blame me for the tragedy that has ensued? Would I be the vessel for their anger?

My chin stayed high as Rogue's grip tightened on my thigh, and I knew what he wanted.

A display. Proof, just as he had in Nautia. What was needed to convince people that I was, in fact, a Storm Bringer and the daughter of Vaelor.

Although if he intended to marry me and place me atop a throne regardless, I supposed it didn't really matter if I had any Fae blood at all…but it would to his people, to know that I was one of them, that I belonged here.

And I did belong, blood or not. In spirit and heart and soul, I was Ravaryn's.

I raised my eyes to the sky and called to it. Without a single cloud in the sky, thunder rumbled seconds before bolts of lightning struck in every direction, encircling us in crackling light.

Coincidentally—or perhaps not a coincidence at all—at the same moment, Rogue's wyverns flew over the town in unison. They roared in approval, the sound mixing with the lightning's cracks in a powerful hymn.

The villagers' eyes widened in shock as if they hadn't seen the wyverns yet, hadn't known their king was chosen, hadn't known he had a mate, much less a Storm Bringer.

Chills spread over my skin as a small wave of pride swept through me.

"Together, we are the Conquerors of Skies. Together, we will offer each and every one of you the peace and safety you deserve. We will bring King Adon or Adonis or whatever damned name he decides to use to his deathbed. We will burn him to the ground in the name of every fallen soldier and offer you his ashes. Celebrate this night, for we are on the precipice of freedom."

The crowd's silence disappeared in a flash of roaring cheers.

"The Skyborn King and Queen," someone shouted from the crowd.

Not someone—Ewan. My eyes found him and our entire group, their pride nearly palatable. Alden had his arm around Mother's shoulders as they watched on with misty eyes, nodding.

The phrase spread through the entire village until that word was the only intelligible sound—*Skyborn.*

We were their Skyborn.

A smile pulled at my lips as I glanced at Rogue, and his grip tightened around me.

We would offer them peace.

I sucked in a deep breath, inhaling every emotion from the crowd as my rapid heartbeat sailed.

We would offer them life. Not just survival, but *life,* without fear and war and overwhelming tragedy.

We—their king and...maybe queen.

For the first time, the title didn't send a fresh wave of panic over me.

As I exhaled slowly, a single thought—a single hope— whispered in the back of my mind. My eyes shifted to Rogue, his gaze still over our people, his expression filled with pride.

Maybe I could wear the crown without being crushed under the weight. Maybe...Maybe I could be Ara Draki without being suffocated by the name.

"Without further ado…" Someone handed Rogue a cup carved from bone, and he raised it in a toast. "May your hearths always be warm, your bellies full, and your hearts happy."

He chugged the golden liquid, some spilling down his chin as he did so. The drops rolled down his neck to his exposed chest, and my attention was helpless to do anything but follow them—straight to the gold chain tucked beneath his shirt. I snaked a hand beneath the fabric, and he watched me, his mouth ticked up in a grin, his throat bobbing with each swallow, as I pulled out a small A charm.

I smiled, shaking my head, before tucking it back in. *Goddess above, I love this man.*

If we weren't seated before thousands of eyes, I would've leaned forward and licked the gold from his skin. His gaze darkened as if he could read my thoughts, but it was more likely that he smelled the desire from between my thighs—because I was *burning*. His eyes flashed as I bit my lip and winked.

Tightening his grip on my thigh, he lifted the mug to our people. "Let the summer begin."

* * *

The night flew by in a blur of colors and treats and sweet drinks. We spent hours dancing until we needed a breath, drinking a special Fae wine that radiated a bubbliness through us, and laughing until our bellies burned.

My family, each and every single one of them satiated and content, if only for a night, was the best birthday gift I could have ever been given.

I reclined on my elbows at the bar as I watched the others dance—if it could be called that. We may be the most uncoordinated people in Ravaryn—at least, all but Livvy. She knew how to move, and Rys and Lee hadn't taken their eyes off her since she started.

Alden joined me, sitting on the bar stool next to me with his own cup in hand.

"Be careful with the Fae wine."

"Why?" My eyes dropped to the goblet half full of golden wine.

It was a delicious concoction, all warm berries and grapes with a hint of chocolate and no bitterness from the alcohol. It could have been a dessert, for all I knew.

He nudged me softly with his elbow. "Because it affects humans differently. You'll get much drunker, much faster. Your Fae half will help a bit, but those two?" He pointed at Liv and Mother, who were clearly already drunk but deliriously happy as they held hands and swayed. "They're goners."

"Oh, let them have their fun," I said, nudging him back.

"I wouldn't dream of spoiling it." His eyes went distant for a second, an echo of sadness sweeping over them before they flicked back to me. "Happy birthday, Ara. I wish Vaelor could be here, for so many things, but especially today. For your birthday, to see that speech. A half-blood on the throne? And accepted, by at least these people? It's…revolutionary. Something he would have dreamed of."

I didn't respond. Not because it wasn't revolutionary—maybe it was—but because I wasn't ready to truly accept what had just happened. I had revealed myself in Nautia for the sake of gaining fighting men and women to our cause, but this felt different. This felt real. It felt life-altering. Kingdom-altering. History-altering.

The thought made my head spin. My hands gripped the wooden bar, seeking stability.

With a mind clouded with wine, a heart nearly exploding, and a soul that was content for the time being, I didn't want to dwell on it.

No, tonight was ours, and I wanted to spend it not thinking or worrying at all.

As a new song began, I tipped the cup up and wiggled my brows at Alden as I downed the contents. He laughed, sputtering on his own wine. Slamming my cup down on the bar, I hopped off the bar stool and dipped into a dramatic bow, extending my arms to the side before reaching a hand to him.

"Care to join me for this dance?"

"Oh, of course, noble knight. How could I ever deny you?"

CHAPTER TWENTY FOUR

He grinned and rose to his feet.

A deep laugh behind me caught my attention, and I turned to find Rogue with his arms crossed across his chest, smiling down at me.

"Ah, better yet, I think I shall join my daughter-in-law. It seems she's in need of a partner," Alden said, patting me on the shoulder as he glided past us.

Rogue stepped closer, tucking a loose strand behind my ear. "You're radiant when you're happy."

"As are you," I replied, resting my hands on his chest as I tilted my face to his.

He leaned down, and the rest of the tavern slipped away as his lips brushed against mine in a slow, drugging kiss. I was beginning to love our soft touches as much as the rougher ones—maybe more. While the rough set me aflame like a raging bonfire, these lit me with a different warmth, slow and permanent. An ember set deep in my chest. One I knew would never flicker out.

My heart ached as he broke the kiss to whisper, "The flowers will be opening soon. Want to go watch?"

"Of course. Let's get the others." I turned to the group only to find they were all occupied with the current song. I paused and turned back to him. Slowly, I slid my palms onto his cheeks, feeling the stubble along his jaw. I ran my thumb along his lower lip, letting my eyes roam over his face. Every part of him was beautiful. His mouth ticked up in a sweet smile, and I pulled him down for another kiss. I needed it, him, his touch.

Each taste was merely a fix until the next.

He groaned into my mouth as he walked me back against the bar. His hands seared a path along my body, snaking beneath the thin fabric of the dress he designed. Nothing was soft now. Not his lips, his touch, the burning desire that had become a roaring inferno, *him*.

Addicting. Beautifully and deliciously addicting.

Breaking the kiss was like moving a mountain, but I gripped his chin and smiled at him with a restraint I hadn't realized I possessed. "I need to see you fall to your knees first, my King."

His eyes darkened as he chuckled, lowering his mouth to my ear. "I would kneel before you right now in front of everyone here if I thought that would guarantee me a taste. Or maybe you'd prefer I just splay you atop the bar and slide that pretty little dress to the side. You seem to enjoy that."

"Later," I whispered, echoing his promise from earlier.

"Later." He kept his heated gaze on me as he lifted my wrist to his lips. "But just know, your desire is the only thing I can smell right now, and it's driving me fucking *mad*."

My heart skipped a beat. Goddess above, I wished I could smell his desire. I had a feeling it would quickly become my favorite scent, something spicy and warm and delectable. My human half prevented it—not that he had ever been shy in showing it.

My cheeks flushed, and he swept his thumb across the color.

"Oh, come on. Let's go get the others before we miss it." I gave him a quick peck and slipped my hand into his.

He gave a dramatic groan as I tugged him back into the crowd.

"You big baby."

Snatching me back, he wound his arms around my waist and pulled me into his chest to kiss the top of my head. "Don't be such a temptress, and I won't be so tempted."

"I could just stand here, and you'd be tempted. Is it really my doing?"

"Entirely." He brushed a gentle kiss over my forehead and paused before adding, "Although not your fault."

My heart sang, but I swatted at his arm as the song came to an end and the others found us.

"Ready to see some magic?" Iaso nearly vibrated with excitement.

Chapter Twenty Five

Rogue

Every day, every moment, every interaction with Ara made me fall more in love with her. If I was lost to her before... I shook my head, tightening my grip on her hand as I led her through the village streets.

Lost wasn't even the right word anymore. She *found* me, revived me, lit me from the inside, and showed me not everything resides in the dark. She blew in like the storms she wields so easily and uprooted my entire life, my entire perspective, my everything.

She had *become* my everything—her laugh and moans my favorite sounds, her rain and desire my favorite scents, being near her my favorite pastime.

No other feeling had consumed me so thoroughly, not the rage or hatred or disgust. No, if I allowed it, these feelings that consumed me now would light the entire realm on fire with their strength. The flames would burn a bright blue as they consumed everything but her, leaving her a shining beacon among the black ash.

Inhaling deeply, I regained my composure and turned to

her. Her silver eyes were lit with a relaxed happiness I had never seen but now could never live without—so bright, she put the moon and all its stars to shame.

"Ready?"

She smiled and nodded. "Show me the magic."

I stepped out of her line of sight, and her lips parted in a soft gasp. The blooms hadn't opened yet, but they were close. The field was on the precipice of flames, the red light shining within the twisted buds.

"Just wait," Iaso breathed at Ara's side, placing a hand on her shoulder. Elora and Livvy joined on the other side of Iaso, and then Thana, Delphia, and Mya, all touching each other in some way—holding hands, bumping shoulders, wrapping an arm around the other.

They were family. I smiled to myself, dropping my eyes. My family.

As the moon rose higher, more town folk joined us, waiting in hushed silence. The bright, full moon peaked, and a beam of silver cast over the field.

The first bloom fell open slowly, dispersing its glowing pollen like embers among the night sky. Then another and another bloomed until the field was lit with floating sparks.

Ara gasped, her eyes following them into the sky as they scattered like fireflies. "Fire's breath," she whispered with awe.

The children darted into the flower field, laughing. As their fingers glided through them, the flowers released more embers, and they swirled in the breeze as the children giggled, waving their hands.

Ara glanced at me, then at the girls. They shared mischievous grins and kicked off their shoes. Lifting their skirts, they sprinted into the field altogether as they spun and frolicked with smiles so bright, I thought they might outshine the blooms themselves.

A small band assembled at the edge of the field, playing a lively tune. Ara held her hands out to the side, spinning with her eyes closed as the tempo accelerated, the rhythm becoming more frenetic. She was beautifully lost to it, and I could no longer tell if it was her matching the music's pace or it matching hers as she spun and spun. She had released her red skirt, allowing the bottom to be coated in the glowing sparks as her bare feet spun in the dirt.

Smiling to myself, I kicked off my own shoes and ran into the field with her. She spun right into my chest, and I wrapped my arms around her as she gazed up at me with nothing but happiness in her eyes—a sight I would chase for the rest of my days.

"Happy birthday, Ara," I whispered.

"Thank you," she replied and stood on her toes as she wrapped a hand around my neck. She pulled me down to her to kiss my cheek. "I love you."

"I love you, too, little storm. More than I can put into words."

* * *

I had been awake for hours.

Last night had been a dream—easily one of the best nights of my life. We had laughed and shared and celebrated with the family we created. We weren't bonded by blood but loyalty, and we were stronger for it.

It was one of the only purely happy nights I could remem-

CHAPTER TWENTY FIVE

ber. If my childhood self could see what we had built, I don't think he would have felt so bad, so alone. To know this was what was to come? It made everything worth it, every single agonizing moment.

Last night was a memory I would cherish, but we were leaving today, and the weight of that overshadowed any lightness of the day before. It had been weighing on me since the moment Ara closed her eyes.

She was scared. She had told me as much as we crawled into bed, facing what would come in the morning. She should be. I was too, but not for myself.

Traveling to Rainsmyre would send us south toward the Cursed Wood. We would skim along the southern border between Ravaryn and Auryna—dangerously close to Auryna's reach. Uncomfortably close. Even so, I would risk my life for the chance of finding the crown without hesitation. I would travel to Adonis' precious capital, to his damned chambers, and rip the crown from his hands if that's what it took; not because it was mine—and it was—but to speak with the wyverns and gain their support in the war.

We were outnumbered plain and simple, and it was my responsibility to tip the scale in our favor. It was my existence that hatched Adonis' convoluted plan in the first place, so I would risk my life for the good of Ravaryn.

But Ara's?

I knew the answer and hated myself for it, had cursed myself a hundred times already.

If Doran's death taught me anything, it was that none of us were invincible, and that reminder, that *fear*, was making every decision right now.

My jaw clenched along with my fists. She lay beside me,

asleep in the late morning hours. I turned to her, running a hand through her hair lightly, carefully, and she leaned into my touch even in her sleep, sighing as she inched closer.

I had declared her my equal last night. The word would spread like wildfire.

King Rogue Draki, the unshifted, the unclaimed, the broken, was no longer. I had been chosen by the wyverns as well as a woman. I was mated. Chosen. Undeniable.

And not just mated, but matched. My equal in every way—strength, power…blood claim.

To my people, my words were clear. I had declared her my equal, and thus, she was. That was the upside to one of Ravaryn's longest-standing traditions: it didn't require a crowning ceremony for the mated one of a reigning monarch, just the declaration. The words made it so.

Ara Starrin. Ara Wrynwood. Ara Draki—one day, *if* she forgave and accepted me after this—was the reigning queen of Ravaryn.

If I fell on this journey, Ravaryn wouldn't be entirely lost. She had a queen—one who would be unprepared and enraged, but a queen, nonetheless. One who would be worthy of the title.

That was one reason I couldn't let her make this journey with us. Reason two, however, was much more selfish, and even knowing so did nothing to dissuade me. I knew I would do it. I would take away her choice. Again.

I could nearly hear her screaming it was wrong, but I was overwhelmingly fucking selfish; therefore, it changed nothing as I slid from the bed without glancing back. I couldn't, because if I did—if I looked back and saw her lying in my bed, asleep and content, because she trusted me so

CHAPTER TWENTY FIVE

much that she could let her guard down entirely—the guilt would crush me.

I dressed methodically and pulled my boots on, all while avoiding her and the mirror. Tying my hair back was the last task I had, but I hesitated. My small bag was already packed by the door, and I stared at it for far too long.

My thoughts were both racing and frozen, a cacophony in my head that wouldn't shut the fuck up. Frustrated, I exhaled forcibly and ran a hand through my hair, tying it back before marching to the bag and scooping it up in one swift motion. I stalked to the door before I could lose my nerve and wrenched the door open, but the sound of her shifting stopped me in my tracks.

She released a breathy sigh, but I didn't look back. I didn't dare. I paused with my eyes closed, my knuckles rubbing my sternum as the ache reappeared for the first time in a long time, and silently closed the door behind me.

I moved through the hallways without thought, letting my feet guide me on instinct. I was numb—the way I used to live day to day. I was without any feelings at all as I burned them away in forced indifference.

When I stepped into the entryway, the others were already gathered, ready to leave. Their eyes found mine, and every smile slipped away one by one. They knew. Without words, they knew.

The mood shifted and sank, plummeting as they understood what I was doing, what I was forcing them to do.

For better or worse, Ara would be safe. That was all that mattered.

"You can't ask me to do this," Alden said, his voice so low that it barely reached my ears.

"I can't let her risk her life for this," I whispered back.

Alden clenched his jaw, averting his gaze as he strode to the front door, bag in hand.

Off to the side, sitting on the step with Ewan's hand on her shoulder was Iaso.

"I'm sorry," I breathed without meeting her eyes.

I had told her my plan. She had disagreed and adamantly tried to dissuade me, but it was for naught. I wouldn't risk Ara's life, not for this, and Iaso knew it as she handed me a small flask.

"She won't be able to track you," she whispered quietly.

My chest felt like it could cave in at any moment as it tightened like a vice around my lungs, but I took the canister slowly and tipped it back, swallowing the bitter contents.

Then I felt it.

Every instinct went on high alert. My heart raced. My gut twisted, bile rising in my throat. Her presence, the warm tenderness that had filled my chest since the moment I claimed her, dissipated from me bit by bit until she was entirely gone. I was disgustingly empty. It was wrong. Cold. It was like a vital part of me was being ripped away in one fell swoop, leaving a gaping hole.

"She will feel the same thing when she wakes. Empty," Iaso muttered. "She won't feel you."

I swallowed hard, standing straighter. The thought of her not feeling our bond would be my undoing. I wanted her to feel me constantly. I wanted to bite her and mark her and fill her until she undeniably belonged to me, and I her. I wanted to fill her so thoroughly that even the moon itself would feel our bond.

But now, we were achingly empty.

CHAPTER TWENTY FIVE

"How long will this last?"

"Maybe twelve hours." I could've vomited at her words. Twelve hours without Ara's soul entwined with mine. "You'll have to take it at least twice a day if you want to remain… unfound."

My jaw clenched as I inhaled deeply. Twice a day. I'd have to take this unnatural monstrosity of a tincture twice a day, rip Ara from me twice a day.

"Thank you, Iaso. I…" Another apology was on the tip of my tongue; I wanted her to know I meant it. I wanted to turn around and run right back up those steps to Ara and beg her to stay of her own accord, for my own selfish peace of mind, but I did neither. Instead, I cleared my throat and turned to the others. "Are we ready?"

A voice that was distinctly Ara's seethed in the back of my mind. *Selfish, lying coward.* I actively ignored it. Nothing I didn't already know.

They all nodded without a word, and in that same, heavy silence, we filed out the door. In the bailey sat our horses and the rest of the men accompanying us. We all meticulously attached our bags to the saddles and mounted them before I clicked, urging my steed forward and closing my eyes as we passed through the gates.

Someone rode up to my side, and it was Lee's voice that broke the silence. "Are you sure about this?"

"Yep," was all I said, the word clipped with a confident finality that I sure as hell didn't feel.

Chapter Twenty Six

Ara

The sleepy haze wore off in soft, easy waves as the warm sun graced my skin through the open window. Stretching, I groaned, popping a few joints, and reached for Rogue.

I sat straight up, the covers pooling around my waist. The bed was empty. My face jerked to the window. The sun had already peaked. It was well past midday.

We were late. I threw the covers back and leaped from the bed, running to grab my clothes and ready myself.

Braiding my hair back, I turned to our bag, but it wasn't by the door. My eyes darted about the room in a frenzy. This was not the time for this. We were already running late, I didn't know where Rogue was, and our bag was g—

My heart stopped.

Our bag was gone. Not lost.

I sprinted from the door and down the hall to Ewan's room. I knocked once. Again. When no one answered, I peeked inside. Empty.

No... I swallowed hard, turned, and ran.

CHAPTER TWENTY SIX

I made a beeline for Alden's office as I entered the library. I didn't bother knocking this time as I swung the door open. It slammed against the wall, the sound echoing through the empty room.

They were gone.

My eyes fell to my feet as I considered my next steps. I didn't need to find Iaso, whom I knew would still be here, nor my mother or Thana or Livvy. They would only gaze at me with sickening pity and offer an explanation or reasoning or some other damned thing I didn't need. No, in this moment, all I wanted was the solitude they so haphazardly thrust upon me against my will.

They—*he* left me.

My chest tightened as my pulse raced. I clenched my fists as my breaths came quick and uneven.

After everything I did, everything I had done, he left me here like some...some prized trophy. As if I were fragile. As if I hadn't proved my worth again and again. As if I wouldn't serve more use *with* him than away. As if... As if...

My mind was as erratic as my breaths. I couldn't finish a single thought; I couldn't even finish a breath. My hand flew to my chest. Sweat pricked along my forehead and down my spine as adrenaline and hurt poured through my veins.

If I could've laughed at this moment, I would have. What sad irony—air evading me just as Rogue did. Perhaps they were in on it together, planning to take away my every choice, even that to breathe.

My vision swam as I hyperventilated. I stumbled back a few paces, and my back hit the wall. Tears brimmed in my eyes as I slowly slid down. As I sat, I pulled my knees to my chest.

I knew the techniques. I knew I should look for the calm, but I didn't want to. The anger and disappointment clung to me like a wet rag, suffocating me in a panic I didn't care enough to dispel.

I wanted to be angry. I wanted to rage at him. I wanted him to know he hurt me, so deeply, that my chest physically ached. It…

My breath left me in a whoosh.

It didn't just ache.

"No… No, you didn't," I choked out. I couldn't feel him. "What did you do? What did you do?" I screamed and screamed and screamed, repeating the question until my words became broken.

Even with a betrayed heart racing painfully and burning lungs that refused to cooperate, I felt nothing. I felt empty.

He was gone.

Even worse, he'd freed himself from me so I couldn't find him.

The man who had offered me freedom and choice and unwavering confidence pulled it all straight from under my feet while I slept in his bed.

Air continued to evade me until my steadiness did as well, followed by hearing and sight and any other sense that tethered me to this realm.

I embraced darkness when it came for me—the only calm I desired to find.

* * *

When I woke, I was still on the floor, alone and utterly exhausted, but the rage had not subsided. Not one bit.

CHAPTER TWENTY SIX

My jaw clenched as I stared at the dark room, looking but not seeing. My breaths were forced but deep and thorough, clearing my head as my thoughts speared at Rogue.

I allowed myself three breaths before I shot to my feet, barely enough time for the dizziness to subside.

"Fuck you and your plan, Rogue."

I stalked out of the office and slammed the door behind me. I didn't know where to go or what my plan was, but I knew I was finding that asshole, and when I did…Goddess help him.

I marched through the winding maze of shelves with a vengeance, snatching every book that could potentially tell me about Rainsmyre—travel, history, merchant logs, even a botany guide of southwest Ravaryn. Once my hands could carry no more, I sat at a table in a hidden corner, dropping the stack in front of me.

Each passing moment wound me tighter as the silence permeated the library, but I didn't want to see a single face or speak to a single person. I could barely contain myself as the rage shifted from simmering to boiling.

My eyes darted across the pages, taking in as much information as I could gather before freezing on a map of Ravaryn. It detailed the roads and paths, including which ones would lead me from Draig Hearth to Rainsmyre.

Looking closer, the path seemed fairly simple: a straight shot through Blackburn back to the Cursed Wood, cross through it, then skirt along the edge of Auryna. Rainsmyre was on the southwest corner of Ravaryn.

I studied it carefully, committing it to memory. I wouldn't need Rogue to lead me there. Hell, with it just being me, I may be able to catch them in a matter of hours. A day, tops.

I couldn't be sure when they left, but it couldn't have been that long ago, and it takes much longer to travel with a group than alone.

I snapped the book closed and jerked to my feet, leaving the books on the table as I hurried from the library. I jogged down the front steps and threw open the door.

The sun was no longer shining. No, now there was an enraged thunderstorm. Heavy rain fell in sheets as thunder rumbled overhead, and I reveled in it. I loved it. Just like every time before, I took and took and took from it. I let it feed my rage, and it fed from mine. Together, we wound tighter and tighter until I feared I may burst. Clouds swirled overhead, the wind whipping my hair.

The eyes of several guards found me instantly as I descended into the bailey. They were all frozen, their faces pale and tight, and my walk slowed. They almost looked scared. I glanced around, but there was no one else in the courtyard.

It was just me, and yet...they were terrified.

My lips parted slightly as I realized it *was just me.*

They were scared of me. Maybe it was the sudden onset of a hurricane or the look in my eyes or the power crackling from me in every direction but whatever the reason...

Good.

They wouldn't dare stop me, and as they subconsciously stepped back as I neared them, it dawned on me that they couldn't if they tried. That was a new realization—a sobering one. This power allowed me to offer *myself* the freedom I had never known, even if it was through their fear.

No man, not even Rogue, would make my decisions for me. It was a promise I made to myself weeks ago, and one I

CHAPTER TWENTY SIX

would enforce tonight.

I stalked across the soaked dirt, and they flung the gates open for me without a word, dipping their heads as I passed. They closed the gates behind me, and once again, I was alone.

Alone. I chuckled to myself, running my hand over my empty chest as another wave of anger pulsed through me.

"Rogue, I will fucking kill you," I seethed under my breath.

Lightning cracked behind me, following me. It got closer and closer, missing me by mere inches, but I paid it no mind. It didn't matter—nothing did.

I still didn't know where I was going. I knew *a* path to Rainsmyre, but I didn't know if that was the one they chose, or if they would be anywhere near it, and I was on foot like a half-wit.

I cursed myself for not grabbing a horse from the stables, but I was already out, and there was no turning back.

Lightning struck closer still, nearly nipping my heels. With a roar of frustration, I jerked my hand to the sky where it happily latched on. It pulled me into its embrace as it had once before, but unlike last time, I had no destination in mind.

I didn't, but it clearly did.

It dropped me somewhere I didn't recognize mere seconds later, the word *ride* still whispering from the recesses of whatever realm had carried me here.

I staggered, breathing heavily as I took in my surroundings. The area was dark in the torrential downpour, the soaked trees creating ominous shadows, the scent of pine needles and wet stone handing in the stagnant air.

Something moved behind me. The ground squelched under my feet as I swiveled on my heel, coming face to face with the guardian wyvern as he gazed at me from within a cave.

I hesitated as we locked eyes. His were a warm amber that reflected my crackling silver like a mirror.

Then, it hit me like a ton of bricks.

Rogue may have untethered himself from me, but he wouldn't think to do so from him. The wyvern would know exactly where Rogue was.

He could take me.

Slowly, my magic seeped from me, crawling over the ground toward him, exactly like it had toward the creature of night all those weeks ago. His eyes dropped to his tipped wing as if he felt me before they shot back to me, but he did nothing. He…let me.

My magic moved through his body until it found his heart—large and powerful. I wrapped around it like a vice and urged him forward. It took every ounce of my strength to move his massive form, and his lips pulled back over his razor-sharp teeth as he threatened a low growl.

"I'm sorry. I need to find him." Guilt panged in my gut, but I continued.

He took one step forward and then another at my command. He stepped from his cave into the rain, his gaze heavy and hard as he regarded me. His wing lowered to the ground, and I stepped closer, taking a deep breath.

"If this is what kills me, Rogue, I swear to the Goddess, I will come back and haunt you," I whispered.

Holding my breath, I reached out a shaking hand and placed it gently on his soaked wing. His head whipped back at me, his jaw snapping audibly.

Tightening my grip around his heart, I urged my magic

CHAPTER TWENTY SIX

through his body, latching onto every flicker of life that permeated him—the very energy that beat his heart and moved his muscles—but he was massive, and it stretched me thin and taut.

I placed my other hand on his wing and began climbing when he didn't immediately throw me across the clearing. It didn't take me long to reach his back, but it felt like hours as I tensed every muscle in my body, waiting for my magic to slip and this wyvern to shred me to pieces.

I deserved it, controlling him like this, but the lightning led me here for a reason. It knew he would help me find Rogue, and if this is how I had to do it, then so be it.

I threw a leg over his back, straddling his spine, and suddenly wished I had a saddle. His scales were slick from the rain, and I had to lean forward at an awkward angle to grab the spikes—the only things that would keep me atop his back, aside from my own trembling legs.

Fear and doubt threatened to force me down, but before I had a chance, he shifted. He took a step forward and then another, moving faster and faster until he was running.

My eyes shot open wide. I hadn't commanded that.

He was acting on his own accord, which meant...

I tightened my hold, my pulse thrumming as a scream caught in my throat.

Dumb. Dumb. Dumb.

The rain let up briefly, allowing my gaze to land on what was ahead of us and offering me a split second of realization before he dove off the cliff to soar straight down.

Not even the Goddess herself could've held back the terrified scream that tore from me.

The force of the wind pushed me back inch by inch as we

gained speed. We were moving at an alarming pace, racing toward the ground or sea—whatever awaited us below. But at this rate, I wouldn't arrive there on his back.

My hands were nearly numb from how tightly I was holding on, but it didn't matter. His spikes were smooth, and I was gradually slipping farther and farther off.

My legs held on for dear life as I slid back, catching nothing to gain traction.

There was nothing else to hold.

I had inches left. Maybe three.

"How are we still descending?" The thought escaped my lips in a shrill screech.

Another inch gone.

"Stop. Please. Sto—" The words morphed into another scream as I lost my hold entirely and flung back.

My vision went black as he flew ahead of me, and I tumbled senselessly, briefly losing consciousness. When I came back to, all I saw were black scales.

He was right below me as I barreled toward impending death.

What? Why wouldn't he—

A heartbeat passed. A painfully slow one.

He's toying with me.

I erupted in a roar of frustration, the cumulative rage from the day splintering from me in a blinding explosion. White light streaked across my vision as adrenaline shot through me like a blazing arrow, lighting every sense. My focus speared at him, my power crackling from my palms in visible bolts. The energy latched onto him and yanked me down, my body hitting his with a thud as the energy wrapped around his spikes and abdomen, anchoring me to his body without give.

CHAPTER TWENTY SIX

He leveled out as if my searing power was nothing but a small tickle against his tough, scaled exterior. His face peeked back, revealing a single eye. It focused on me with such depth that he had to have known exactly what he was doing. There was too much age in his yellow irises, too much knowledge, for what he'd done to be anything other than intentional.

"Was this what you wanted?" I seethed, exasperated as my eyes welled once again.

He turned forward again, flying in a direction I could only hope would lead to Rogue.

My breath hitched, and I harshly wiped my cheek as a tear slipped. The rain may be pelting my face relentlessly, but I wouldn't let tears over Rogue soak my cheeks. Not yet.

I was tired, angry, and frustrated, but most of all, hurt, and I just wanted the one thing I wished I didn't. Every part of me screamed for Rogue. I wanted to fall into his arms and sob and bang on his chest before finally resting in the steadiness he always offered, but he *hurt* me—deeply and thoroughly. He lied, tore his soul from my chest, and left me with nothing, not even a note.

I wanted to hurt him, too. I wanted him to know what I felt right now and suffer through the same feelings. *How did he think I would react? Did he even feel bad about it?*

Dropping my face to my hands, I scrunched my eyes.

I wanted to demand he explain himself, demand he admit he was wrong, to grovel and beg me to stay, because my presence was so vital—to him and the mission.

Not merely liked or desired or enjoyed. Not even just loved, but utterly indispensable.

For once in my entire life, I just... I wanted to be needed.

I wanted *him* to need me because I had somehow found

myself desperately needing him. If I had to learn the feeling wasn't mutual, that would be heartbreaking, and even that felt like an understatement. If Rogue Draki didn't need me, my world would tilt on its axis.

But the worst part of it all? I *thought* he had.

That was what really hit me in the gut. I was completely blindsided. We spent the night in blissful celebration, and then this?

A blade would have hurt less. The ache that burrowed in my chest with his absence and betrayal was too deafening. At least a bleeding wound could heal with a little tonic or salve from Iaso.

"Well, fine. Now, find him, please," I uttered with what strength I had left, dropping my hands and leaning forward to lie on the wyvern. I tucked my hands under my cheek, letting my magic hold me aloft.

I needed answers and an explanation straight from his mouth.

If he didn't need me, then I wanted to hear the words.

* * *

I could feel my heartbeat in my throat.

A group had set up camp ahead, a small fire giving their location away. It had to be them, and the sight reignited my anger.

I was angry at them all. They had all left me there without warning, but it was at Rogue's orders, and he was about to deeply regret that decision.

My lightning cracked from cloud to cloud seconds before the wyvern let out a warning roar, announcing our arrival.

CHAPTER TWENTY SIX

They all jerked to their feet, squinting into the sky to pinpoint us in the dark of night.

The clouds had blotted out any moonlight, so the only light illuminating our forms were the bolts of white that cleaved the sky.

I spotted Rogue, and my jaw clenched. His face was tight as he swiveled to a nearby clearing away from the others. The wyvern followed him and landed gracefully, extending a massive wing, which I quickly climbed down as rage boiled in my veins.

Unfortunately, it wasn't regret that painted Rogue's features.

No, it was unfettered rage. The mirror to my own.

The second my feet hit the grass, rain poured, soaking us both to the bone.

"Have you lost your mind?" he shouted, stalking to me as he gestured to the wyvern.

I stopped, my mouth falling open before twisting into a sickening grin as a low chuckle escaped. I felt the energy sizzle across my irises before I saw the light reflecting on his face. When he was within my reach, my hand pulled back and slapped him. *Hard.* His head snapped to the side with a satisfying crack.

"Have *I* lost my mind? Me?"

A muscle feathered in his jaw as he slowly turned back to me. His eyes were a glowing fiery orange.

"Yes, you. You could have been hurt. Worse, you could have died. What were you thinking *riding* a wyvern?"

"Rogue, are you—Did you hit your head while you've been out here or have you always been this dense?"

He tensed, anger flashing on his face, the fire flaring in his pupils.

"You left me there! You left me there while I slept in *your* bed without so much as a note, and worse, you…" I turned away, throwing my hands up.

He gripped my hand, swiveling me back to him. His mouth was pressed in a tight line. "What? I what?"

His words were softer than I anticipated. I expected a fight—shouting and screaming and arguing, but not this. Not gentleness.

"You…you…took you from me." My voice cracked as I tapped my chest. "And you don't get to do that. You chose me. You devoted yourself to me, and I to you, and now you're mine, you selfish dick. You don't get to take it back and leave me behind like some worthless—"

His palms found either side of my face. "You are *not* worthless."

"Just not needed," I breathed.

His brows furrowed. "In what world would you get that impression? Not needed, Ara? Perhaps you truly have lost your mind."

I jerked my face out of his grasp, but his hand slid under my chin and pulled me back.

"Don't you get it?" He released me to run a hand through his hair. "You are *so* needed, *so* overwhelmingly important to me, that I left you behind, Ara. I left you. I clawed you from my chest so you wouldn't follow us"—he scoffed—"and we see how well that worked out."

"You're not making any sense. None of this makes sense! Why would you declare me your equal, just to turn around and prove you don't actually believe that?" My words shook harder with each syllable as my throat tightened.

CHAPTER TWENTY SIX

He stared incredulously for a moment before laughing—actually laughing—and it grated my already raw nerves.

I swiped his dagger from the sheath and leveled it at him. "So help me, Rogue, if you don't stop laughing, I will cut your tongue from your mouth."

"I'm sorry," he said, shaking his head as he caught his breath. "I'm sorry that I am so…so fucking bad at this, at us. I can't even protect my love without hurting her and giving her all the wrong ideas."

My heart stopped as my breathing quickened.

"I never meant for…" His words trailed off as his eyes fell on my face again. "Fuck, I'm so sorry, baby." He closed the distance in one large step and cupped my face. His mouth brushed against mine, and my lip quivered. "I love you, Ara. That's why I left you, because you are more important to me than anything in this realm, more so than my own kingdom. Of course, you are my equal, mighty Storm Bringer. You are my incredibly strong force of nature who could turn the tides for us. Hell, I don't even know if *I* qualify to be *your* equal."

A tear slipped from my eye, and he gently wiped it away with his thumb.

"I left you because I couldn't imagine a world where you no longer existed. I couldn't risk your life for this—not for me, not the crown, not even for Ravaryn. I left you there because the thought of losing you made me want to carve my own heart from my chest and lay it in the grave with you."

"Why didn't you say anything? Why did you think *this* would be better?"

"Would you have stayed if I asked nicely?" My lack of response pulled another chuckle from him. "Exactly."

"Well, that wasn't your decision to make."

He inhaled deeply, exhaling slowly as his gaze roamed over my face. "I know, and for that, I'm sorry."

It wasn't enough. An apology wasn't enough.

I needed more. More reassurance. More—

"Vow to me. Vow to me that you will *never* take my choice away again. For any reason. Under any circumstances."

"Ara…"

"Vow to me," I seethed.

He took a breath and slowly unsheathed his sword. Lowering to one knee, he held the blade out to me in offering. "I swear it, upon the Goddess and everything under her stars. Upon my own beating heart, I swear to you that I will never take your choice away again."

"Ever."

"Ever," he echoed, rising to his feet.

I nodded once and dropped my eyes, but he tipped my chin back, forcing my gaze back to him. His face was solemn, his brows furrowed.

"I'm hesitant to ask, but…forgive me?"

"Not yet," I answered honestly, and he swallowed hard, dipping his chin in acceptance. "Maybe when I can feel you again. At least I understand your dysfunctional thought process." I rubbed at my sternum, still achingly empty. "Sort of."

"Horrible, isn't it?"

"Horrendous," I replied as we strolled toward camp.

"For what it's worth, I regretted leaving you the moment we exited the gates. I'm happy you found us." His eyes flitted to his wyvern as the guardian leaped into the air, creating a wave of wind that shook the nearby trees. "Although your means of doing so was incredibly reckless."

CHAPTER TWENTY SIX

"Would have been much less reckless if I had left on a horse at your side."

"Fair," he said. "That was dangerous but clever. How did you even think of that?"

"I didn't." I could nearly see the questions on the tip of his tongue, and they only reminded me of how exhausted I was. This wasn't something I wanted to explain in the middle of the night. "I'll explain tomorrow."

He nodded, wrapping a hand around my head to pull me in. He kissed my hair before sliding his hand back into mine and leading me to his small tent.

I waved as we passed the others, Alden and Ewan giving me apologetic looks. I hadn't forgiven them yet, but I didn't have it in me to be angry right now.

Inside the tent was warm, and the makeshift bed in the corner was calling my name the second I stepped in. I walked over and plopped down, my eyes closing as I pulled the covers over my form—and then realized I was soaked.

With a deep groan, I rolled out of bed. My hands fumbled with the clothing as it clung to me, but I stilled when I felt Rogue's fingers glide down my spine. Chills followed in his wake.

Suddenly, I gasped as a lightness rushed through my chest, spreading out like a ring of warmth from my heart to the tips of my extremities. My head tipped back, my eyes closed, and I inhaled deeply as if I had been suffocating for the past few hours and this was my first real breath. It was like stepping from the frigid winter into a heated, candlelit cabin.

When the feeling dissipated, I felt the bond. It was back; *he* was back.

"I will never do that again," Rogue swore, resuming the

motion along my spine. When he reached my lower back, he took his time sliding his finger back up. He exhaled slowly and whispered, "There's something else I need to tell you, and you're not going to like it."

I tensed but didn't turn. The sleepiness left me in an instant as I clenched my jaw. Of course there was more.

"What?"

He sighed, his hand pausing at the base of my neck. He slid my wet hair over my shoulder before sliding his hand around my throat. My breath hitched as he pulled me back until I was flush against him. His grip locked me in place as he lowered his face to my ear. "You are the Queen of Ravaryn."

I rolled my eyes, annoyance flaring as I tried to pull away. "Rogue, I'm tired. I don't—"

"No, little storm. Your reign has already begun. That is the other reason I left you behind, because if I die trying to find this damned crown, I wanted to make sure Ravaryn still had her queen and that is you, Your Majesty."

I was as still as stone. My heart beat once. Twice. And then I elbowed his gut, turned, and reared back.

Before he had time to react, my fist connected with his nose in a hard crack.

Chapter Twenty Seven

Rogue

"Still looking great, I see," Alden hummed, stifling a smile.

Three days later, and my eyes were still blackened. Ewan elbowed Alden and laughed. "Our girl sure did a number on him."

"I'd say he looks better like this," Alden said.

"At least someone put him in his place," Delphia said from behind me.

I swiveled to find her already on her horse, her bags secured for the next day of travel. With a deep sigh, I led my steed to Ara and outstretched a hand to help her up. Her face was tightly sealed as she stepped around me and mounted without a sound, disregarding me entirely.

She had been riding with me begrudgingly, even holding the reins, as she refused to have my arms around her. It put me at an awkward angle, but I wouldn't put her on a horse with anyone else. She had studied the maps and learned our path before she left, so we rode in silence. She hadn't spoken much of anything to anyone, and any words she did say were never directed at me.

While I loathed it, I deserved it—and much worse—so I took it on the chin, giving her as much space as possible, but it was all I could do to not fall at her feet and beg for forgiveness.

After she settled in the saddle, she glanced back over her shoulder to check if the group was ready I presume, but her gaze fell on me instead. To my surprise, she didn't immediately look away when our eyes made contact.

It was much worse.

Her gaze lingered without an ounce of warmth. Her brows furrowed as she studied my face before swallowing hard and turning forward again without any acknowledgment at all. Nothing.

The feelings that sank in my gut were a painful combination of guilt and regret—not for making her queen, but for the pain that clearly burdened her. Pain *I* had caused her.

While my decision to declare her my equal was solid, I had taken her choice away and told her so right after my declaration to never do that again. The words had been as bitter as poison as they left my mouth that night because I knew they would hurt her.

But if I was honest with myself, I wasn't sure I ever intended to say them to her, not in this life.

Maybe there was a small part of me that hoped I would never have to breathe them aloud, that I would die on this journey and leave Ravaryn in much better hands than my own. Maybe I was foolish enough to think she couldn't hate me in death.

Every choice I made with her was a misstep, and *that* is what I deplored—that I couldn't learn my fucking lesson.

CHAPTER TWENTY SEVEN

It was a mistake I would never make again. I meant my vow to her, and I would ride this steed to hell before I broke it.

Her choices were hers to make, a simple truth I couldn't seem to get through my thick skull before, but it was clear as day now as she sat with her back to me, just as she had for days.

She would beat it into my head if that's what it took—clearly, if my broken nose was any indication—and I would let her.

She was *so* good, even in the face of everything she had been through. She had this admirable talent of keeping her head straight without sacrificing anything, not even her honesty and certainly not her thoughtfulness.

I didn't deserve her. I never had. I still couldn't fathom why she chose me. Maybe it was luck or a blessing or a fluke made by fate, but whatever it may be, I was still here, jeopardizing the best thing that had ever happened to me, and for what? To keep her safe? Flimsy reasoning at best.

I should have known she would risk her life if only to find me and give me a piece of her mind. I should have expected it, but to see her flying in on a wyvern?

That was unexpected in every possible way. She couldn't have chosen a more dangerous path. No person in the history of Ravaryn had ever ridden one. No person other than Draki blood had ever even touched one before her and Iaso.

It was all uncharted territory, and she tested fate because of me, risked her life which meant more to me than anything else, because of me.

I had to do better, *be* better, and I would. For her.

Because this was torture.

I wanted to hear her voice again, even if it was just an angry scream, an insult, a death threat. I wanted to touch her, smell her, hold her, *drown* in her. I would let her rage against me, hit me, shove me, choke me if it meant I could feel her touch again. I would let her suffocate the very life from me if it meant her scent would replace the air in my lungs.

I needed her. All of her. Every inch, every insecurity, every hating thought, and loving touch.

I just need you.

Given enough time, I would gain her forgiveness. Whether it be today or tomorrow, a week from now, a year from now—one day, I would adequately repent.

Whether she chose to trust me again…

Well, that was a different question. A different dream.

At least, the sun was shining today, which eased my heart. After three days of rain, the clear skies allowed me to breathe, even through the stifling humidity.

As we started moving, Alden joined our side, and I peeked over at him.

"She just needs more time," he mouthed with a knowing look.

I nodded in response.

She could have all the time in the world because regardless of her choice, I was hers. I always would be. From the moment we locked eyes in that tavern back in Auryna, I was hers—wholly and unconditionally, and that was a choice that had long been out of my control.

We were on her time.

* * *

CHAPTER TWENTY SEVEN

The stench of decay reached us long before we laid eyes on the Cursed Wood, strengthened by the stagnant humid air. The mood of the group was tight as the ominous shadows came into view, greeting us like an old enemy.

Ara tensed as I wrapped an arm around her waist, but she said nothing as we neared the edge. Our horses became antsy as soon as we crossed into the shadows, the temperature dropping a few degrees with each step further into the forest.

This entrance into the woods led down a much shorter path than the one we had previously walked when bringing Ara into Ravaryn.

"Stay on high alert, and stay quiet." My voice carried to the rest of the group, the only sound in the eerily quiet forest. "We'll be through in an hour."

The minutes ticked by rather quickly as we were left undisturbed, and before long we could spy the exit. It was a lonely hole cut from the brush, barely big enough for a horse and its rider.

The sight of it pulled a relieved breath from Ara, and I forced myself not to react. She had allowed my hold to remain for the entire hour—the closest we had been in days—and I didn't want to push her boundaries now.

We were mere feet away from the exit when the rustling of underbrush whispered through the silence, and a few thin tree trunks swayed briefly.

"Men," I breathed, and we tightened our circle.

The horses pawed and huffed anxiously as we froze, studying the tree line. A minute passed with no other sounds or sightings of movement.

I started to give the order to move when something bounded through the trees—something much larger than us.

A dozen swords unsheathed simultaneously as the darkness around us deepened, even in midday light. Shadows swirled along the ground, caressing the horses' uneasy feet. They neighed and shuffled, pulling at their reins with a newfound panic.

"If I tell you to run, Ara, *please* run," I said, but she didn't reply. "Ara—"

I peeked over her shoulder at her face. She wasn't scared; she was listening. Her eyes were glued to the south, her ear tilted in that direction.

"Ara," Ewan shouted as he reigned his horse closer, moving in her line of sight.

Her gaze flicked to him momentarily before she smiled and leaped down.

"What are you—" I started.

"Just trust me." She turned to the darkest part of the forest.

"That's an awfully big ask right now, Ara," I breathed, but she didn't seem to hear a word as she stepped into the shadows and disappeared.

Panic colored my vision red. I jumped from my horse and sprinted after her. Grabbing her shirt, I snatched her back into my chest as a massive feline beast appeared, armored from head to tail in slick black scales—a creature of night.

Two soulless abysses stared back at me as it growled, slowly stalking forward.

Ara tapped my arm. "I'll be all right."

"No." I didn't release her. "There's no way in any hell I am letting you walk into his clutches."

She turned in my arms and rested a hand on my chest. "Rogue, I'll be fine. I don't know how I know, but..." She

CHAPTER TWENTY SEVEN

peeked back at it. "This is the same creature of night I controlled during the battle. I can just feel it. *She* remembers me somehow. I can…I can still feel the remnants of my magic on her. It's like I left a part of myself with her."

Ara shoved at me gently, and against every screaming instinct, I released her. My heart thrummed in my chest as I watched her edge closer to the creature of night, closer to death.

She stopped a foot away from it, hesitating. My jaw clenched as the beast stepped closer, cautiously sniffing her hair. Its breath blew her strands of brown away from her face, and Ara laughed lightly.

Then…the beast purred like a simple house cat.

My mouth fell open as Ara placed a hand on its snout, rubbing between its closed eyes as it sank to the ground. It flattened beneath Ara's touch, reveling in her pets.

Alden's voice rang out behind us as the others joined me. "What…"

"It remembers her," I whispered, peeking at them.

"Her power continues to defy all reasoning," Alden said. "They may be deemed Storm Bringers, but it is much more than that. It's the manipulation of energy…of life itself. I fear there may be no bounds to what she can do."

"You fear?"

"With all magic comes a price. If she left a piece of herself with this creature, it begs the question… What piece?"

My gaze shifted back to her. Ara sat on the ground, cross-legged as she scratched behind the beast's ear.

She controlled this beast and the wyvern, if only briefly. That's two—two creatures who owned bits of her, whatever or wherever those bits came from. Her soul, her magic…her life.

"All right. I can't stay much longer. You see those guys?" She pointed a thumb back at us. "They're waiting on me."

It whined as she stood and dusted her trousers with a sigh.

"Don't worry. I'm sure we'll be passing through these parts again soon, and I'll bring you a treat. Promise."

With one final pat, Ara turned back to us. The beast remained on the ground with its paws tucked beneath its chin as it watched her return.

No one said a word as she passed. She swung onto our horse and settled in the saddle.

"Ready?" she asked with arched brows.

Alden and I startled before returning to our horses.

With a renewed breath, she smiled. These were her first smiles in days, and my first real breaths. I remained on the ground, taking the reins to lead the horse. Ara furrowed her brows but said nothing.

This opening was small and always set my nerves on high alert.

I stepped through the opening first, feeling a bit lighter than I did moments prior. Green rolling fields and an abundance of wildflowers swayed in the breeze, glowing under the bright summer sun. Small birds flitted about, sucking the nectar from various buds between the abnormally tall trees scattered among the hills.

"It's beautiful," Ara said. Glancing over my shoulder at her, my eyes roamed over her pale form atop my pitch-black horse—a beautiful contrast. The breeze blew her hair, the sun glinting off her cheeks, slick with a sheen of sweat.

"Yes, still just as beautifu—"

Squelch.

CHAPTER TWENTY SEVEN

An arrow struck the horse's shoulder, and Ara shouted as it reared back. She gripped the horn, narrowly preventing her fall.

"Take cover!" I shouted to others as I jumped out of the line of impact as its hooves came crashing back down.

Ara yanked the reins back, and her horse turned as a rope fell around her shoulders. Her horse galloped forward as she was jerked back, falling from the horse. She hit the ground with a hard thud, choking and gasping as she clutched at her chest. The rope went taut, and she was dragged back several feet as if it was attached to a running horse.

Jerking my hand out, the rope lit on fire and disintegrated, releasing her as I sprinted to her side. I wrapped my arm around her, and my hand met wet warmth. I slowly pulled it away to reveal blood coating her back.

She hissed as I wrapped my arm under her shoulders and lifted her. She rose to her feet, stumbling as I guided her back to the forest as quickly as she could move.

"Where are they?" she whispered.

"I don't know," I answered, keeping an eye over our shoulders.

I couldn't see our attackers, which meant they must have been hiding somewhere—either behind the trees or in the ditches between hills.

"Down!" Alden screamed as he strode from the forest, his hands crackling.

We dropped, and I covered her head as arrows struck the ground all around us. Ara screamed, tensing as her hand shot down to her leg. I clenched my jaw as I peeked.

An arrow protruded from Ara's calf.

My teeth could've cracked under the pressure of my

grinding as I slowly rose to my feet. A wave of heat rolled over my body as black smog covered us. Bones cracked and joints popped as the scales crawled over my skin.

The rage and adrenaline poured through my veins, preventing any pain at all.

As razor-edged teeth tore through my gums, I dropped the smoke veil, revealing my dragon form to the humans for the first time—massive, blood-red, and *enraged.*

The ground shook beneath us as I roared a deep, guttural warning, echoed by the roar of flames. It was aimed in their general direction, and satisfaction rang through me as screams bellowed, the scent of burnt flesh permeating the air.

A bolt of Alden's blue lightning raced toward them and landed on the structure they hid behind. It sizzled up and over, shattering the shield like pieces of broken glass, shards tumbling to the ground before they disappeared into thin air.

My breath caught.

It was more than a small group of soldiers.

At least a hundred men stared back at us, armed and ready, only a small fraction blackened.

Nobody moved. Nobody even had time to before the wyvern Ara had flown down on swooped and leveled part of their army with his massive wings, throwing them back into each other. Those who were narrowly missed scattered, distracted and disoriented by the sight of a wyvern they didn't even know existed.

With that, I flapped my wings and leaped into the air, creating a gust of wind that tousled the trees of the Cursed Wood.

One of their men shouted an order, and the ranks ran

forward with swords at the ready.

I glanced back to Ara as our small group joined her. She rose, parts of her soaked in her own blood and her eyes crackling as if she contained the storms themselves.

Her gaze met mine, and her lips twisted into a devilish grin seconds before the sky darkened. Ominous thunder was their only warning.

Lightning struck at the core of their army and ricocheted in every direction, illuminating their terrified faces enough for me to see where their higher-ranking officers were stationed.

* * *

Ara

Rogue's enormous form would have cast half their army in shadows if it wasn't already as dark as midnight.

Liquid fire spewed from his mouth, consuming the backside of their ranks as the front lines raced toward us.

We were greatly outnumbered, but not out-powered. Not this time. Not even the sickening scents and sounds of war could overtake me as my panic was tightly leashed.

Ewan, Lee, Delphia, Alden, and our few soldiers raced forward on horseback, slicing through at least a dozen men. Alden's magic struck the hearts of several soldiers, and they fell to the ground mid-step as they were electrocuted.

The last time we faced Adonis' leagues, I had been forced to the sidelines, helpless to do anything but watch.

Not today.

No, today, I was one of the most powerful people in this

field.

Today, I was Queen of Ravaryn, and I would defend my people with my life.

Swiveling back on my heel, I sprinted to our horse and started to swing onto his back when my creature of night crept from the forest. Her eyes were darker as shadows poured from their sockets.

She stalked forward with a low growl.

"Hungry?"

* * *

Rogue

My fire was diminishing, but the back half of the army was in ash, as were all of their supply wagons.

The air was thick with smoke as I dipped my wing, turning back toward Ara, when my blood went cold.

Ripping through man after man was Ara's beast with her seated firmly on its back. Ropes of crackling light held her atop it as a dozen more bolts struck those around her.

Wait.

Not struck.

Pulled.

She held her trembling hands out to the side, back bowed as lightning sizzled in pulses toward her palms, returning to her as if it had belonged to her all along. A dozen men dropped, and her head shifted forward slowly as her beast continued in a spray of blood and screams.

A mass of dark shadows surrounded them on the ground,

swallowing those the beast wasn't tearing into. When it dissipated, all that remained were the soldiers' blackened bones.

Veins of glowing white crept up Ara's arms, her shoulders, her neck, her face—all reaching for her illuminated eyes, now bright enough to light the entire field.

It was like staring into the sun if it were an icy white.

I dove down and landed beside her with pride in my chest. Her gaze greeted me briefly before I turned and swiped the men running at us with my spiked tail, shredding them before they hit the ground.

Another idiot raced forward with a raised sword, and I lowered my head, giving a low warning growl before opening my mouth and incinerating him. Nothing—not even his sword—remained.

My magic's well was tapped, but at least I had rid the world of one more imbecile.

Who charges at a fucking dragon with nothing but a sword?

My laugh came out as a rumble as I turned forward and snapped my jaw around another soldier, tossing him to the side.

I swiveled at the sound of hissing and was met with a loud squelch.

A deep roar released from my lips as a spear embedded through my wing and into my front shoulder, anchoring me in this position. Blood trickled from the wound, pooling at my feet.

Before I could react, Ara strode toward me, her entire form glowing like the moon.

Her eyes flashed to me as her hands gripped the wooden rod.

"Sorry," she said with a tone that was less than apologetic and yanked.

Another roar ripped from me as the spear was torn from the muscle in my shoulder. Another yank and the barbs of the spearhead shredded the leather skin of my wing.

She dropped it as pain sliced through the wound and blood spurted from my shoulder. It must have hit a vein or artery, if the amount of blood flowing down my leg was any indication.

I was losing it fast—too fast. My skin went cold within seconds as my head began to swim. I stumbled a step then another before falling to the ground with a thud.

Ara didn't waste a second. There wasn't a speck of fear on her face as she rested her hands on my wing, and her veins of white sank beneath my skin. My entire body clenched as it sizzled and burned its way through my body to my shoulder. I could feel every bolt, every crackle, with excruciating clarity.

It was nearly unbearable until the pain dimmed. The blood stopped flowing. The wounds scabbed. Another few seconds and they disappeared entirely.

She gasped as her electric vines withdrew from me back into her palms.

"Go."

I was about to leap into the air when another spear shot through the air and struck the neck of her creature.

"No!" Ara screamed, sprinting toward her.

The creature hit the ground with a thud, the shadows seeping from its eyes. By the time Ara made it, the sockets were empty, and her beast was gone.

She fell to her knees before it, her hands hovering over the wound, but even her magic couldn't heal the dead, and when she realized, her cries were the only thing I could hear.

CHAPTER TWENTY SEVEN

My eyes darted to where the spears were coming from and back to her. I stepped closer, nudging her with my snout.

She turned to me with rage and sorrow in her eyes as she seethed. "Kill them all."

I launched into the air. In the distance was a large crossbow with another spear loaded in it and three terrified soldiers standing on the platform. One of them pissed himself as I started to descend with the intent of crushing it, but I leveled when I felt it.

Not only had Ara healed my wounds, but she had also refilled the well. I was nearly overflowing with power. The hardened scales along my body could barely contain the firestorm within, raging, begging, *demanding* to be released.

With a deep breath, I relinquished control.

Flames poured from my throat. The large bow shattered in a violent explosion of splintering wood, and every soldier in the general vicinity screamed, thrown back several feet before they were also engulfed in flames.

My fire blazed everything to the ground, and I didn't stop until the well ran dry again.

The entire army had fallen, diminished to a smoking pile of bone and ash.

Chapter Twenty Eight

Ara

The battle was over, but my skin could barely contain the power I had taken from those men in the form of their lives.

"What was that? How did they know?" Lee shouted as he and his once-white horse galloped back, now stained a deep, violent red.

I had killed.

I had killed *a lot*.

"I…" The word was barely audible as their conversations faded into the background.

I stood off to the side as the others congregated, questioning, shouting, recuperating. No one on our side had been killed, which was a miracle, but their side… Not one soldier had survived our wrath. It was warranted, but wrath all the same—a slaughter, and they might as well have been nothing but an offering, an army of lambs.

My hands shook. They were stained red, but not from our decimated opposition. This blood was mine and Rogue's, and my now-dead beastly friend's.

CHAPTER TWENTY EIGHT

I had no need to pierce the soldiers' flesh to drain the life from them. It hadn't been their blood I was after. No, it was their *lives,* the energy that beat their hearts and moved their muscles. What had allowed them to be born into this realm and breathe and live.

That was what I took from them. Their essence. I had consumed it and now...

Now, I had dozens of lives inside me. The power that *was* dozens of lives.

My whole body shook.

I was going to implode. My skin was going to split, and this power would return to the realm that had given it.

I turned slowly, my breaths and lips quivering. Whatever light came from me cast the others in a silver-white.

I couldn't stop it, couldn't control it.

It was too much, the power lighting me from the inside as it tried to rip free.

A tear slipped from my eye when Rogue's gaze landed on me.

His face fell, and he shoved the others out of the way as he sprinted to me.

"Hey, little storm, hey," he whispered, his hands roaming over me without touching. "It'll be all right."

Power thrashed at the thin vessel my form provided. It was too much, and I wasn't enough.

Lightning in a flimsy bottle could not be contained for long.

"I killed them."

"I know. To protect your people, *our* people, against those who would hurt them. You *saved* them."

I jerked a nod, inhaling harshly, trying to rationalize it

the way he did, but as much as it tore at me, it didn't matter. Morals and understanding didn't matter. Nothing did, because their lives were about to explode from me.

"You're hot, Ara," he whispered cautiously, and my brows furrowed. "Your skin…It's burning up."

"I'm overflowing." Another tear dropped as I ground my teeth, clenching my fists. "I can't—I don't know how much longer I can hold it. I can't be around you, any of you, not when…"

I stepped back, shaking my head. I may have taken lives today, but I wouldn't take theirs, too.

"I am *not* leaving you," he seethed, deathly serious.

"I know," I muttered. "I'm sorry…"

It would destroy them, destroy everything.

My lip quivered. Thunder rumbled in the distance as lightning raced across the sky. I was about to reach my hand up and let the sky consume me once and for all when Alden stepped forward.

"Expel it." His face was pale and tight, his chest rising quickly. "Throw it. Force it. Get rid of it. *Now*."

I locked eyes with him as my heart raced. I could barely hear him, barely see him, any of them.

"Before it destroys you, Ara. Get rid of it, in any way you can."

Get rid of it.

"Run," was their only warning, my voice booming and barely contained, and run they did.

I was vibrating by the time they hit the forest line. Delphia hung back, holding my gaze before she threw a shield over them, protecting everyone from the inevitable.

The second I could no longer see them, I erupted.

CHAPTER TWENTY EIGHT

My eyes rolled back as a flash of white shot to the sky seconds before the power exploded from me in every direction. The grass incinerated. The air electrified. The smell of rain and smoke filled my lungs as my hair stood on end.

Bolts of lightning reached for anything and everything—from me and the sky.

I pushed on every possible outlet. A torrential downpour fell from the clouds that blotted out the sun as the lightning struck again and again without end.

Then, like my worst possible nightmare, energy from my hand struck a burnt corpse and it—*he* flinched before his limbs moved. He rose to his feet as if being pulled by strings, a soulless vessel of energy.

Oh, for Goddess' sake.

I screamed and yanked the magic back before throwing it to the clouds, and he dropped to the ground.

Better left dead.

A bolt formed from me to the sky—an unyielding connection from my palms to the plains above us. I forced the power upwards in pulses again and again in an almost endless explosion.

My throat shredded as incessant screaming filled my ears.

How had I taken so much?

The bolt remained, sizzling and crackling until it had taken everything I had to offer. Only then did I collapse to the ground, which was now at least ten feet beneath me.

I free-fell, landing hard with a thud that knocked the breath from my lungs, but at least everyone was safe from me.

Rogue found me within moments, cradling my head on his lap.

"You know, it's funny," I mumbled as exhaustion clawed its

way through me. "To save your life, I took from the sky... Now, I have returned its power tenfold." I coughed and lay limp in his lap as the rain fell in a slow, miserable drizzle. "Do you think it appreciates that?"

He laughed, but it sounded broken. "I do. I really do."

My eyes were closed, and I couldn't bring myself to open them again.

"It's gone." Delphia's voice rang out from the distance, a faraway sound that hung heavy with sadness. "As far as I can see... it's gone."

* * *

Peeling my eyes open, I groaned at the pounding headache that stabbed behind them.

I ran a hand down my face before glancing around and sitting straight up. I was alone in a small tent, the sunlight shining through the tarp. *Where—*

My eyes dropped to my hands, my clothes. No filth. No blood. I was dressed in clean, dry clothes.

My stomach sank, and I swallowed hard as my throat tightened, threatening to choke me as Rogue's words came back to me.

You saved them.

Somehow, the sentiment didn't feel like enough to satiate the guilt that permeated my being. Maybe it was the fact that I knew, we all knew, Adonis had another hundred men armed and ready. Hell, maybe even another hundred thousand. His endless supply of bodies was his greatest asset.

Or maybe it was the fact that I hadn't hated the act. The

rush of power, the thrill of turning the odds in our favor with my own two hands...

I had felt indestructible. Formidable. Terrifying.

As a woman in a man's world, that feeling was an addictive, dangerous thing—a dangerously eye-opening thing, revealing just how fragile a man can be in the face of a powerful woman.

I should have felt irredeemable. I should have been disgusted and wracked with guilt, but I wasn't, and that was what I hated—that I didn't hate myself for it.

The creature of the night, however...her death cut me deep. She was only there for me, and it was because of me she was killed. I had hopped off to pull the spear from Rogue, leaving her vulnerable, and then I couldn't save her in return.

Tears pricked my eyes as I stood with a deep, shaky breath and found my boots. I pulled one on and was lacing the other when Rogue entered the tent. His eyes shot wide as he rushed to my side.

"You're awake."

I cocked my head, raising my brows. "Yes...?"

"Ara, it's been a full day."

I rocked back, reclining on the pelt. "Oh."

"How do you feel?" he asked hesitantly.

"All right. I have a splitting migraine, but I'm fine," I sighed as I finished lacing up the other boot. I stood and took a step toward the opening flap. "Where is everyone else?"

His arm barred my way, his jaw clenched, and my heart jolted.

"What?"

"There's something else you need to know." He ushered me back to where I was seated and sat with me.

"You're scaring me," I said with a nervous chuckle. "Wait, did I hurt someone?"

"No. None of our own." He inhaled deeply. "Do you remember what happened after the battle?"

I dropped my eyes, searching for any recollection. "There's only bits and pieces. I remember feeling like I was going to explode…and the lightning…and…" My gaze darted to his. "Oh, dear Goddess, I rose a dead body."

His face fell in shock, his eyes wider than I had ever seen. "You what?"

"Exactly what I said. A bolt of energy hit a corpse and he…stood like a puppet. He moved, but he was definitely dead."

Rogue stared blankly at me and blinked once. Twice. "I didn't know that."

"I didn't like it."

"I wouldn't assume so, but we should definitely tell the others about that," he said.

I nodded. "It seems like vital information. *Alarming* information."

"I agree," he mumbled, shaking his head. "But back to what I was getting at. Well, when your power erupted like that, it went in every direction. Up, down, and *out*. You…It…The—"

"Spit it out. You're scaring me."

"Your power incinerated the Cursed Wood. Not all of it, but at least a third."

I inhaled sharply and shot to my feet. "What?" He gripped my wrist, but I jerked it free. "No, I need to see."

I stalked from the tent and froze.

"Where are we?" I asked to anyone nearby as I stared over a charred wasteland.

CHAPTER TWENTY EIGHT

A hand landed on my shoulder and turned me slowly. I resisted for a moment before following its lead to find what remained of the forest, the edges charred and leafless.

A choked sob broke from me. "And the creatures?"

I peeked up to find the hand belonged to Alden, but he didn't answer.

"What of the creatures?" My words were becoming increasingly shrill as panic set in. I jerked my face to him when he remained silent, and his eyes swam with tears as he shook his head. "Oh, Goddess. Oh, no."

The world spun beneath my feet as nausea rolled in my gut. I reached out, latching onto Alden's shoulder as I retched. Standing, I wiped my mouth and sent out the feelers of my magic.

I found creatures small and large, scattered through the remaining forest but they were far, far away from here. Safe from me.

"I killed them," I whispered.

"It was an accident," Rogue said, his voice soft.

"Do you think they'd care if it was an accident?" I screamed, but he didn't flinch.

Rogue didn't deserve my anger; it wasn't him I was angry at. It was myself. *I* killed those animals, and I didn't want comforting words. I didn't deserve them. I needed to be angry. I needed them to be angry at me because I destroyed a forest, an ancient wood booming with life—or *was* booming. They *should* be angry.

Rogue's face was tight. "I think they would forgive you, if beasts from the Cursed Wood could do that."

My face flushed, and I shoved at his chest as tears slid down my cheeks. "I doubt it. I think they would have preferred to live, but I killed them. I killed them all—the humans, the animals, the trees. I'm a murderer, Rogue."

"Then what of us?" Alden questioned lightly behind me.

I swiveled around to find him and Ewan standing side by side with matching looks of empathy.

"What of you?"

"If you're a murderer, then what does that make us?" Alden asked.

I opened my mouth to respond but stopped, snapping it shut again.

Ewan stepped forward. "The casualties of war do not make a murderer, Ara."

"If not them, then it would have been us," Alden said. "While the creatures' deaths are regrettable, you took down at least a third of those men alone. You are a force to be reckoned with, and that power *saved* us. It helped save Ravaryn."

My lip quivered. "None of that matters to me right now. Maybe it makes me a horrible person, but the death of those innocent animals hurts me a lot more than those soldiers. They didn't have a role in this, and yet they were incinerated all the same."

Rogue threw an arm around my shoulder and swiveled me back to him in a tight, breath-stealing hug. "No, it does not make you a horrible person. It just means you have the biggest heart." He kissed the top of my head. "I'm so sorry."

"It's not fair. Those poor animals…" Another cry broke from my lips, and I clutched his shirt in my fists.

"It was an accident, Ara. I know those words don't mean much right now, but they are the truth."

Maybe I would believe it one day, but right now, I just felt

CHAPTER TWENTY EIGHT

sick. Disgustingly sick.

I don't know how long we remained there as I sobbed into his chest, Rogue solid as stone with his arms wrapped around me, but when I had no tears left to cry, I took a deep breath and released him.

Even with my swollen eyes and pounding headache, it felt like they deserved more mourning. It would never be enough.

Rogue led me to a nearby rock and set me on it like he was scared to leave me as he went to help pack up camp. I sat while the others flitted about. Though I knew I should get up and help, I couldn't bring myself to move.

I just stared off, looking but not seeing, as the feelers of my magic searched repeatedly for any other sign of life, but there was nothing. It was the same every time. The same trees, the same plant life, the same creatures until—

I sat up straighter, cocking my head to the side.

A small flicker of life caught my attention, something so minuscule, I hadn't noticed before, but it almost felt... familiar. I waited for the thump of a beating heart and took off sprinting.

"Ara!" Lee shouted behind me. "Guys, she's—"

I ran to the rocky terrain—invisible when shrouded by trees, but now exposed and blackened—and searched, following the small thumping heart.

Tucked away in a crevice was a tiny creature of the night.

Another choked breath broke from me as I sank to my knees. "Oh, little guy, I'm so sorry." I reached my hand in to grab him, but he nipped at my hand with razor-sharp fangs, and I hissed as blood spots speckled my skin. "I deserved that."

He was no bigger than a kitten with eyes just as dark as his mother's, but where her skin had been scaled, his was bare and soft, and based on his size, he was much too small to hunt.

He was vulnerable.

I turned as the others came running up behind me and held him up.

The guys' faces fell while Delphia jogged to my side and reached for him. "Aw, poor thing. He's tiny."

I handed him to her, and she cradled him to her chest.

"He'll need us," I said. "He'll never make it out here."

"No, he's too small to hunt for himself, and this"—she gestured to the blackened ground—"wouldn't provide him anything, even if he could."

I dropped my eyes as the guilt returned full force, weighing in my gut. Clearing my throat, I walked to Rogue's side, and he slid an arm around my waist.

"The little guy can come with us," Rogue said. "Just another wild creature to add to the growing list of odd pets at Draig Hearth."

"He'll fit right in," Delphia cooed as she raised him to her face and kissed the top of his head. He growled—or tried to, but it came out as more of a mewl—and she laughed, tucking him close to her chest again.

* * *

Monotonous days of riding passed, and my body was stiffer than it had ever been.

We rose early this morning, beating the sun to the road, and had been going for hours. The sun was past its peak, and the heat was stifling as the afternoon set in, the air thick and

CHAPTER TWENTY EIGHT

sticky.

We took frequent breaks, filling our flasks and letting the horses drink from the streams, but it was still rough. The horses—and people—were slick with sweat. The closer we got to the coast, the more humid it was, our sweat clinging to us like an irritating wet blanket rather than cooling us.

"How much farther until Rainsmyre?" I asked.

"Just a few hours," Lee said.

"Goddess, I forgot how hot it is down here, especially in the summer," Ewan groaned as he dipped his hands in the creek and poured water over his brown curls.

"I kind of like it," Lee said with a smile. He was reclining beneath a tree with Delphia, slicing an apple. He offered a bite to the small creature, but he refused.

"I'm worried about him," Delphia said, her brows furrowed. "He hasn't really eaten anything. Not fruit, cheese, not even the jerky."

"Maybe he's supposed to be drinking milk?" Rogue said as he stood from the bank, his hair and white tunic soaked.

My eyes raked over his form, reveling in the way the fabric clung to his well-muscled chest, and my ogling didn't go unnoticed. When my gaze crawled back up his body to meet his, he offered me a smirk and a wink before joining them under the tree.

"Well, we definitely don't have that," I said, crouching beside Delphia and the creature.

Delphia handed him to me, and he studied me just as I did him. I set him down to explore, and he took small cautious steps, creeping toward the edge of the water and sipping from it.

The breeze blew, and we all sighed, lifting our faces.

"That was a gift from the Goddess. I just know it," Alden said, his thick, long hair piled on top of his head. "We need to get thinner clothing in Rainsmyre, some more suited to this heat. Surely they have that, right?"

Rogue and Lee howled with laughter, but it was Lee who said, "You two are just big babies, you know that?"

"Well, some of us haven't spent our lives traveling. The east coast isn't this…sticky," Ewan said, wiping his face with a cloth. "I miss it."

"Me too," Alden and I said at the same time, pulling another round of laughter.

Rogue smiled down at me as he wrapped an arm around my shoulder, pulling me against his side. "We'll return home soon."

"Until then, let me go, because it is way too damn hot to be this close to anyone." I dipped out from under his arm.

He laughed and slid his hand under my chin to tilt my face to his. "As if you don't want to be *much* closer than this," he whispered low enough for only me to hear.

My cheeks flushed, and he gave me a quick kiss before releasing me.

I chuckled, dropping my gaze to our little beast. His snout was in the air, sniffing for something. "Hey, look."

He followed his nose in a slow, clumsy run. Delphia and I followed after him as he cut through the grass and found a dead rodent. We both peeked at each other, grimacing, as he devoured it, consuming the decayed rat within minutes. When he was finished, he licked his paws in contentment and flopped over on his side, his belly bulging.

"Oh my," Delphia said, her face nearly green.

"He's a scavenger." I scooped him up and took him back to

CHAPTER TWENTY EIGHT

the creek. He thrashed and fought as I rinsed him off, but at least he no longer smelled like decay. "He'll be easy enough to feed."

He napped in Delphia's lap the rest of the journey to Rainsmyre.

As the city came into view, the stench of fishing boats and dirty ports drifted in our direction, and I held back a gag as I dreamed of the sweet warm scent of Nautia.

"Ah, yes, the stench of Rainsmyre—its most telltale sign that you've made it," Lee said, inhaling deeply.

"Nothing like Nautia." Alden covered his nose with a cloth.

The city was much larger than Nautia, the buildings taller and wider. They were made of dark, worn wood, some painted, some stained with age.

"It's got its own charm, though. You just wait." Lee hummed with excitement. "I believe one of my old pals still lives here, too."

"I don't know if I want to see these 'charms,'" I said, my eyes flitting to him with suspicion.

"You don't like seafood and good music? This is a fishing village, after all. They have the best fish you'll ever eat, and the fishermen work in swing shifts, all hours of the day. They have to go somewhere in their off time when they aren't sleeping, so the taverns are always lively. There is always some kind of music playing, as the fishermen have developed a taste for that, and they have the coin to support it."

"Believe it or not, Rainsmyre is a hot spot for musicians hoping to make a living by playing," Rogue added.

My brows were nearly in my hairline as I studied the streets ahead of us again. People walked on both sides of us along the dirt paths while we rode down the roughly paved streets. The women wore wispy, colorful dresses that blew in the wind while the men were dressed in trousers and sleeveless, linen tunics, some revealing their legs in cut-off pants, the edges frayed around the bottom. Everyone's hair was cut short, even the women, their hair barely reaching their shoulders.

"Now see, they know how to dress for this heat," Alden whispered, gesturing to them as they walked by.

"Are you going to cut your hair and trousers too, then, Alden?" I teased.

"Never," he said with mock offense before his face softened. "No, my Ara liked my hair long, so I haven't cut it since she passed away."

The smile slid from my face a fraction. "Oh. I didn't know."

He shrugged, offering a light smile. "Well, I've never told anyone."

Lee led us to a tavern he had been to before. It was a large building with two floors and several windows, some cracked open and coated with a white fogginess. I squinted at it closely. It was as if the windows were…

"They're frozen," I said.

"There are some with water magic who can manipulate temperature, and they are paid *handsomely* around here. When they freeze the windows, the air that blows through is pretty damn cold. It can cool the entire building within a few hours, and they'll stay frozen indefinitely."

My mouth fell open. "That's genius."

"Revolutionary. Let's go in there," Alden said in a rush, and Lee laughed. "We need food, anyway. My stomach is about to eat the rest of me."

"That was the plan," Lee said. "A friend of mine used to own this place."

CHAPTER TWENTY EIGHT

As Rogue settled a glamour over himself, he opened the door and motioned us in.

Lee lifted a brow as Rogue's wings disappeared and the red in his eyes diminished to a deep brown.

"Better to be safe than sorry." Rogue shrugged.

Chapter Twenty Nine

Ara

Lee's friend, Kal—a seven-foot-tall behemoth of a man—was more than welcoming.

He wore a stained apron tied around his waist with his blonde hair tied back in a ponytail as he moved behind the bar, handing out plate after plate. A crooked grin was plastered on his face the entire evening as he served us and his patrons.

"It is quite the pleasure to meet you, Your Majesty. Not something I thought I'd see in this lifetime," he said, his voice deep and flecked with an accent I couldn't place. "And you, too, Ara Wrynwood. Now, I did meet your dad years ago, out on the other side of the kingdom. In Nautia, I believe? That's a nice little town."

"Aye, it is," Ewan said.

"No formalities. Please, call me Rogue." He stuck a hand over the bar and shook Kal's hand.

"How did you meet Vaelor?" Alden said as he finished his third bowl of stew. "He was my son."

"Ah, so you are the legend who sired him? He spoke highly

CHAPTER TWENTY NINE

of you," he said.

Alden grinned. "Aye, that I am."

"Well, I was young, we both were, and I was traveling the realm. I just happened to be in the tavern—the Sopping Sailor, I believe—at the same time as him. Now, that man could drink anyone under the table, including me, which is a feat to be sure."

Alden and Ewan laughed. "You got that right. He had a special talent."

Kal sighed, turning to Lee. "So, care to tell me why you're really here? Because I have a sneaking suspicion it's not just to see me."

Lee swallowed a swig of mead and cleared his throat. "We're actually here looking for someone."

"I figured as much. Not many people come this way for anything else. Who ya searching for?"

Lee's eyes flitted to Rogue, and Kal's gaze followed.

"My grandfather, Drakyth Draki."

Kal's dropped his eyes to the bar as he wiped the counter with a rag. "Well, I'd say you're about thirty years too late."

"Damn," Rogue muttered under his breath. "We thought we might be."

"How did he…?" I asked.

His warm, brown eyes shifted to me. "His son, Adrastus."

Rogue's jaw clenched as his eyes flicked to Alden. "Of course, it was."

"We found letters between Drakyth and my son, Vaelor," Alden said, shaking his head. "Drakyth had started to express concerns that Adrastus would do something before they stopped suddenly."

"Everything I know are just the stories that have been told, as I moved here after his death." A patron stumbled into the counter and interrupted Kal to order a shot, already too drunk to care what we were discussing. Kal grabbed a bottle of liquor and tipped the nozzle down, pouring the liquid into a tiny glass as he continued. "He burned the entire house down, Drakyth included, but not before…" He paused, clearing his throat as the patron tipped the shot back and slammed the empty glass back on the bar with a sloppy grin. Kal glared at him, and the drunk staggered off.

Turning back to Rogue with a sympathetic gaze, Kal leaned forward on his elbows to whisper, "He removed his wings, sheared them straight from his back. They were found nailed to the wreckage."

My mouth hung open in disgust, my gut twisting. Rogue's wings flinched behind him, his shoulders tensed, hands clenched around his mug.

"From the stories I've heard, Drakyth was well-loved in the town. His son? Not so much, and after the murder, he was hated. *Deeply.* Rainsmyre was glad to hear of Adrastus' assassination, to be truthful. I heard more than a few people celebrated the end of his life."

"I think most people were glad to be rid of Adrastus," Alden said, his own jaw tight and brows furrowed. "I knew Drakyth briefly. He was a good man, just scared and scarred by the war and the loss of his family. I hate to hear he came to such a brutal end."

"My dear old dad sure knew how to ruin lives," Rogue uttered and downed the contents of his mug. "Well, I suppose it's not the person we're looking for as much as it is something that was in his possession."

Kal's face piqued with curiosity.

CHAPTER TWENTY NINE

"We're looking for the crown. *The* crown."

"Ah, yes, the Obsidian Crown. Speaking of…" Kal said, dropping behind the bar as he crouched. Alden leaned over the counter to look, and Rogue's mouth opened to speak but snapped shut when Kal popped back up with a broad smile and an intricate blue decanter. "Ah, here we are."

He popped the cork out and poured seven shots—one for each of us and one for himself. He slid them in front of us, and we paused, confused, as Kal lifted his glass.

"A toast to the beasts who came before us and will be here long after us." Rogue's head cocked to the side in question, and Kal's laughter bellowed. "The Wyverns, of course."

Hesitantly, we clinked glasses before downing them all in a burning gulp.

"Well, that cost me a small fortune, but best believe it was worth every cent to drink with my King and Queen, the Skyborn of Ravaryn."

I choked on my chaser of mead and wiped my mouth. That had been only days ago. How had the word beaten us here?

"It truly is the greatest honor to meet you, to drink with you." Kal dipped his head to Rogue, and to my utter surprise, Rogue's cheeks tinted pink. My mouth fell open in a surprised smile.

A woman stepped up beside us then, asking Kal for another drink.

As Kal turned to skim the shelves of alcohol at her request, I leaned over and swiped a thumb over Rogue's burning cheeks. "That's a sight I never thought I'd see. Rogue Draki, embarrassed?"

He laughed under his breath, shaking his head and swatting my hand away. "Don't get used to it."

"So, how did you hear about that?" I asked as Kal turned back to us.

"Oh, everyone's heard it. Word travels far and wide, particularly when it's about a chosen Draig and his half-human queen who possesses the magic of the skies." Kal lifted his brow, nodding.

Rogue and I peeked at each other, my own cheeks flushing now.

"You know," Kal said, leaning on his elbows again, "I was actually wondering when this would get brought up. I'm quite curious. What are they like, the wyverns?"

Rogue's grin matched Kal's as he chuckled. "Magnificent. Larger and more powerful than anything you could ever imagine."

Kal let out a low whistle, shaking his head. "I would love to see one in person someday."

I smiled, peeking at Rogue.

Pride shone in his eyes as he nodded. "You will. A few are already here, and when I have the crown, the rest will follow."

Kal stood straighter. "Ah, yes, the crown. I'm assuming since you're here, Adrastus didn't take it with him?"

Rogue shook his head. "No, and since only those with Draki blood are able to touch it, no one else could've moved it."

"So it must be at the house, then." Kal ran a hand over his chin before he clicked his tongue. "Everything there was burned to the ground, though; I don't know if it would've survived the flames."

"It wouldn't have burned," Alden cut in. "Obsidian is forged by the flowing veins of fire within the ground. Nothing up here could torch it."

CHAPTER TWENTY NINE

Kal glanced about the tavern, walking around the wooden bar when he found who he was looking for. He strode to a barmaid and whispered something to her. She nodded without so much as a glance in our direction before continuing on her way.

Returning to us, he pulled his apron off. "I'll take you there myself."

* * *

Drakyth's house was outside of town, sitting in its own meadow carved from a vibrant forest.

Remnants of the structure were left—the blackened floorboards, a few crumbling walls—but nature had reclaimed most of it. Vines of green and blooms in an array of colors contrasted the crumbling, burnt pieces as they consumed the house. A few trees had sprouted through the cracks in the floors, still thin and growing. Even the sound of birdsong carried over the small meadow on the breeze.

Everything but the burned evidence of tragedy was beautiful, as if nature herself were trying to erase the death from the location.

Rogue swallowed hard as he studied the area. "I don't understand. Where could the crown be? There's not a room left. Not a closet or cupboard. Nothing."

"I don't know," Kal replied.

"We can still check the area, see if there are any loose floorboards, hidden doors…" Ewan said.

Rogue gave a defeated nod and walked forward down the overgrown dirt path.

We searched every remaining inch of the house as well as

the surrounding field. There was nothing—no sign of Fae life or the crown.

"This doesn't make sense," Rogue said, pacing with wisps of smoke trailing his steps. "I know Adrastus didn't have it. He may have been a tyrant, but he wasn't a clever one. He was boastful and egotistical. We would have known, and in Stryath's office, I saw where the crown would have been. I saw the hole cut from the wall that would have held the crown when it wasn't claimed."

"Someone has to have taken it," Lee said.

"Who could have done that?" I asked, but the blood drained from my face as the words left my mouth. I stopped and waited for an answer—any answer—but when there was none, I said the only possible name. "Adonis could have taken it."

Rogue's face whipped to me, his eyes burning orbs of fire as his chest rose and fell quickly.

"He wouldn't have known where it was. He was cast from his father's house before he could even walk," Alden said, waving his hands about.

"Are you sure?" Ewan asked. "Is there any possibility he could have taken it?"

Alden shook his head. "There's no way to know for sure. What I do know is that Adrastus' manor was far from here, and Adonis and his mother would have had to travel a great distance to end up here. Even then, how would he know where Drakyth lived? Where he hid the crown?"

"That's the only lead we have right now," Delphia huffed. "Have we considered that when Drakyth said the crown was safe, maybe he wasn't referring to a place? Maybe it was a person. If he left it with someone, then…" She stepped back,

CHAPTER TWENTY NINE

her eyes dropping to her feet.

That made my head spin. I sighed deeply as I sank to the ground and sat on the lush grass. The little creature ran over to me and crawled into my lap as I crossed my legs. If she was right, the crown could be anywhere in Ravaryn. Hell, it could be in Auryna. It could be anywhere with anyone. It would take entirely too long to find it—if we ever did.

It seemed everyone had the same realization as I did as the mood plummeted. They all sat around me in a circle.

"Someone here has to know," I said, breaking the silence. "He wouldn't have left the crown in the hands of a single person without some kind of plan. Someone has to know, has to be on the lookout for when the next chosen Draig came looking. Whether it was you or someone a hundred years from now, *someone* would have been chosen eventually, and they would have followed in our exact footsteps. They would've come looking."

Rogue nodded, his face tight.

"You're right," Alden said. "Unlike his son, Drakyth was intelligent, and he valued family. He wouldn't have left his *worthy* descendants stranded."

"Surely not," Lee said as if he were desperately clinging to his last strands of hope.

"If that someone is still here, we *will* find them, my King," Kal vowed. "Tell me what I need to do."

And right here, in this knocked down but never defeated circle of mismatched family, was where our last ditch plan was hatched.

* * *

Delphia and I entered the tavern, scantily clad in small dresses. Our hair was curled and loose, our lips lined with rouge.

I could feel eyes on us as we walked to the bar where Kal stood, greeting him like any other patron would. He handed us two mugs of mead, and we took them gratefully before turning to recline our elbows on the wooden bar.

My eyes grazed over our men, seated around a discreet table in the corner. Rogue's wings were once again hidden behind a glamour so as not to draw attention.

Our plan was half-baked at best, but we wanted to act as soon as possible. If Adonis was already sending more men, then we were running out of time. Magic had its limits, and we were outnumbered. We *needed* the wyverns in our ranks, and the only way to do that was to open the line of communication between them and Rogue.

Still, with Drakyth being a loved member of the community, those who pillaged his home and stole his belongings, even after death, were not likely to willingly come forward with that information. So, here we were, posed as helpless, beautiful women to talk drunk men out of their secrets. They were all too easy to manipulate—clueless, overconfident creatures easily distracted with a little cleavage and batting eyelashes.

If it was left with someone, we would find them. If the crown was stolen, we would find them, too—one way or another.

Our first target appeared in my line of sight, snapping me from my thoughts—a desperate man.

"Hi, there," Delphia drawled as her fingers slid along her necklace that hung dangerously close to her exposed

CHAPTER TWENTY NINE

cleavage.

It did not go unnoticed as his eyes followed like a starved man.

It didn't take long before he led us back to his group of drunken men. We sweet-talked them until they were completely intoxicated, their slurred words getting more rambunctious by the minute.

"So, have you all always been fishermen?" I asked, scooting closer and leaning on my elbows in feigned interest. They smirked as their eyes fell to my cleavage, and I could've sworn I smelled faint wisps of smoke.

I resisted the urge to look back over my shoulder at Rogue as they answered.

"Oh, aye. All our lives," a man missing a few teeth said. He leaned forward, and I stifled a gag at the stench of his breath.

"All your lives?" I asked, raising a brow. He nodded, and I hopped into a chair closer to him. Delphia eyed me closely as she leaned in to listen. "Then you must know the legend. We heard there used to be a Draig here. Is that true?"

His face lit up like he held the answer to all my problems. "Oh, a Draig he was. Mighty and quite bitchy."

I reclined in my seat as their group howled with laughter, huffing as I crossed my arms over my chest.

"Oh, sweetheart, don't be like that," he drawled, reaching a hand out to my thigh.

There was definitely smoke in the room.

I shifted and pulled my leg from under his palm, crossing it over my other one as I rested on my elbows and leaned forward again. "Then tell me. Whatever became of him? Does he still terrorize these parts?"

"No, he doesn't. He died a long time ago," he said and

THE LAST DRAIG

gulped down the contents of his mug.

"What about all his treasure?" Delphia hummed, her face bright and intrigued. "Don't dragons hoard treasure?"

His brows furrowed before shaking his head. "Trust me, everything was ransacked ages ago, but his murdering bitch of a son took most of what was left."

My heart sank. My smile sank. My hopes sank. My eyes dropped to my lap as I sat back, swallowing hard.

"What was left… What does that mean? Where did the rest go?" Delphia asked.

"Oh, his…" He turned to the rest of the group, who had lost interest in our conversation. "What was that guy who took Draki's shit when he died?"

"His apprentice," a rail-thin elderly man answered.

"Ah, yeah, his apprentice. He was always hanging out with that guy. Followed him around like a lost pup, he did." He laughed, taking a fresh mug from a barmaid who peeked at us with furrowed brows before flitting to the next table.

"Oh, so he took all the good treasure, then?" Delphia asked, rolling her eyes dramatically.

"Sure did. Left nothing of value for the rest of us," he groaned as if he was actually inconvenienced.

Disgust rolled through me. A man was killed, brutally, by his own son, and this drunk had the audacity to feel inconvenienced that there was nothing left for him to steal. These were exactly the type of men we were after. Any woman showing them a bit of interest—or a little leg—was like honey to the flies.

It grated my nerves, but I plastered the prettiest fake smile I could muster on my face. "Do you know where he went?"

The guy shook his head, slamming the mug down. "Why

CHAPTER TWENTY NINE

are you pestering me with all these questions? You should be showing me your tits and taking my coin, whore."

This piqued the interest of the rest of his group, and their eyes found us again with renewed enthusiasm. My heart thumped in my throat, but I swallowed it down with a large drink of whiskey.

The room was fogged with smoke even though no fireplaces were lit—not in the dead of summer. Kal opened a few more windows.

"Perhaps we are thieves on the road, and the current owner of a Draig's hoard seems like the perfect target." I slid my hand along my thigh, splitting my dress so he could see the dagger strapped to my thigh. His eyes followed, his mouth falling open before he gulped. "Do I not seem…dangerous to you, sir?"

"As dangerous as they come," the man replied with a disgustingly cocky grin. "Alas, I don't know where the lad went. I couldn't tell you, even if I wanted to." His gaze slid over me, hips to breasts. "And Goddess, do I want to."

He licked his lips and started to reach for my waist.

"Then our business is done here," I said as I jerked to my feet.

His eyes were round as saucers as his face twisted with outrage. "Like hell it is."

His hand circled my wrist and yanked me down into his lap. His other arm wrapped around my waist, locking me in this position.

"Wrong choice, buddy," was all Delphia said as she sipped her drink.

With a breathy laugh, I reached my arms back and wrapped my hands around his neck. He started to speak when the lightning crackled in my irises. The rest of his men blanched and stumbled back, knocking chairs over.

"What are you fools—"

The drunk didn't finish his sentence. Energy raced from me into him and wrapped around his heart like a vice as flames licked at his legs, confined to a small circle beneath him. I released him slowly and stood, smoothing my dress out as I did so. He was anchored in the seat, unable to move as I controlled the life within him.

I clicked my tongue as I turned to face him. The man thrashed against my hold, his eyes brimming with tears as he tried to scream through a sealed mouth.

"Oh, what was that? I couldn't hear you." I turned my ear to him, lowering closer to his face. "Oh, you're sorry?"

He nodded so hard, I thought he might break his neck.

"Too late," Rogue seethed as he stepped up behind me.

Based on the man's widened eyes and cowering, I imagined Rogue's powerful wings were on full display, his eyes a menacing, fiery orange. Pride swelled in my chest at Rogue's ability to inflict fear in people like this—sadistic cowards—with nothing more than his powerful stature.

The drunk stilled as the fire at his feet disappeared, but not for long, as his eyes lit with flickering flames—the mirror to Rogue's. Smoke rose from his skin as Rogue burned him from the inside out. Blackened char replaced his eyes as his form slumped before falling to the ground with a thud.

A wave of satisfaction washed over me.

It was then I realized the tavern was silent. I looked up slowly, dreading what I knew I would find.

All eyes were on us, their faces stunned. My heart raced, and I turned to Rogue, grabbing his hand. He lifted it to his

CHAPTER TWENTY NINE

mouth and kissed my scar, not an ounce of embarrassment or regret on his face. Walking past me, he pulled me after him as we stepped over the drunk's corpse nonchalantly and strolled through the winding maze of tables and chairs toward the door.

"Long live the Skyborn king and queen," Kal whispered as we walked passed. He lifted a glass to us with a smirk before tilting his head to the body. "And good riddance."

The eyes of every person sitting close enough to overhear his words widened, lingering on us. Time seemed to slow for a few seconds as the gears turned in their minds, but it didn't slow enough. The whispers started, spreading like wildfire from one person to the next.

They had heard of us—their Skyborn.

I would never understand how word traveled so fast across such a vast land. It was mind-boggling, and I wasn't sure I liked the idea of the entire realm knowing I was their queen. Actually, I knew I didn't, because I wasn't even sure I wanted the title, much less it being common knowledge, but it was well on its way.

If this side of the realm hadn't already known Rogue had declared his queen, they would soon.

I clenched my jaw and tipped my chin to Kal in goodbye before pushing the door open and stepping into the night.

Disheartened and severely disappointed, I turned to Rogue. "Maybe we should just retire to an inn."

He nodded as the others piled out after us, Lee right on our heels. Ewan's mouth was downturned as he and Alden strode to me. Delphia was the last out the door, unbothered as she took the creature of night from Lee.

Alden's hands hovered over my form but didn't touch me.

"Are you all right?"

"I'm fine," I sighed.

"Can't say the same for that damned fool," Lee said, elbowing Rogue with a grin.

Rogue glared at him, and Lee held up his hands in front of him. "Hey, he deserved everything he got."

"Yes, he did." I tightened my grip on Rogue's hand.

This night had been a failure. We knew the crown was gone, but had no lead as to where—not even an inkling—and we had imploded our plan by killing that man, blowing our cover. After that, I just wanted to get out. There were too many lingering eyes.

But damn, he deserved it. The confidence and lack of hesitation in the man's attempt told me he had done this before, successfully, and the thought sickened me. He never would again, though, and I could take solace in that, regardless of the way he died. A small part of me wished it had been more drawn out, more painful, as I knew there were most likely women out there still healing from his vile touch.

Closing my eyes, I sighed and tried to push the thought from my mind. I opened my eyes again as Rogue pulled me in down the street, strolling slowly.

It was past midnight, but the streets were lit with flickering lanterns. People strode down the side paths, chatting and laughing as if it were the middle of the day. The smell of cinnamon pastries and coffee almost overpowered the scent of the harbor.

I glanced in both directions and sure enough, next to the tavern was a little bakery, its large serving window still open to the public.

CHAPTER TWENTY NINE

"A town of swing shifts." Lee shrugged. "I think the inn is down the way a bit."

We followed Lee as he walked past the window, but my feet slowed. My mouth watered at the swirled desserts, coated in spices and icing. Small balls of chocolate and different sugared candies were scattered around the baked goods.

"This one, please," Rogue said.

The short, elderly woman grinned and pulled the roll from the display, wrapping it in a crinkly brown paper before handing it to me—not him—with a knowing look in her unnaturally green eyes, wrinkled around the edges from a lifetime of smiles. I laughed and took it gratefully as Rogue handed her a few coins.

Her eyes widened. "Sir—"

She started to give some back, but Rogue held his hand up. "Keep the change."

She smiled, giggling to herself as she sat back in her chair and counted the gold pieces.

"That was nice," I muttered before taking a bite. I rolled my eyes back dramatically, moaning at the sweet warmth. "Oh. My. Goddess. This is—"

A woman cleared her throat behind us, and we swiveled. I swallowed down the bite, wiping my mouth quickly with the back of my hand.

It was the barmaid, the same one who had eyed me when Delphia and I were speaking with the men. Her eyes darted around the street before jerking her head toward the alleyway.

I peeked at Rogue, and we cautiously followed behind her, the others on our heels. The alley was dark and isolated, the stones slick with runoff and growing algae.

She stopped and turned to face us. "I've been waiting on you for a good while."

"What are you—"

"The apprentice, Terran, is in Canyon, and he has what you're looking for."

My mouth fell open, my heart skipping a beat.

Rogue's voice was hesitant but hopeful as he asked, "How do you know what we're looking for?"

"He has it. He stays at the inn at the far end of the market, the one with the symbol of a bee. He takes his supper in the pub below *every* night, just after sundown. That's where you'll find him. Look for a man with long, dark hair and a scar down the right side of his face."

We didn't have time to ask any questions before she dipped into a deep curtsy and strode around us back to the tavern.

"Wait!" I shouted. She paused, peeking over her shoulder. "How does he have it? I thought only the blood of—"

"That's all I have for you this night. Good luck on your travels, and…" Her eyes flicked back and forth between me and Rogue. "Long live the Skyborn."

She bowed once more and disappeared around the corner.

Chapter Thirty

Rogue

"We're nearing Canyon," I called back to the group. It had taken us two full days of riding to get here, as we had to cross the mountains that divided the land between the coast and the desert. The trek was easy enough, though. We passed straight through the valley—a pathway cut from the mountains eons ago.

Canyon wasn't too far from Rainsmyre, but the terrain was completely different. The expanse of land was covered in dry, red dirt, as it rarely saw rain. Sparse bushes and prickled vegetation scattered across the land, but what really drew focus were the desert mountains—massive, jagged stones jutting from the ground with sides too steep to climb. They were highlighted by the rising sun, casting them black against the sky's vibrant pink.

"In between two of those mountains is Canyon," Ewan said to Ara, gesturing at the western horizon.

"The creator of this place had the ability to split the ground," I explained. "He created this place a long, *long* time ago before magic had been diluted down to what it is now, back when it was more elemental and *much* stronger."

I peeked over her shoulder to watch her face fall in awe.

She might not agree with the summer heat, but it definitely agreed with her. Her brown hair, braided down her back, had tinted a bit golden on the ends after days in the sun, her skin tanned. Freckles like her mother's had appeared along her cheekbones and over her nose. Even the sheen of sweat that clung to her skin called to me.

"Someone *created* the canyon?" she asked, raising a hand to cover her eyes as she squinted in the direction Ewan had pointed.

"Yes," Alden replied, "for this exact purpose: to create a safe haven for those who needed it. It has developed into a black market of sorts, but it's safe."

"Safer than anywhere else in Ravaryn," Delphia muttered before dropping her eyes to the creature nestled in her lap. "Isn't that right?" she cooed, and Lee grimaced.

"Are you going to talk to it like that when it's ten times your size?" he asked.

Her eyes shot to him. "Yes, and he'll love it."

"Sure, it will. Right up until it eats you."

Delphia looked down at her pet, cooing again as she said, "Well, he only eats dead things, isn't that right?" He popped his head up, purring as she ran her hand along his back. "As long as I'm not dead and decaying, I don't think I'll be very appetizing."

Lee gawked at her before snapping his mouth shut.

"She has a good point." Ara shrugged her shoulders. "He's a little scavenger."

Lee shook his head, turning away as a grin spread across his face.

CHAPTER THIRTY

"Perhaps we should name him Vulture," Ara added, glancing at Delphia.

Delphia laughed—loud and genuine. It warmed my heart to see Delphia coming back to herself, even if it was this little creature doing so.

"Vulture," Delphia repeated, thinking it over. "I like it."

"Vulture, it is," I said as Ara grinned at me over her shoulder, swaying with the horse.

"I think I'll just call him V," Lee said.

"Aw, you already have a little nickname for him," Ara teased. "I think you secretly like him more than you let on."

"Maybe," Lee replied with a chuckle.

The mountains grew larger as we neared them, reaching high into the sky. The one we walked along cast a dark shadow as we followed it down the narrow valley to the market entrance.

When we had reached the end, facing a large wall of solid stone, Ara asked, "Well? Now what?"

"We're going to let the others continue forward, but we'll hang back. I have somewhere I want to show you," I said.

Her mouth tilted up in a one-sided grin as the others leaped from their horses and led them forward. They huddled around the middle of the wall—exactly where the symbol was carved. They whispered their promises and swore the blood oath before glancing back at us.

"We'll join you inside. I'm going to show Ara the Silver Hollow."

"See you soon," Lee said as he disappeared into the stone, the others closely following.

Ara's eyes were wide, her mouth hanging open as she slowly peeked up at me.

"The blood oath is how Canyon stays as safe as it is. You'll see when we enter, but first…" I turned our horse.

"First, we see this Silver Hollow," she hummed, shimmying her shoulders.

We didn't have to go far on horseback, merely a mile or two until we were at the base of the peak it sat atop. I swung myself off before turning to grab her waist and lower her.

"I can get myself down," she said, swatting my hands.

"Yes, but why should you when I'm here?"

She rolled her eyes as she shook her head and glanced around. She walked forward with her arms out to the side. "I don't see silver or a hollow."

I laughed and ran, scooping her up before taking flight. She squealed and wrapped her arms around my neck.

"Patience, little storm," I drawled as I landed and set her on her feet. Her jaw was slack as she stared. "Rendered speechless, hmm?"

I slid my arms around her waist and pulled her back into me, joining her in the view.

The Silver Hollow sat atop a plateau that overlooked the surrounding desert. It was given its name for its pools, all cast silver by the crystals that grew along the bottom—not small crystals, but massive towers that reached towards the surface in every direction. Some of them broke through the water along the outer banks, their peaks glinting with the sunrise.

Ara walked out of my grasp and crouched on the bank, poking one of the crystal tips with her finger. "This is breathtaking."

"The Silver Hollow is a special place. It's said this is where the Goddess herself bathed every morning, just so she could

CHAPTER THIRTY

watch the sunrise from the best spot."

Ara laughed, running her fingers through the water before standing.

She stilled, reclining her head ever so slightly as I slid my hands over her waist and skimmed under her shirt. Goosebumps prickled her skin as my hands skimmed over her belly button, higher between her breasts, and back down to her hips.

I tugged at the hem of her shirt, and she lifted her arms as I pulled it overhead. She turned to face me, smiling lightly as she ran her hands over my abdomen before tugging my shirt off and tossing it to the side.

I didn't pull my eyes away from her as we undid the buttons of our trousers and let them fall to the ground.

My fingers slid over her waist, her breasts, to her shoulder as I brushed the hair back. "You are glorious, Ara."

"As are you," she replied, tracing my scar from hip to shoulder with her finger before she found my jaw and pulled me down as she stood on her toes. Her mouth brushed mine, and I could feel the smile on her lips.

I pressed forward, showering her with gentle kisses. She tilted her head back with a giggle as I kissed her cheeks, her eyes, her neck. Looping my hand in hers, I turned her to the pool, and we slowly waded down the steps carved from stone.

I reclined on the stone edge with Ara between my legs, and we watched the sunrise in ethereal silence as the sky shifted from pink to bright blue.

My arms wrapped around her shoulders, and she placed her hands on my forearms, resting her chin on them.

"I can feel the magic here—the energy, I mean. It *is* different than other places," she whispered.

"It's everywhere." Even I could feel it in the air; I couldn't imagine what she must be feeling.

"But especially here." Her voice was barely louder than a breath as she sank lower into the water and laid back, floating on the surface with her eyes closed.

I enjoyed watching her relax for a few moments before she peeked an eye open.

"Well, come on."

I sank down and dipped my head under the water, reveling in how cool the early morning water felt before reclining to join her.

* * *

When the heat of the day began to sink in and we had long since dried on the shore, we returned to the valley, to the entrance.

Ara followed me to the stone wall, watching closely as I gestured to the symbol carved into the wall—a circle with six triangles etched around, creating the outline of a sun.

"Repeat after me," I instructed. "*Vidi neminem.*"

She repeated the words fluently. "I saw no one?"

"You know the ancient language?" I lifted a brow to her.

"I'm an avid reader who also happened to have a tutor who was adamant I learn to speak it."

"This place was meant to be a safe haven, so that's the promise. You come and you go, but you never name who you encounter here. Everyone is no one in Canyon."

"Ah. So, what now? The blood oath?"

"Yes," I said as I pointed at the wall.

CHAPTER THIRTY

The list of requirements had revealed itself with the phrase, the rules etched into the stone just under the symbol.

To enter, you must abide by the rules and there are three:

1. All who enter are equal and shall be treated as such, or may you forfeit your soul to a lifetime of forced servitude. There are no kings, just as there are no slaves.

2. No blood shall be spilled with ill intent, or may your own be boiled in your veins.

3. Thievery is prohibited, or may the nasty and rotten have free reign to take whatever they so choose from you, including but not limited to any and all belongings, body parts, soul remnants, and magic.

Think carefully upon these rules, traveler, because there is no return. When you swear your oath with blood upon the symbol, your fate is sealed while within my walls.

I pulled the dagger from the sheath and grabbed Ara's hand.

Tilting her palm up, I asked, "Ready?"

She nodded and watched carefully as I slid the dagger across her palm, wincing as the drops of blood formed. I lifted my own palm and sliced across.

"Blow it at the symbol."

Her brows furrowed with confusion, but she did so. The blood became ash on our breath, drifting to the symbol. It stuck to it as if it were wet and filled in the carved sun with deep red ink. The wall flickered and dissipated, leaving a burning sun hanging in the air for a moment before it disappeared, too.

Towering stone walls shadowed either side of the market streets, carts and vendors set up at their bases. People were everywhere, chatting, shopping, eating, resting.

Down the way, chambers were carved from the stone wall itself and turned into all kinds of business—taverns, shops, apothecaries, inns. Canyon had everything and anything anyone could ever need.

We took our time perusing the market, working our way through the smaller carts to the massive shops that had taken up residency in the rooms. Ara slowed as we walked by an antique shop, chock full of disorganized trinkets. Tables and piles were scattered about the room, creating narrow pathways to walk through.

She strolled into the shop as if in a daze. As we entered, a short, elderly woman stood, her eyes a piercing green. Her gaze roamed over my face as if she recognized me, and an uncomfortable chill spread over my skin.

"Ah, he who was named in hopes of what he would become." Her head tilted to the side. "Tell me, Rogue Draki, did you become the rogue your father wished you to be?"

Ara's face swiveled to mine. My jaw tightened, smoke drifting from my clenched fists. "No. No, I did not."

She smiled and nodded. "I'm glad to hear he did not get to wield ye as a weapon, deary." Her eyes flicked to Ara. "I imagine you're another's weapon now."

"Yes. Ravaryn's." Ara's voice cut through the tension, laced with restrained anger.

The woman's eyes flitted back to me, her smile deepening, her eyes an unnatural emerald.

"Wait, we know you," Ara said cautiously, squinting at the shopkeeper's face.

CHAPTER THIRTY

"Know my sister, do ye? Bless your bones. I'm surprised she didn't fatten ye up."

"Ah, the baker," Ara said, turning her eyes back to the shelves.

"Something pull ye in here, Ara?"

My eyes widened as I studied her, unease settling in my gut.

"I don't know," Ara replied as she shook her head and continued her exploration.

"Nobody comes in here for nothing."

Ara's gaze lifted to the shopkeeper then, words on the tip of her tongue, but she froze, her gaze dropping to the dusty, glass case at the woman's side. She followed Ara's line of sight.

"Ah, come take a look," she said, motioning Ara over. "Fancy jewelry, do ye?"

"Not particularly." Ara stepped closer, studying the case before she straightened, her gaze flashing to the woman with what nearly looked like fear.

I joined her, standing at Ara's back as a chill ran down my spine.

"Find what called ye in?"

Ara swallowed hard and nodded, her mouth pressed into a flat line. The shopkeeper pulled a brass key from her bosom, unlocked the case, and raised the lid.

Slowly, Ara reached her hand forward and pulled out a ring. I stepped to her side to get a better look, but it seemed simple. The center stone was a dainty, light blue diamond bound by a thin silver band.

"Have you seen this ring before?" I asked.

Her face was pale, her chest rising and falling quickly. "This was mine...I mean, my mother's. She gave it to me when Evander tried to force me into marriage, but I thought it got stolen when you kidnapped me." She gave me a pointed look. "I thought *you* stole it."

I shook my head. "No, I never even noticed it on your finger."

"Kidnap?" The woman's eyes flashed between Ara and me. "Aren't you two quite the interesting lovebirds, eh?"

Ara held the ring, but her face lowered back to the case.

"See another that snags your attention, do ye? That doesn't happen often."

Ara lifted another ring—a plain silver band with a metal oval and a flower imprinted in the middle.

The lady leaned over for a better look and paused before pulling back, her face grim.

"Woman's revenge, that's the flower stamped. It's a beautiful bloom, easily mistaken for daffodils, but produces a nasty powder on the stem. Deadly, it is." She took the ring from Ara and slid a fingernail under the metal oval. It popped open, revealing a tiny chamber inside. Along the bottom was a dusting of white powder. "*This* ring was used to store its poison." She held it back out to Ara with her eyes distinctly on me. "The perfect place for a woman to hide her revenge. There's not enough left in there to kill a man, but it'll bring him to the brink of death for a short while."

Ara took the ring cautiously. "I've never seen this before, not even the flower."

"Ye don't have to have seen it before. For whatever reason, fate decided ye needed it. That's what my shop is—Fate's Offering. The only fools who set foot in this chaos are those who are called by something inside."

CHAPTER THIRTY

Ara slipped them onto her fingers with a sigh. "How much?"

"We don't deal in money here. These things find me, and I just return them. Take them, deary. They belonged to you long before today."

We left the shop with a solemn heaviness between us.

"That was odd," she whispered, fidgeting with the rings.

I stopped walking, and she strode forward a few steps before noticing.

"What is it?" she asked.

"I understand your mother's ring calling to you, but why that one? Do you… Do I make you feel threatened or unsafe in any way? You can be honest. I would never mean to—"

She closed the distance between us and took my hand. "No, never. You may anger me sometimes, annoy me occasionally, perhaps get under my skin for a moment or two, but no," she said and chuckled as I cracked a grin and started to pull my hand away. She tightened her grip. "You don't scare me."

"You swear?"

She wound her fingers through mine and kissed the back of my hand. "Yes, I swear."

"All right." We started strolling again, hand in hand. "It was odd. Though, I think the old hag may have unnerved me more than anything."

"Oh, shh. I thought she was kind of nice, given the circumstances."

"If you say so."

We strolled through the booths without really looking until Ara stopped, her eyes wide. A smile spread across her face as she swiveled back to me.

"A bookstore," she said.

"By all means, let's go in." I gestured forward and followed closely behind her as we stepped inside.

Both of our mouths fell open.

From the outside, it appeared to be the same size as any other shop, but from the inside, we could see it in its entirety. Floors and floors of books spiraled up through the stone, dim but lit with flickering candles and lanterns. Dust covered most surfaces, cobwebs hanging from ceiling corners and between shelves, but it didn't smell musty. Rather, the smell of coffee and old books permeated the air.

While people sat in the chairs and tables dispersed across the bottom floor, all reading or working, the store was mostly quiet, the only sounds that of flipping pages and whispering voices.

Ara inhaled deeply, moaning as she exhaled. "If someone could put this scent in a candle, I would burn it night and day."

A man appeared then, as ancient as the bookstore seemed. His wispy white air glided along the smooth floor as he hobbled toward us with his wooden cane. It was only when he got closer that I noticed his eyes had no irises—they were solid white.

"Welcome. Feel free to wander. Get lost if you desire and stay as long as you wish. There are enough books here to keep you for a lifetime."

"Oh, thank you. I do believe I could spend a lifetime here," Ara joked, and the man smiled, revealing two long, sharp canines.

"I would enjoy the company," he replied with a raspy laugh. "But alas, I believe your life is already promised to another." His gaze shifted to me, and he sank into a stiff bow. "Your

CHAPTER THIRTY

Majesty"—his gaze flicked back to Ara—"Majesties. Should you find a book or several worth your fancy, do let me know. I'll be just over there." He gestured to the desk he had come from.

With that, he turned and walked back to reclaim his seat. He crossed his legs, lifted his metal goblet, and sipped from it as he flipped through a book.

"I like him," Ara said with a smile. "Let's go."

We roamed for an hour or two as Ara cataloged which floor was which, and I was happy to follow, holding two steaming mugs; although, I probably could've disappeared entirely, and she wouldn't even notice, if not for her missing coffee. She was in her element, lost in her world of books.

We finally made it to the top floor—six in total. She went to a shelf, and her fingers grazed over the books. With a satisfied grin, she pulled one out. Clutching it to her chest, she finally faced me. "Romance."

"Ah, so we'll be here awhile, then." Glancing around, I found a group of reading chairs and plopped down in one, setting our mugs on the nearby table.

She found a book—a forbidden love story she said she'd already read once before—and joined me in the chair next to mine.

"Read to me?" I asked.

She peeked up at me with a grin and crossed her legs in her lap as she faced me, moved a candle closer, and cracked the book open.

Her voice was mesmerizing, her story-telling enthralling as she read, and within a few chapters, I was ensnared in the story. The rest of the world was distant as we sat alone on this floor, absorbed into the story of a prince and a maiden.

Her voice faltered halfway through the book, her cheeks flaming a soft red.

"What? Don't stop now. He's about to confess his love, isn't he? I knew it. That bastard is no better than me. He's head over heels for that woman. You better continue."

She blinked, stifling a smile. "Rosalyn paused outside the gates of the manor, her eyes brimming with tears. He called her name again, softer, breathier, as if her name itself breathed the very life into him.

'What? What could you possibly have left to say?'

'Not much...' He closed the distance between them as drops of rain fell slowly. 'Just three measly words.'

Her eyes tracked him closely.

'I love you.'

Rosalyn's face fell, blanching as the drizzle soaked her hair. 'You...'

'I love you, Rose. With all my heart and being, I love you.'

She ran back to him and threw herself in his arms. His hands slid along her waist. They slithered over her body, taking in every agonizing inch that he had tried and failed to deny himself. She moaned into his mouth, and he wound his hand into her hair, pulling her face back to gaze into her eyes.

'Tell me, Rose. Tell me these same feelings consume you as thoroughly as they do me. Tell me you return my affections, and I will whisk you away. We will leave this night and never return.'

'I love you, Elric. I love you like the moon loves the stars, like the sun loves the flowers of summer. Take me. Take me now, this night. Take me, have me, forever.'

His arms encircled her, one hand on her lower back, the

CHAPTER THIRTY

other in her hair as he lowered his mouth to hers, reclaiming her lips with fervent hunger. He walked her back and lowered her to the ground. They reclined at the base of the tall oak, the cool, soft grass gracing their skin in the summer night's heat.

He pulled back, smiling as his hand slipped beneath her long skirts. He slid it along her calf slowly—"

Ara jumped, gasping as my fingers grazed along her calf.

"Read, little storm."

Her breath was uneven as she continued, "His hand slid along her calf slowly.

'Please,' she whispered, her breaths quickening.

'Have you ever been touched here?' he asked as his hand slid under the back of her knee.

She shook her head.

'And here?' His finger trailed over her bare thigh, and her innocent eyes were wide as they followed the movement.

She shook her head slowly."

Ara's own breathing had quickened as my hand followed her words. She hadn't pulled her eyes from the pages, but I kept mine on her blushing face as she read.

"'Then I'll be your first?' His exploration continued higher over her hip, dipping low to the inside of her thigh. Her breath hitched, her legs snapping closed around his hand.

'Do you wish for me to continue?'

She nodded breathlessly.

'You must say the word, Rose. I will not push you.'

'Yes.'

He pulled her legs apart gently, and they fell open for him. He moved his hand an inch higher, drinking in her every reaction—the way her back arched, her fluttering eyes as she watched him. Her breaths quickened as he slid a finger higher, higher until he was teasing around the spot he knew she wanted him.

'Please,' she whispered again, and he smiled, cupping her between her thighs as she moaned.

'I can feel how wet you are already, even through your undergarments. Poor Rose. How long have you been starved for my touch?'

Her cheeks flushed a deep wine red, her eyes wide. He teased along the edge of her thin undergarment, pulling it away from her skin as the backs of his fingers slid through her slickness."

Ara's eyes fluttered as I slipped my own fingers beneath her trousers, but she wasn't wearing anything beneath them—at my command. She was already soaked, shifting uncomfortably as her legs widened to give me better access.

"Such a good girl," I whispered.

She swallowed hard and continued. "'It may hurt the first time,' he said, 'but I'll be gentle, and please—tell me to stop at any time.'

'I want this,' she said, reclining on her elbows.

He grinned—*a devilishly good-looking grin*, she thought. She knew he was trouble from the second she had laid eyes on him, and that was all she had wanted ever since.

Trouble. Delicious, forbidden trouble.

He shifted her skirts above her waist, baring her to him as he pushed her legs wider and sank beneath them.

'Beautiful,' he whispered before leaning forward to place a kiss on her most sensitive spot.

She gasped, her back arching. 'I...'

'Do you like that?'

CHAPTER THIRTY

'I...Yes, very much.'"

Ara's trousers were on the ground beside me, her own cunt bare to me. Her legs were raised over my shoulders as I copied every action Elric did to his poor, starved Rose—not unlike my poor, starved Ara.

"Someone will see us," she whispered, looking at me for the first time.

"There's no one for at least four floors, little storm."

"They'll hear us." Her eyes widened, imploring.

"Then, I guess you'd better stay quiet," I said, smirking before I lowered, keeping my eyes on hers as I ran my tongue over her.

Her head fell back on the chair and my hand flew to her mouth, suppressing the moan that slipped from her lips.

Chapter Thirty One

Ara

Nothing had ever made me feel more alive.

My heart pounded as Rogue worshiped me with his tongue in deliciously slow circles. I could feel his heated gaze on me as he feasted, his eyes devouring his prey just as his mouth did.

"You enjoy it, don't you?" he whispered, sliding two fingers into me with one hand while the other was still firmly locked over my mouth. "The thrill of potentially getting caught? Of someone seeing you splayed before me, so needy, so desperate, so…soaked?"

My eyes snapped back to him as I mumbled against his hand, and he clicked his tongue.

"That's not being quiet, Ara." He pulled his hand out slowly before thrusting back in with another finger. I closed my eyes, cheeks flaming, the wet sounds of my burning desire the only thing I could hear over the pounding heartbeat in my ears. "Based on how *starved* you are, I would say you like it quite a bit."

He watched his fingers as they thrust into me slowly—

CHAPTER THIRTY ONE

painstakingly slowly. I wanted to scream, move, *beg* for more friction. My hips bucked, and he chuckled.

"Maybe you even like the idea of someone spying, watching you writhe beneath my tongue, listening to every breathless moan you try and fail to stifle."

I moaned into his hand at his words alone. They wound me tighter, higher, because he wasn't wrong. He groaned, moving his fingers faster.

"It'd be the last thing he'd ever see. Make no mistake, I *would* kill him for laying eyes on what's *mine*, but I'm a generous man. I'd let him watch you come first, grace his eyes with the way your back arches and your cheeks flush, as it'd be the most beautiful thing he'd ever seen. A true blessing before a swift death."

He lowered his mouth, running his tongue over me in one long swipe.

"He'd die a happy man," he said against me before he dove in mercilessly.

His tongue licked and swirled as he curled his fingers inside me. I tried to hold back the moans, stifling them as best I could, but he moved faster, curled faster, set me on edge faster. It was blinding, building in my core all at once.

"Come for me, but don't let them hear those pretty little cries," he commanded. "Those are only for me."

His hand stayed firmly in place over my mouth as I fell apart beneath him, clenching around his fingers as sparks clouded my blackened vision. Nothing—no one—mattered at this moment. There was no one else here, not in the store, not in Canyon, not in Ravaryn.

As I came down, he sat back on his heels and slid his fingers past my lips. I sucked them clean, and his eyes flamed, a smirk ticking up the corner of his mouth.

"Naughty," he said, shaking his head. "So naughty for such a good girl."

* * *

It was mid-afternoon when we finally found the others surrounding a blacksmith's booth.

While Delphia was distracted with Vulture, Ewan held a sword at eye level, Alden and Lee leaning over his shoulders as they examined the blade.

Ewan glanced at us as he checked the sword's balance. "She's a beaut, huh?"

He handed the sword to Rogue. It was made entirely of black Damascus steel, sharpened on both sides, the hilt just as intricate. "Oh, yes. The craftsmanship is phenomenal," he said, handing it to Ewan.

He checked the pommel for the blacksmith's mark and pointed out a flaming bird.

"Aye, that's my crest," the middle-aged woman said as she glanced over her shoulder.

She leaned back over the hearth, sparks flying as she hammered the piece she worked on a few more times. With her blonde hair braided in a circlet and sleeveless tunic that dipped in the back, the head of the same flaming bird revealed itself, tattooed between her shoulder blades.

She set her tools down and turned, wiping her hands on her apron, blackened with ash and dust. Her skin was bronzed, her eyes a warm honey brown.

"So, you made all of these weapons?" Delphia asked.

"Oh, aye. Every one," she said. "I've been here for decades,

CHAPTER THIRTY ONE

just working my heart away. No better trade for someone who wields the flames."

"Your attention to detail is impeccable," I said, lifting a small dagger that reminded me of the one I used to carry. A blue stone was cast in the handle—the same kind mine used to have. "What stone is this? I think a dagger I used to have had the same stone in it. The entire blade actually looked incredibly similar to this, but it was silver instead of bronze. It was always my favorite." My eyes cut to Rogue. "But *someone* threw it in the lake, never to be seen again."

He gave me an apologetic smile.

"That blade is the sister to only one other," the blacksmith said. "The stone—Storm's Eye—was a favorite of the late king Vaelor, so he commissioned a blade with it. He brought two stones that day and told me to keep the other as a gift since the stones are rather rare. You say you had a similar one?"

She lifted a brow, stepping closer. Her eyes raked over me in a way that made me shift on my feet. I nodded.

"Ah. You wouldn't happen to be *the* Ara Wrynwood, daughter of our former king, now would you?"

I smiled, dropping my eyes as I replaced the blade back on the table. "One and the same."

"Well, it is an honor to meet you." She stuck a hand over the table, and I shook it. "And that must mean you are Rogue Draki, King of Ravaryn, no?"

"The wings didn't give it away?"

"Aye, they did, but you know what they say about assuming." She laughed and picked up the dagger again, handing it back to me. "Here. You should have this. It only seems right that the stone stays in the family it came from."

"How much is it?" Rogue asked, reaching into his coin bag.

"Consider it a gift to my king and queen." She dipped her head and started to turn back to her work.

"Then consider this a gift to a loyal subject," he replied, taking her wrist and placing the small bag of coins in her hand.

Her eyes locked on where their hands connected as her face blanched. She blinked rapidly and jerked her hand away. The bag fell to the ground, the coins scattering with a clatter and rolling under her table.

"Oh, I'm sorry. I shouldn't have—I'm sorry." The words tumbled from his mouth as he reached down to grab them. He set it on the table, but she didn't reply. She shook her head, staggering back until she hit the side of the hearth. "Truly, I am...so sorry. I shouldn't have touched you."

Her eyes were glazed over as she nodded, gesturing a hand in a wave to leave.

I glanced at Rogue and slid my hand into his. Worry and regret pressed between his brows and burrowed within my gut at the sight of him. He hadn't meant to disturb her, but it didn't matter what his intentions were as she was clearly unsettled.

"Are you sure you're all right?" I whispered back at the blacksmith. "Would you like us to fetch you some water or food? Perhaps...a healer?"

Her eyes snapped back to me before softening. She took a deep breath. "Yes, I'm quite fine. Thank you. Enjoy your blade, Storm Bringer."

As we walked away, the woman sank into her chair and dropped her head to her trembling hands. Rogue peeked back over his shoulder, taking a slow, deep breath before

CHAPTER THIRTY ONE

turning forward again.

"It's getting close to sundown," Alden said. "We should make our way to the other end of the market and find him. He'll be taking his supper soon."

Rogue nodded with a deep breath, and we made our way to the pub where Terran dined each night—if our source was to be believed.

We strolled past every pub and inn, checking for the bee symbol, but we didn't find it until we reached the very last shop. It backed into another exit from Canyon with a false wall, but from the inside of the protection spell, we could see straight through it. An empty, narrow valley greeted us from the other side, the sunset perfectly framed by its cracked walls.

I glanced up at the wooden sign swinging above the entrance to the pub that doubled as an inn; Honeyed was the name, and under it was a carved bumblebee.

"Here's our place," Lee said, staring at the sign alongside me.

"Yep," Rogue replied.

None of us moved. I think we were all equally as hesitant. This could be it. The keeper of the crown could be in there with the long-sought-after solution to our problems, just on the other side of those swinging doors.

Or he could not be. It could all be wrong—misinformation or even trickery. It could be a trap; although, the blood oath would protect us from any physical harm.

We wouldn't know until we entered and saw for ourselves.

I sighed, attempting to settle my rising nerves, and stepped forward. My hands shook as I pushed the door open.

The tavern was large and full of eating patrons. The scent

of honeyed mead and bread, cooking meat, and a faint waft of fire filled the room, pulling an audible growl from my stomach.

Rogue chuckled, but it was short and clipped. He sounded as nervous as I felt.

"There," Delphia whispered as she pointed.

Sitting alone, hunched over a bowl of stew, was a large, dark-haired man.

"Terran," Delphia called loudly.

Rogue tensed, and Lee elbowed her, but we all froze as the man's eyes snapped up. A long scar stretched from his hairline across his eye and down to his chin—on the right side, exactly as the barmaid said.

With another deep breath, Rogue strode over and sat across the table from him as we stood at his back.

"I'm assuming you know who I am," Rogue whispered, leaning forward on his elbows.

"Aye." Terran's gaze skimmed over Rogue, snagging on his wings. "Are you as dreadful as your father?"

"Goddess above, I hope not," Rogue answered.

"No. He is not," Alden said, his voice tight.

Terran's eyes shifted to him, and he froze. "Well, hello, Alden. I didn't expect to see you here…with him."

"Nor did I you," he said.

"You know each other?" I asked.

"Yes," Terran said. "We met briefly when Drakyth still lived at Draig Hearth."

"You know what we're here for," Rogue said.

"Have you been chosen, then? Have you earned it?"

"Yes."

Terran nodded and glanced around the tavern. "I keep it on

me, to keep it safe. The rules say no thievery, but the crown doesn't truly belong to me, now, does it?"

Lifting his satchel, he pulled out leather gloves and slid them on, followed by a pair of chain mail gloves, which topped his leather ones.

I eyed him with a lifted brow.

"You don't want to see the burns and blisters that result from touching it. Only Draki blood—you'd be wise to remember that."

Cautiously, he pulled out an unremarkable box made of plain, unmarked wood. Even the latch was simple. He clicked it open, glanced around once more, and opened the box. His hands grabbed something carefully but kept it beneath the table, away from prying eyes.

My heart was in my throat as we leaned over the table, nearly bursting with nerves.

There it was.

A crown made of obsidian, carved to resemble a wyvern. The wyvern was curled in on itself with his tail in his mouth and his wings tucked at his sides, all shining, black stone.

I didn't need confirmation from Rogue or anyone to know this was it. It radiated ancient power in a way I'd never felt. The strength of its energy echoed its purpose; it held the unbreakable bonds to the hundreds of wyverns that awaited their king.

Its power was one that had been here long before we were born and would remain long after we were gone.

"That's it," Rogue breathed. "I can feel it calling to me as the wyverns did."

Terran replaced it in the box and closed the lid before sliding it across the table. "Then, my work is finally done."

Alden grabbed it quickly and shoved it into a satchel of his own.

"We'll have the crowning ceremony as soon as we get back. The crown will merge with me, and then…" Rogue turned to me with such hope in his eyes, my chest swelled with it. "Then, we'll have done it. We'll have turned the tides."

Relief was clear on his face as if he could fully breathe again.

"We did it," I said, laughing as my eyes watered. I placed a palm on either side of his face and kissed him.

"We did it," he repeated, nodding.

Lee, Delphia, and Ewan smiled at each other as Alden clapped Rogue on the shoulder. "Proud of you, my boy."

"We couldn't have found it at all without your help, Alden. Thank you," he said, placing his hand on top of Alden's.

Alden nodded once, patted his shoulder, and turned to me. "I say we have a celebratory drink."

"Oh, yes," I replied, and Rogue laughed.

"Tonight we celebrate," he said, sliding a hand around my waist and kissing the top of my head. "Because this was no small victory."

* * *

And drink we did.

We drank and ate and danced. Lee had already booked us rooms with the innkeeper, so we were merry and relaxed for the first time since we had set out on the journey.

While Delphia sat off to the side with her creature most of the time, it seemed hope had found its way into each of us. It felt as if every step before this night, before we had found the crown, had been us grasping at straws, trying to resolve

CHAPTER THIRTY ONE

whatever mess Adonis had made.

But now? Now, we had made our first move. We made the first step, and it was one he knew nothing about. We had a secret weapon—*weapons.* Hundreds of powerful beasts they would never see coming.

I smiled to myself from my seat against the bar as I sipped yet another mug of Fae rum. It was delicious, tracing a warm path down my throat that spread throughout my body to my limbs and especially my head.

While I sat at the bar alone and had been for the last half hour, I was thoroughly content. It was nice to watch in silence as those around me were genuinely happy, drinking and conversing with their friends—but the first alone time I'd had in days ended as Ewan joined me.

He flagged down the barmaid as he climbed onto the bar stool beside me.

"This is a good feeling, being ahead of Adonis for once," he said with a lopsided grin.

"Yes, it is. Thank you for coming with us."

"Of course. As if I would be anywhere else."

"With Iaso, perhaps?" I wiggled my brows.

He sighed deeply and sipped from his cup. "Iaso is…way too good for me. She's too good for everyone in this realm."

"Those are words from a man in love."

He paused and stared at the swirling brown liquid in his cup. "Aye, they are." He smiled, glancing up at me for a second before reaching into his pocket. He pulled out a small, wooden box. Opening it, he turned it to me.

It was a ring—an absurdly large emerald centered in the middle with golden vines wrapped around it, setting it in place.

My hand covered my mouth as my eyes stung.

"I'm going to ask her to marry me, and hopefully, she'll have me." He snapped the box closed and shoved it back in his pocket. "I'm not a powerful, high-ranking official, or even a powerful Fae, but I'll love her better than anyone else. Even on my deathbed, her name would be on my dying breath. I live and breathe for that woman." When I didn't immediately respond, he asked, "Too much?"

"No. Oh my Goddess, no. You are worthy of Iaso, just as she is worthy of you. You are both kind and loving and selfless." I wiped my cheek as a tear slipped. "And the ring, Ewan? I don't believe you could have found a more perfect one."

"Thanks, Ara. I...I appreciate that more than I can put into words." He threw an arm around my shoulders and pulled me into a hug. "Your father would be so proud of you. I know I've said that a dozen times, but I'll say it a dozen more because it's the truth."

I wrapped my arms around his waist, hugging him back. "I'm so happy for you."

"Me too," he chuckled.

With that, Ewan strolled over to Lee, who had joined Delphia's side at her table. Ewan plopped down beside them as Delphia smiled and poured a few shots. I covered my mouth, laughing as Lee offered the rum to her creature, and she swatted his hand away with a scoff.

Rogue was still sitting with Terran, as he had been most of the night. He asked him any and every question he could about his family, and Terran answered each one happily.

* * *

CHAPTER THIRTY ONE

The pub started to clear out as the night came to an end.

Ewan and Lee had already retired to their rooms, but I sat with Rogue and Terran. The hours passed like minutes as I listened intently to each tale Terran relayed. It was fascinating. Terran had been friends with Drakyth for centuries, so he had an endless amount of stories to tell—about him and the Draki family—and he seemed happy to have someone to tell them to.

He was in the middle of one when Alden tapped me on the shoulder.

"You heading to bed?" I asked, resting my chin on my hand.

"No, but...can I speak with you about something?" His eyes darted toward Rogue and Terran. "Alone?"

The smile slid from my face, my hand dropping away as I sat up straighter. "Of course. Come on." I stood and leaned over to give Rogue a quick kiss on the head. "I'll be back in a few."

He smiled and grabbed my chin, pulling me in to kiss my lips. "All right. I'll be here."

I chuckled and walked to the side with Alden, glancing around to check on Delphia. She had spent most of the night by herself, bouncing from table to bar and back.

Panic set in when I couldn't spot her. She hadn't said goodbye, so I didn't think she'd retired to her room yet.

"Ara, I didn't know how to say this earlier, but it's about Terran. He's—"

"Alden, have you seen Delphia?" My eyes darted from face to face.

My words cut short when my eyes found her whispering with a man I didn't recognize. His face was tight as he said something unintelligible, and her head shook side to side until her eyes locked with mine, wide with complete and utter terror.

My heart thumped as I shoved past Alden and ran to her. She met me in the middle of the pub.

"Poison. Someone has poisoned the drink within the last hour or so. He said a man just choked and died in the alley. H-he wanted me to relay the message. Ara, w-we need to go. We need to get out of here and take some kind of antidote." She started to ruffle through her bag from Iaso. "She had to have put something in here. Go. Get Rogue."

I nodded repeatedly as I turned. As soon I swiveled toward Rogue, his eyes were on me. I jerked my head to the door, and he stood and followed us out.

The air was crisp as we stepped out of the pub into the streets. Delphia waved and walked over to the side of the shop, out of the flickering light.

She had pulled four vials from her bag. "I don't think Lee and Ewan will have been dosed. I think they left early enough…right? We don't think so?" The questions spilled from her mouth in panic as she passed out the vials, popped the top off hers, and swallowed.

We all did the same.

"This should prevent any side effects of poison if we took it soon enough," Alden explained, tossing his vial into the trash bin. "It's a cure-all—if it's the same antidote Iaso usually makes—but it also won't hurt if we weren't dosed, by some luck."

"We need to tell the others," I said and turned on my heel.

Delphia grabbed my wrist, yanking me back with surprising strength. "And what? Cause mass panic? We don't have any cures for them. That was all we had."

CHAPTER THIRTY ONE

My brows furrowed. "As opposed to what? Leaving them to chance? There are other healers here with antidotes, I'm sure. They need to know."

"No," Delphia said. "They don't."

"What are you—"

With her hand firmly latched on mine, she stepped through the invisible wall, pulling me with her. Once we were outside of the protection spell, I could no longer see the streets of Canyon. I couldn't see anybody until Rogue stepped out enraged, Alden closely following.

"Delphia, what do you think you're doing?" Rogue asked, pulling me back into him.

She waited without answering, and then I felt it.

A wave of exhaustion hit me like a ton of bricks. I stumbled into Rogue, blinking rapidly. He swayed but caught us both on the stone wall. Alden wasn't so lucky; he stumbled and fell forward, cracking his knees on the hard ground.

"What is..." My words were heavy.

"It's a sedative," Delphia said, shaking her head as I sank to my knees.

I stared at her in confusion when her energy crept out to me, seeping into my fingers like...pure darkness. Her energy was so *wrong*, black and twisted as the cloud consumed her mind—the same darkness I saw clinging to her mind upon our arrival, overwhelming and soul-consuming.

It was eating her alive.

"Delphia, you're l—"

Rogue stumbled and hit the ground beside me. I reached a hand out to him, and he took it, grasping tightly, as if for dear life.

"Delphia, you're letting your grief destroy you. I can feel

your energy, dark and low and so unlike the *real* you. You are happiness and warmth. You always have been." Getting the words out in intelligible sentences was like pulling teeth. It took my sole concentration as the fog settled over my mind, beckoning me to darkness.

"Grief?" She laughed, cold and humorless. "Is that what you think this is? Grief?"

I pulled back and fell, my back hitting the stone wall with a thud. My eyes flitted to Alden and panic struck me. He was flat on the ground.

"Delphia, whatever it is, we can help you," Rogue mumbled. He was the last one still upright, if only from his knees.

"Help me? *You* help *me*? You are the reason Doran is dead. He thought of you as a brother, Rogue. He trusted you!" She leaned over him, pausing, before planting a hand on his shoulder and shoving him back. "And you killed him. You ran your own sword through his heart like he was *nothing*."

"What? No—" I started.

"How could you say that? You *know* that's not what happened. You were there, Delphia. You watched Evander kill him."

She laughed again, but it was angry, horrifying, as she shook her head and stepped back. The mass of dark energy around her mind shifted and swirled, deepening.

I focused on it, on her. The feelers of my magic reached out to her and when they encountered her mind, I physically recoiled as a wave of nausea rolled over me.

"Rogue…" I breathed. "It's not…I don't think…"

Men stepped from the shadows.

Human men.

My heart dropped, my eyes flashing from Rogue to Delphia.

CHAPTER THIRTY ONE

"No," Rogue breathed. He shook his head. "No, D, no, you didn't."

"I had no choice. My brother's murderer cannot run free. I can't—won't allow it. He deserves more than that. He deserved more than you."

I wanted to reply. I wanted to argue, to knock some sense into her, to convince her she was wrong, but I struggled to do more than keep my eyes open. They slipped more closed by the second...

Until a flash of red hair caught in my peripheral vision.

Chapter Thirty Two

Rogue

"You have got to be fucking kidding me," Ara seethed. My eyes snapped to her before following her line of sight and landing on that freckle-faced redhead, Finley.

Rage pulsed through me, burning away some of the sedatives. My legs shook as I slowly rose one leg at a time, my eyes burning a fiery orange.

"You're dead," I said, locking eyes with him.

Finley, standing behind two soldiers, laughed and nodded. "Yeah, okay, and how do you plan on doing that?"

My shift started before I could control it. Talons tore from my nail beds. Sharp teeth extended from my jaw. Scales rolled over the skin, starting between my shoulder blades.

The fire pouring through my veins burned the remaining sedative, but it also drained my magic, and if I didn't shift fast enough, I would be left magic-less and unconscious.

It all ceased when I felt a pinch in my neck. My hand flew to the spot as I turned to see the man Delphia had been speaking with in the pub.

CHAPTER THIRTY TWO

He had jabbed me with something, and—

I swayed and fell with a thud, knocking my head on the stone floor.

"We thought you might need a little extra," Finley said, walking through his men toward Ara and me.

"Do not…"

"Do not what? Touch her?"

He slid a hand over her head, smoothing her hair, but she was too weak to move. Her face was tight with rage as she tried to flinch away from him.

"What will you do, oh mighty Draig, hmm? Because to me, it seems like you're quite…useless."

* * *

Ara

He dies tonight.

I don't care if I die with him. If it's the last thing I do, Finn dies tonight.

"I do believe I'm allowed to touch my bride however and whenever I want," Finn said.

My eyes snapped to him as nausea rolled in my gut. Rogue growled, and flames licked over his arms.

"Never," was all I could manage.

"Oh, Ara, forever the stubborn one. Time will change that."

My jaw clenched, nearly breaking my teeth from the force as my eyes shifted back to Delphia. She stood to the side with her arms crossed over her chest, but she met my gaze with almost regret.

"Now what, General?" a human asked. Surely not to Finn...

But it was Finn who answered. *Dear Goddess, Adonis is dumber than we thought.*

"Now, we do what we came here to do. Load them up."

My eyes darted to Rogue, my heart pounding. I wanted to reach for him, but I couldn't move a muscle. I was as completely immobile as he was.

"What about that one?" A human pointed at Alden.

Delphia interjected, stepping forward. "Oh, he wasn't involved. He's innocent. He didn't—"

"Dispose of him." Finn waved a hand in dismissal.

"No!" I screamed as the man pulled a dagger from his sheath.

He gripped Alden's hair, lifting his head, but Alden's eyes were wide open. He lunged and grabbed the man by the throat, electrocuting him.

The soldiers jumped into action. Two more dropped like flies as bolts of energy shot from Alden's palms—but then a squelch echoed over the shouts.

Dead silence.

Nobody moved.

Alden's eyes shifted to me, and I already knew.

Before his hand moved to his abdomen, I knew.

Before the dark red coated his white tunic, I knew.

He collapsed back to the ground, and I stilled. My mouth hung open, my body trembling. I heard nothing, could process nothing.

Tears poured down my cheeks.

"No!" Delphia shouted and sprinted at the man, but another soldier threw a dagger that struck her in the shoulder. She stumbled back into the wall, clutching at the wound. He

CHAPTER THIRTY TWO

stepped closer and stabbed another dagger into her other shoulder. She screamed as he hit it with the hilt of another, shoving the blade into the stone, anchoring her to the wall. She slumped, blood seeping from each wound.

As she started to lose consciousness, the darkness in her mind faltered. Flickered. Faded a bit.

It…waded like wispy black tendrils of smoke, the same kind I had seen in my nightmare all that time ago.

The same darkness I had felt in her mind several times and attributed to grief, to pain. The last few weeks flashed through my mind, connecting like shuffled puzzle pieces that had finally fallen into place: her avoidance, her hatred, her aggressiveness. Everything was so out of character for her… because she *thought* she was living with her brother's murderer.

It was as if a wave of ice-cold water poured over me. *Oh, Goddess.*

It was Adonis' doing. All of this.

All that time she was missing…

Bile rose in my throat. When she was grieving and in pain, he had her. When she should've been burying her brother and comforted by her family, that *monster* had her. I clenched my jaw painfully tight, my breath quickening as rage seethed through every inch of me.

He had changed her, mangled her mind, and shifted the atrocity of Doran's death to his own brother, changing the warm Delphia we knew to the icy shell she had been over the last few weeks.

My heart broke for her, for what she was about to experience, to realize.

My arm was like lead as I lifted it, but I forced it upwards, forced my palm to reach toward her, and pulled. The energy was disgusting, utterly vile as the black tendrils visibly reached for me, but I took it all, emptying her mind of him.

When the last of his control was gone, Delphia tensed. Her face blanched, and I could nearly see the horror behind her eyes as she came to, processing each event with painful clarity.

When the realization struck home, she screamed—a blood-curdling, earth-shattering sound. The stone around us shook, pieces tumbling to the ground. Everyone's hands flew to their ears, and when the sound ceased, blood dribbled from my ears as they rang.

"What—what did I *do*?" Her face twisted in utter devastation, worse than when Doran had been killed, worse than I had ever seen. Her breath quivered, her entire form shook, as her eyes shifted from me to Rogue to Alden, and she realized what had been done. What *she* had done. "I'm sorry. Alden, I'm—Doran. Oh, Doran. Oh, Goddess, what have I done?"

She sobbed, clutching at her heart rather than her wounds as her head fell forward.

"I'm sorry. I'm so sorry. I can't— I failed you, Doran. I failed you all." Her eyes were on the sky as she fell apart, sobs wracking her body. Blood poured from her wounds at each shuddering cry, but she didn't seem to notice or care. "And Thana. Oh, Goddess. She will hate me. *I* hate me. You *should* hate me. Doran, I'm so sorry! I'm—"

A soldier struck her head with the hilt of his sword, and she slumped forward, unconscious.

My rage was boiling now, a violent ocean thrashing painfully against my chest; I was overflowing with the need for an outlet.

CHAPTER THIRTY TWO

"Sedate her, you fools!" Finn cried, unwittingly offering himself as my target.

My lip quivered as my face slowly turned to Finn.

He stumbled back, tripping over his own feet. "Sedate—" He was cut short as I wrapped my magic around his heart and crushed it. Painfully. I squeezed and choked. He was beet red, deprived of air and blood as I forced his legs to walk toward me. When he was directly in front of me, I snapped his femurs. He screamed bloody murder, and I sealed his mouth shut as I yanked him down, breaking his kneecaps.

My hand gripped his throat and searched his mind for any trace of the black magic that shrouded Delphia.

But there was none.

I pulled his life from him slowly. I wanted it to be agonizing. I wanted the last moments of his miserable life to be the worst he had ever experienced—pain that would literally drive him to the brink of death so I could shove him over.

"You're here of your own volition... You're not even being forced to do this," I whispered, my lip curling back in disgust. He listened intently, hanging on every word. "You should've taken no for an answer. Now, you will die here instead, at my hand. Your body will be ravaged by the land of the Fae, food for the worms, as you would not be worth anything more. You are *nothing*, Finley. Nothing but burning, worthless flesh beneath my palm, soon to be forgotten. Enjoy the afterlife that awaits you. I'm sure you will deserve every second."

I pulled every bit of life from him that I could and released him. He slumped to the ground with a thud.

His life staved off the sedative, if only for a few moments, and I staggered to my feet, eyeing every human. Their faces paled with fear, bodies trembling. Rogue was lying flat, but his eyes followed me as I stumbled to Alden, watching with tears of his own.

I dropped to Alden's side as sob after sob broke from me. His breaths were ragged and uneven as he reached for my hand, his skin already cold.

Something stabbed me in the neck, and I jerked back, sucking the life from the human in an instant. He didn't even have time to flinch before he dropped to the ground.

His energy staved off less than the last. This sedative was stronger.

My heart pounded in my ears as I blinked rapidly and held my shaking hand over Alden's wound, willing it to close. I imagined the skin stitching together and the blood flow ceasing.

Nothing happened.

Again.

Nothing.

My magic was waning, each passing second dragging me closer to falling unconscious. The only thing holding me upright was the blinding panic building in my chest as more blood pooled around him.

When I really, actually needed it, it wouldn't fucking work.

A frustrated cry tore from me.

"Someone grab that bag," I shouted, pointing at the satchel Iaso had given Delphia. Nobody moved. "Grab it, damn it! Grab the—"

"Ara," Alden managed, coughing. Blood coated his lips as he shook his head and squeezed my hand. "It... It'll be all right. Nothing in that bag could help me now."

"No, Alden, don't. I need you. You're my friend, my grandfather," I cried. I could barely breathe. My chest

CHAPTER THIRTY TWO

was tight, my eyes blurred with tears. I wiped his shirt as they dripped onto the fabric, but it was for naught as they disappeared into the darkening red. "Please."

"You'll be all right. You are strong," he choked, covering his mouth as he coughed more blood. "Strong and brave. You will save Ravaryn, just as your father did before you."

I couldn't speak through the force of my cries. I clutched his hand to my chest.

"Stay strong and stay true, Ara Wrynwood, my granddaughter. I am so proud to have known you," he whispered as his eyes lifted to the sky. A faint smile graced his lips as his chest hitched. "Now, I finally get to see…my Ara. My son."

He stilled. I screamed, shaking his shoulders. "Alden?"

A faint wisp of blue electricity left his mouth and drifted to the sky, disappearing among the stars.

"No…" The sight broke me. My chest caved in, and I collapsed in on myself as the breath left my lungs. "Alden, I'm sorry…"

"Ara," Rogue whispered. "Ara, hey."

I started to turn to him. I needed him. I needed Rogue—his steadiness, his hold. I needed to fall apart, to pull my hair out, to scream and collapse. I felt like I was imploding. It was too much—the emotion, so blindsiding and devastating, the exhaustion that clung and settled between my bones, beckoning me to the ground.

I didn't care about the soldiers. I didn't care about the dead humans scattered around us or even Delphia's unconscious form. I didn't care that Lee and Ewan knew nothing at all in their drunken slumber.

Nothing mattered because Alden was dead.

Alden was *dead*.

The kind, ancient man who greeted me when I first arrived. The one who welcomed me with open arms and helped me every step of the way.

My grandfather was dead.

I couldn't tell if I was screaming or sobbing or both, the sound echoing against the stone, strangled and broken.

I started to reach for Rogue, but Alden's bag snagged my attention. My heart beat once. Twice. I snatched the box from it, ripped it open, and grabbed the crown.

Searing pain raced through my hand as blisters bubbled at the contact, but I clenched my teeth and launched it to Rogue. He jerked enough that the crown skimmed the skin of his fingers.

It was enough.

The wyvern woke and slid beneath Rogue's skin. It crawled under his sleeve and peeked above his shirt collar before winding around his neck. Flames licked at Rogue's throat as the wyvern made a full circle, biting its own tail as it settled in its final resting place as if the tattoo of a black wyvern had always been there.

Another prick in the neck, and my hand flew to the spot. I vaguely heard Rogue roar my name as my vision tunneled until it was entirely black.

"I love you," I mouthed.

Rogue's form engulfed in his own flames was the last thing I saw before tumbling into the icy, silent darkness.

Chapter Thirty Three

Rogue

My mouth was dry, my throat on fire.
I shifted, my body stiff and wet, and white-hot agony raced through my back.

My breath left me in a whoosh as my eyes snapped open, but my mind was still fogged. I was lying face down as the world spun around me, black and charred and dark.

"Where…"

The ground around me was burned, a blackened wasteland. Slowly, I gritted my teeth and turned my head, sending another burning wave of pain down my spine.

The Cursed Wood stood on the other side.

Why is the ground wet?

My head pounded.

Ara. Where is Ara?

I was already losing consciousness again, wave after dizzying wave pulling me back under. I tried to sit up, to look around for her, my mate, but excruciating pain knocked the breath from my lungs, and I fell back to the soaked ground.

Why is the ground wet?

It was red—so dark, it was nearly black.

My heart raced.

I was lying in a pool of blood...with something off-white crumpled and sitting just outside of it, speckled with red.

What is that?

With a trembling hand, I reached for it, wincing as pain laced through my every muscle. My heart raced as I realized it was paper—a folded, dirtied letter.

> *I rather enjoy the game we're playing. Although, I did think you had an advantage, so I had to level the playing field. Now, we're both ground-bound.*
>
> *Your turn, little brother.*

The note burst into flames in my hand, and I closed my eyes, my breathing ragged, as I slowly lifted a hand to my back, clenching my jaw as my stomach curdled.

A roar tore from me, shaking the surrounding wood and the ground beneath me as my vision tunneled.

An answering call, the echo of a whisper, met mine on the breeze as a distant island shuttered and woke.

Fire erupted from me in every direction, out of my control as it sucked whatever energy I had left and incinerated *everything.*

I collapsed, losing my grip on reality as I sank back into the darkness when the claws of a black wyvern scooped beneath me and lifted.

Chapter Thirty Four

Ara

The throbbing in my skull woke me first, quickly followed by the sharp bite of pain at my wrists and ankles. The distant sound of dripping water echoed through the hollow room, which was sickeningly warm and humid.

Goddess, the heat.

It was stifling. I inhaled deeply, my eyes refusing to open against the spinning behind my eyelids. The thick, stale air slithered down my dry throat, and I erupted in a cough that ricocheted through my already pounding head like a sledgehammer in a pottery shop.

A muffled groan escaped me. I stirred, my aching muscles screaming as I pulled a hand down to cup my forehead...only to realize I couldn't move far.

My eyes snapped open as the memories flooded me, accompanied by a fresh wave of pain and nausea. I choked on a silent sob as my chest seized, each cry a blade down my shredded throat.

I didn't want to be awake, to be reminded of what brought

me here, who we lost in the process. I wanted to remain lost in the darkness, unseeing and unfeeling. At least then, the agony couldn't pierce my chest in fervent waves, not if I wasn't in this realm, present and at the mercy of overwhelming grief.

As my eyes adjusted, I examined my whereabouts. The room was dark, the floor and walls made entirely of stone, damp with condensation. The dripping continued in the corners, repeating incessantly every few seconds. The area was dimly lit by waning candles, leaving ring after ring of melted wax along the floor, but it was enough.

The light illuminated what they wanted me to see.

What I was to understand.

To bear.

To suffer.

What they had done.

Screaming filled my ears, my skull, my soul, but I was frozen. Every muscle. Every thought. Every breath. Choked off by a horror that twisted and grew into utter, inconsolable, unforgivable devastation.

Every part of me came to a screeching halt as I shattered, releasing a broken wail I barely recognized as my own.

Directly across from me, nailed to the wall, bloodied and broken, was a pair of maroon wings.

About the Author

J.D. Linton is the Amazon Bestselling debut author of The Last Storm, book 1 in the Rogue x Ara series.

She's married to her high school sweetheart and a mother of one. She enjoys reading and writing spicy fantasy romance, and as with most writing mamas, she's also a midnight writer—up all day with her real baby and up all night with her fictional babies.

When not writing, you can find her reading, making a million tiktoks, or at the park with her son.

Writing has truly changed her life, and she's even more thankful for the incredible community it brought with it.

You can connect with me on:
- https://linktr.ee/authorjdlinton

Also by J.D. Linton

The Last Storm
Ara Starrin's entire life has been a lie.

Hidden in the shadow of her controlling father, General Evander of Auryna, Ara has never tasted true freedom. For most of her life, she's been locked away in his estate as he is determined to protect her from the bloodthirsty Fae across the border.

But as her twenty-sixth birthday comes and goes, he decides it's time for her to marry, against her wishes and completely unbeknownst to her.

Ara's fate is sealed the moment he announces her engagement.

Rogue Draki's entire life has been a painful truth.

Raised at the hands of his father, the merciless king of Ravaryn, Rogue has never tasted an ounce of kindness. Now that his father is dead, the crown has been thrust upon him, and it is his responsibility to save his people from the wrath of Auryna.

It is for that reason he crosses the border into Auryna to spy on the court in the Capitol—for secrets, leverage, anything.

Rogue's fate is sealed the moment he lays eyes on Ara Starrin.

For the Love of Fritters & Frights
"Halloweentown if it was a Hallmark movie with spice"

For the Love of Fritters & Frights is a fun, almost cozy Halloween novella that will leave you feeling warm and fuzzy just in time for the holiday. It's perfect for those who need a nice little romantic pallet cleanser chock full of cozy, fall vibes, fun Halloween events, and a variety of amusing creatures.